THE MARQUIS DE FRAUD

THE
MARQUIS
DE FRAUD

PHILIP REED

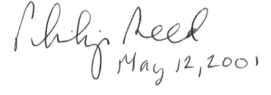

May 12, 2001

EPIC PRESS
LONG BEACH, SAN MATEO, CA

Published in the USA by Epic Press, Long Beach and San Mateo, California. Contact the publisher at: Epicpress@aol.com.

Text design by Richard Cheverton/Waypoint Books; cover design by Diane Suzuki; cover art by Eric Peterson.

First edition. Printed on acid-free paper.

ISBN 0-9708722-0-8

Library of Congress Card Number: 2001086778

To horse trainers everywhere;
to their hard work
and their undying dream
of creating a champion.

ACKNOWLEDGMENTS

I COULD NEVER HAVE WRITTEN this book without the help of Jeff Bonde, one of the top thoroughbred trainers on the West Coast. Jeff let me observe every aspect of his job as he trained and raced horses at tracks such as Bay Meadows Race Course, Hollywood Park, Del Mar and Santa Anita. He openly shared his knowledge of pin hooking—buying yearlings, breaking them and training them for racing—and patiently answered my endless questions. The devotion Jeff, and his wife Martha Bonde, show to horses, and horse racing, represent the best of what makes this sport so special.

Also, I wish to express my gratitude to the following people: Louis Lebherz, for introducing me to his brother Phil and for reading the early drafts; Richard Cheverton, for making critical connections and laying out the book so beautifully; Eric Peterson for the vivid cover illustration; Diane Suzuki for bringing together the elements of the cover design; Ann Haley and Marilyn Iturri for their careful and perceptive editing; Jim Riordan and Bud Sperry, at Seven Locks Press for showing me a better way to put a book in print; Jackie Green for her invaluable assistance with publicity; the Mavericks Writers Group for critiquing the book as it emerged; John Hawkins, my agent in New York and Irv Schwartz, my film agent at AMG, for their support and comments; Kevin Hawke for proofreading and suggestions; my father, Thomas Reed, for his notes and enthusiasm for the story; my good friend Mark Stevens for his overall critique and one important idea in particular; Mr. James Ullrich Esq., for introducing me to Texas and Texans; Pat Baylo for reading the manuscript so many times and always inspiring me with her enthusiasm; Barbara Reiter for her thoughts on the ending; Sharon Lebherz and her friend Helen Hobbs for their perspective on horses, mysteries and justice; Dr. Tom Amberry for the hats; David Hood, in London, for the wonderful day at the races; Dr. Lou Boxer for his constant encouragement; and to all the booksellers who have been so helpful but especially to Sheldon MacArthur at the Mystery Bookstore, in Los Angeles, and Joe and Bonnie, at the Black Orchid in New York City.

PREFACE

A FRIEND OF MINE called me one day, his voice filled with excitement. "I have the premise of your next book," he said. "It's something that actually happened to my brother. It's about horse racing. And it's about life on the backside of the track." He gave me the number of his brother, Phil Lebherz, who lives in the San Francisco Bay Area.

I called Phil the next day and was glued to the chair for two hours listening to a story of a stolen thoroughbred racehorse, a charming con man and an international chase. When I hung up, I knew I had to write the story.

Still, since this was going to be a work of fiction, there were characters to be created and many situations to be invented. I began researching the world of horse racing—which really meant hanging out at the track a lot. I began writing the book and the opening section flowed nicely. But eventually I ran into a barrier and I couldn't go any farther.

In the story, the two main characters leave for England and

Scotland to chase a stolen racehorse. I had a rough idea what would happen, but I was low on details and the locations seemed sketchy. When I told Phil the book was stalled, and why, he considered the problem. Then, with characteristic boldness, he said, "Come on. Let's go find the ending to your book." A week later we were on a flight to London, filled with a sense of mission.

Phil and I covered a lot of ground while we were in the U.K. We went to the track on a stormy March afternoon and saw the horses thundering over the jumps in the driving rain. We met trainers and toured their stables. We talked with jockeys and bookies. We took an express train to Scotland and walked the streets of Glasgow where the con man in my story had been raised. We also spent the night—all night—in a Glasgow bar drinking with native Glaswegians. By the time we flew home, I knew that somewhere in our experiences were the ingredients for the ending of my story. When I finally got back to my desk, the rest of the book seemed to write itself.

Here then, is *The Marquis de Fraud*, a blend of reality, speculation and fantasy. I hope you enjoy it.

Philip Reed
Long Beach, California
Jan. 2, 2001

THE MARQUIS DE FRAUD

PROLOGUE

HE SAT ALONE in his car, in the hot night, the duct tape slippery in his hands as he hummed that tune, "Taking Care of Business."

That's all it was, he thought, just taking care of business. Making sure the deal goes through, making sure the money would flow to him, that his life would keep going along nicely. This is the way things should have turned out anyway. Just helping 'em along.

Taking care of business.

He tore off a long strip of tape and wound it around his neck from his collar to where the mask started. Only it was hard to work the tape with his hands shaking so bad. Shaking and sweating and the tape sticking to everything but the skin he needed to protect. Must steady the nerves, he thought, reaching for the bottle of Chivas and tipping it up. Yeahhhh . . . . The scotch burned nicely, coating his teeth, coating his throat, coating his nerves. He went back to work.

Now he was taping the exposed flesh of his wrists between his cuffs and his gloves. Must be careful. Must always be protected. Can't risk even the tiniest scratch, he thought, looking in the rearview mirror. Jesus, he even scared himself—a masked specter with reptilian layers of tape around his neck. The sight alone might kill poor Sonny.

If only it were that easy—that easy to take care of business.

He opened the car door and stepped out into the heat.

It was a quiet side street. Parked cars here and there. Big old live oaks lining the sidewalks. And locusts buzzing high up in the dark limbs. Buzzing in his brain as he waited, waited, waited to do this thing he actually *DID NOT!* want to do.

Quick glance at his watch, 2:05 a.m. That meant the Silver Fox was closed now. That meant that Sonny would be coming down the street here to his car. Just as he did every night.

But this night would be different. Tonight fate would finally catch up with him. When your number's up, your number's up. No escaping that.

And here he came now, a distant figure strolling down a dark sidewalk and—thank God—Sonny was alone for once.

Get ready now, he thought, ducking behind a live oak. He slapped his pockets. Left pocket held the plastic bag. Right pocket held the club he'd made by sliding a steel rod inside a length of garden hose. Yes, I'm ready. Ready to take care of business.

Sonny passed right in front of him. So close he could hear him breathing, could hear him humming a tune they'd played that night in the club. So close he could reach out and touch him.

And there was his unsuspecting head bobbing right in front of him. Walking toward his car now, bending to unlock the door. But he wouldn't get to do it. Oh no. Because the club hissed through the air and—*Smack!*

The blow caught him nicely behind the ear. But Sonny didn't go down. Not like he was supposed to. He stumbled forward, catching himself on the door handle and turned, one arm raised, as if he could stop what was going to happen—as if he could stop fate.

Sonny's sweating face shone in the weak light, looking up at him, looking up at this masked specter with tape around his neck. And in that moment, as he picked his spot for the next blow and as he kept hesitating—Jesus, why did he hesitate?—Sonny's hand flashed out and tore off his mask. And in doing so he felt one of Sonny's fingernails rip a gash down the center of his forehead.

"Well shit," Sonny said in that nasal West Texas drawl of his, "I mighta known."

Sonny reared back and spit in his face. Spit right into the gash, into his open flesh.

Jesus! He's trying to kill me!

That did it. The membrane holding his anger ruptured and his fury hemorrhaged into the night. The club rose and fell. The quiet neighborhood became filled with the fleshy smack of the club, the obscene grunts of exertion, of one man beating another without mercy.

Sonny dropped face down in the tall grass. *Finish him! Finish him!* He pounced, straddling the still form. He worked the plastic bag over Sonny's head, pulled it tight and held it there until every last twitch and flicker of his life was gone. Until the man beneath him was dead.

He stood, panting, recovering himself, feeling the regret, the loss, the end of something. But it was done now. No going back. Now, the policy would pay. The money would flow. And the good times would continue—in another city perhaps—but they would continue. That was the point.

He peeled the duct tape off his neck, balled it up and threw it away into the tall grass. Then, suddenly, he felt it—the hot wetness. The blood trickling down his forehead. And he remembered the gash Sonny had torn in his forehead. He remembered how Sonny spit into his wound.

He ran back to his car, tore the door open and jumped inside. In the mirror, he saw the scratch was deep and ragged. And there was blood. Lots of blood. His blood. And Sonny's, too. He grabbed the bottle of Chivas and poured it over the laceration, feeling it burn, praying that the alcohol would purify him.

He poured more whiskey into the torn flesh and sat there in the car, in the hot night, scrubbing the wound. Scrubbing and scrubbing and scrubbing it and beginning to feel that things would never be right again.

PART ONE

PIN HOOKING

THIS ROW OF SEATS, halfway up the grandstands at Bay Meadows Race Course, was Cliff's office. He was sitting here now, in the predawn cold, the tools of his trade in his lap, two stopwatches and a pad of yellow lined paper with the names of his horses on it: Mr. Doubledown, Epic Honor, Good Times Roll. He was here every morning. Only thing different about today was he had two Styrofoam cups of coffee on the seat beside him instead of just one.

Looking down the aisle, he saw Dan Van Berg working his way up the stairs. Big guy. Pushing thirty. Friendly face. But the way he moved—turning his shoulders, powering up the stairs on the balls of his feet—showed he had a hungry streak in him somewhere.

Cliff held the coffee out to him. "Thought you might want to see your horse work. Ramon's gonna breeze him here in a minute."

Dan eased himself into the seat, peeled the lid off the coffee cup, took a noisy sip.

Cliff said, "How's business?"

"Travelin' too much. Just got back from a seminar in Houston. How ya been?"

"You don't wanna know. Here! Here he comes now." He handed Dan a stopwatch. "Clock him when he passes the eight pole."

Dan tried to set down his coffee, burned himself, said, "Ah! Jesus!" He took the watch and turned toward the track.

Cliff already had their horse in his sights, could spot him from across the track even though there was a pack over there, each one looking pretty much the same in the early light. He picked out Ramon in his orange vest, saw him come around the turn on Epic Honor, then saw two horses coming up from behind, challenging him the way they do sometimes in the early morning at the track.

"*Now,*" Cliff said to Dan, pressing the stopwatch when Epic Honor shot past the eight pole and started down the stretch toward them. The other two horses were coming on strong.

But then Ramon set him down. Nothing big, just a slap on the rump telling him, *Let it out, boy.* Epic Honor laid his ears back and took off like a rocket. Watching, Cliff was connected to the horse, could feel the raw power flowing through him, could feel him reach down and stretch out.

Epic Honor pulled away by a length . . . two lengths . . . . The other jocks let their horses drop away, trying to save face, like they weren't really trying.

Cliff clicked off the stopwatch as the horse blurred past the finish line. "Twenty two and change. What'd you get?"

Dan was still juggling the coffee and the stopwatch. "I—I screwed up. Sorry, man."

"Twenty two and change," Cliff said again, smiling, feeling good because that was why he was out here, to cross the finish line first, and there hadn't been much of that lately. Not since the rains started. Since the track went dark and he lost his best horses. Yeah, he'd almost forgotten what winning felt like.

Dan said, "Who'd those other horses belong to?"

"Zacco."

"Nik Zacco? We kicked Zacco's ass?"

"Feels good, don't it?" Cliff said. "Let's hope we can do it for real on Thursday."

Cliff wrote *22 3/5* next to Epic Honor on the yellow pad. Looking across the grandstands, he saw Zacco was in *his* spot. Every trainer at Bay Meadows had staked out a place he worked from. Zacco was turning away, like he hadn't just seen his horses get beat. Cliff found himself resenting the smug bastard for his $200 haircuts, for his Derby win last spring, for his long list of Hollywood clients. In this business it's contacts, Cliff thought. Who you know and, in Zacco's case, who you blow.

"So our horse's workin' good," Dan said. "That why you asked me to swing by?"

Dan was smiling, trying to read him. Salesmen were like that. So no wonder Dan was making big bucks selling insurance. He even started his own company. But at least Dan was in a good mood. It would help Cliff with what he had to do.

"Actually, there was something else I wanted to show you."

Dan laughed, blowing steam off the coffee. "I kinda figured. So what's up?"

Cliff looked across the track to the sun coming up over Mount Diablo on the other side of the San Francisco Bay. The sunlight warmed him. And it felt good.

Cliff said, "You ever hear of pin hooking?"

They were standing beside a corral out behind the stables looking at a leggy colt that was staring back at them with an attitude like
Yeah? So what do you want? He was a roan with a white brush stroke
down his nose and the aura of raw power, like a young Mike Tyson.

"His daddy was Relaunch," Cliff said. "He was a great stallion,
won about a half a million bucks. They shipped him to every track
in the West and he never broke down. Horse was like iron. So this
guy comes to me yesterday from a ranch down in Texas. He sells
me this one for seventeen. He was Relaunch's last crop."

"Last what?" Dan asked, looking the colt over.

"The last colt Relaunch ever sired. You're lookin' at the last
Relaunch right here. Thought you might want a piece of the action."

"Nice lookin' horse," Dan said, stalling, thinking it over.

Actually, he wasn't much to look at, Cliff thought. Not with
those crooked legs. When he first saw the skinny teen-ager he
wanted to laugh. But then he saw him move and bells went off in
his head. *Speed.* That's what he saw.

It happened like that sometimes at auctions, or at the races, or
at the stables on the backside of the track. Nothing you could put
into words. Just a voice inside saying, *This one's the real deal.*
Besides, Cliff had seen plenty of good-looking horses finish last.
Like he always told his clients, there were a million ways to lose a
race, but only one way to win—cross the finish line first.

Cliff slipped into the corral and advanced on the colt. "C'mere,
you." He held out a Lifesaver. The colt looked at it and Cliff saw
the attitude again. Like he wanted the attention, but didn't want to
ask for it. *If this horse were a human,* Cliff thought, *he'd have red*

8

hair and freckles. The colt went for the Lifesaver and Cliff stroked his neck, his ears, rubbing him the way he knew horses liked. When Cliff turned away and ducked back under the railing, the Relaunch colt followed.

"How long's it gonna be before you can race him?" Dan asked.

"Ain't gonna race him. Gonna pin hook him. In a pin hook, you buy an unbroke yearling, get a rider on him and get him up to a quarter mile breeze where he can show himself. Sell him six months later at auction. And you look to double your money."

"In six months? You've done that?" Dan asked, showing that hungry streak he had.

"Done better." Cliff dug in the pocket of his windbreaker, pulled out a dirty envelope and handed it to Dan. On the back, handwritten in smudged pencil, were two rows of figures.

"Them's the last eight pin hooks I've done—what I bought 'em for, what I sold 'em for."

Dan focused on the numbers. Cliff waited, smelling the wet straw and manure hanging heavy in the air. Nearby, two grooms were hosing down a gray filly, whistling along with a Mexican radio station as they worked. Hot walkers and exercise riders passed, nodding to Cliff. Early morning at the track. This was Cliff's life; he'd been raised on the backside of the track.

Dan pointed a thick finger at the numbers on the envelope. "You're telling me you bought a horse for forty-five grand and sold him only six months later for— "

"A hundred and a half," Cliff finished. Then, in that even tone of voice, he added, "That was a winning situation."

Dan laughed. "More like big casino. But why's the horse worth so much more after only six months?"

"When the horse is growin' fast, lotta bad stuff can happen. Could buck a shin, could break down. I get 'em through that phase, I got a two-year-old that's ready to race. That's what they'll pay top dollar for at auctions—the Japanese, or them sheiks."

Dan rubbed his jaw, thinking it over. And when Cliff saw him smile, he knew he'd made his decision.

"I'm in," Dan said. "But I gotta tell you, this is a bad time for me. I want to build my own house. I got the property but I don't have the cash to start building. My wife would kill me if I told her what I was doing. So, I can only go five."

"Five's good." Cliff pushed his hat back on his head and breathed out, "I'll need a check in thirty days."

Cliff extended his hand and they shook. No contract. No receipt. Just a handshake. That's how it's done at the track.

Dan swallowed the last of his coffee. "How big a piece of this horse do you have?"

"I'll hang on to five, like you."

"Who's going to pick up the rest?"

Cliff shrugged, trying to play it cool. "That's something I wanted to ask you about. You got any fat cat Silicon Valley clients might want in on this horse?"

Dan understood it all now. "You were workin' me, weren't you? You were working me this whole time."

"I wouldn't call it that exactly."

But then Dan thought of something.

"I can't believe this. I just met this guy, an investment counselor I wrote some policies for. He was telling me he was looking for a horse. He's this young guy—type that likes to play the game hard. Know what I mean?"

"I know exactly what you mean."

"He's got this scar on his forehead and one eye is screwed up—from some auto wreck he was in. But he's Scottish and his accent just charms the shit out of everyone. And his wife—man, is she gorgeous. And, this is funny—she carries this little rat dog everywhere with her."

Dan was seeing the scene, laughing.

Cliff asked, "So, is the guy for real or what?"

"Well, he claims to handle forty million dollars worth of investments." Dan waited as Cliff absorbed that. Then he added, "So, you want to meet him?"

"Forty million bucks?" Cliff asked. "Now what do you think?"

Mr. Gastin opened a strongbox and removed a fanfold strip of checks that were tied to his money market account.

"Okay," he said with a heavy sigh. "What's my total?"

Malcolm Ravling punched numbers into his calculator with the tip of a thin gold pen. He looked at the total, touching the scar on his forehead as he did so.

At last he spoke. Soothingly, thoughtfully, with absolute conviction: "One hundred and seventy thousand, five hundred and sixty dollars." He wrote the amount on a piece of paper and placed it in front of Mr. Gastin.

"And I make it out to— ?"

"Ravling Financial Advisors. Or just *RFA*."

Mr. Gastin bent over the check, his thick fingers holding the pen. He hesitated, afraid to write such a frightening number. At last the pen began moving. He tore off the check and extended it to Malcolm, the edge fluttering.

"That's our life savings," he said to Malcolm. "Right there in your hands."

They stood up. Malcolm turned to Mrs. Gastin, who had been sitting to one side in the small living room. "Irene, thank you so much for the tea," he said in his lyrical Scottish brogue. He hesitated, almost shyly, then hugged her, feeling a wave of protectiveness toward this woman, blinded as she was by diabetes. He pictured the Gastins' excitement when they received the first statement on his gold-embossed letterhead, showing how much money he had made for them. They wouldn't be nervous then.

Outside, Malcolm moved easily down the walk leading from the modest bungalow toward the black BMW. He was medium height, but thick across the shoulders. Brown hair fell across his forehead into his eyes, giving him a schoolboy look.

Malcolm slid into the driver's seat and his wife, Becca, who had been waiting in the car, asked, "Did you sell him?"

"Of course." Malcolm stabbed the key into the ignition.

"What took so long?" she asked, stroking the little Pekinese in her lap. "Nookie and I were getting *soooo* lonely. Weren't we?" She kissed the top of the little dog's head.

"It was a big decision for him."

Becca laughed. "What was that guy's problem? It's like, *hello,* doesn't he know you're going to make him a fortune? You know? I mean, like, *hel-lo.*"

"We're due in Portola Valley at four, for the seminar," said his assistant, Gordon, from the back seat. Gordon was a year out of college with a thin, pimply face and spiky black hair. He wore a leather jacket over a crisp white shirt and tie and he kept Malcolm's schedule in a big black planner.

Gordon produced an elegant little cell phone. "I better call them."

"Why?" Malcolm started the engine, which gave an understated German growl.

"It's a hour's drive."

"Gordon," Malcolm smiled. "Give me a little credit here."

Malcolm pulled out and drove slowly down the street. When he turned the corner he put the accelerator to the floor. The car shot forward, blew the stop sign at the intersection and barreled up the freeway ramp onto I-880 northbound.

"Any calls, Gordie?"

"Dan Van Berg rang," Gordon said.

Malcolm couldn't help noticing that, although Gordon was *very* California, he was developing a slight Scottish accent and was using some of Malcolm's phrases.

"He's coming to the seminar. Says he found a race horse for you."

"A race horse, aye?" Malcolm smiled. "Brilliant."

Ahead, across the bay, they saw the TransAmerica pyramid building and the cluster of skyscrapers huddled improbably on the tip of the San Francisco Peninsula. The black car darted in and out of afternoon traffic, its speed still building. Becca let go of all feelings of control. But the little dog in her lap whined pitifully for the entire trip.

An explosion of applause followed Malcolm's presentation at the seminar in Portola Valley.

He looked out into the sea of smiling faces, mostly blue-haired ladies his mum's age, all clapping, nodding and talking to each other, saying how *smart* this young man was. How *charming*. How *clever* he was with finances. How much money he had made for Mrs. So-and-so. That's why he put on these "free" seminars. He didn't actually tell them anything. Just convinced them he was the right man to handle their estates. To help them avoid inflation and offset a variety of evil taxes.

Becca stepped up on stage and handed Malcolm a sweating bottle of Evian. She wore that clinging white top and tight black pants that defined her slim hips and long legs.

Behind her was Van Berg and another guy, the horse guy—a short, tough character in a green mackinaw, dark hair combed back hard, a baseball cap in his hands. Maybe thirty-one, thirty-two. Hard to tell with that weathered face. Malcolm could fairly *smell* the track on him.

Dan stuck out a big hand for Malcolm. "Great job, man. You had 'em eating out of your hand." He leaned in close and added, "For insurance? Me, okay? I can take care of anything you need. Anything."

Dan turned to the other guy. "Malcolm Ravling, Cliff Dante. Best trainer in Northern Cal. He's got a deal for you."

Malcolm felt the calluses on Cliff's hand as they shook.

"Got a horse I need backers for." Cliff's voice was low and intense. "Dan here said you might want a piece of the action. It's a pin hook deal."

Malcolm waited for more.

"Way it works, you buy an unbroke yearling, get him up to a quarter-mile breeze, sell him at auction for a profit."

Becca's face lit up. "A race horse? *Cool.*"

Cliff continued his pitch: "Horse with big-time pedigree goes for a bundle—"

"Mr. Dante, please. I've been around horses all my life. My father took me to the races every Sunday afternoon in Glasgow. So what're you selling then?"

Cliff looked uncomfortable. But he plowed ahead. "I got a yearling. Looks like a real athlete. Good mover. I got him for seventeen. I'm offering a share for seven."

Malcolm snorted. "Seven thousand? Chicken feed." Then something occurred to him. He eyed Dante, realizing this was exactly who he had been looking for. Dante knew thoroughbred racing, all the players in the game, how to move money and horses around. But like a lot of trainers, he probably wasn't too bright. Yes, he'd do quite nicely.

"I'm in," Malcolm said, offering his hand. Cliff accepted the handshake.

Becca laughed and said to no one in particular, "I don't *believe* this. He just bought a race horse."

"When do I get to see our horse run then?" Malcolm asked.

Cliff squinted at him. "Got to get him broke first."

"I *know* that. I want a horse I can wager on. I'm a punter at heart, you know. That's the fun of it, aye Dan?"

Dan said to Cliff, "What about Epic Honor? You got any shares to sell?"

"Epic Honor?" Malcolm asked, watching Cliff closely.

"He's a three-year-old. Small horse, but precocious—lots of speed. But, like I say, he ain't big. He could run under that table over there."

Becca laughed. She looked like she enjoyed the way Cliff talked.

"Matter of fact, Epic Honor's racing Thursday at Bay Meadows. I know an owner wants to cash out. I can give you a piece for twenty, but—"

"I'll take it."

Becca shivered with excitement. "I don't believe this. He just bought another race horse."

"Awright!" Dan said. "We've got the Relaunch colt for a pin hook—and Epic Honor's our runner. We're a team now. Team Dante."

Several elderly women stood nearby, booking appointments with Gordon. Malcolm was about to turn away when he thought of something. This was separate from the pin hook deal. But he saw the opportunity and couldn't stop himself.

"How're you set for investments, Mr. Dante?"

"Doin' all right, I guess."

"Where've you got your money?"

Cliff shrugged like it was obvious. "In horses."

"That's all well and good. But you can't ignore the long term."

"That's what my wife says. She don't like the fact I don't even have a will."

"A will?" Malcolm looked Cliff up and down. "I could take care of that for you—as a favor for my trainer. Gordon will make an appointment. Get it done in a half a tick." He glanced at the waiting ladies, then he looked back and winked: "See you at the track, aye?"

Everyone was gone for the day and she was watching the sun set from the 39th floor of her Houston office building when she heard someone enter the front office door. She walked down the carpeted hallway and found him standing in the reception area, tall, grace-ful—*dangerous*—like she remembered him. He removed his Stetson.

"Ellis," she said, taking his hand and finding his fingers long and cool and elegant.

"Linda." His voice was soft and velvety. "Been awhile."

"It surely has." She laughed, a little nervous. "Come on back to my office."

She settled behind her desk. He sat facing her, crossing his long legs, his jeans sliding up on a pair of snake-skin cowboy boots. He was her age, mid-forties, but his hair had already gone completely white — not gray like most guys—and it flowed down over his collar. This gave him an exotic appearance that went with the other things she had heard about him.

She lit up and saw him realize he could smoke, too. A pack of cigarettes appeared in his hand as if it was a card produced in a magic trick. He fired up a chrome Zippo and she saw that he wore a gold ring on his little finger, embedded with dia-monds. That reminded her to check—no, he wasn't wearing a wedding ring.

"Well, I hear you've come to no good," she said, blowing smoke out.

"I wouldn't say that exactly."

"You look well-heeled. How're you makin' a living?"

"This 'n' that. You know how it is."

"High stakes poker games is what I heard. Shootin' pool."

He smiled easily. "Variety of things, really."

"I remember in high school how you were always bettin' on the football games, horse races. What is it about other people's money that holds such an attraction for you?" Her tone was challenging but he didn't react. It seemed to remind him of a game they used to play.

She glanced out the window and saw the sun was down now, somewhere far away over West Texas, where they knew each other last. It was nearly dark in the office now, but she didn't turn on the lights. It was always easier to say things in the dark. Besides, the lights of Houston lit up the room like candlelight. And candlelight was always kind to a woman's face.

"I understand that you *do* things for people."

"How do you mean?"

"Things people can't do themselves." As if to explain she said, "I went back to our 25th reunion out in Odessa. Ran into Bo Coker. He told me what you did for him."

"What I did . . . ?"

"About that drunk that hit his wife, killed her and their kid."

He gestured with his cigarette. "It's sad, but folks just aren't getting satisfaction from the courts anymore."

She nodded, feeling suddenly like crying. Maybe it was because she knew he would understand when she told him what had happened.

"I called you because of something that happened to my little brother," she said.

"Sonny. He was something else. Whatever happened to him?"

"He was a deejay at KMEQ, then he got a steady gig at the Silver Fox. He was very funny, very quick. Everyone thought he was a hoot."

Ellis listened, watching her through a veil of smoke.

"He hit a bad stretch a couple years ago. Not workin' any, so he came and lived with me. I'm single again, so I didn't mind the company. And that's when it happened."

She drew a strand of her hair through two fingers. Her blond hair was her one really good feature. Everything else seemed plain to her, her body tall and lean, almost masculine. Maybe that's why she did well in business, because it was a man's world down here in Texas, and she looked a bit like a man, acted like one, too.

"Last year about this time, Sonny—" She stopped, feeling her voice begin to shake. Ellis just watched her, and she was reminded of a time when they parked in his Chevy pickup beside the river, drank beer and smoked Luckies. Now, they were together again, with the feeling of many years between them and the knowledge they might have spent that time together. And maybe then they would have been happy.

"I need your help. I heard you were willing to—to go *further*, than a private investigator for instance. Maybe even use force if necessary. Is that true?"

He spoke carefully. "Like I said, when people are wronged, they want satisfaction. They just ain't getting it from the courts anymore."

"Satisfaction. That's what I want. In fact, after you get some information about this deal—I'm going to join you. I need to do something about this situation myself."

"So I'm not going to work with Sonny?"

"No. You'll just be dealing with me."

"Okay." He smiled.

Buying time to let her emotions settle, she picked up the folder on her desk and took it to him. He watched her cross back to her desk and sit down again.

"You'll find some money in there for travel expenses."

Ellis opened the folder and found the fat envelope packed with hundreds. "Where am I going?"

"Wherever you have to—to find him. I heard he was out in California now. Pullin' the same kind of stunts he pulled here. He changes his name, uses Social Security numbers from people that are dead now. His photo's in there."

Ellis found the photo and angled it so it caught the light in the dim office. A man's face looked back at him. It was exactly the type of man Ellis hated. He knew just what to do with a man like this. And he'd have fun doing it.

From the darkness, across the room, he heard the hatred in Linda's voice as she said, "Let me tell you what that son of a bitch did to my brother."

When he got home from the seminar, back to his ranch in Pleasanton, Cliff went upstairs to do some bookkeeping. He was feeling pretty good about selling the two shares of the Relaunch colt. When Malcolm and Dan came through with the dough he could pay off some of these frickin' bills. He sat there in front of his computer looking at what he owed and the money he had coming in.

Cliff rubbed his eyes. Why the hell couldn't he focus?

He knew why. Knew all too well. It was just too damn quiet here. Usually, this time of night, this place was a madhouse. Jamie would be trying to get their three-year-old girl down while he gave Davie a bath. Jesus, he missed the kids.

And Jamie, too, with her honey-colored hair and her country-girl looks. They'd been married seven years and she'd always been there for him. Until now.

It had been a week since the big blow-up, Jamie sobbing, "I can't go on like this. Something has to change."

"You knew when you married me I was a trainer. You knew there wasn't no steady paycheck."

"But I thought you'd be winning by now," she said. "Besides, you're always gone."

That fried his ass. She didn't mind him being gone when he won a big purse from some stakes race. Like last year, when he took first in that graded stakes race at Santa Anita, he bought her a new Lexus. He'd cleared a hundred grand three years running. But this year was a different story.

First, he lost his biggest client, the president of Golden Eagle Investments, when the son of a bitch took his horses over to Nik Zacco. Then his best runner got a virus and was scratched from the last three races. And then the rains came and the track went dark and Jamie said she couldn't live like this anymore so she drove off with the kids in the Lexus he had given her. And now the house was a morgue. What he needed was a winning horse. What he needed was another Golden Eagle. What he needed was to hold his family in his arms again.

"Cliff!" His grandmother called from downstairs. She had a house across the way, but she had been staying with him since Jamie and the kids left. Probably wanted to make sure he didn't go off the deep end.

"Cliff!" she called again. "Vannie's here!"

He looked out the window, watched the truck and horse trailer below, backing up to the barn, delivering the pin hook, the colt.

"What'd you buy?" his grandmother asked as he headed through the kitchen. She was doing the dishes, leaning against the countertop as she worked.

"A yearling by Relaunch. Saw him last month when I went to that auction down in Texas. Wanna see him?"

"Not tonight. Don't trust myself two steps out the door. I fall and bust my leg, you'd call a vet and put me down."

"Not you, Grandma. I'll keep you around just to stop me from gettin' a swelled head."

Cliff put on his muckers, stepped out the back door and headed for the barn. The smell of the earth was heavy in the air. The lights of San Francisco glowed over the mountains to the northwest. Dark winter clouds blew in from the Pacific.

Cliff saw that Emerson had come out of his room in the barn and was standing there, waiting to see the new horse. The old man wore his customary flannel shirt and tight jeans, showing how bowed his skinny legs were. He moved toward the trailer with scuttling, crab-like steps. He'd been Cliff's assistant for eleven years, living in the tack room in the barn, all of his possessions in the suitcase he kept under the neatly made cot.

The driver climbed out of the pickup, leaving the motor idling, radio going. He was a young guy, lanky, greasy hair leaking out from under a baseball cap.

"Got a horse here for Cliff Dante."

"You're in the right place," Cliff told him.

"Rained like a bastard all the way up. Had a hell of a time finding the turnoff."

Cliff and Emerson said nothing, standing under the arc light on the side of the barn, watching the driver as he lowered the ramp and entered the dark trailer. They heard him inside, impatient with the horse, saying, "Come on, you!"

"Hey, hot rod," Cliff called to the driver. "Easy with him. He's just a youngster."

"What'd you pay for him?" Emerson said to Cliff. He always spoke in a whisper—his voice was blown out from cheering too many horses across the finish line.

"Seventeen. I'll take a third. Already found backers for the rest."

"Anyone I know?" Emerson's eyes twinkled under the drooping lids.

"Dan Van's in for five." Emerson nodded. "Rest belongs to this guy Malcolm Ravling. He's this young guy, Scottish or something. Kinda arrogant. Claims to handle forty million bucks worth of investments. His old lady goes everywhere with him, carries around this ugly lookin' mutt."

Emerson wheezed with laughter, shook his head.

They heard the driver's angry voice inside the trailer. "I ain't got time for games, ya son of a bitch," then the slap of a hand on horseflesh. The horse whinnied and they heard the heavy tread of his hooves booming on the trailer floor. Cliff jumped up inside, threw the driver up against the wall of the trailer.

"Touch my horse again," Cliff said, "I'll disfigure you."

The driver looked at Cliff, shorter than him, but in his face big time. He backed off saying, *shit,* stumbled out of the trailer.

Cliff stood there in the dark, sensing the horse's fear, and its pride, too. *A teenager with red hair and freckles,* he thought again.

"This here's your new home," he told the colt, touching his muzzle, stroking the velvety nose. A moment later he knew he could take the halter and lead him outside.

Stepping into the light, Cliff watched Emerson's eyes move over the horse, taking in the crooked legs. He looked at Cliff, shocked, but said nothing.

"I know, I know. But he's a good mover."

Emerson moved around the colt with his sideways shuffle, running his hand along his neck, his back, then down his rump. He bent to look closely at his legs and hooves. The colt danced back a few steps. Emerson chuckled. "Light on his feet."

The driver shoved a clipboard at Cliff. "Sign this and I'm outta here."

Cliff ignored him. "Watch him walk now," he said to Emerson. He led the horse in a circle. Emerson watched, thinking how he would work with him, imagining what he would be capable of in six months, a year. He saw him winning races and smiled.

"I had a feeling about him," Cliff said. "I think he's gonna show real nice."

Cliff finally accepted the clipboard without looking at the driver. He signed, handed it back.

"Good luck with him," the driver said, pulling the visor of his hat down.

"Luck's what we need, hot rod. Drive careful now."

The pickup and trailer pulled away. Silence returned to the ranch and the two men with the horse as they looked into the future. The future was always golden when you got a new horse. Because, Cliff knew, you were buying the promise of the horse, not the horse itself. And the promise was the same: *This one's the real deal.*

The wind picked up and brought a few drops of cold rain. Cliff instinctively looked up. Clouds were shooting across the sky, moving unnaturally fast.

"Let's get him inside."

They started walking the colt toward the barn as the rain picked up and Cliff said, "You believe this frickin' weather?"

"Shit no." Then Emerson paused and asked, "So, this English guy, is he for real, or what?"

A long black leather couch faced an enormous TV in the otherwise stark room. Becca lay on the couch watching "Braveheart." She was wearing a silk nightie, pinched in tight around her breasts with frilly lace across the top.

Images of sword fights and horseback riders and epic battles raged across the screen without provoking a visible response from Becca. One of her hands was moving under the nightie. Her breath was short, eyes glassy.

To one side of the TV a large window looked out on Marin County, the San Francisco Bay and the city across the broad stretch of water. The Golden Gate Bridge spanned the two bodies of land and the headlights of cars, crossing the bridge at this late hour, moved silently through the air like distant jets.

With a shuddering sigh, Becca stood up, knocking over the wine glass at her feet with a *ting*. She left the movie running, bare feet slapping on the hardwood floor as she unsteadily moved down the hallway past a bookcase holding hundreds of videotapes and into a dark study where Malcolm sat in front of a computer. She stood behind him, watching him work. At the top of the screen, above a column of numbers, it said, "Trainer Stats." His hands roved over the keys, as if his fingers were tiny animals in search of bits of nourishment. He still wore his suit pants and white shirt. Beside him on the desk was his open briefcase. Multicolored checks lay scattered over a deeper layer of contracts and documents.

Malcolm glanced up at her, returned to his work.

"You said you'd watch it with me tonight," she said.

"Go ahead and start. Be in in a sec."

"It's half over. You missed your favorite part."

Malcolm chuckled. "I ran a Dun & Bradstreet on Mr. Dante, the trainer. Checked his assets."

"And?"

"He's an empty suitcase."

"He still might be a good trainer."

"For my purposes, he might be just perfect."

The computer screen flickered and came up with a new page of information.

"Malcolm, you work all the time," she whined. "You need to do something besides make money."

"What could be more fun than making money?"

She smiled down at him. "Well . . . ."

A whispering sound diverted his attention from the computer screen—the sound of silk sliding over a woman's soft skin. As she lowered her arms again and dropped the nightie to the floor, Malcolm saw her breasts were free. Gloriously free. Calling him. He dove in. She laughed and pressed his face into her cleavage. He fed greedily. First on one precocious nipple, then the other. Her hands loosened his belt. His mighty sword sprang free. He lifted her up onto the edge of the desk, just the right height now for him to—he stabbed it into her. *Yes! God yes!* She leaned back and let it happen, feeling complete and full until, somewhere halfway through, when everything was going up and up, she opened her eyes, and saw that his right hand was back on the keyboard, working the numbers and getting very hot about whatever it was that he saw.

PART TWO

GLORY DAYS

IT WAS THURSDAY. Race day.

Dan was trying to clear his desk so he could head out to the track. He was in his office in downtown San Mateo, checking his e-mail. He had a two-room suite over Bob's Barber Shop, off El Camino Real, right down 25th Avenue from Bay Meadows. It was big enough for a start-up business. Only problem was, this old computer was so damn slow. He wished he had the bucks for a new system.

Dan's assistant, Veena, appeared in the doorway. "Dan, there's someone here to see you," she said in her musical voice with a slight trace of an Indian accent. "Mr. Dante. Cliff Dante."

He looked past Veena into the outer office. "Hey, hey! My man! Come on in, buddy!" He glanced back at the screen: seven messages. Maybe he could skim them before Malcolm showed up. They were all supposed to ride out to the track together. Malcolm was due any second. But the guy was always late.

Cliff was standing in front of his desk now, and Dan saw he

was all decked out. No green windbreaker and baseball hat today. He was wearing a shirt and tie under a navy blazer. His hair was combed back hard, a pair of wrap-arounds were parked up on his head.

"Lookin' sharp."

"Gettin' ready to get my picture took."

Dan laughed. "Wanna look good in the winner's circle, huh?"

"That's the plan."

"So how's Epic Honor?"

"Workin' real nice. Only problem is, we're up against this three-year-old of Nik Zacco's. Horse called Charlie—he holds the track record."

"Yeah, well, we kicked his ass last week. We'll do it again today."

Cliff gave a half-hearted smile as he stood there, shifting his weight, something on his mind. Dan waited, thinking, *Come on. Out with it, man.*

"Malcolm just called," Dan said. "I told him you were comin' here and he said he'd swing by and pick us up. Said he had a surprise for us. He's supposed to be here at —" He groped the desktop for his planner.

"Twelve-thirty," Veena said. She was still standing there with her clipboard and the to-do list, always ready to help him.

Cliff shifted again. "Look, I had a question on something . . . ."

"Fire away."

"Malcolm comes out to the ranch yesterday, goes over my finances with a frickin' electron microscope. I told him I just wanted to do my will."

Dan knew what was coming. He had used the old will trick

himself. Tell a client you need to see his finances to set up a will. Then, when you know where his money is, you know how to sell him insurance, investments, whatever.

"Now he's got me movin' money all over the map. Money-market crap here, IRAs over there. And he wants me to take my last $40K I got in a CD and buy some tech stocks. I go, 'Hey, I do my gamblin' at the track. Comes to money management, I stick it in a CD and forget about the son of a buck.'"

"Nothin' wrong with that."

"To hear Malcolm tell it, the stock market's free money."

"Lotta people're makin' big bucks these days."

"How about you? You play the market?"

Dan folded his arms across his big chest and frowned. "If I had more cash I would. My money's tied up in this property I own."

"He even wants to take out an insurance policy on me, 'cause we're in the racing deal together. Some horse kicks me in the head, he gets a bundle."

"In partnerships, that's not unusual."

Cliff suddenly held out a wad of papers. "Look this over, tell me what you think." Dan saw the gold embossed letterhead for *Ravling Financial Advisors*. It was a portfolio splitting up the forty grand into funds selected from Morningstar financial services. He had laid it out on a spreadsheet linking it to IRAs and additional insurance policies, all nicely diversified. Slick presentation. At a glance, it looked good. Still . . . .

"So what's your question, Cliff?"

"My question?" he seemed irritated. "Is the guy kosher or what?"

"People are throwin' money at him."

"That don't make him legit."

"True."

Suddenly, Cliff was heading for the door. "I gotta go see our horse."

Dan stood up. "Wait a second. Why don't you ride out to the track with us? Malcolm's gonna be here any second."

"I'll see you there."

And he was gone. Funny guy, Dan thought. Asks for my advice, then he splits before I can say anything. He glanced back down at the papers in his hand.

Veena cleared her throat. He looked up and saw her standing there with the to-do list and a mysterious smile in her dark eyes. Indian women always looked so *wise*. Hell, she was wise—she kept the business going, not him.

"Yes, Veenaben?" He used the formal construction of her name.

"In most cases, when you meet a new associate, you run a check on him."

"True."

"You haven't done that with Mr. Ravling."

She was right, of course. Here was Malcolm Ravling, writing millions of dollars of insurance through his company, and he hadn't even checked the guy out. That's because he bought the image—the flashy suits, the fancy car, the diamond-studded wife. And now it took Cliff and Veena to ask if he was kosher.

"Okay, get Hershel to run an inspection report on him."

"Very good."

A flash of light on glass caught his eye. Down in the street he saw two stretch limos pull to the curb.

"Is this . . . ? Oh my God," Dan laughed. He was trying to see through the limos' black-out windows. Could this be Malcolm? The drivers were getting out of the limos, looking for the entrance next to Bob's Barbershop. A moment later there was a knock. Veena went to meet him at the door.

"Mr. Van Berg?" The limo driver was a big blond guy squeezed into a chauffeur's suit. He had a big grin on his face like he knew a joke you didn't.

"Mr. Ravling sent a car for you. And another car for Mr. Dante."

"Mr. Ravling sent a car—for *me*?" It sounded like a line out of an old English movie. No doubt about it, Malcolm really knew how to live.

"Why did he send two cars?" Dan asked. "I think we could all squeeze into one."

The driver smiled. "You'll see."

"Well, you missed Mr. Dante. But I'm ready to go."

As he headed for the door, Veena was on him again. "Your wife called earlier. The contractor needs you up at the property for a site inspection."

"Tell him I'll be there first thing tomorrow."

"And a Mr. Gastin just called."

"Who?"

"He had a question about a policy Mr. Ravling sold him. It's written through our company."

Dan stopped, frowning. But then he waved it away. "I'll call him tomorrow."

"I'll see that I remind you. And Dan . . . ? Good luck."

"Thanks, Veena."

Dan walked downstairs, waved to Bob, cutting the last few hairs on some chrome-dome's head, and out into the street. Rain from last night was still dripping off the trees. But it was sunny. Clear and sunny and warm. Stunning. Dan took a deep breath, inhaling the smell of flowers. Sunny skies were ahead.

Dan slipped on his shades and approached the limo. The big blond driver opened the door, the grin still pasted on his face. Dan ducked inside, forgetting to take off his sunglasses. In the darkness, the door closing behind him, the scent of the leather interior mixed with an expensive perfume. How could this be? Malcolm was supposed to be in here.

"Mr. Van Berg?" It was a voice out of a wet dream.

"Yes." He whipped off his shades, eyes still adjusting to the dark.

She was leaning back into the leather seats, arms thrown wide, one leg up, skirt stretched tight across her thighs.

"Who are you?" *Man, was he cool or what?*

"I'm yours."

"Mine? For what?"

"Whatever you want. Compliments of Mr. Ravling."

He was about to say something when the limo shot forward, throwing her into his arms. She laughed like a tiger purring. He fought bravely, trying to free himself, hearing himself laugh, a goofy lecherous laugh and all the time thinking, *Cliff, buddy, you don't know what you're missing.*

When he got to the track, Dan hung out at the paddock, people-watching while he waited to hook up with Malcolm and Cliff.

The rail-birds were there already, guys with racing forms and pick sheets in their hands, checking out the horses as they were led into the paddock for the fourth race. Dan liked to try to figure out people by the way they dressed, the way they talked. Some of these guys were studying the horses, making notes in their programs like they knew what the hell they were doing. Others were working the stats in the Racing Form. Other guys were trying to get tips from their buddies. Everyone was busy working an angle. Except that tall guy across the way, white hair flowing out from under a Stetson. He lounged against the rail smoking a cigarette, looking dangerous. What was he all about?

"Daniel."

He turned to find Malcolm in front of him, expensive dark suit and crisp white shirt, Ray Bans hiding the bad eye. Becca was standing next to him—looking lost without her little rat dog to hug—and Gordon trailed behind, waiting for commands.

"Malcolm," Dan returned, "you're looking prosperous. How's life treating you?"

"Life is good. Have a cigar." Malcolm whipped out a long black cigar. "Arturo Fuente—Opus X. Cost me thirty bucks apiece."

Dan took the cigar and smelled it. Wow. It was exotic and subtle, bringing back memories of college poker parties and the occasional round of golf with clients.

"Enjoy the ride over?" Malcolm winked.

"Yeah, well, I gotta tell you," Dan said. "I'm married."

"What's the relevance?"

"The girl you put in the limo. I don't go for that kind of thing.

I mean, I do but—I don't want to screw up my marriage is what I mean. Besides, if I did anything, I'd feel so damn guilty."

Malcolm looked amused. "Guilt isn't in my repertoire. Maybe Cliff was more adventurous."

"You missed him. The limos came after he'd already split."

"Damn."

Malcolm produced a lighter, a gold affair that looked like a miniature arc welding set. The flame popped to life and they bent in to it. Between puffs Malcolm added, "What's the point of privilege if you don't take advantage of it?"

Dan's cigar was on fire. He stepped back, waving the flames out.

"Malcolm, I'm hungry." Becca walked toward them, taking teeny weenie steps, wearing a skirt so tight it showed everything she wasn't wearing underneath it.

"Hello Becca," Dan said, puffing the big cigar. "You're looking lovely today."

"Why thank you, Mr. Van."

Malcolm growled: "It's Mr. *Van Berg.*"

Dan laughed. "Everyone calls me that. *Dan Van I'm your man.*" He was enjoying the cigar, acting like a fat cat. *Privilege.* Maybe Malcolm was right. Maybe he should loosen up.

Cliff looked at his watch. Thirty minutes to post.

"Guess I'll head on over to the paddock," he said. But he didn't move. He just stood there in the quiet stall on the back side of the track, a pigeon cooing in the eaves above, sunlight slanting in from the window high on the cinderblock wall. He stroked Epic

Honor's neck; the chestnut coat was like velvet. The horse was calm—very calm for a three-year-old who could run like a dream. Cliff ran his hands down the horse's dark legs, thinking, as he sometimes did, how unlikely it was that a one-ton animal was supported by matchstick legs. Bone, tendons, a sheath of muscle. That was it.

"You iced his legs yet?" Cliff asked.

"Thirty minutes. Is that what you wanted?" It was always thirty minutes, for every horse before every race. But Emerson would check with his boss to make sure he got it just right.

"Thirty should do it."

Cliff removed the muzzle from Epic Honor. On race days he only got a couple scoops of grain. So they had to use the muzzle to stop him from eating his bedding.

"I'll leave the wraps on till I get him over to the paddock," Emerson said in his whispery voice, gray hair combed back, mustache neatly trimmed, watching the horse and watching his boss, too.

A high-tech tweedling noise came from somewhere, out of place in this stall with the smell of the earth and animals in the air. Cliff pulled a cell phone from the pocket of his navy blazer. He always wore the blazer for stakes races. He'd won a bunch of races in it so he knew it was good luck and always wore it. Unless the purse was above fifty grand—then he wore the suit.

He unfolded the tiny phone. "Cliff Dante."

"Malcolm Ravling here. It's race day. You nervous?"

"I been here before."

Malcolm laughed. "Well said. Well said."

Epic Honor sensed he no longer had Cliff's attention. He tried to bite the cell phone. Cliff fought him off as Emerson wheezed with laughter. The horse's big teeth bit the loose material of Cliff's sleeve and shook him playfully.

"Thought I'd ring up and let you know . . . ." Malcolm was saying, "I bought those funds for you."

"Sorry?"

"The mutual funds we discussed, to anchor your financial package. Write me a check when you get a second."

Write you a check? Cliff thought. You're the one owes me seven grand on the pin hook, and twenty for Epic Honor.

Malcolm felt Cliff's hesitation. "Then too, perhaps you want to put your money somewhere else . . . ."

"It's not that. I don't know nothin' about this stuff. I mean, I'm just a dumb horse trainer."

In the background, Cliff heard another voice, Becca saying, "Malcolm, come on!"

Malcolm came back on the line. "Meet for a quick one before the race?"

"Sure thing. I'll be at the paddock in fifteen."

Cliff flipped the phone shut and turned back to Emerson. "You believe that shit? He didn't even ask me. Just bought 'em."

"Who was that?"

"Malcolm Ravling." He saw the questioning look in Emerson's eyes, so he said, "the Slimy Limey"—just like that. It just came to him so he said it.

Emerson nodded, knowing now who he meant.

"Okay. I'm outta here." Cliff left the stall.

The stables were quiet as he began the long walk to the paddock. As he stepped outside, he heard the bell across the infield. It was from the starting gate for the third race. As he moved into the tunnel under the track and over to the grandstands, he heard the crowd cheering the horses around the clubhouse turn and into the stretch. Just hearing it did something to him. He felt the excitement building in his gut.

By the time he came out the other side of the long tunnel, the crowd had settled down again. The winners were cashing their tickets and buying drinks for their friends. The losers were studying their pick sheets, asking who looked good in the fourth, dreaming of winning again next time.

Just like he was.

At the paddock, he saw them all standing there: Malcolm and Dan Van smoking stogies, and Becca and Gordon standing nearby looking bored. They all saw him coming and applauded his entrance. He smiled, feeling uncomfortable, wanting to just concentrate on the race. But no, this was part of the job too. Make the clients feel like he was worth the dough they were shelling out for him to train their horses.

"Cigar, Cliff?" Malcolm asked.

"Thanks. For later, maybe." He tucked the cigar away in his inside coat pocket, next to the ones he had brought.

"Are we going to win today?" Malcolm asked, his voice coming from behind a cloud of blue smoke. Becca waved at the smoke, wrinkling her nose and saying, "Ewwww."

"I always come to win, Malcolm," Cliff said, his eyes narrowing.

A squeal of joy from Becca. They all turned.

"Look at our horse," she said, clapping her hands excitedly. "He's *sooo* beautiful."

Epic Honor was being led into the paddock by a groom, Emerson shuffling along beside them carrying the saddle. They guided the horse into the stall beneath the number six, posted on a large blue plaque, the same blue as the jockey's silks.

Time to saddle up. Cliff approached this ritual the way a ballplayer laced his cleats before a big game. He threw the saddle over the horse's back, then bent to slip the strap through the buckle and cinched it tight across the Epic Honor's belly. He checked the bridle and the position of the bit in the horse's big mouth, feeling the muffled clicks of teeth on steel as he did so. Using his hand turned sideways for measuring, Cliff checked the tension of the headstall. Then he crouched beside Epic Honor and stripped the wraps off his forelegs with short, deft motions.

Cliff stood up and looked at his horse. Epic Honor tossed his big head and nudged Cliff's hand, wanting his affection. "Go get 'em, buddy," he said in his horse's ear, rubbing him just the way he liked.

They followed Epic Honor down the narrow runway between the grandstands, walking on the springy cedar chips, and emerged into the open with the crowd behind them, murmuring, getting set for the fourth race. Ahead of them, Nik Zacco walked beside the big black horse named Charlie, talking to the jockey, a young hot shot named Duran. Zacco shot a look back at Cliff and nodded, exuding ease and confidence.

In the saddling area, just below the grandstands, a jockey swaggered toward them, small but intense, like a rooster in blue silks. A riding helmet was perched on his head, his goggles pushed up and the crop held loose in his hand.

"Hey, Niko," Cliff said, smiling through the wrap-arounds.

They shook hands.

"Cliff."

"Que paso?"

"Hangin' in there, man." Niko Lopez stifled a yawn. "So what've we got here?"

Just another race for him, Cliff thought. *For me it's blood and guts.*

"You got a lot of horse here—fastest in my barn. Lotta gas so don't be afraid to go for the lead," Cliff said.

"Where do you want me?"

"You got speed on the inside so I want you to break clean and get out front. If you miss the start, make a move in the turn and close big." Cliff stroked Epic Honor's nose. "Like I say, horse's got plenty of gas. He wants to run."

"Don't worry, Cliff, I ain't gonna choke him."

"All right, man. Catch us a break out there."

Catch us a really big break, Cliff thought. *Come on, turn my luck around. Turn my life around.* First place money was forty grand—minus ten percent to the jock and ten to the trainer. That left 24K split three ways. Then there was the two hundred cash he'd put on the nose. If Epic Honor finished first that would mean he'd have plenty of money for groceries, a little breathing room. He'd pay some bills, then buy some gifts and take them over to Jamie and the kids. Let Jamie know the good times were back.

Cliff gave Lopez a leg up onto his mount. He bounced once, one foot in the stirrup, and climbed aboard. Now he was looking down at them all. He flashed a big white smile at the owners. The groom turned Epic Honor's head and led him toward the track. Watching the horse go, Cliff felt nervous for himself and nervous for his horse, protective, wanting to share the victory but knowing he had to shoulder the disappointment of a loss, too.

Ten minutes to post.

They moved up the steps toward Cliff's box in the Turf Club, which had seats and tables instead of just the concrete steps and steel railings in the grandstands. They were right above the finish line, the grounds sprawling below them, with the neatly raked dirt track and the smaller, inner oval of turf. The starting gate was distant across the infield, and then there were the stables and ramshackle buildings on the back side of the track. And beyond that were the offices of Silicon Valley—Intel, Apple, Oracle—where a whole different type of gambling was going on.

Malcolm looked at Cliff, his voice quiet, soothing, as he slid an envelope out of his inside coat pocket. "Here're the funds I got for you."

The envelope flashed white in the sunlight. Dan watched the exchange.

"I don't know why I need all this," Cliff said. "I mean, I just wanted to do my will. What's so hard about that? I kick the bucket, it all goes to my old lady."

"You say that now. What if Epic Honor turns out to be a Derby winner?" Malcolm asked, pronouncing it "darby." "What if our pin hook, the Relaunch colt, goes for half a million at auction? You want all that to go up in taxes?"

Dan seemed eager to agree. "You aren't prepared, taxes can be a real bite in the shorts, man."

"And in this market, Cliff, the future is always bright." Malcolm smiled, suddenly unpretentious. Cliff saw how the boyish looks, brown hair falling on his face, the off-kilter eye, could all come together and be charming. His gut was telling him *Go slow.* But then, what did he know? He was just a dumb horse trainer. Besides, Dan seemed to think the guy was for real.

Gordon and Becca slowly approaching the box now, Becca sipping a plastic cup of white wine.

"Gordon, fetch Dan 'n' a round of the best malt whiskey they have here." Malcolm flashed a hundred dollar bill. Gordon snapped up the bill and disappeared.

Becca saw the envelope in Cliff's hand, with the gold-embossed letterhead reading RFA Inc. "Oh! You're investing with Malcolm?"

"Just doin' my will."

"He'll make you a fortune. Seriously. Did I tell you what he did for my father?"

Cliff squinted at her, shook his head.

"He used to work at Target. Okay? Malcolm took his savings and made him a fortune. Now he spends all his time on the golf course."

Cliff opened his program and checked his notations on the race. He looked at the tote board. Malcolm watched Cliff studying the odds and reading his program.

Malcolm said, "So, who're you going to put your money on in this race?"

"Told you, man. I don't bet." Cliff slid the wrap-arounds off the top of his head and into place, hiding his eyes.

Dan shot a look a Malcolm, having fun. "No. Of course you don't bet. But say you did, who looks good? Besides our horse, the six horse, to win."

Cliff took a last look at the horses below them, ready to run. He consulted his program filled with mysterious marks and symbols.

"Epic Honor to win. So I'd take six, eight and three," Cliff said.

"In what order?"

"Just like I say: six, eight and three." Cliff smiled at them, cocking his head. "Five minutes to post. Think I'll get a quick one before the race. Be right back." He stepped out of the box and disappeared up the steps.

Dan and Malcolm traded a look, sensing the confidence in Cliff's prediction.

"You know, Dan, it might spice things up to put a few dollars down on our horse," Malcolm said.

"I was thinking the same exact thing," Dan said.

"Back in a tick," Malcolm said to Becca, stepping out of the box.

"Me too," Dan said, following Malcolm.

Standing near the betting windows, keeping an eye on the TV monitors hanging from the ceiling, Dan said to Malcolm, "Did he say six, five and—?"

Malcolm was digging in his inside coat pocket. He hauled out a big wallet, one of those continental jobs with room for weird-sized bills. "No, no. Six, *eight* and three."

"I'm going for an exotic. Just for the hell of it." Dan laughed, pulling out a few singles. "I'll go for the trifecta. Stay loose and bet a deuce."

Malcolm gave a disgusted laugh.

Dan said, "Hey, trifecta's a junk bet. If you win it's big casino. But it's a long shot."

"Unless you've got an inside source."

Dan felt the excitement stirring but said, "Look, if Epic Honor wins we split the purse—thirty grand. That's excitement enough for me."

He was about to head for the betting window when Malcolm grabbed his arm.

"Fuck, man." But with his accent it came out *foock mun.* "Don't you see what we've got?"

"What?"

"Look at these punters." He waved his cigar at the lines of people waiting to bet. "They're just pissing in the wind, hoping they hit something. But Dante *knows.* He knows the trainers, the jockeys, the horses."

"There's stats on all that stuff."

"But our man's got the eye. The *eye.* He reads horses like I read the market. Don't be a pussy. Put down some real money."

Malcolm planted the cigar back in his mouth and turned away, leaving Dan looking at the bills in his hand, which suddenly seemed like chump change.

The betting window was clear now, four minutes to post. The window seemed to be beckoning Dan. The cashier, a middle-aged woman with dark-frame glasses, sat there smiling neutrally, wearing a green blazer. He thought of what Margo would say if she knew what he was doing. He thought of the house they wanted to build. Then he glanced at the monitor. Their horse was going off at twelve to one. If it won, it'd be big casino. If he hit the trifecta that would be . . . *holy shit.*

He stepped up to the window.

"May I help you?"

"Fourth race, Bay Meadows. Trifecta baseball. Six, eight and three."

"How much?"

"Twenty."

"Anything else?"

"Same race. Six horse. On the nose."

"How much?"

"Two hundred."

She punched in his bet and his betting slip popped up out of the machine. When he took it and put it in his pocket, it felt like a million bucks.

Ellis had heard them calling her Becca when he watched them in the paddock. Now, Becca was left alone in their box in the grandstands, sipping a glass of white wine, the sun shining on her silky blond hair, while the men went off to place their bets. He couldn't help noticing what a pretty little thing she was. He felt certain she wouldn't mind if a stranger with an easy Texas drawl asked a few innocent-sounding questions.

"Pardon the intrusion," Ellis said. Surprised, she looked up at the man with the flowing white hair, leaning over the railing, holding his Stetson in his hand.

"Yes?" She smiled uncertainly. She looked to him like a child, a little lost child. Of course she had a body that could burn a house down, but still . . . .

"Gentleman that was here a moment ago, believe I've met him. But I can't for the life of me think of his name."

"Which one?"

"One smoking the cigar."

She thought that over. "They all had cigars."

He laughed lightly. Who said blondes were dumb? He gave her

a better description, recalling the photograph Linda had given him. It was hard to imagine that the man he saw here today was capable of doing those things to Linda's brother. But Ellis knew a man's face seldom revealed what he could do in the darkness.

When she gave him the man's name, Ellis carefully committed it to memory.

"Reason I ask, I believe I've crossed paths with him in Texas. Did he ever reside in the Houston area?"

"I—I don't really know."

Ellis noticed the big rock on her finger, 24 carats glinting in the California sun. Funny, it was hard for him to tell which man she was with; it was hard to tell who was with who, really. Like that weasel with the thin face and the spiky black hair. Where'd he fit in?

"He'll be back any second if you—"

"No, no. I don't want to intrude. Just had to satisfy my curiosity."

He started to leave.

"And your name was?"

"Ellis."

"Ellis what?"

"Ellis is enough." He nodded, smiling. "Bye now."

He moved out of the box, placing the Stetson on his head. Coming in the opposite direction, down the aisle, was the skinny little weasel carrying a tray of drinks. He eyed Ellis sharply as they passed. When he reached the little lady, Ellis heard her say, "Gordon! Where have you been?"

Gordon? Ellis filed the name away for future use.

Gordon asked, "What'd that guy want?" But by then Ellis was out of earshot, taking the stairs with long strides, threading his way through people hurrying to the windows to place last-minute bets.

Ellis decided to call Linda now, then come back and watch them some more. Either that or he might try to catch Gordon alone, see if a few free drinks would loosen his tongue. Maybe he could find out where all that money was going. Assistants, secretaries—underlings of all sorts—were a good source of information. 'Cause they usually had a bone to pick with their boss. Ellis would find his dissatisfaction and exploit it.

Ellis found a phone booth, stepped inside and shut the door. He dialed. Linda picked up on the first ring.

"Found him," he said.

"That was fast."

"Wasn't much to it, really. Cop friend of mine ran a few of those socials you gave me. Just saw him and verified it."

"Where are you now?"

"Racetrack near Frisco."

There was a pause during which he heard her lighter scratching in the background. He pulled out one of his own and the phone booth filled with the wonderful smell of fresh tobacco smoke. It made him think of the card games he played in the dark rooms filled with smoke, men talking in low voices.

"So how's our man doing?"

"Doing quite well by the look of things."

"You have his number? His address? All that?"

"His office, yeah."

"What about his home?"

"I'll get it if you want."

She waited, putting it all together in her mind. "Get everything you can on him until I get there."

"When're you coming?"

"Soon as I can get away. I'll need you to pick me up at the airport. Where're you staying?"

"Little fly speck motel near the airport. Looks out at the bay."

"Sounds lovely. Get me a room there, would you? I'll be there mañana."

They were quiet for a moment, each reacting to the idea of being together again and feeling okay about it. They had this business between them, so there would be no expectations—even though they weren't the type to have them.

"Say, Ellis?"

"Yes ma'am." His voice was lazy and slow.

"Make an appointment with him. I'd like to meet him. Face to face. I want to see what kind of a person could do a thing like this. Tell him—" she chuckled. "Tell him I have this big pile of money I'm bringing into the state. I need some advice about insurance or tax shelters or—I'm sure you can think of something."

"I'll make the appointment . . . . as long as you let me come along."

He heard her draw hard on her cigarette, then breathe out, her voice husky as she said, "From here on in, sugar, I won't go anywhere without you."

Three minutes to post.

Cliff leaned against the rail in their box in the grandstand, his stomach grinding as he watched the horses being led to the starting gate for the fourth race. Cliff had seen thousands of races, watched hundreds of his horses run with big bucks riding on the finish. But that didn't stop him from getting that clawing nervousness, like he'd swallowed a cat and the damn thing was raking his guts. A lot was riding on Epic Honor—the last of his ready cash, trying to impress his two biggest clients, maybe even the future of his marriage. *Jesus, put some pressure on yourself, why don't you?*

"*The number six horse is approaching the gate . . .*" the track announcer said over the P.A. system.

Cliff saw Epic Honor being led into the gate. He could see Lopez getting the feel of the horse underneath him, his knees up high, adjusting the reins, pulling his goggles down into place.

"He's very calm," said a whispery voice beside him. He turned and found his assistant trainer Emerson moving into the box.

"All set?" Cliff asked him.

Emerson nodded and flashed the betting ticket at Cliff. He had put $200 on Epic Honor for Cliff because Cliff never went to the window himself. Someone might follow him, see who he was betting on, try to jiggle the odds. All sorts of bad shit could happen. So Cliff always sent Emerson to bet for him. It was better this way.

Malcolm and Dan came back into the box. Malcolm picked up one of the whiskeys, drank it off and said, "Where's Gordon gotten to?"

Before Malcolm got an answer, Becca took the betting slip out of his hand. She read the amount and dropped her jaw. "You put all that on our horse?" She covered her mouth as if she had let something slip.

Malcolm shrugged and said, "Just a thousand—a kilobuck on a sure thing."

Becca turned to Emerson, and asked him, "But isn't horse racing, like, really dangerous for the jockeys?"

Emerson blinked at her, a little amazed, and said, "Yes."

"I mean, do you think the jockeys ever worry about falling off?"

He considered this question carefully. "If they do, they're finished."

"The number three horse is approaching the gate . . . ."

They all stared across the track at the starting gate. Cliff saw the last horse being walked into the gate. A groom shoved the horse into the tight space and quickly closed the door behind him.

"The flag is up!"

Cliff thought *Here we go,* and felt the nervousness ratcheting up.

"And they're off!"

Cliff heard the bell and saw the horses explode from the gate and sprint for the rail. He searched the pack for a dark chestnut horse and the blue silks, and saw him three back on the rail. *Shit man! I told you to break clean and grab the lead!*

Epic Honor was in third. But Cliff had to like what he saw: His horse was moving with long even strides, still calm, poised, holding back as they went into the turn, keeping his position on the rail and waiting for his chance.

The horses were close enough to see with his own eyes now. He turned and saw them halfway through the curve, bunched tight in a pack, flowing over the ground like a single enormous beast rippling with muscles, eight riders on one animal throwing off a spray of dirt and sweat. And now, here they came, closer . . . closer . . . breaking into two groups, Epic Honor still third but boxed in on the rail, seeing the stretch opening up in front of him but with nowhere to go.

Cliff could feel the horse's calmness giving way to something else, to blind determination, the wild joy of wanting to run as fast as his muscles and heart could carry him. They were moving out of the turn now and he saw that Lopez was taking him wide. *Too wide! Jesus, don't go six wide!* Now he had a longer race to run—he had to cover more ground. And he had to make up the extra distance in the stretch. No one could do that. Unless Epic Honor had a fifth gear. This was it. It was time to find out what he had.

Let him run, Lopez! Cliff was screaming inside his head, frantically sending the message to his jockey. *Turn that son of a bitch loose!*

And that's when he saw Lopez set him down.

In the gate before the race, Lopez had been thinking how Epic Honor was in the six hole and that wasn't good because there was a lot of speed on the inside and the first horse to the rail might win the whole enchilada. Six furlongs wasn't much more than one long turn and a stretch to hold on for the finish. With a big purse on the line, every horse and rider out here would be going tooth and nail for the finish line. And once the winner's purse was cut in pieces the jockey would take 10 percent for risking his ass out here among hurtling bodies and flying hooves.

Epic Honor was walked into the gate and the doors closed behind him. Lopez felt the horse relaxing underneath him, so he worked to keep the horse's head up, his attention focused on the race, his weight balanced and ready while the last horse was finally shoved into the gate. A second of silence, then—

BBRRINNNGGGG!

The doors flew open. Lopez dug his heels in and Epic Honor shot forward, sprinting for the rail but—too late. Two horses got there first and now he was eating the spray of dirt the leaders threw up. Lopez looked for daylight between the horses, feeling the energy of the three-year-old surging between his legs, and got that breaking-loose-inside feeling as he realized he was on top of a real runner. *Plenty of gas,* Dante had said. No shit, man. This horse wanted to go to the front. If only there was the room to get there.

Into the turn now, still boxed in on the rail. Epic Honor was so close to the lead horses he was afraid they'd clip hooves. Lopez pulled him in a little, trying to hang on and hope it opened up in front of him or else he would have to go wide on the outside. But there wasn't time now, he thought. He was coming out of the turn now and he saw the stretch a quarter mile down the track.

Holy Jesus, this horse was fast! Epic Honor was practically pulling the reins out of his hands, ready to claw his way over the backs of the horses in front, or squeeze in along the railing. Damn shame, Lopez thought, all this speed and nowhere to go but wait for another day, another race.

And then it happened.

Lopez almost wanted to laugh with amazement. The lane to the right opened up and there was daylight inside. Beautiful wide open daylight. Nik Zacco's horse, the gray named Charlie, was moving up the outside and the horses in front of Epic Honor sensed him coming and went outside, leaving just enough room to—

Epic Honor saw the opening at the same time as Lopez and he put the crop to him thinking, *Okay let's see what fifth gear's like.* He felt Epic Honor leap through the opening and begin chasing Charlie with the raw desire of a young champion. So here they were, closing on Charlie with five lengths, gaining ground with each stride.

The jock on Charlie saw them coming and turned the horse's head to show him they were being chased. Charlie veered left as they closed and bumped Epic Honor, coming on fast, startling the horse and making him falter. Then he regrouped and poured it on, down the stretch, two horses locked in a dead heat for the finish line with two lengths to go, running their hearts out.

Up in the box, Cliff saw his horse get bumped in the stretch, and when he saw how the race finished he slammed his program into his hand and yelled *Dammit!* and burst out of the box.

The board was flashing **"Inquiry"** as he ran down the steps to the track with Dan behind him shouting, "He did it, man! He closed big time!" But Cliff had seen more races than Dan and he was getting a bad feeling. A real bad feeling because he knew the stewards didn't want to take down an odds-on favorite like Zacco's horse Charlie.

Cliff was thinking, *Not this time. I need first, not some nice-try-bullshit second place finish.* He had reached the track now and could feel the soft dirt under his feet and saw Lopez galloping out with his arm raised, signaling a foul.

Epic Honor circled back and stopped in front of Cliff and Dan. The horse was breathing hard, blasts of hot air shooting from his nostrils, and a calm part of Cliff thought, *This horse's got a great set of lungs.*

Malcolm was charging into the group now with Becca struggling to catch up with itty bitty steps. "Do we have a winner?" Malcolm demanded, red-faced.

Lopez jumped off, landing in front of Cliff. "Don't worry man. We've got this race."

"Bullshit!" Cliff was really pissed. "What the hell happened? I told you to get out front and hold on. Instead we get hung six wide."

"You over-trained your horse, man," Lopez sneered. "He fell asleep in the gate."

A slap in the face to Cliff. But before he could answer, Lopez saw the horse named Charlie circle back. Duran jumped off. And Lopez went for Duran. The other jock saw Lopez coming, and knew why, and was ready for him as Lopez waded in, throwing quick little punches, arms pumping, their helmets falling away as Cliff and Dan jumped in to break it up.

Malcolm stood back, laughing, watching the action from behind his sunglasses.

Zacco appeared out of nowhere and jumped into the middle of it, throwing an elbow at Dan who felt the pain stab below his eye. Dan said, "Oh yeah?" and hauled off to take a swing at Zacco's big face. But someone dragged Dan backwards and he fell over the two jockeys, locked together and fighting like pit bulls. Cliff pulled Lopez off and stepped between them and everyone stood still, breathing hard, then brushing themselves off and feeling a little foolish.

Cliff held Lopez by the arm, dragging him back, yelling at Zacco. "Get a leash on your jock, man. You guys been to too many rodeos to pull this kind of shit."

"Your man cut me off!" Duran said, spitting pink saliva in the dirt.

"Watch the video," Lopez said. "Then I'll finish you off." He broke loose and lunged at Duran again, but then Becca screamed,

"Oh my God!" They turned and saw the lights on the board flashing "**OFFICIAL**" to show the final results were in:

Win 6

Place 8

Show 3

Dan looked at Malcolm, stunned. Malcolm smiled and said, "Unbelievable."

Cliff let go of Lopez, who brushed himself off, dabbed a nostril that was leaking blood and said, "So okay. So you happy now or what?"

It was sinking in. Dan slugged Cliff in the shoulder and yelled, "We won! I can't believe it. We won!"

You couldn't tell much from Cliff's expression. All he said was, "I never seen 'em take down an odds-on winner."

"Yeah, but we won!"

Cliff wasn't even smiling. He'd trained himself to do that. But inside, he was going nuts, starting to calculate the payoff, starting with $200 on the nose at 12 to 1.

Zacco saw what was happening and charged toward the officials, fuming like a home run hitter called out on strikes.

Lopez gave the other jockey the finger and turned to pick up his helmet.

"Come on man," Dan yelled to Cliff. "We won!"

When Cliff didn't react, Dan slapped him on the back and yelled, "Big casino, baby!"

Cliff finally smiled, "Hey, I told you we came to win. You think I was kidding?"

They were moving toward the winner's circle now, Cliff starting to work the numbers, thinking, *Our share of the purse is forty grand, minus the jockey's cut . . . so we'll split about . . . . Plus a hundred at 12 to 1 makes two and a half K. That means I can cover the price of our pin hook, the Relaunch colt. Hit Malcolm up for the rest and . . . .*

"Cliff! Cliff! Get in here!" Becca grabbed his arm, squeezed it tight against her breast, as she towed him over to stand next to Malcolm, lining up for the photo. Epic Honor stood nearby, as calm as ever. Cliff's cell phone cut through the chatter. When he hung up a moment later, Malcolm saw his expression and asked, "Who was that?"

"Eddie Voss—biggest owner in California."

"He hear about our horse?"

"Hear about him? Hell, he wants to buy him."

"What'd you tell him?"

"I go: 'Get in line.'"

"Well done, lad. Well done." Malcolm said, putting his arm around Cliff's shoulder, laughing. They all smiled. And the photographer froze the moment.

After calling Linda, Ellis had returned to watch the men in that box in the turf club. He had seen Gordon and the little blonde having words about the stranger who had stopped by. *Looks like I stirred up a hornet's nest*, Ellis thought. Then, just before the big race, Gordon took off. Now did that make sense? *I think not.* So on a hunch, Ellis followed him, thinking he might learn who fit with who or—more importantly—who was conning who. Then, when Linda flew into town tomorrow, he could lay the whole thing out for her.

Only problem was, they were stuck in traffic on the north-bound lanes of the Golden Gate Bridge, Ellis in his rented Chevy Lumina and Gordon in a Saab convertible several cars ahead. Ellis could hear his radio, see the little weasel twitching around, moving to the music, slapping the steering wheel. Generation X. *Shit.*

Ahead of them, across the Bay, an enormous mountain of rock rose out of the water. Marin County. Afternoon traffic had moved a grand total of a quarter of a mile in the last fifteen minutes.

Traffic stuttered forward, then stopped.

Looking around at all these Californians, in their Acuras and BMWs and Land Rovers, Ellis hated them all, believing that his hatred was proof of his loyalty to the Lone Star State. But the hatred he was feeling this afternoon actually sprang from a deeper, more personal, source. He had first noticed the hatred infecting his system when his gambling skills began to deteriorate a few years ago.

The decline had started one afternoon on the golf course. In those days he made his living hustling in the country clubs around San Antonio and Austin. He was facing a four-footer to win the press on eighteen and the match. The putt was worth $750. Setting up over the ball, he heard a voice in his head say, *What if you miss?* It was the voice of doubt, softly whispered, that undercut his confidence. And confidence, in the final moments of any game, was what had always carried him to victory. The putt slid past the hole. It was the first of many misses that eventually drove him out of the game.

Pool was next. His confidence held for several years and he made a nice living, choosing his opponents carefully, slowly increasing the bets. But the day came when the shots that should drop didn't. All the close calls seemed to go against him. It wasn't technique or nerves. It was that damn whispering in his head: *What if you miss?*

And so he finally arrived at the card table, where motor skills were not part of the equation. Here it was card sense and the ability to read people. He was making out quite nicely. But he knew his luck with cards would end, too. And all he would be left with was the hatred. He decided, then, to make the hatred work for him.

Traffic on the Golden Gate Bridge moved another hundred yards, then some more. It was breaking up. Soon they were on land again. Ten minutes later, he watched the Saab convertible pull into an office building on a side street, a three-story structure with exposed redwood beams, built against a mountainside. Gordon took the outside stairs and let himself in through a glass door with those Levelor blinds across them.

Whose office was this? And who did Gordon work for? Ellis was sure he was an assistant; he had that toady look to him, like he was used to kissing hind titty. Funny how ready a lot of these assistants were to sell out their bosses.

Time for a little walk, Ellis thought, feeling restless and cooped up in the cramped, impersonal rental car.

The sun was down now, so Ellis moved easily, with a rolling gait that suited his tall frame. He stepped lightly on the stairs so as not to shake the flimsy building. Beside the door was a sign: RFA Inc. Looking through the blinds, Ellis saw the front office was dark; a light from the rear illuminated Gordon as he sat, intently staring at a computer screen. At one point, Gordon glanced up quickly, looking toward the front door as if he thought someone was coming. Why did he look so guilty? What the hell was he up to?

Ellis returned to the parking lot, circled the building and climbed the back stairs. He found himself directly outside the office in which Gordon was working. Back here, he was shielded from the street, up against a hillside which was dark and leafy; the faint gurgle of a stream mixed with the hum of distant traffic.

Staring through the rear window at this Gordon character, Ellis realized that without meaning to, he had begun scheming. Among other things, money had been misappropriated from Linda's brother. Dirty money was here somewhere. Ellis surely would like to know where it was now. He'd never steal someone else's hard-earned money. But dirty money? That was another thing entirely. That was fair game.

Two hours later, Ellis had smoked three cigarettes. He carefully stubbed out the butts, shredded them and scattered the paper and tobacco on the plants down below. He was just beginning to wonder if ole Gordy was going to pull an all-nighter when he saw the weasel stand up and leave through the front door.

Ellis moved to the end of the rear balcony and watched Gordon's Saab pull away. Then he returned to the rear window he had been looking through and slipped the knife from his boot. The long blade caught the rays of a distant streetlight as it moved steadily toward the latch. Odd, Ellis thought, that doing something like this didn't make him the least bit nervous. That's because he knew he was hunting for justice. And no one could stop a man who had justice on his side.

After their big win, Dan, Malcolm and Cliff had cashed their betting slips and, their wallets fat with hundred dollar bills, they drank some more and bet on a few more races. Then they called a limo and had the driver take them all over to Scoma's on the waterfront in San Francisco.

After a bacchanalian feast, with the best wine in the cellar, Malcolm ordered a round of Louis the XIIIth brandies at $110 a shot. He sat back and said to Dan and Cliff: "You know, in France, they protect this brandy with armed guards."

Malcolm was feeling nicely pissed, like he was floating in a bubble above the table. All in all, it was a very fine scene. Nearly perfect, except for one nagging concern.

Where in hell was Gordon?

Becca had told Malcolm about the visit from the tall white-haired stranger at the turf club, and how Gordon left shortly after that. Malcolm had his eye on Gordon lately because he sensed his assistant was restless. He was around all that money every day and he probably wanted a bigger share. That was only natural. But it meant Malcolm had to watch his back now. Strangers asking questions about him, his assistant disappearing—this wasn't good.

"Armed guards?" Dan laughed. "Come on, man. You're full of it."

"You'll believe me when you taste it—or when you smell it. This brandy is so strong, when the waiter brings it, you'll smell it clear across the room."

"Stuff I drink's like that, too," Cliff said. "But it don't cost a hundred a pop."

"Becca, you've tasted it. Tell them how—" Malcolm said, but he turned and saw her vacant chair and remembered seeing her wobble off toward the loo.

"I gotta hand it to you rich guys," Cliff said, "you can sure spread the bullshit thick. Now these ain't expensive but—" he pulled a slim cigar out of his pocket. "Caribbean Rounds. They ought to go nice with that Louis the Whatever brandy."

"No, no. I got this covered," Dan said, reaching into his coat pocket. "Macanudo Pantigas," he announced proudly, holding up a much thicker and longer cigar.

Dan offered the cigar to Malcolm, except Malcolm was reaching into his inside coat pocket, casually saying, "I purchased these on the black market while I was down in the Bahamas a few months ago, setting up an offshore trust for a client." With a flourish, he whipped out the thickest, longest stogie any of them had ever seen. "Cohiba. Care to try one?"

"*What* are you doing?"

They turned and found Becca looking at them, as each held up his own cigar as if it was a symbol of his manhood. She covered her mouth and began to giggle, and seeing themselves as she did, they had to laugh too. But in the end, they all accepted Malcolm's black market Cohibas and fired them up.

A waiter appeared and Malcolm gave him detailed instructions about bringing coffee with the brandies. Dan elbowed Cliff and whispered, "What'd I tell you about this guy? He really knows how to live."

"Cigar's my way of celebrating," Cliff said. "Picked up the habit from my father. He won a claiming race, it'd be one kind of cigar—he won a stakes race it'd be a better one. If he won a featured race, he'd go out and get the biggest damn stogie he could find, chew on it the whole rest of the day."

Malcolm began sniffing the air. "Wait," he said sniffing some more. "I think . . . ."

Dan turned and saw the waiter approaching with a tray of brandy snifters. "You saw him coming!"

"*Smelled* him coming."

"You're so full of it," Dan said. But he was laughing, enjoying Malcolm's style.

The brandies were distributed and Malcolm raised his glass. "To victory."

They were silent a moment, swirling the amber liquid, then sampling it.

"Good stuff." Cliff said, smiling. A rare smile. Malcolm was beginning to see Cliff was a reined-in kind of a guy. Nothing like a little Louis the XIIIth to loosen his tongue.

"I'm tellin' you, nothin' feels better than kickin' Nik Zacco's ass," Cliff said.

"Yeah, but he's a great trainer," Dan said.

"You ask me, the guy couldn't train a goat to eat shit. I hate the son of a bitch."

"Why?"

"Me 'n' Nik got the same taste in horses. So if I'm at an auction and he sees me bidding, with all that money, he just runs right over the top of me."

"Not anymore," Malcolm said, punctuating his point with his cigar. "From now on, I'll back you—all the way."

"This one time," Cliff said, "a guy named Birdie Jolly called me up, says he's onto a horse he thought I'd like, horse called Traces of Gold sellin' for seventy-five. The horse is runnin' in Texas, but they ship her to OakLawn. She's runnin' two times a month. This horse was iron. And only seventy-five grand, okay?

"So I've got first shot at her because it's the one time Birdie was onto a live horse. But I knew Birdie worked with Zacco too, so I send Nik a fax, 'Check this out—only seventy-five grand and she's runnin' Group 3 at OakLawn.'

"Pretty soon I get this message on my machine and it's Zacco. He says, 'Don't you *ever* call me with no jackrabbits from Texas. What are you? Brain dead?' He goes on and on about what a dumb piece of garbage I am.

"So I get him on the phone, and I say, 'Hey Nik, I'm tellin' you, your clients and everyone else, I don't want to talk to you no more. And if I run into you again, I'm gonna hurt you. You don't feed me, I don't feed you.'"

"So what happened?" Dan asked.

"So I buy the horse. She winds up making seven hundred grand, and they sell her for five hundred grand as a brood mare after she's retired from racing."

Malcolm's laughter rumbled appreciatively as he thought of all that money.

"Nice horse," Dan said.

"The horse was iron," Cliff said. "So now, every time I run into Zacco at a yearling sale or whatnot, he runs right over the top of me. It's not his money. What's he give a shit?

"This one time, he outbids me, then starts mouthin' off about it. I go up to him and I go, 'Nik, you better stop with your smart one-liners, or I'm gonna disfigure you.'"

Dan exploded with laughter. "Ask my wife if you don't believe me, she was there. I go to him, 'I don't think you know how to fight. And we're gonna find out right now.' Then he's all apologetic. 'Oh, I didn't mean nothin' by it.' And blah, blah, blah."

They all laughed. They drank.

Malcolm smacked his lips. "This brandy reminds me . . . . My old dad, when he was pissed, man, he was a mean old sod."

Malcolm looked up and saw that Gordon had just entered the

restaurant and was heading toward them. Good. He liked this story—he would lead the laughter at the punch line.

"One night I come home late for tea. My old dad's standing there at the top of the stairs, drunk as a sailor. He says, 'You'll be comin' home on time or you'll nay come home at all.' *Boom!* He throws me down the stairs. Then he says, 'Aye sure! Now cry ya little baby, cry to your mummy!'"

Gordon stood near the table listening. Malcolm saw it must be raining out again because drops of water glistened on the shoulders of his coat.

"Well, I pick myself up, I go chargin' up those stairs and *boom!* smashed him right in the foockin' mouth. He reels back like, looks at me out of one eye and hands me the bottle. 'Aye, you punch like a man—now you can drink like a man.'"

A thunderclap of laughter. Malcolm watched as everyone laughed, applauded. Except for Gordon. Malcolm saw he was just standing there, silent. Normally, he'd be leading the laughter and keeping it going.

"Oh did we get drunk that night!" Laughter dying down now. "Sadistic old sod, he was." Malcolm raised his glass. "To first place. Well done, Cliff." He finished his brandy.

Fortified, Malcolm finally faced Gordon.

"Decided to join us then?"

"We have a problem."

"Oh we do? What type of problem?"

"We need to talk—alone."

Dan said, "Oh, so it's *that* type of problem."

Malcolm finished his brandy and said, "Very well then." He stood up. They all began getting unsteadily to their feet.

"I'll take care of this," Malcolm said, grabbing the bill which had just appeared.

"No way," Dan said. "It's gotta be—"

"Dan, Dan. Next time we win, you can do the honors. Besides, it was my idea to order the Louis the XIIIth."

Malcolm produced a cube of credit cards bound with a rubber band. He chose one but Becca stopped him.

"That one's full," she said softly. He sorted through the plastic and lifted out another. She shook her head. Leaning in, she pulled one out and said, "This one's okay."

They all moved to the front door. They stood outside under the awning and Malcolm saw that it was, in fact, raining. Raining very badly. He stood there feeling Gordon's eyes on him and had the strange feeling that a moment was approaching that he'd dreaded for a long time.

"Becca, you lot—take the limousine. I'll go with Gordon. He came in my car."

"Malcolm, please." Becca took his arm. He hated her clinging like that. He really hated her. He needed to think clearly now because it was starting. That time he knew would come someday. It was here now.

"I'll be home soon. Don't wait up."

"Shit," she said. "You're always gone, running off to Europe or—"

"Cliff," Malcolm put his arm around Cliff's shoulders as they watched the limousine circle the parking lot, coming toward them, "after what I saw today, I want a bigger piece of the action. Think you could put together a list of horses I could buy into—say maybe a hundred grand worth?"

Cliff nodded. "Sure thing. I'll call you tomorrow."

The limo pulled up and Dan, Cliff and Becca disappeared inside. The door closed and the limousine pulled away.

Malcolm stood there watching the rain jump on the pavement, falling on the boats along the wharf, hissing as it beat on the surface of the water. He turned to find Gordon staring at him.

"Okay, Gordie. What's this problem then?"

Gordon waited, searching Malcolm's face. "I think you already know."

"I have no idea what you're talking about," he said. But inside Malcolm was thinking, *He knows now. He knows everything.*

PART THREE

TRUE COLORS

WHAT THE HELL'M I doin' here? Cliff wondered, listening to Becca going on and on as they sat together in the back of the limo, heading to her house in Marin County. Dan had bailed out at a CalTrain Station to catch a train back to his office, where he'd left his car. And Malcolm had gone off with Gordon, so that left him in the hot seat, listening to a steady stream of Dear Abby from his biggest client's wife.

Except that, with the booze and glow of the race and the hunch that his luck was turning, Cliff was actually listening to Becca and, you know, it was starting to make sense. And that was, like, kinda scary. Besides, the rain outside and the hum of the tires below them, moving them through the night, made it cozy in here together. All in all, he was feeling better than he had in quite some time.

"So I'm like telling this friend of mine how I got this really cute exercise suit at Nordstrom. And my friend goes, 'But Bec, you're like *so* not into working out.' And then I go, 'Didn't I tell you Malcolm bought a race horse?' And we both start laughing and she goes, 'That's *so* typical of you.'"

Cliff didn't know what the hell she was driving at, but he laughed anyway, a laugh that sounded kind of phony to him. Kind of like *heh heh heh.*

She didn't need his laughter to keep her going. She touched his arm and said, "You don't know about me, do you?"

"No. But I been catchin' the drift here pretty quick."

"Malcolm is always saying all I think about is clothes—not the thing I'm going to do in them," she continued. "I go, 'That's not true. I like to sunbathe and I don't wear *anything* for that.'"

She covered her mouth and laughed, turning to face him.

"I know that sounds like so *extreme* but I think people should feel free about their bodies. Don't you?"

"Oh yeah. I think that's an excellent idea," he said, shifting his seat.

"I mean, like when Malcolm and I were house hunting, the only thing I said was we've *got* to have a house with a yard where I can sunbathe in the nude. Cause I *hate* those white lines the straps leave."

"I hate it when I get them things, too."

She slapped him playfully. "*Shut up.* I'm just saying, people shouldn't be so uptight about their bodies. That's all. Subject closed." She turned away and pretended to pout.

He touched her shoulder. "Sorry. I didn't mean nothin' by that." He could feel the warmth of her body under the thin fabric. He forced himself to pull his hand away.

She turned back to him. "You think I'm a complete ditz. Don't you?"

"Yes."

"Okay, then I won't say what I was going to say."

"Come on. I want to hear it." Christ, he was acting like he was in high school.

"I mean, that stuff about buying an exercise suit, I brought that up for a reason."

"I knew that."

"Yeah, *right*. Okay, what was I going to say?" He was caught flat footed. "See? You can't figure me out. You think you can but you can't. Ha ha!"

"Gimme a break. I'm sittin' here trying to follow all this. And I can tell you, it ain't easy."

"That's cause you don't know me yet. Once you know me you'll listen and just think, *Okay, whatever*." Her laughter ran up and down several octaves. "You must think I'm such an airhead."

"Just go ahead and tell me the thing you were going to tell me in the first place." He paused, hearing what he'd said. "Shit, I'm starting to sound like you."

She swung at him, another playful slap, but he caught her hand.

"You're fast," she said as he held her hand.

"Gotta be around you."

He released her hand, glanced out the window and saw they were winding through side streets, climbing the side of a mountain, probably close to her house now. Then what? Would she ask him to come inside for milk and cookies?

"Okay. Are you ready for this?" Her face was bright with expectation. It was amazing, being with a young woman, Cliff thought, even if she was one taco short of a combination plate.

"I want you to give me riding lessons."

"*Me?*"

"Yes you. You know how to ride, don't you?"

"Course I do. But I'm a trainer."

"So train me to ride. I want to dig my heels in and go really fast." She bit her lip and made a suggestive expression. "Did I say that wrong?" Laughter. "See, since Malcolm is buying horses all the time—"

"All the time?"

"That's why he goes to England so much. He goes to auctions over there and buys horses. He didn't tell you that?"

No, he sure as hell didn't happen to mention that particular detail, Cliff thought.

"With horses, like, all around me all the time, I can't stop thinking about them. They're so, you know—" She stopped herself. "I had this dream the other night where—No. I don't think I better tell you that one. But seriously. Would you teach me to ride? Pleeeeease."

Okay, let's start with a bareback lesson right now, he thought.

The limo slowed. The driver's voice came to them, muffled. "Which one is it?"

"The third on the left." She peered through the windshield. "Malcolm's not home yet."

The car stopped in front of a three-story white house built into the side of a hill with picture windows facing the Bay. A double garage opened directly into the street. A wrought iron gate led to a tiled staircase along one side of the house. Cliff looked up and saw the windows were dark, streaked with rain. It was coming down pretty good. Now that they were stopped he realized the day was coming to an end. He felt glum.

"Shit," she said, her voice losing its sparkle. "I *hate* going into the house when Malcolm's gone. It freaks me out."

"You got an alarm, don't you?"

"Yes. But Mr. Spaceman forgets to turn it on." She whirled on him. "Would you come in with me? The driver can wait or—I'll drive you home."

"Naw. I gotta be at the track at five in the morning." But then Cliff thought of his own house, dark and empty.

"It'll just take a few minutes and—and you can tell me about the horses. Oh say yes. *Please* say yes. Malcolm would thank you for helping me." She took his arm, a child afraid of the dark. Hell, he didn't mind being the big strong hero, looking behind doors for the boogie man. Been a while since anyone made him feel like a hero. For that matter, it had been a while since he had done any bareback riding.

"Well, okay. But I gotta be on my way pretty quick."

"I'll just get changed and then I'll run you home in the Mercedes."

They piled out of the limousine and thanked the driver. The big black car slid off into the night. Cliff imagined the driver chuckling lecherously. Screw him, Cliff thought as he found Becca taking his hand and leading him up the walkway to the big dark house.

"I've been with you for about a year now, and I've had a lot of suspicions, lots of little things. But I never really knew for sure what you were doing. Then, this afternoon, at the track, when that guy from Texas came up and started asking questions—"

Gordon paused, looking over at Malcolm to see how he was taking it. Malcolm sat behind the wheel of the big black BMW, staring at the road between swipes of the wiper blade. Light from oncoming cars splintered and moved across his grim face.

"I went back to the office," Gordon continued, "and—and I got into your files."

Malcolm slowly turned to him. "You did *what*?"

"Your computer files. I know your password. There's that picture, behind your desk, and in the reflection in the glass I can see your hands on the keyboard. So I watched and—I got your password."

The car hurtled into the turn. Malcolm could feel the tires gripping and slipping. Gripping and slipping. The road straightened out, then he saw the turnoff, the sign flashing at them between beats of the wipers. The only sounds were the ticking of the turn signal and the creak of leather as Malcolm shifted in his seat.

"Let me explain something to you," Malcolm said. "There's a reason my files are protected. The way I handle money is . . . unorthodox. That's how I make so much for my clients. I mean, think of it, lad—you don't get rich doing things the *normal* way."

Gordon was silent.

"So for you to think you can break into my records and understand what I'm—"

"You know," Gordon interrupted, "My mother used to say, if something looks too good to be true, it probably is."

"What the foock does that mean?"

"I thought you were, like, psychic or something, the way you read the market."

"That's my job, to be one step ahead. I'll show you. When we get to the office."

"*Right.* You don't have to do this anymore Malcolm. Not with me. "

They were pulling into the lot now in front of Malcolm's office building. The headlights swept the empty parking spaces, the dark windows reflecting back their high beams. They climbed the stairs in silence. It was nearly midnight and the neighborhood was quiet around them, rain falling steadily, soaking their hair, their jackets, soaking the hillside and the streets and earth beneath it.

Malcolm fed his key into the lock and shoved the door into the dark office. It felt unfamiliar in the dead of night. They squinted as the fluorescents came on. They moved into Malcolm's office.

"When I first started, I noticed you positioned your desk so you could see the front door." Gordon waited, watching Malcolm's face, smiling, letting him know he knew his secrets. "I thought it was like weird, okay? Like *why?* But after I saw that guy at the track, it clicked. You're afraid someone's going to come get you. Someone from the past that you'd—cheated." There, he'd finally said it.

Malcolm felt he couldn't stand this anymore, the way that Gordon was smugly exposing him. He felt he might explode. But he forced himself to say, "A cheat, aye? That's what you think I am?"

"Well, my mother used to say, if something looks too good to be true—"

"I don't give a foock what your mother said."

A wave of fury hit Malcolm. He felt dizzy, like he might black out and do God knows what. Must keep his hands busy. Must keep calm. He reached into a cabinet by his desk and removed a bottle of Chivas single malt and two cut-glass tumblers.

"Let's have a wee goldie, shall we? Then we can—" He felt a draft and turned. The window was ajar. *"Great.* You're in here muckin' about and you leave the bloody window open."

"I didn't—" Gordon shut the window and locked it. Turning, Malcolm thrust the tumbler into his hands. He clinked his glass, urging Gordon to drink.

"Pull up a chair. I'll show you how it's done." Malcolm pressed the computer's power button and waited. Something was wrong. The screen remained dark, displaying the message "Disk not found."

"What in the hell have you done?" He slowly turned to Gordon. He could feel the hot blood rushing to his face.

"It was working when I left." Gordon's confidence was evaporating, his evidence gone. The whole thing was backfiring on him.

Malcolm stared in silence at the computer in front of them; it stared back with its single eye, dark and lifeless except for the message, "Disk not found."

"Hello," Malcolm said, looking at a pile of small screws on his desk. He saw that they fit into the now-empty holes on the computer case.

"Someone's taken it apart," Gordon said.

Malcolm slid the tin box back, then tipped it up like the hood of a car. There, below, were the guts of the computer. Lying across the tangle of wires and computer boards was a broad electrical strap with a plastic connector on one end.

"Someone's taken the hard drive," Gordon said.

"I wonder who could have done that?" Malcolm responded sarcastically. He felt suddenly calm as he fixed Gordon in his stare.

"Malcolm. It wasn't me."

"Course not, laddie. But say it was, what would you be planning to do with it?"

"What do you mean?"

"Let's just say you took the hard drive. Now you'd think you have leverage against me. Aye?"

"You mean, like *blackmail* you? No way."

"No? What were you going to do?"

"Offer to help you."

"Help *me*? Do what?"

"Get people's money. And, since I was sharing in the risk, I deserved, well, a bigger piece of the action. Because, I mean, you're making a fortune here . . . ." His voice trailed off as he watched Malcolm's face.

The silence of the night pressed in on them. They looked down at the pilfered computer, then back at each other.

"But I didn't take the hard drive, Malcolm. You've just got to believe me."

Malcolm poured more scotch for himself. He was ominously quiet. Then, deliberately, he filled Gordon's glass. He raised his glass, urging Gordon to do the same.

"Good stuff, this."

Gordon took two big swallows. Malcolm's expression seemed almost dreamy as he said, "Lucky. I've got everything backed up on my laptop at home." His voice was unexpectedly friendly. He looked Gordon up and down.

"Tell you what, let's pop over to my place. Talk this over. I'll tell you how the whole thing works. Then, when we're done, you can tell me what you did with the hard drive here. How's that sound? Hmmm?"

"Malcolm, I—"

"Yes, yes. I know. It wasn't you."

Malcolm drank off the rest, set the tumbler down and said, "Drink up."

Gordon drained his glass.

"Off we go then." Malcolm gestured for Gordon to precede him through the doorway. They clicked off lights as they went, then shut and locked the front door.

Descending the stairs, Malcolm looked down at the top of

Gordon's head bobbing in front of him so vulnerably, making him flash back to that night last year in Texas when he dealt with Sonny. At the same time, he remembered what Gordon said earlier. *You're a cheat.* The rage boiled up again and he impulsively slapped the side of Gordon's head, boxing his ear.

"Ow!" Gordon turned on the stairs, clutching his ear in pain as he looked back up at him with a hurt expression on his young face.

"You stupid little shit!" Malcolm roared. "You have no idea what I'm doing. People *trust* me. That's why they give me their money. Because they *trust* me!"

Gordon was cowering, his back against the railing halfway down the stairs. Seeing him there, so pathetic, rain glistening in his spiky black hair, Malcolm couldn't stop himself. He smashed his fist into the thin face. Then he seized Gordon by his coat and threw him down the stairs. Standing above, powerful again, Malcolm wished his father was alive to see him handling this situation, see how he stood above Gordon, who was struggling to find his feet. Malcolm descended heavily, step by step, saying, "I gave you a chance to work with me. And you do *this* to me! People wouldn't give a little shit like you one penny."

Malcolm had reached Gordon, who was wobbling on his feet. He grabbed the back of his coat and his belt—bouncer style—and ran him at the big BMW. The car bucked on its springs as Gordon's head crashed into the door post between the front and back windows. He crumpled and slid to the ground, face down to the pavement.

Suddenly, Malcolm's anger vanished and he felt sorry for what he had done. Malcolm knelt next to Gordon. He stroked the back of his head, smoothing his hair. The young man didn't move.

"Gordon," he said softly. "You have to understand. I'm going to pay all my clients back. Every last penny. Because they trust me." He shook Gordon ever so gently, as if to rouse him from sleep. "Do you hear me? Every last penny."

He shook Gordon again. And again he got no response. It was then that he noticed the blood flowing out of Gordon's ear and forming a sizable pool on the wet pavement.

When they reached the front door Becca rummaged in her tiny purse for her key as wild yelping came from the other side of the door. Little mutt was getting so excited it might pee the floor, Cliff thought. The big door swung open on the still, dark interior. She flipped on a light.

"There. Phew! What a relief!" She crouched beside the dog, petting it and cooing, "Nookie, Nookie. How is my precious little Nookie?"

All sorts of inappropriate comments formed in Cliff's mind concerning the use of that word.

She stood up and Cliff saw her wet dress was pasted to her breasts, her nipples pinched tight from the excitement and the cold. She saw Cliff was enjoying the sight.

"*Cliff!*"

"Better'n a wet T-shirt contest."

"Want me to dance?" She pulled her dress away from her skin, adding, "Don't answer that." She waved him into the living room. "You can wait here while I get out of these things."

It was a high ceilinged room with hardwood floors. He looked around at the sparse furnishings, a long white leather couch facing a large-screen TV, a rack of videos—not what he expected from Mr. Money Bags. Cliff found Becca was still standing in front of him, looking expectant. He felt he was rushing toward something inevitable, the claiming of a gift—her body—and it was a dangerous and wonderful feeling he hadn't experienced for a long time. He remembered it from years ago, being a teen-ager and wanting like hell to do it with some hot babe and then realizing that she wanted it just as much.

"I'll just get out of these things," she said again, backing away, a move that invited him to come along.

But he didn't follow. His feet turned to lead and he stayed put, alone in the living room as she disappeared, still yacking about something or other. She opened a door and stepped out of sight.

Cliff turned and saw the dog staring up at him.

"What do you want? Huh Nookie? Huh? Ya little rat." He bent to pet the dog and it flopped on its back. He scratched its ribs, saying, "Go on now, fiddle. Fiddle." The dog's hind leg kicked orgasmically.

What the hell was Becca doing in there now? Cliff wondered. He pictured her bare-chested, rubbing herself with a big fluffy towel.

"Ah, Cliff?" Her voice drifted down the hallway.

"Yes ma'am?"

"*Cliff.*" A little more urgent now. "I, uh, need you."

Need me? Well, we all have needs, he thought, hearing a voice in his head: *Get your spurs on cowboy! Time to rodeo!* His feet were moving now, toward the light, thinking he could at least get an eyeful before saying he really shouldn't. The other voices, the other spectators that he carried with him through his life, were stepping back, aghast, as he moved down the hallway.

It took him a half dozen strides on his way to marital disaster before he realized the "need" Becca referred to was something else. He heard her voice, muted, but quietly hysterical saying, "Don't. . . Please don't . . . . " and "Just leave, okay?" And a strange man's soft, menacing voice.

Cliff reached the door, his system exploding with adrenaline as he saw the scene framed in the doorway, a scene which didn't make sense at first: Becca, in panties, clutching a shirt to her chest, one arm extended to ward off a tall, rail-thin man with long white hair, his arm reaching out to Becca.

"Hey shithead," Cliff said. "Who invited you?"

The man's head snapped toward Cliff's voice but his hand was still extended toward Becca. She screamed, "He's got a knife!" And then Cliff saw it, long and curved and wicked.

They all froze.

A scrabbling of nails on hardwood floor. Nookie came barreling through the door, yelping and snapping at the intruder.

The tall man's eyes moved to the dog. Cliff kicked at the knife. The man rolled away, turned full circle and lunged at Cliff, the knife zeroing in on his heart. Cliff danced aside like a bullfighter avoiding the horn, and felt a burning line spread across his chest. His feet got tangled up in the dog and he fell back against the wall.

The man's tall frame was rushing past Cliff. He stuck out his foot. The man went down in a heap, the knife sliding across the floor. They both dove for it—the guy got the knife and Cliff landed on the intruder's back. More powerful than he looked, the man rose, lifting Cliff, then threw him off. Cliff landed on his feet, focused on the knife, ready to block the thrust with his arm, sacrifice his arm to save his life. But then the guy just stood there smiling.

"You want it?" the guy said to Cliff, holding out the knife. "You want it so bad, come and get it."

Cliff moved at him, faking, and the guy smiled. "You and me—all the way—next time. What do you say?"

"Anytime, pal."

The guy smiled again, nodded politely, said, "Bye now," and disappeared out the French doors into the rain. One moment he was there and the next he had vanished.

"Oh my God!" Becca was beside Cliff, still clutching the shirt to her chest, staring in horror at him. He looked down and saw a red line spreading across his white shirt, his tie hanging, partially severed.

The pain suddenly hit Cliff. He gritted his teeth, hissing, "Shit, shit, shit!" He stumbled into the bathroom, tearing his shirt open, frantic to see how bad it was. Blood spilled from a long gash across his chest. But nothing was spurting and his pain was on the surface—burning like a sonovabitch.

"Are you all right?" Becca moaned, rocking back and forth, looking a little green.

"Sit down," Cliff ordered. Last thing he needed was to have her keel over and split her gourd open on the bathtub. She sat down heavily on the closed lid of the toilet.

"Sorry. I'm gonna get blood on your towels."

"Should I call 911?"

"Not yet." He was at the sink, running hot water on a washcloth. He washed the wound clean and looked at it in the mirror. Not too deep. He could see where the knife had skittered off his ribs.

"Who was that guy?"

"He was at the track today—asking about Malcolm."

"Asking what?"

"I don't know . . . ." Her eyes were unfocused; she was going into shock.

Cliff said, "I need to take your car. I'll try not to bleed on it."

She laughed weakly. "I'm so sorry. I just wanted you to tell me about the horses."

"We'll do that some other time."

"*Sure.*" Tears were in her eyes. "This was our chance. You won't be back."

Cliff took off his belt and refastened it so it held the washcloth over the wound. He went into the bedroom, where rain was blowing in through the open double doors. He closed and locked them. Turning, he saw the light was on in an adjoining room, an office by the looks of it. Drawers were pulled open, papers strewn across the floor. The guy had been looking for something. What?

Back into the hallway now, Cliff saw Nookie licking up a trail of blood droplets leading into the bathroom. He found Becca where he left her, sitting on the toilet bowl, shoulders heaving. His legs felt shaky as he walked back to her.

"Keys. I need your keys."

"In my purse. In the bedroom." She didn't move. She didn't turn to look at him.

He rubbed her bare shoulder. "Next week, come out to the ranch. I'll get you set up on a horse. Show you a few things if you want."

She turned and looked up at him, still clutching the shirt to her chest. "Would you really?"

"Sure. Call me." She stood up, sniffling, and Cliff saw a tattoo of a butterfly winking at him above the elastic of her panties. As she pulled the shirt up over her head Cliff glimpsed her breasts. But there was no pleasure in it now. Nothing like a knife across your ribs to take the fun out of things.

Malcolm stood there in the night, in the woods, breathing hard after several attempts at wrestling Gordon in behind the wheel of the BMW. The problem was Gordon kept waking up and fighting him. Malcolm had to thump him again—not hard—just a stunner, to make him easier to handle. He didn't want to inflict any obvious injuries. He wanted all the cuts and bruises to come from the accident itself.

Must try again, must get this done, he thought, getting his wind back. He grabbed Gordon under the armpits. This way he could keep away from the blood on Gordon's face, keep away from the mucousy fluid running out his mouth and hanging in long ropes from his nose.

The BMW idled patiently, its headlights shining down on the surface of the water. It had taken Malcolm a long time to find a lake by the side of the road, one en route to Portland, Oregon, where he knew Gordon's mother lived. When they found the car (*if* they found the car) he would say Gordon told him he was leaving to visit his mother. She was an alcoholic and she was having some problems now (true enough, Malcolm thought, recalling their conversations). Gordon had been tired when he left San Francisco. Been drinking a bit, too. Malcolm had tried to talk him out of leaving at night but he was in a panic to help his mum. Anyone would be. It was all quite understandable. Quite tragic.

He had Gordon's arse on the seat when his head flopped forward onto Malcolm's shoulder. *Bloody hell! Get off me!* Malcolm shoved him backwards and he fell across the passenger seat.

Gordon groaned and said, *"No,"* or *"Oh,"* or something like that.

"In ya go," Malcolm grunted, swinging Gordon's legs in near the pedals. Done. Now, I must get the car in gear and—

"Malcolm?" Gordon's eyes had opened and were looking at him. His eyes were surprised and confused, gleaming in the weak dash lights. Gordon's hands came up, feebly, reaching for Malcolm. They were dripping with mud and blood. But they kept coming at him.

Best thump him again, Malcolm thought, looking around for the stone he had used before. He turned back, holding it. And Gordon's hand closed on his tie.

"Let go, you—!" He raised the rock, but he was too close to swing it. Gordon was dragging him into the car. "Shit! Let go!"

"No . . . . Please . . . ." Gordon moaned, crying.

Malcolm slid the knot down on his tie, pulled it off. But it was in Gordon's hands now. He got a good grip on it, putting one foot on Gordon to hold him in the car, and ripped it out of his hands. Didn't want to leave that kind of evidence behind. Besides, it was silk—a $200 tie. Tidy it up a little, it'd be good as new.

Gordon was sobbing now, head lolling back on the seat, his face splotched with blood. *Get in there!* Malcolm slammed the door shut, but Gordon was reaching out and it smashed shut on his fingers. Malcolm swung the door again. Christ, his hand was still in the way! Malcolm swung the door over and over until it finally closed. He stood there, breathing hard, seeing his hot breath in clouds against the headlight beams.

Okay then, we'll do it this way, he thought, circling the car. He opened the passenger door and carefully cracked all the windows an inch or two. It would fill with water faster. He could hear Gordon sobbing inside the car. Then his head flopped forward and blasted the horn. *Damn these Krauts with their earsplitting horns!* How close was that house he had seen? Would anyone hear and come running?

He pulled Gordon back off the steering wheel, feeling his shoulders heaving, his body wracked with sobs.

"Sorry. But you brought it on yourself, lad," Malcolm said. "Snooping about. Asking questions. You behaved poorly."

Checklist: He had taken his cell phone to call a cab back to San Francisco; the windows were down, the motor was running. *Wait!* Almost forgot. He turned on the dome light. He looked to make sure the driver's seat was at the right position. Yes, Gordon's feet touched the pedals easily. It might be the kind of thing the police would check. Or an insurance investigator. When he filed for a claim they would be looking for ways to deny it. Penny pinchers. And here he was, out a brand new BMW.

Okay then, here goes.

Malcolm slid the gear lever into drive. The big car bumped forward. He pulled back out and slammed the door. The car crept forward, picking up speed, bumping and rocking on the rough terrain. It was really moving now, faster, faster until it dropped over the edge and—

WHOOSH!

A wall of water rose up around it. The big car wallowed, then settled in. Bubbles still came from the exhaust. Then, sinking lower, the engine cut out. It was quiet now. Very quiet except for— what was that? A bumping sound came from inside the car. Irregular, but frantic as if—*Holy mother of God! Gordon was trying to get out!* And then he heard the screams, rising higher and higher, in a frenzy of desperation and anguish until, with a final belch of bubbles, the car roof disappeared under the water. And quiet returned to the night. Soon, all that was left were the headlights. And in the muddy water, those soon disappeared, too.

"Hey, hey! It's Dr. Death!" Cliff said to the vet as he walked into Epic Honor's stall on the backside of the track. It was 6 a.m. and, with only three hours' sleep, he was feeling kinda lightheaded. But the energy of the big win yesterday was still with him.

"Morning." The vet spoke cautiously, looked up from examining the horse. He didn't know how to take the greeting.

Epic Honor heard Cliff's voice and turned to him, tossing his head. Cliff looked into his big dark eyes and remembered the fire he'd seen there yesterday after the race, like a world class athlete with his game face on. Now, the eyes were soft and warm as if to say, *Did I do okay?*

"I got a question," the vet said, putting his things away. *Oh Jesus, here it comes,* Cliff thought, bracing for bad news.

The vet was a young guy, sincere, the type that looked sympathetic as hell when he told you your horse just ripped a tendon and would never run again. Yeah, Cliff thought, the vets were the only guys at the track that never lost.

"I just wanted to ask you—did you give him Lasix before the race?"

"No."

"Okay then. Everything looks fine."

"His legs are good and all?"

"Legs are fine. Lungs are clear. Everything looks good."

"Okay, then. I take it all back. You're not Dr. Death."

The vet laughed, still not sure how to take him.

"I wouldn't have thought nothin' but Lopez comes to me after the race, says he pushed him hard in the stretch. I knew he wasn't a bleeder, but when you take a horse, and really torque him down you never know."

"His lungs are completely clear. No trace of blood. That's why I asked about the Lasix."

"That's all I wanted to hear. 'Cause I got plans for this guy," Cliff said, pulling the muzzle close to him. The horse's big lips mouthed Cliff affectionately. He was a mouthy horse, Cliff thought, always trying to kiss you, grab your phone or your watch. Anything shiny.

"I heard he ran a great race yesterday. You thinking Golden Gate?"

"I'm thinkin' the Santa Anita Handicap."

"Santa Anita," the vet whistled. "The big time."

Cliff saw one of the exercise riders passing the door. He barked: "Ramon! Baye con caballo!" The rider turned and went off in the other direction.

Cliff reached high on the horse's neck, rubbing under his mane. Epic Honor let out a satisfied sigh. Cliff reached higher until—a stab of pain tore across his chest as the stitches pulled. The vet saw him wince.

"You pull a muscle or something?"

"You wouldn't believe it if I told you. Thanks for your help, Doc." They shook hands and Cliff stepped outside into the new day.

Cliff reached for the list in his pocket thinking, *Now, where was I?* He'd been jotting down the names of horses Ravling could buy into. Speed Calling, that big gray named Firecracker, and Mr. Double Down. That would cost him about a hundred grand. Maybe he could spot a winner down at the Barrett's auction next week in Pomona. If Malcolm was buying horses overseas—and why the hell was he doing that?—maybe he'd fire for some chips at Barretts. They could go there before the Santa Anita Handicap.

His cell phone rang. He dug it out of his windbreaker pocket. "Hello."

"Hey, Cliff. It's Dan Van."

"Yeah, Dan. Where you at?"

"Heading for a big meeting downtown. Fidelity West. If I make the deal it'll be big casino, baby."

Cliff laughed, remembering Dan's excitement at the race yesterday, waving a fist full of hundred-dollar bills he'd won and yelling, *Big casino, baby!*

"Reason for the call," Dan continued, "You said someone wanted to buy Epic Honor."

"Eddie Voss. But I told him we were runnin' him at Santa Anita first."

"I was thinking, what if there was a way to make a deal now, *and* let him run."

"Whatcha got in mind?"

"I'll call Voss and say, let's settle on a price, then we let him run under our colors, and split the purse if he wins."

Cliff laughed. "Voss ain't gonna go for that."

"You never know. Okay if I give it a try?"

"Fine by me."

"So what's our price on Epic Honor?"

"Well, here's the thing. I only want to sell half interest," Cliff said.

"Half?"

"Horse means a lot to me and my family."

"Okay. For half interest, how much? Think of a dream price."

"One ninety. Two hundred."

"Two hundred it is."

Pause. Cliff realized Dan was doing a sales pitch on Voss in his head.

Dan said, "I need one good line."

"What do you mean?"

"If you were pitching Epic Honor to a buyer, what would you say?"

He thought over. "I'd say, 'He ain't the fastest horse in the barn, but he never gets sick, and he's always ready to dance.'"

Laughter came over the line. "That's beautiful, man. That'll clinch it right there. I'll let you know what happens."

Cliff disconnected and tucked the phone back in the pocket of his windbreaker. Two hundred for half interest Yeah, *right*. Voss would never pay that. But just the mention of the money lifted his spirits, gave him that old feeling of confidence. Maybe his luck was finally turning. Everything was coming together.

Cliff heard the whistle as the CalTrain approached the station on the other side of the track, bringing the first race fans down from San Francisco, the rail-birds. He stood there breathing in the new day. It felt like spring, like the beginning of something new. It was a good day for what he had to do.

Back at his house, Cliff changed into a clean pair of jeans and the red polo shirt Jamie had given him for his last birthday. He scooped up the presents he bought and headed out.

On the way to the car he saw Emerson was out in the field driving the Relaunch colt on long reins. He watched the yearling with its fluid, powerful steps, and the old man behind him with his brittle sideways shuffle. Emerson would turn him first to the left, then to the right. Occasionally the colt tossed his head, annoyed by the bit in his mouth.

Cliff moved to the corral, ducked under the fence. The Relaunch colt saw him coming and tossed his head. Angry? Happy? With this horse, it was hard to tell. A moody teen-ager. Cliff stroked his nose.

"Be ready for a rider soon, Cliff."

"Put Ramon on him. He's good with the young ones. Don't let him push him. Take it slow and easy."

"You got it, Cliff."

The colt suddenly laid back his ears and bared his teeth.

"What's that for?" Cliff asked, holding his ground. The Relaunch colt nickered and tossed his head again. "All right, all right. We're all watching so you can stop now."

Emerson wheezed laughter.

The colt pulled free and ran around, dragging the reins.

"Watch he don't trip on them reins," Cliff said. Then, ready to go, he added, "Wish me luck. I'm off to see Jamie now."

Emerson got a faraway look in his eyes. "I hope you can work things out, Cliff."

"Me too. But you know Jamie, she's got a wild streak in her."

Cliff had driven halfway to the gate leading out onto the highway when he saw a car coming the other way, a big silver Crown

Victoria. It stopped even with him. The window rolled down to reveal Malcolm's smiling face.

"Mornin' Cliff."

"New wheels?"

"Rental. Gordon took the BMW. He had to drive up to Portland. His mum's in hospital."

Cliff remembered Gordon showing up last night saying, *We've got a problem.* So that's what it was all about.

"I owe you a tremendous debt, Cliff. I came home last night, police cars were everywhere. Did that maniac hurt you badly?"

"Fifteen stitches. But it wasn't the first time they had to sew me back together. What'd the guy get?"

"The police think he was after my guns. I collect a few revolvers. Just a hobby of mine. But seriously. Thank you."

"No problem. Look, I got somewheres I gotta be."

"I came to see your grandmother. She wanted to go over a few things with me."

"Oh. Well, good luck. She's a tough old gal."

Time to hit him up for the money, Cliff thought, drawing a breath. But then, as if reading his thoughts, Malcolm said, "Should be something in the mail for you tomorrow. Call me when you get it. And the mutual funds I got you—up two thousand already." He gave Cliff thumbs up. "The profit's yours. But you need to get me that check."

"Maybe at Santa Anita next week. You comin' down for the race?"

"Wouldn't miss it for the world. Cheers."

As Cliff drove forward he looked in his rear view mirror and saw the silver car stopping near the fence. Malcolm got out and leaned on the railing, watching Emerson work with the colt. Cliff found an opening in traffic and pulled out.

When Cliff drove up, Jamie was in the front yard of her mother's house, hands on her hips, watching Davie push a toy lawn mower through the grass. Seeing her there like that, in jeans and a western-cut red-checked shirt, Cliff felt a lot of things deep down inside in a way he hadn't experienced for a long time. But most of all, he was glad he hadn't jumped Becca's bones after all the night before. Now, he was here with a clear conscience.

Davie saw Cliff's car and came tearing toward him. He started grabbing for the bag of toys, hopping up and down. Cliff danced away, saying, "I didn't bring you nothin'! These ain't for you!" But he said it in a way that just made the little cowboy more intent on getting his hands on the goods.

"Hey, don't I even get a hug first?" The little arms wrapped around his father's neck and squeezed. Cliff soaked it up, then set him down. Davie found the plastic golf set he'd brought him.

Cliff turned to Jamie. "How 'bout you? I get a hug?" He took her in his arms, lifted her off her feet. But she wasn't really there.

They stood watching Davie taking huge divots in Grandma's lawn.

"Where's Lady Emily?"

"Napping."

"Can I see her? Just a peek."

"In a minute. I just got her down."

"So how you been?"

"As well as can be expected," she said.

The breeze was blowing her honey-colored hair across her eyes, which were narrowed, challenging, the way he remembered her from their first days together, before she was his.

"We won the featured race at Bay Meadows yesterday." He paused. "Purse was 40K."

"Your share?"

"I walk away with ten. Plus, I had a little action on it myself. That'll go a long way to paying the bills."

Davie yelled, "FORE!" and a whiffle ball sizzled past Cliff's ear.

"I got two new clients should be good for a whole string of horses. One guy's gonna be my new Golden Eagle."

"Cliff, this isn't just about money. I know you think it is, but it isn't."

"Well hell, what is it about then? I'm listening."

She looked him in the eye and said, "I'm thinking about going back to school."

"Back to school? Why?"

"I want to become a vet."

Cliff laughed. "A vet?" He could see his laughter was pissing her off. He took it down a notch. "A vet. I see. Okay."

"That way, if we stay together, we've got common ground."

If we stay together. Cliff felt a wave of anger and panic. He tried like hell not to show it, not to react because he knew, if he wanted to, they could have a big old fight right now, all the unresolved shit gushing up to the surface.

Davie had the club up on one shoulder now, like a baseball bat. When he swung at the ball, he spun around and fell on his butt.

The kid was such a bomber. Cliff showed him how to keep his feet in one place while he swang. The next effort launched the ball up in the air and the wind caught it, holding it in place against the sky for a moment.

Cliff turned back to Jamie. "Kid's a natural."

She allowed a smile. They relaxed again.

Cliff handed her an envelope. She looked at him.

"Go on, open it."

Inside was an airline ticket. She looked at him for an answer.

"First class to LA. Epic Honor's runnin' at Santa Anita next week. It's a big race. I want you there—for luck."

She looked away.

"He's a special horse, Jamie. He wouldn't be here now if it weren't for you—the way you fed him after the mare died. Remember how Davie used to sneak into his stall?"

She struggled to keep her voice even. "But we said we'd give it a month."

"Just one day. Fly down late afternoon, come back after the race. I want you to meet the new clients. They been askin' about you."

She was silent. That was better than saying no.

"I bought a new colt, from a ranch down in Texas. He's lookin' real good."

"I don't want a new horse. I want to go back to school. I want to remodel the kitchen." Her tough looks dissolved into an expression of despair, as she said, "I want to change something, but I don't know what it is."

Cliff couldn't stop himself. He took her in his arms. The wind blew her hair across his face and he breathed in her natural smell. He stroked her hair and whispered in her ear. "I want you to come

on home now." He felt her quiver and yield to him. Then she twisted away and ran into the house. But she took the plane ticket with
her. Maybe that was her way of saying she'd be there for him when
their horse ran.

Linda left the comfort of Delta's first class cabin and moved
down the jetway toward the terminal. A sea of faces appeared in
front of her and, scanning them, she saw Ellis's head above them
all. Hard to miss. She skirted the crowd and stood in front of him.

"Hey there."

"Hey." He smiled down at her, seemingly pleased with the way
she looked, the simple outfit she wore, tan slacks, a white cotton
shirt and black leather jacket.

He took her bag and they began walking.

"Pleasant flight?"

"I survived. How've you been?"

"Busy."

"Oh?"

"Yeah. I'm making progress. How long did they cut you loose
for?"

"My company pretty much runs itself," she said. "I'm not
going back until I get this deal resolved."

They were moving through the terminal now, walking side by
side, and Linda knew the people around them probably assumed
they were husband and wife.

In the parking garage, Ellis popped the trunk on the rental, a
white Chevy Lumina. Linda saw a laptop computer in the trunk.

"Didn't figure you to be the computer type."

"That's part of what I've got to tell you."

They climbed in and he began driving. He said, "I happened to come into possession of Mr. Ravling's financial records."

Linda laughed. "Ellis, I swear. You are something else. *You happened to come into possession of Mr. Ravling's financial records.* What'd you do, swipe his laptop?"

"No. I took the hard drive out of his office computer."

"So what's with the laptop?"

"I took the hard drive to one of these little computer chop shops. Got them to put the information from the hard drive onto a laptop. Had them install the program to access it. Sentinel Investor."

"It tracks investments. Sure, I use it."

They circled a wide ramp and found themselves joining a stream of traffic heading north toward downtown San Francisco. Born and raised in Texas, she was used to being surrounded by prairie. Here, the water cut in and out around them. It didn't seem right.

"So this is San Francisco."

"This is it."

They topped a rise and saw a sea of bungalows jumbled together on cramped lots, the freeway worming its way between them. She shook her head. "My God, how can people live like this?"

"Come to a place like this, you realize how spoiled we are in Texas."

After a moment she said, "So why're you doing all this with the computer?"

"You told me how he ripped off your brother. You're aimin' to get his money back, aren't you?"

"Think we got a shot at doing that?"

"I think there's a pretty fair chance we can squeeze money out of him one way or the other. That's what you want, isn't it?"

She was silent a moment, then said, "Not exactly."

"Well, we're meeting with him tomorrow. You better tell me what you've got in mind before then."

"I surely will. Till then, I guess you're just gonna have to trust me. You trust me, don't you?"

"As much as I trust anyone."

He turned the Lumina into the parking lot of a motel, the Knight's Rest. She saw Ellis was right—it was a fly speck motel, or at least San Francisco's version of one. Inside the office, a door behind the counter opened and an Indian desk clerk appeared, still chewing his lunch. Checking in, she realized why they were there— they weren't being recorded in some national computer system. The clerk wrote their names on index cards and put them in a plastic file box he kept under the counter. Linda couldn't help noticing that Ellis had registered them both under his last name: Ransom.

They ate dinner at a seafood place on Market Street, then he pointed the Lumina across the bridge and Ellis showed Linda the office where they would meet with Mr. Ravling in the morning. From there they drove to Ravling's house on the hill overlooking the bay in Marin County. They sat in the car smoking and Linda looked up at the big windows. The weak blue light of a TV flickered inside.

"You been in there?"

"Briefly."

"What's it like?"

"Like they just moved in. No furniture. No pictures on the walls. Just a bunch of big old empty rooms."

Linda watched the TV light moving in the window.

"He married?"

"Yep. Got hisself a pretty little wife, all dressed up with jewelry and such. Big rock on her finger."

A wave of anger swept over Linda as she pictured it, trash like Ravling living in luxury, thinking he got away with something.

"My brother's money went to buy that place." Linda's voice was husky. She threw her cigarette out the window. "Let's get the hell out of here."

"Got a bottle in my room," Ellis said when they got back to the Knight's Rest. "How about a nightcap?"

A man and a woman. A cheap hotel. A bottle of booze. It was like a Hank Williams ballad. But Linda didn't care. This city had her off balance and feeling empty inside. A drink might take some lonesome out of the night.

"Sounds good."

It was a small room with barely enough space to move around the bed. The shag carpeting was matted and worn in a trail from the bed to the TV, the bed to the bathroom, the bed to the door. Everything seemed to lead to the bed. Sitting in the only chair, she saw the laptop computer was on the desk. Next to it was a copy of the *Daily Racing Form*.

Ellis got glasses from the bathroom and poured from a bottle of Johnnie Walker Red.

He handed her a glass and sat across from her on the bed. She lit a cigarette.

"There's this story in my family, about me and Sonny. See, he never could take care of himself. Kids in the neighborhood used to shove him around. There was this one kid, Tab Kelly, took Sonny's bike or hurt him or—I don't know. When I heard about it, I went on the warpath. I caught this Tab Kelly in the weeds out back of his house. They were diggin' a hole, making a clubhouse or something. Well, when I finally got ahold of him, I threw him down in the hole. Wouldn't let him back up."

Ellis chuckled. He kicked off his boots and reclined on the bed, hands behind his head.

"I had a big sister too," Ellis said.

"I didn't know that."

"She was twelve years older than me. More like a mama to me, really."

"Where is she now?"

"Died when I was about ten. She took sick real sudden. I came home from school one day and there was an ambulance out front of my house. Everyone left and went to the hospital. I didn't know what to do so I went down to the barn. My daddy put up a basketball hoop in there so I could shoot baskets come rain or shine. Only thing was, I had to shoot the ball over the rafters. I had my one rafter shot, my two rafter shot and my three rafter shot."

Ellis paused to sip the whiskey.

"My daddy came out to the barn and told me Suzie passed away. He said it was a fever. I don't think they ever really knew for sure. Anyway, he told me to come up to the house. But I didn't want anyone to see me crying. So I just stayed out there, shooting baskets, tears running down my face."

Linda knew now that she could tell it. And if she cried, fuck it. She wasn't a machine. She had been keeping it to herself for months, touching it in her mind like it was something red hot, then dropping it before it burned her. She would give it to Ellis now, the hatred, and let it burn him, too.

"I told you sometime back about how Mr. Malcolm Ravling got Sonny's money and all, by those phony investments. But there was a lot more to it than that."

"Kinda figured that."

"Reason Sonny came to live with me, see, he tested positive for HIV."

Linda watched Ellis, thinking he might say something smart. But he just nodded.

"He'd been working some as a deejay, and when word got out what he had, they fired him. When he got sick I took him in..."

She took a drink of the Johnnie Walker Red, held the glass up to the light and looked through the amber liquor.

"You ever hear of something called a viatical?" she asked.

Ellis shook his head.

"It's for when someone is terminal. See, Sonny had a life insurance policy he'd paid into for years that was worth a half a million. It was the one smart thing he did. But now he was fixin' to die. So he sold the policy to an investor who gave Sonny two hundred grand up front to cover his medical costs. Then when he died, the insurance company would pay a half million to the investor."

Linda kicked off her shoes and put her feet up on the bed, next to Ellis's outstretched legs.

"Well, sure enough, Sonny got his money—which he needed for treatments and all. But then a funny thing happened. They started giving him these drug cocktails. And he started getting better. He started working again and—and everything looked like it was going to be all right. The only loser was the investor who bought the viatical 'cause he couldn't collect until Sonny died and now Sonny was okay."

She stopped herself, feeling her voice beginning to shake. She hated it when her voice shook because it made her feel weak and she had trained herself to always be strong. But she was close to something now and had to continue.

Her feet were cold so she wormed them in under Ellis's legs for warmth. They were touching now, touching again for the first time in years.

"Last summer, one Saturday night, Sonny had a gig at a club, the Silver Fox, in south Houston. I woke up the next morning and saw the door to his room was open. He hadn't come home. Along about noon the police called. They found him lying near where his car was parked. They said he'd been lying there a while but no one saw him 'cause the grass was so tall."

She took a sudden deep breath.

"When the cops found out he was HIV positive, well, that was enough for them. They didn't want to do much about it. Finally I got ahold of the report—such as it was. It said Sonny had head injuries. The cops said that was 'cause his heart failed, and he fell and hit his head and it was all natural causes stemming from his disease. But there was one thing in the report I couldn't stop thinking of—they'd found a wad of duct tape near his body. That and the head injury got me thinking. I called the insurance company and found that, sure enough, they paid off the person who bought the viatical."

Ellis was ready for it when she said, "You'll never guess who had bought Sonny's viatical."

"Mr. Malcolm Ravling."

"You got it. Only, of course, he was using a different name then, Mr. Butler or something like that. So this man, this Butler or Ravling or whatever, had talked Sonny into investing all his money with him, stung him for thirty grand. Then, when he found out Sonny was sick, bought the viatical. When Sonny started to recover Ravling went to the club, followed him out and—left him there."

She was crying a little now, adding, "Left him there. That was the worst part, Ellis. He left him to lay there all night, alone, in the grass, like an animal."

"You tell the cops all this?"

She touched her eye with the back of one finger, sniffed, then said, "They agreed to question Mr. Malcolm Ravling, but they couldn't find him. By then, he was out here in California with his new wife, in his big house, living the good life."

"So you called me."

"Yes. I didn't want to have just anyone do it. I wanted someone who knew Sonny, someone who would understand what I was feeling. You understand, don't you?"

"I understand." He looked like he was turning it over in his mind, considering the angles. "Only problem is, now that he's out of state, got a new name and all, it's gonna be hard to prove what he did."

"Prove?" She laughed bitterly.

"That's what you're after, isn't it?"

"Far as I'm concerned, you don't have to *prove* anything. Far as I'm concerned, it's cold fact."

"Then what are you after?" He asked carefully.

She laughed as if it was obvious. "I want to kill that son of a bitch."

"Okay, sure, I can do that."

"Ellis, you aren't listening. I said, '*I* want to kill that son of a bitch.' I want the great pleasure of doing it myself. I'll need your help. But I want to do it myself."

She saw a slow smile spread across his face. "I like it," he said finally. "I like it a lot."

There was nothing else to say, at least at this moment. So, after the silence had lengthened, and turned from being one thing, into another, he patted the bed next to him. "Come on over here now. Come on."

Maybe she'd been waiting for him to say this. And now that she had told her story, she felt drained and relieved. So she left the chair to lie down beside him, her head on the pillow next to his, looking into his eyes, the warm light of a single lamp spilling across them.

For Linda it had been two broken marriages ending in bitterness. After that it had been an occasional chance encounter while she was on the road in a distant city. These encounters began with the idea of physical gratification and were sometimes successful, sometimes disgustingly hollow. But she took nothing away with her. And now it had been a long time for her. So long, in fact, that she wondered if it would ever happen again. Not the Great Love, no, forget about that. Just reasonably good sex.

For him it had often been a sport, like a well-placed bet that ended in a quick burst of pleasure and then a reassuring return to solitude. The only time it was anything else was once in Dallas, ten years back, when that cocktail waitress had something in her words that evoked a sense of what could be. But after two weeks living together in the room above a bar, she took off on him and he went back to being exactly as he had been before, only more so.

It seemed as if Linda and Ellis had both arrived at a point in their lives where both sex and love were behind them, where they had set down their expectations for the last time. They were on the edge of a new phase of their lives—the last phase—where the years would accelerate, their habits would solidify and they would glide into the darkness alone.

But on this night they came together again and picked up a thread that had been cut many years ago when, due to miscommunication, or mismatched timing, they had split up, left their small town and gone on to separate lives. Now, in this cheap hotel, when Ellis stroked her hair and looked into her eyes, they found that those early encounters were very much with them. The memories had been lying undisturbed all these years, in case they were needed again.

And they felt young again.

He kissed her with exaggerated laziness, as if she might say, *Stop this foolishness now,* and he could say, *I was just kiddin' around.* But she didn't say any such thing. She kissed him back and held him tight and he could feel her eagerness as she opened her legs and worked herself against his thigh.

They lay like that for a while, kissing and not going any further, but then her hand was inside his shirt, stroking the hair on his flat hard chest, and he unbuttoned her blouse and saw that her secret was a body touched lightly by age, still lean and athletic. Soon they were naked, under the sheets—still unhurried—with the light turned off and a warm glow coming in through the curtains and a foghorn out in the night and the rumble of a jet in the air and a spark, deep inside each of them saying, *I forgot it could be like this.*

Afterward, they lay there talking, and just as she was getting drowsy, she heard his voice in the dark.

"Where do you suppose it is?"

"What?"

"All that money he's taken off various people."

"Ellis, I got plenty of money. Forget the money."

"That's your money. All I'm saying is, where do you suppose that dirty money is?"

In his words, she felt him pulling away from her. So she repeated a question she had often spoken to him, trying to answer it as she asked it again: "What is it about other people's money that holds such a fascination for you?"

It was money, or the mention of money, that had always opened doors for Malcolm. The casual, confident mention of large amounts of money always got him what he wanted, particularly in a place like this, this enormous bank on Market Street, rising like a pillar of financial stability in downtown San Francisco, as permanent and unmovable as the rock below it, anchoring this elegant city of wealth.

These thoughts were in Malcolm's mind as he walked into the spacious lobby early that morning, his $500 Italian shoes clicking crisply on the polished cut-granite floor, his Hart Shaffner & Marx suit hanging just right on his frame and the brass-edged leather folder carried lightly in his hand. He smiled and nodded to the faces around him as he boarded the elevator and blasted off for the top floor.

Moments later the leather folder was open on Mr. Roland

Debosky's desk. Mr. Debosky's head, with carefully trimmed graying hair, was bent over the pie-charts and bar graphs Malcolm had prepared last night as Becca watched a movie alone in the living room.

Running a finger up one bar on the chart, Malcolm intoned, "And the bank's capital was used to realize a quarterly growth of nearly 35 percent."

"From existing accounts?" Debosky asked to show that he was following all this.

Malcolm thought it over, or rather, he looked like he was thinking it over while he considered what would look best.

"The existing accounts were maximized and there was a strong influx of new clients," he answered softly. Then, as if it just occurred to him he added, "One of my new clients owns the biggest blood stock ranch in the area—fifty acres in Pleasanton. She's decided to sell it and invest that capital with my firm."

"Fifty acres in Pleasanton. I wonder what a place like that is worth?" Mr. Debosky asked dreamily.

"It's listing for ten," Malcolm answered as if they were in a club that spoke its own language, omitting the word "million" when it was obvious.

There it was, that casual, confident mention of money. Malcolm watched Mr. Debosky react. It was a chain reaction really, one that went something like this: *If he's making that much money, and I have a piece of it, then I'll make this much money for the bank* . . . . Mr. Debosky returned from his pleasant daydream and looked at the "growth" bar Malcolm had indicated in blue on his color chart. He checked his file on Ravling Financial Advisors.

"Let me see here . . . the initial loan was —"

"Three hundred."

"And this new application is for three hundred thousand also."

"This filing is short term, though, to carry the firm through this real estate transaction. Certain changes will be required to restructure so funds are needed for legal and accounting services. The bank's return on this money will be substantial."

"Yes, yes, I see that."

A voice from the doorway interrupted. Mr. Debosky looked up. "Yes, Pat?"

Malcolm turned to see an attractive middle-aged woman, Mr. Debosky's secretary probably. She looked very smart, very efficient.

"Ah, you were asking about the file on R.F.A.?"

"I have it here. Thanks."

"There is an addition. Something just came in."

Mr. Debosky read her tone. He frowned slightly, annoyed.

"Excuse me." He stood and left the room.

Malcolm rose and stretched. His eyes glided out the window to the stunning view of the financial district, then, looking north, to the sparkling Bay and the Golden Gate Bridge. He had always thought of this as his kingdom, like he was a modern-day William Wallace in "Braveheart." He ruled this city with his courage, with his boldness, with his superiority over weaker men.

In the other room, the voices were hushed but intense. He moved closer to the doorway, as if inspecting another angle of the view.

"Whenever an inquiry is made, any further applications are flagged," Pat was saying. "We had a call from an insurance company in San Mateo. They had discovered something on an inspection report and were following up."

"So?"

"So until this inquiry is answered the application is frozen."

"According to who?"

"Mr. Chevalier. He called a few minutes ago. He thinks this could indicate a—a problem." She was nervous, but insistent. Very smart. Very efficient.

"I *hate* when this happens. We've got this opportunity and then—"

Still looking out the window, at the Bay and the bridge and the buildings, all under a perfect sun, it seemed that the picture before Malcolm suddenly dimmed, as if the light behind it receded, as if the vividness—the reality of it—diminished, and when Mr. Debosky returned he looked at Malcolm with different eyes.

There would be a hold on the application, he said, because of a change in regulations and *blah, blah, blah* . . . . Malcolm didn't really listen to the shit Debosky was saying until he heard: "So we are unable to act on this today."

"But this needs your attention immediately. That's why I took the time to come here personally. Because I thought we had a relationship. Because I thought you understood the speed at which business of this kind progresses."

"Yes, but the problem is at a level where, well, frankly, we need to verify several things."

Malcolm was silent. He was deeply disappointed in Mr. Debosky. But the man stared back at him with defiance in his eyes.

"Right then." Malcolm snapped his folder shut. "I'll be at my office this afternoon. Call me when it goes through."

"It won't be today."

The short phrase hit Malcolm hard. For the first time in quite a long while he couldn't think of what to say. He rose and shook hands.

Before turning to leave he gazed at the view again, at his kingdom. There was a problem out there, he realized. A problem in his kingdom. And he was beginning to realize who was responsible for it.

Linda emerged from the shower, put on a simple navy blue business suit and headed next door to Ellis's room. Her hair was still wet, turning her blond hair brown, and she was finishing a cup of really awful coffee from the motel's so-called "Continental Breakfast." Opening the door, she saw Ellis hunched over the laptop, reading a spreadsheet with dozens of entries. Next to the computer, on the worn desktop, was a nickel-plated snub-nosed .38 revolver.

"You're not going to tell me you flew on an airplane with *that*?"

"Uh, no," he said, looking up at last. "Picked it up when I got here."

She finished her coffee and tossed the Styrofoam cup in the wastebasket by the desk. They had skipped breakfast and opted for cigarettes and coffee instead. Her stomach was too tight for food now anyway.

"Tell me, how do you 'pick up' something like that?"

He smiled and she saw him decide to come clean.

"Let you in on a little secret. When I was up at Mr. Ravling's house the other night, I saw that he had a small firearms collection. I wanted the cops to think this was your garden variety burglary, so I lifted this one. Figured it might come in handy before this is over."

Linda picked up the revolver. "So I'm gonna use *his* gun on him."

"Yes."

Linda smiled as she felt the weight of the gun in her hand. The barrel was pointing at Ellis's lower body.

He said, "Whoa," and stepped aside. "It's loaded, you know."

"Ellis, I know how to handle a gun. My daddy used to take me down to the creek, shootin' water moccasins with a .22."

"So, you want to test fire it?"

"Why?"

"You don't want any screw ups."

"It'll be easy. We go in, if he's alone I'm going to tell him who I am, why I'm doing this, then . . . ."

"At least snap it a few times. Get a feel for the action." He took the gun from her, released the cylinder and emptied the bullets. He handed it back to her.

She held the gun at arm's length, sighted an imaginary target, and pulled the trigger five times, enjoying the solid feel of metal-on-metal. She looked at Ellis.

"That should do it."

"Then what?"

"Wipe the prints off. Then throw the gun down next to him and we leave."

"Okay." Her voice sounded odd to herself. She looked at her watch. "Let's go."

"There's one other thing," he said slowly. "In a closed room, it's gonna be loud."

"I know that, Ellis."

"Very loud. Like getting your ears boxed. A .38's got more bark than a .22."

"Why are you telling me this?"

"I don't want you to drop the gun or anything."

"I'm *not* going to drop the gun." She smiled at him. "You've got to learn to trust me. You trust me, don't you?"

"As much as I trust anyone."

She looked at him a long time, then said, "Let's go see Mr. Malcolm Ravling."

Now that's more like it, Cliff said, pulling the Ravling Financial Advisors envelope out of the stack of mail on the kitchen table. Guy finally coughed up the training fees he owed on Epic Honor. I take it all back, Cliff thought, slitting open the envelope with a paring knife and reaching inside.

The envelope was empty.

Shit.

Cliff stood there in the kitchen, the empty house silent around him, wondering what the hell was going on. He'd been looking forward to making the trip south with all this settled. Well, maybe the guy wrote out a check and *forgot* to put it in the envelope. That was possible. He reached for the phone.

A voice answered on the first ring. "Hello."

"Malcolm?"

"Yes. Cliff my boy! How are you?"

"Confused."

"Why?"

"I got an envelope from you today."

"Yes."

"There's nothin' in it."

"Right."

"Normally, people put things in envelopes. Like checks."

"Checks?"

"For horses, for training costs. I thought you sent me the money for the pin hook."

"Oh that. This is much more important. It was my way of making a point."

"Well, I don't think I got it."

"Yes you did."

"But there's nothin' in the envelope."

"That's my point exactly. You see, that's what your wife and children will get if something happens to you without a current will and insurance policy."

Cliff threw the envelope over his shoulder and turned around, wrapping himself up in the phone cord and almost pulling the telephone off the wall. He thought of saying a lot of things, but he kept his mouth shut.

"Cliff? You still there?"

"Right here, Malcolm."

"You see the point I'm making? Everything's smashing now, you're winning races and the money's pouring in. But we don't know what the future holds. That's why you need to prepare. So we need to get those things taken care of. Agreed?"

"I've never been in disagreement with you. It's just a matter of timing. I'm looking at $200 a week training and boarding fees. I've got transport and vet bills—" A rap on the kitchen door. Emerson stuck his head in. His face was flushed.

"Hang on a second," Cliff cupped the receiver. "Yeah."

"Ramon is on the Relaunch colt. You gotta come down and see this."

"Malcolm. I gotta go look at our horse."

"Which one?"

"The pin hook—the Relaunch colt. We got a rider on him."

Over the phone, Cliff heard a voice in the background calling faintly.

"Must ring off now. My eleven o'clock is here. Investors from Texas."

111

"Listen, I made a list of horses you might want to buy into. Let me show you what I've got and we can settle all the business at once."

"Brilliant. Let's do it at lunch. One o'clock at the track?"

"See you there."

Cliff hung up. Emerson was holding the door open for him. In his whispery voice, he said, "You aren't gonna believe your eyes."

At exactly eleven o'clock Linda opened the door and stepped inside the offices of Ravling Financial Advisors. Her purse was heavy in her hand, her fingers slick with sweat. Her heart was punching a hole in her chest.

Looking around: a wood-paneled office. Empty receptionist's desk. Leather upholstered chairs. A painting of some English castle on the wall. Movement from an inside office. A voice saying, "One o'clock at the track?" Then the sound of a phone hanging up and the voice again: "Hello?"

A man appeared, a man she'd seen in photos but never in the flesh.

"Mr. Ravling?" Ellis asked.

"Please, just call me Malcolm."

He smiled pleasantly. He wasn't at all what she expected. She had pictured someone predatory. This guy was boyish, with one eye that didn't look at you, and made you feel sorry for him; but he had a classy feel to him, foreign, educated, refined.

Ellis said, "I'm Mr. Keller from Texas. I called to discuss a—"

"Yes, yes. Been expecting you. Usually my assistant, Gordon, would be here but—" he nodded at the empty desk "—family emergency."

Good! He's alone, Linda thought.

Ellis said, "This is Miss Nightingale, our CEO."

Malcolm shook her hand and gave her one of those evaluating glances which salesmen use to qualify prospects.

"Nice to meet you. Come in. Come in," he said, waving them through a doorway.

They followed him into a rear office where two chairs faced a large wooden desk. A computer sat on a table to the right. It was brand new, she noted; boxes with the Gateway logo were still in the corner. Malcolm sat behind his desk.

"Please, have a seat," he gestured at the two chairs.

Ellis looked at Linda questioningly, like she might do it now. But she wasn't ready. She wanted to give significance to the execution. It wouldn't be complete unless the bastard knew why he was dying. They sat down.

"You're from Houston, is that right?"

"Right," Ellis said. "But we're considering a move to relocate here."

"You couldn't find a nicer place to live. Actually, I'm not from the area myself—or couldn't you tell?"

He waited for them to laugh. She forced herself to smile but she was actually choking on her rage. It was hard to be this close to Sonny's killer and stay calm.

"As I indicated on the phone, Miss Nightingale here," Ellis gestured to Linda, "has an import business down in Houston. We had been told that we should open a California office, at least on paper."

Malcolm frowned, thinking. "For what purpose?"

"Taxes," Linda said. "You see, we have a substantial sum of money we need to find a home for. We were told that you knew the tax laws, could save us a great deal of capital in the long run."

"Of course. But tell me, how much are we talking about?"

Linda said, "Somewhere in the neighborhood of two-point-three." Pause, then: "Million."

"I see. Okay. That's—that's—I can see why you would want to act wisely. There are a variety of ways we could go. Scenario one: You retain me as your financial manager to oversee the establishment of various funds and trusts. Scenario two: This could be structured as work for hire—half of my fee paid up front, half on completion. What I would do is . . . ."

Linda tuned him out as she thought how Sonny must have sat before this same man and heard the lies falling from his lips like hunks of rotting garbage. She opened her purse and reached inside.

"But tell me, Mr. Ravling," Ellis was saying, "Say we wanted to maximize our money, even with high risk situations, what would you recommend?"

"There are a variety of things you can do, actually, depending on your investment philosophy."

"And just what is *your* investment philosophy?" Linda asked. "Make as much money as possible, regardless of how you make it?"

Malcolm paused, searching her face. "How do you mean?"

"I mean, for example, you might want us to put our money into viaticals."

"They're very hot right now. But there's a risk."

"A risk? Not for you. You learned how to take the risk out of them."

"I'm not sure I'm following you."

"Suppose you heard of a man, a young man, who had a terminal disease. We'll say for purposes of argument that he had AIDS. Are you with me?"

"Or anything really," Malcolm added, warily. "There are a variety of things that someone might—"

"I'm not talking about *a variety of things* now." She leaned forward. "I'm talking about a young man who is dying—that's a terrible thing. Did you know, when a young man believes he's going to die, he cries continually? From despair."

Malcolm sat back, folding his arms and frowning.

"So we'll say then that this young man is so desperate he's ready to try anything."

"It's unfortunate, yes. I've had friends myself who had AIDS."

"Have you really? And did you buy viaticals on them?"

"I lent them money, actually," he said, trying to understand her anger.

"Let's say instead that this young man sells you a policy on his life—"

"That's not how it works exactly. You see—"

"I know it's not *exactly* how it works. But that's the gist of it. So what if this young man uses that money to treat himself and he recovers. And he even begins to believe that he will live. And the long fits of crying in despair and loneliness end. And he rejoins the life forces. Are you with me?"

"Yes, it happens sometimes."

"I know it happens. But my question now, *Mr. Butler,* is—"

He jumped at the use of that name. "Ravling. My name is Ravling."

"It's Ravling now, sure, but when you were in Texas it was Mr. Butler."

Malcolm made a tight laughing noise that wasn't really a laugh at all. Linda became aware of Ellis beside her smiling, enjoying all this.

"But let me continue, Mr. Butler, because I haven't finished the story of this young man. As I said, this young man began to recover. And everyone was happy except for one person. Do you know who that was?"

Rather than answer, he said, "The prudent investor has to be ready for this kind of a situation."

"That's just my point! You were ready, weren't you? But Sonny wasn't ready for you. So you followed him to the Silver Fox in Houston. And you made good on your investment, didn't you? And you left him dead in the grass like an animal. And you collected your money. But I'm just wondering—what was the duct tape for?"

"The—*what?*"

"Duct tape. There was a ball of tape found near his body. That's what made me think it wasn't natural causes, like the coroner kept saying."

Malcolm sputtered indignantly, saying, "If you think that I had—this is absolutely outrageous—"

"You don't know what outrageous is," Linda said. She stood up suddenly and pulled the revolver from her purse. "Now this, *this* is outrageous."

Malcolm held out his hands, as if he could push away the bullets. He made sputtering noises and pushed back in his chair. But the sight of the gun loosened his tongue.

"You mentioned Mr. Butler. Okay. I think I understand now how you could think that I—but you see, I'm *not* Butler. Butler was another broker I met. I knew nothing of the policies he was buying."

Malcolm suddenly bent toward the desk, saying, "Let me see if I have an address for—"

Ellis flew out of his chair.

"*NO!* Back away from the desk now. Just sit tight and listen to the lady."

Malcolm straightened up. He looked away from them as if searching his memory.

"I can see how you would be bitter about what happened but—we can work something out. I'll help you get the money back—if that's what you want."

"What I want from you is what you took from Sonny," Linda said. Her hand tightened on the revolver. *Any time now,* she thought, *any time.*

Malcolm turned to Ellis, pleading his case. "Butler was always coming to me with investment schemes, some of them were borderline, admittedly. He said viaticals pay forty—sometimes fifty percent. I told him I'd go for it but I didn't want to know *anything* about the person who held the policy. It wasn't right, admittedly, but—fifty percent."

NOW! Linda's mind screamed, *NOW!* But she loved seeing him squirm. She was in control at last, extracting pain that would pay Sonny back. This was justice.

Ellis towered over Malcolm. "So you're saying we should talk to this Butler character. Is that it?"

"Yes. Butler's the one."

"Where is he now?"

Malcolm looked at Linda, then quickly looked away.

"Here in San Francisco. After Houston we both came up here and—I could take you to him. Settle this right now. How would that be?"

"It's not up to me. It's up to the lady." Ellis looked at Linda. "What do you think?"

"Maybe we should . . . ."

The look of terror on Malcolm's face turned to hope.

"But I don't think we will," she added.

Malcolm's face went ashen.

"Now do you see how Sonny felt?" Linda asked. "He thought he was going to live. But then you killed him. You thought we were going to believe your bogus story about Mr. Butler. But we're not. Now do you see how my brother felt?"

"Yes," Malcolm said. "Yes I do."

"Not completely," Linda said, lifting the gun, and pointing it at the center of Malcolm's chest.

This is for you, Sonny, she thought. *This is for you, wherever you are.*

Over the cell phone, Eddie Voss sounded like a Vegas mobster. This made Dan feel like he was playing a scene in a B-movie.

"Like I say, we want the horse if the price is right. But we ain't about to pay no two hundred for a share of some 3-year old got lucky and won one race."

"Eddie," Dan said, "How many times have you paid big bucks for some horse, only to have him break down after a couple of races? Then it goes from being worth, say, four hundred to zilch in a second."

Dan paused, negotiating the freeway ramp. He was coming back from a follow-up meeting with Fidelity West's CEO. They wanted to get a look at him before they closed the deal. Contracts were being drawn up. When they were signed it would mean a nice influx of cash—some of which would wind up in Dan's pocket. Then he could call the contractor and give him the go ahead on the new house. Margo would like that.

Finally, Voss broke the silence with a grudging, "What's your point?"

"Let me put it this way. Epic Honor may not be the fastest horse in the barn, but he never gets sick, and he's always ready to dance." Dan felt the beauty of the line as he delivered it. It was huge. Hell, this was more fun than selling insurance. "The horse is all heart—and you can't put a price tag on that, can you?"

A dry rasping noise came over the phone. Dan realized it was laughter. "Okay Mr. Van Berg. You're very persuasive. I'll go two hundred for half share."

"And race him at Santa Anita under our colors."

Voss heaved a tired sigh. "I must be out of my fuckin' mind. But, yes, as long as we split the purse if he wins."

"Right."

"I'll fax you a contract. What's your fax?"

"It's 650 —" Dan stopped. He could swing by Malcolm's office on the way, invite him to lunch. If the contract was there they could review it over lunch. Besides, he wouldn't mind showing Malcolm the deal he negotiated. A little *in your face* action. He flipped open his planner. Here was Malcolm's number. He gave it to Voss and disconnected.

Malcolm's office was dead quiet when Dan opened the door. He called out, "Malcolm?"

From the inner office he heard movement, then Malcolm's oddly eager voice answering, "Yes! Yes! In here!"

When Dan reached the door he said, "Hey man, did you get a fax?" But he stopped when he saw the two visitors in the room. It was one of those weird things where you feel like you've walked into the middle of something heavy, Dan thought. The woman was stuffing something into her purse.

Dan said, "Sorry to interrupt but —"

"No, no. Come in, Dan. Come right in." Malcolm rose, his face pale. "You can't imagine how glad I am to see you. Dan, this is—oh dear I've completely forgotten—"

The tall white-haired guy nodded and said, "Keller. This is Karen Nightingale."

The woman looked at him. *If looks could kill,* Dan thought.

Malcolm was smiling, indicating his visitors, saying, "They're from Texas!" and laughing.

Texas? Dan thought, recalling something Veena had said when he called her that morning. He remembered her careful words.

"The inspection report on Mr. Ravling came in from Hershel," Veena had said. "There's something on it from Texas."

Something? Dan wondered what it was. But he had that big meeting with Fidelity West and he'd forgotten all about the inspection report he had ordered on Malcolm. He'd see the report when it came in. Besides, Hershel was still making calls, trying to find out the status of a questionable loan Malcolm had with a San Francisco bank.

"Yeah, well, I wouldn't have barged in like that, but I had a contract faxed here—for Epic Honor. Wait till I tell you about it. I'll wait in the front while you finish."

"No, no. We're done."

"For now," the woman said. Man, was she a hard-ass.

Dan was backing out of the room saying, "Your fax machine is in the front room?"

"Yes," Malcolm said. "Dan?"

"Yeah?"

"I'm so glad you decided to pop in. Wonderful to see you."

"Uh, yeah. Same here."

"This is no good," Dan said, shoving Voss's contract away from him. They were sitting in the kitchen on the backside of Bay Meadows where the track workers hung out. The kitchen, as the track rats called it, was a low, dark room. Sandwich counter along one wall, coffee and Coke machine, cooler. Probably the last place in San Francisco where you could buy a coffee for under fifty cents. The tables were packed with exercise riders, grooms, trainers, jockeys and the occasional owner who came by to see his horses work.

"In a typical sale, who pays the sales tax? Buyer or seller? Cliff?"

Cliff was watching someone across the room. Dan recognized Nik Zacco with his white hair, designer jeans and health club physique. He was talking to another man who was so short he could only be one thing.

"Who's the jock?"

"Roberto Torres." Then, disgusted: "I knew this'd happened sooner or later."

"What?"

"Zacco's trying to buy him away from me."

"Jockeys can ride for any trainer they want."

"Roberto and me hung together in high school. His mom was always fixing me these homemade tortillas and cordidas. He came up ridin' my horses. Now he's hot, Zacco's gonna try to lock him up."

"Roberto's that good?"

"Fastest out of the gate, bar none."

"You gonna put him on Epic Honor at Santa Anita?"

"I asked him. He ain't got back to me yet." Turning back to Dan he added, "Zacco, man, he'd cut your balls off to win a race. Sales tax is paid by the buyer."

"That's what I thought."

"But hell, that still means we're getting one-eighty-six for a horse we got for sixty. That's . . . a hundred-and-twenty-six grand of profit."

"Forty two thousand each," Malcolm said, setting a tray down in front of them. He had bought them all hot dogs and coffee.

"But this guy's trying to screw us," Dan said. He grabbed his dog and began dressing it with ketchup, relish, onions and mustard. He took a big bite, then licked ketchup off his fingers as he dialed his cell phone.

"Eddie Voss, please."

"What the hell're you doin'?" Cliff was panicking.

Dan smiled at him. "I got this under control. Just sit back and enjoy this."

Malcolm sipped his coffee. The hot dog sat there cooling. He said to Cliff: "Got that list of horses for me?"

"Right here." Cliff dug the envelope out of his back pocket. "So far, I got about ninety-five tied up in four horses. Thought you might want to fire for a few chips at Barretts next week."

"Barretts?"

"Auction for two-year-olds in training. Down in Pomona, near Santa Anita. Thought I'd stop in before the race next week. It's where we'll sell the Relaunch colt later this year."

Malcolm rolled the idea around in his mind. "I might just do that."

"Mr. Voss," Dan said into the phone. "Dan Van Berg. There's a problem with the contract. In deals like this, the buyer pays the sales tax." He listened. "I understand. But *you* have to understand our position."

Cliff muttered, "Shit. Voss's gettin' hinky now."

Dan continued, "See, if we're going to pay the sales tax, then the price of the horse is going up."

Cliff grabbed at the phone. "The hell're you doin'?" Dan dodged out of reach. Cliff turned to Malcolm. "You don't talk to Eddie Voss that way."

"Our price? Our price is two fifty—we pay sales taxes."

"He blew the deal," Cliff said, shoving his half-eaten hot dog away.

Malcolm watched Dan, a small smile of appreciation showing through.

"Okay Mr. Voss. Thanks." He shut the phone and sunk his teeth into the hot dog.

"Well?" Cliff asked.

"Huh?" Dan said with his mouth stuffed. He was playing with them now.

"What the hell'd he say?"

"He went for it!" Dan let out an explosive laugh. "Is that unbelievable or what? He's faxing us a new contract."

Cliff was stunned.

Malcolm was very quiet, watching Dan. He slowly turned his eyes to Cliff.

"You said you had some news about our Relaunch colt."

Cliff was eating again. "Oh yeah. Lemme tell you guys something. We're in tall cotton with this horse."

"What do you mean?" Malcolm asked.

"I put Ramon on him today. Well, he comes in, all excited. First thing he says is, 'What's the pedigree on this horse?' I tell him no one special, why? He goes, 'This colt's gonna run the balls off any horse out there.'"

"That's fantastic," Dan said, leaning forward.

"And Ramon knows his stuff, lemme tell you. So we'll get some times on him, then ship him to Florida for the rest of the winter. It's hotter there, gets them in shape, makes his coat look good for the auction at Barrett's."

"I've got an idea," Malcolm said, then paused, enjoying their attention. "I'm off to Europe next week. They have an auction at Tattersall's in Newmarket. I could stop by and talk up this Relaunch colt. Maybe I could find a buyer straightaway."

Dan looked at Cliff. "No harm trying."

"Maybe I should take the ownership papers on the Relaunch colt, just in case," Malcolm added. "You never know. If we don't get our price for him, then there's always Barretts."

"Them Limeys are big on American pedigree right now. Sorry Malcolm," Cliff nudged him, smiling. "Sell him sight unseen, then those crooked legs won't turn anyone off."

The loudspeaker above the snack bar crackled to life, announcing the second race. A couple of guys got up and left, heading for the track.

"Hey Cliff," Dan said. "Who looks good in the third?"

"I heard Kona Gold's been workin' large. But he's up against this horse called Something Special that's owned by Dicky Freemont—he's a pretty fair trainer."

"Make a pick. I feel lucky today."

"Take Something Special."

"Something Special it is. I'll see you over there."

Malcolm watched Dan disappear out the door. From his inside coat pocket he drew out a sheet of R.F.A. letterhead. He smoothed it flat on the table in front of him.

"You'll like this." He ran his finger down the list of mutual funds, each with the corresponding account numbers. "All set up in your name. You've already made almost twenty five hundred dollars. Do you want to draw it out as profit or reinvest?"

"Been meanin' to talk to you about that," Cliff answered. "We lost the checks connected to our IRA. So I phoned the company and had 'em send out a new batch. Should be here any day. Soon as they come in I'll write you a check."

"Brilliant." Malcolm stood up, leaving the financial statement with Cliff. "I'm off."

"Not going to the races?"

"I've got a few things to get squared away. I'll see you in Los Angeles. And don't forget to get me the papers on our horse. Maybe I can make us a pretty penny from the Limeys. Aye?"

When Cliff boarded United Shuttle Flight 21 to Los Angeles the following week, he saw the dark clouds rolling in and thought, *Here we go again. It's El Nino time again.*

Cliff took his seat and began mentally reviewing the instructions he had given Emerson for Epic Honor and recalled, with relief, that he had remembered to bring the papers on the Relaunch colt. The checks for the IRA hadn't arrived yet, but hey, he didn't really mind stalling Malcolm a little longer. Maybe the Slimy Limey would actually pay him for the training bills and transport fees.

The 737 barreled down the runway and Cliff saw the rain was falling heavily now. As the jet accelerated, the drops on the window became horizontal and then blew away completely. The lights of San Francisco appeared below between gaps in the clouds. The jet banked, then turned south, the lights thinning, then giving way to vast areas of darkness.

Closing his eyes, Cliff settled back into the seat and saw Epic Honor breezing yesterday morning before he put him on a trailer and shipped him south. Twenty-one and change. What a horse. He was gonna win at Santa Anita and then they'd sell half interest in him. A sale like that, Cliff could clear his bills and have some left over for new horses.

As Cliff dozed, pieces of his life circled in his flickering consciousness, horses and faces and thoughts of money. He saw the Relaunch colt running in the field down by the barn, crossing in front of the big eucalyptus grove at the bottom of the hill and coming back up the slope, Ramon riding up and saying, *Hombre! Que caballo!* He was some horse, all right—the best pin hook he'd ever made.

But that wasn't all. It was the *way* he ran—like he'd done it all before, like he didn't really need to be trained. Like he knew what it took to win better than the jock on his back. Every once in a while you found a horse like that, one that ran so fast it didn't make sense—just a freak of nature.

Stirring, Cliff looked out the window and saw they were over the Los Angeles area. He looked east as if he might see all the way to Santa Anita. Here he was in the big time, the biggest track in California, the biggest stakes race of the year, the Santa Anita Handicap with a $160,000 purse. And Jamie would be there to see him win it.

Cliff leaned back into the seat, closed his eyes and reached for a few minutes more of sleep. But it was no good. It had started. He was seeing Jamie's face, hearing her voice, and thinking that tomorrow night they'd be together again.

When Malcolm finally found Cliff at the Barretts Auction the next morning, he was slouched in a chair in front of a wall of video screens showing slo-mo replays of stretch runs by the thoroughbreds that would be for sale there that day. Other trainers and owners, dressed in jeans and boots, milled around in the dark room, whispering to each other, nodding occasionally at the video screens, making notes in their auction catalogs.

"There you are," Malcolm said. "Been searching everywhere for you."

Cliff's dark eyes never left the screen. His hair was slicked back, a clean shirt flashed white from under the green windbreaker. As the shot cut to a new race, Cliff finally stirred. He opened his catalog and wrote a few notes next to an entry headed "Chestnut Colt" with several dense blocks of print listing its pedigree.

Looking up, Cliff said, "This horse coming up next, want you to take a close look at him. If we could get him for eighty it'd be a steal."

"Why?"

"His daddy was a great sprinter. But they never put a decent jockey on him so he didn't win much. They took him back East to stud and bred him with a miler. The colt should be—look, look!"

Malcolm turned to see a two-year-old working at a track somewhere. Under the horse was a digital stopwatch showing its time as it passed the eight pole, through the stretch and then at the finish line.

"See him change leads like that?"

"Leads?"

"His lead foot. Horse gets tired runnin' on his left side through the turn. He needs to change lead front legs so when he gets to the stretch he can hit the gas." Cliff laughed. "I'm tellin' you, we get that horse for eighty, even ninety, it'd be highway robbery."

Cliff turned to Malcolm for the first time. "How was your flight?"

Before Malcolm could answer Cliff said, "Got three horses I want to try for. But competition's gonna be tough."

"From who?"

"Japanese. They come in here and out-price guys like me. But I know the pedigree lines better then they do so I get a steal now and then."

Malcolm looked disdainfully at the crowd gathering outside the auction room, at the lunch counter and the bar. "Cliff my friend, I want to make something clear. You see a good horse, you go for it—regardless. Understand? We're not going to be outbid."

Cliff smiled. "I'll take that action. Bidding's gonna start here in another hour. Let's grab a bite."

Cliff was tearing into a club sandwich when a voice came from behind them.

"You hear what's happening up north? El Nino's back in town."

They turned to find Nik Zacco smiling at them, wearing a white shirt, expensive jeans and boots. They shook hands.

"I was watching it on CNN in the hotel this morning," Cliff said, still chewing. "Looks like they're takin' it in the shorts. They're getting nuked, man. Houses surfin' down the sides of hills. It's brutal."

Cliff nodded to Malcolm. "Nik, this here's Malcolm Ravling, one of the Epic Honor owners."

"You the one took a swing at me?" Zacco asked, laughing.

"That was my partner. It was the heat of the moment. Know what I mean?"

"That's horse racing." Zacco laughed some more. "I think I met you once before. You're a stockbroker?"

Cliff said, "He's an investment guru. Give him a few bucks and he'll turn it into a fuckin' fortune for you. People're throwin' money at him."

"Is that right? Maybe we should talk. Guy I've got's not doing much for me."

Malcolm pressed a business card into Zacco's hand. "Give me a call."

"Thanks. Cliff, can I have a word with you?"

Malcolm took the cue. He rose. "Anyone fancy a beer? Nik?"

"No thanks, Malcolm. Hey, nice to meet you." Zacco never stopped smiling.

Malcolm dissolved into the crowd at the bar.

"Wanted to make sure there was no hard feelings from that little fracas last week," Zacco said.

"Hell no. I thought it was funny, them two jocks dukin' it out."

"Duran's a hot-headed son of a bitch."

Their laughter died. Nik lowered his voice.

"Listen, I wanted to ask. You close that deal with Voss yet?"

"We reached an agreement. But we ain't passed papers yet. Why?"

"Here's the thing. I've got some people who could be interested in Epic Honor. I thought I'd approach you because I know you don't really want to deal with Voss."

"I dealt with Voss before, he never burned me."

"My people're willing to top whatever Voss promised you."
Cliff put down his sandwich and carefully wiped his hands.
"I'm listening."

It was late in the afternoon, the bar was packed and the auctioneer's voice was going like a machine gun. Cliff suddenly banged down his half-finished beer.

"Jesus! They're up to 106. Our horse is comin' up!"

He took off, shouldering his way through the crowd with Malcolm two steps behind. People nodded to Cliff as he passed, standing back when they saw the intense look on his face, a look they'd seen at the track just before getting their butts kicked in some stakes race. They respected the intensity since they knew it flowed down from trainer to jockey to the horse.

Cliff pushed into the auction room and they slid into vacant seats. The room was like a theater with rows of seats slanting down to a small stage bordered with flowers. Two doors led to the empty stage and a bank of video screens poured out images of galloping thoroughbreds with times, earnings and pedigrees. Three auctioneers sat at a table barely visible above the stage. Spotters in green blazers roamed the room and worked the crowd, looking for bidders.

Cliff turned to Malcolm and spoke behind his hand. "I'm just prayin' no one sees what I see in 108. Look at the pedigree on him." He peeled back the catalog to expose the bloodline on Hip No. 108, listed as Chestnut Colt. "His daddy's Robahush—a great stallion. See what he won?"

Cliff shot a look behind him. Standing in the back of the room were three Asian men dressed in suits. One was bidding, the other was talking on a cell phone.

"I sure as hell don't want to bid against Tokyo," Cliff said. "I'll go a hundred and a half. But he could get anywhere up to three hundred."

A groom led a new horse onto the stage with the number 108 painted on his rump. His mane was braided, his rich brown coat shone under the stage lights. Even his black hooves glowed. His flanks rippled with muscle as he danced nervously, eyes wide.

"Now we come to Number 108, Chestnut Colt by Robahush," the auctioneer said. "This two-year-old missed equaling the fastest eighth mile by only twelve one-hundreds. So who'll start us out here? Who'll give me seventy-five? Seventy-five. Seventy?" His voice broke into an unintelligible stream of rhythmic sounds and sudden exclamations; the only part that could be understood were the numbers.

The spotters scanned the room for bids.

"Seventy? How about seventy? Sixty-five then. Sixty-five. Folks, he's a handsome one! Sixty-five to open the bid. Sixty-five, sixty-five. Okay then fifty-five. Who'll give fifty-five? Fifty-five?"

The spotters searched the sea of faces, looking for a blink, a wave, a nod. The horse tried to rear. The groom flicked the bridle, distracting his attention. He danced around, showing his other flank.

The auctioneer stopped his patter and looked down at the audience.

"Folks, let me remind you this is a Robahush colt. In his 35 starts Robahush earned two hundred thousand with five first-place finishes. And this beautiful colt has nearly set the track record for an eighth mile."

The auctioneers talked among themselves briefly, then turned back to the crowd.

"Now, who'll start us off with an opening bid of fifty? Fifty thousand dollars. Who'll give me fifty? Fifty?"

An older woman in a fringed suede jacket raised her program.

"Ho!" The spotter yelled, pointing at her.

Cliff whispered to Malcolm. "It's starting at half a yard. We're in the game."

"I've got a bid of fifty. Fifty. Do I hear fifty-five?"

A man in a plaid cap raised a finger.

"Fifty-five. The bid is fifty-five. Who'll give me sixty? Fifty-five, sixty? Sixty? Who'll give me —"

A bald spotter with bright blue eyes extended his arm to the woman in the suede jacket. She nodded.

"Ho!"

"Sixty. I've got sixty. Do I hear seventy?"

"Ho!"

Cliff whispered, "Slow down now. Slow down."

"Seventy do I hear eighty?"

"Ho!"

"Eighty, do I hear ninety? Eighty, do I hear ninety? Ninety?"

The spotter pointed at the woman in the suede coat. She sat very still. The spotter extended his arm to her, wiggled his fingers, as if to tickle a bid out of her. She nodded.

"Ho!"

"Ninety is the bid. Who'll give me a hundred. Ninety—one hundred? Ninety—one hundred! This is a Robahush horse! Who'll bid one hundred?"

"Are you going to buy this horse or not?" Malcolm hissed.

"Let the action die down a little first."

"Want me to handle it?"

"Keep your fuckin' hands in your lap!"

"Ninety-five then. Ninety-five?"

The spotter gestured to the man in the plaid hat. He stood up and walked out.

"Ninety-five—a hundred?"

Cliff sat up straight. The spotter's eyes locked on him, asking him silently for a bid. Cliff nodded.

"We've got a hundred. Do I hear one-ten? A hundred—one ten? One ten?

The woman in the suede coat raised her program.

"Ho!"

"One ten! We have one ten—one twenty? One twenty?"

"Getting' a little rich for my blood." Cliff said, folding his arms.

"Why?"

"You said you'd only go —"

"One-ten—one twenty? One-ten going once—"

"You want the horse?" Malcolm asked.

"Hell yes."

"Get your bloody hand up! I'll cover it."

"One-ten going twice."

The spotter had moved up the aisle and stood in front of them. Cliff met his eyes, nodded.

"Ho!"

"One-twenty! We've got one-twenty! Who'll give me one-thirty? One-twenty—one thirty?"

The spotter was staring at the woman in the suede coat. She looked down at her program.

133

"One-twenty going once. Going twice . . . ." The room became very quiet. No one moved. "Sold! For one-hundred and twenty thousand dollars. Number 109 is out. Number 110 is a brown filly. Folks this is Cal-Bred from Meadowbrook Farms . . . ."

Malcolm pounded Cliff on the back. "Brilliant!"

"I don't believe I got this horse for one twenty."

A woman in a low-cut gingham dress came up the aisle with a clipboard. She leaned in to them, showing some cleavage. "Congratulations, Mr. Dante. Beautiful horse."

Cliff signed and she tore a copy off for him.

Malcolm shook Cliff's hand. "Well done. Your strategy worked."

"I can't believe it. The Lord must have looked down at me and froze up them other fuckers. Let's go see our horse."

They were on their way to the barns when Cliff looked at his watch.

"Damn. I gotta get Jamie at the airport."

"I'll call a limousine."

"Fuck the limo, man. I gotta be there." Cliff stopped, realizing something. "Hey, would you pick up the papers? Show 'em this," he gave him the carbon copy.

"Be glad to. What about dinner? I'd love to have the pleasure of—"

"Uh, Malcolm, this is kind of a special night for us. We ain't seen much of each other lately, so we're—"

"Say no more," he laughed. "Tomorrow night then. After our victory."

"Tomorrow. And don't forget the papers."

"Don't worry. And you said your wife might be bringing those checks . . . ."

Damn. Cliff had forgotten about that. "She's supposed to. I'll let you know."

"See you at the track. And Cliff? Have a nice night, aye?" he winked.

Cliff walked away from Malcolm's laughter and headed for the rental car in the lot. It was dark now and the night was clear. He dug the cell phone out of his pocket. Might be able to catch her at the ranch before she left for the airport. She was going to stop there and get some clothes she needed.

Ring . . . Ring . . . Ring . . . Might be too late. Ring . . . Ring . . . Someone picked up.

"Jamie?"

"Cliff. Where are you?"

"Headin' to the airport to get you. I got to stop at the barn, check on Epic Honor, but I'll be there on time."

"You better be."

"Hey, I heard it's a little wet up there."

"I've never seen it rain like this before."

"Reason I called, those checks from our IRA come in?"

"You're not going to buy another horse."

"This is for long term investments. Stuff for you and the kids. The checks were supposed to come in the mail today."

"Oh my gosh!"

"What?"

"Ah, nothing. Yes, I think they're here."

"Bring 'em along. And bring your appetite. I'm takin' you to this fancy steak joint tonight."

"Sounds delicious."

"Bye."

Cliff was at the car now. He disconnected, slid the phone back into his pocket.

As soon as Jamie hung up, she yanked open the cabinet door under the sink and saw the trash bag was empty. *Damn.* She had already taken the trash out. She got out her big green golf umbrella and stepped outside. It was raining so hard she could hear the drops hissing through the air as they fell. Two inches of water stood on the lawn. It was falling faster than the earth could soak it up.

The trash barrels were lined up along the side of the house. She opened the first barrel and found the plastic bag she had dumped there earlier. Peeling back the edges of the bag she saw the stack of envelopes she had thrown away while she was straightening up. Cliff sure wasn't much of a housekeeper.

She found the envelope marked Morganstern & Fremont and pulled it out. Why did they make these things look so much like junk mail? Yes, now she could feel the block of checks inside. She brushed coffee grounds off the envelope and headed back into the house through the rain, jumping mud puddles, and thinking, *Wow, that was really lucky.*

On the drive back from the airport Cliff kept glancing over at Jamie—just looking at her face and thinking how great she looked. A little makeup, but that was okay. Showed she cared. And he'd never seen that blouse before, kind of see-through so he could make out something frilly underneath.

They pulled into the Old Ranch and found a parking space up close. She jumped out before he could open her door and they walked between split rail fences and wagon wheels. Kinda hokey, sure, but the food here was great.

When their steaks arrived and she took her first bite, he asked, "Well?"

"Not bad."

"Not bad? Come on, it tastes great." He poured some more wine for her. He would have rather had a beer, but there was something about sharing a bottle of Dago red that brought you together.

"You trying to get me drunk?"

"I would if I thought it would help."

She shot him a look which he deflected with an innocent smile. They were always busting each other. And that was okay when things were easy between them. But now she seemed to take everything the wrong way.

"You know, I was giving some thought to what you said the other day, about going to vet school."

"Yeah . . . ." She was immediately on guard.

"There's a lot that's gotta be worked out. But it might not be a bad idea."

"What's got to be worked out?" She was chewing slowly.

"Oh, you know, who's gonna watch the kids. Gramma's gettin' a little old to be chasing Davie around the barn."

"My mother said she'd take them twice a week. What else?"

"Well, I just wanted to know, after you get your vet degree, are you gonna work out at the track, or you just gonna take care of kitty cats and doggies?"

She set her knife and fork down.

Damn, shouldn't have said that, he thought.

137

"See, it's that kind of attitude that really gets me."

He tried to pass it off with a laugh. "I'm sorry, it just came out kind of funny. Actually, this could work out really good. It might be a way for us to see each other more—if you were at the track. So is that what you're thinking?"

She held his eyes for a moment, then slowly picked up her fork and began eating again.

"I haven't decided what direction I'm going in," she said. "I just thought I'd start school and see where it takes me. Of course, horses are what I know best, so I thought of that immediately. But I wouldn't want to rule out the possibility of opening a clinic. If the clinic were at the ranch, then . . . ."

Jamie kept talking and he kept listening. Not to the words, but to her voice. Truth of the matter was, he didn't want her to be a vet. But he thought it was all right if she had some room in her life, something other than raising kids. Then, when he got on the top of the heap, she'd forget about all that vet-school crap. Because then she'd realize that winning was enough for both of them.

Later that night Cliff got out of bed and stood naked at the hotel window. You could see the track from here, the grandstands and the enormous parking lot surrounding it and then the dark shapes of the mountains beyond—the San Gabriels.

He hoped Epic Honor was comfortable in his stall, dreaming of victory tomorrow, his muscles relaxed, rested, ready to give it everything. Like a video clip, he could see his horse stretched out, flying across the line, the jockey's fist raised in triumph.

Hands slid around his waist from behind.

"Don't tell me that's all you've got." Jamie's voice was husky.

"Hell no. I thought you were asleep."

She pressed her body into him. She felt hot. Or was that him? He could feel her breath on his neck; her breasts pressed into his back. Now her hands were moving down. Slowly, *oh so slowly* . . . and when they got there, he was ready.

"The flag is up!" he said.

"So, have I got your attention, or what?"

Turning, he crushed her to him and said, "You're the only thing that could take my mind off the race tomorrow."

It was almost like someone tapped him on the shoulder and said, "Hey Dan! Wake up!"

His eyes opened and he instantly felt awake. He lay there in the dark, trying to think what woke him up. A sound maybe? The rain on the roof?

"Dan?" Margo's voice reached him in the darkness.

"Yeah?"

"Why did you wake up?"

"I just had this goofy dream. We were all at the track—but it was in Texas. Don't ask me why. Anyway, Cliff and me are trying to figure out if Epic Honor is going to do well in the race. And Malcolm says, 'He comes from an impeccable pedigree.' And blah, blah, blah—Malcolm can really lay it on thick. And then he gets huffy and says, 'If you don't believe me, look at this.' And he gives us this statement done up on R.F.A. stationery with gold embossed numbers and everything. And we go, 'Wow, that's great!' And we were so impressed we forgot about the horse and the race and everything."

Dan waited for her reaction. Silence.

"I don't get that," he said. "What's that all about?"

More silence. Then he heard her heavy, rhythmic breathing.

"Yeah, amazing dream, Dan," he said to himself.

At the office, Dan told his dream to Veena. She nodded, listening carefully. But said nothing when he finished.

"I mean, do you believe there's any meaning in dreams?"

"Sometimes there is great meaning in dreams. Sometimes nothing."

"Yeah, but how do you tell?"

"If it fits with other things." She waited politely, smiling sympathetically, then said, "With the rain, you better get an early start."

He said, "Start?"

"We've got that booth at the San Francisco Convention Center. You wanted to stop by. Fidelity West was going to be there."

He was kinda spacey. He'd been up since four, when the dream woke him.

"You're right. I'll get going." He pulled on his coat. His umbrella leaned against the wall, a puddle forming around the base of it. Glancing outside, he saw it was coming down harder than ever.

"You catch the weather this morning? Is it raining in L.A. yet?"

"No. But the storm is moving south."

"Man, I hope it holds off until Epic Honor runs. Okay, I'm outta here. Oh, if that Fidelity West contract comes in, call me. I want to get that wrapped up as soon as possible."

"I'll take care of it."

"I know you will. Bye."

Driving on surface streets to the freeway, he went through a flooded intersection and could feel the water blasting the underside of his old diesel Mercedes. Half a block later the engine stuttered, like someone slammed the engine block with a hammer. *Damn.* He'd have to take it easy. Didn't want to conk out on the freeway.

When he merged onto I-80 northbound, he saw there wasn't much to worry about. Traffic wasn't moving. Through the wipers he saw a line of brake lights disappearing into the rain. The downpour pounded on the roof of the car.

He picked up the phone and punched his speed dialer.

"Yeah? Hello?" Cliff's voice was typically deadpan.

"Hey Cliff, it's Dan. Can you hear me?"

"Dan-the-Man. Sure, I can hear you."

"It's raining like a son-of-a-bitch up here. What's it like down in L.A.?"

"Bright and sunny."

"I hope it holds. I heard this's moving south. Where are you?"

"Headin' to the track."

"You with Malcolm?"

"He's here somewheres."

Dan thought about telling him his dream from last night. But Cliff probably wasn't into that touchy-feely dream stuff.

"Malcolm fired for some big chips at the auction yesterday," Cliff said. "Bought a two-year-old by Robahush."

"How much?"

"I was gonna go to a hundred and a half—got him for one-twenty."

"That's great, man."

Traffic was starting to move. He accelerated, leveled off at sixty-five. Better keep his mind on the driving. He was about to say 'good luck' but he bit his tongue. Trainers were so damn superstitious. Better not say anything.

"Call me after the race."

"I'll do that. Talk to you later."

Dan could hear the tension in Cliff's voice, and he felt his own stomach tightening. Looking ahead, through sheets of blowing rain, it was hard to imagine it was sunny anywhere. Here, it looked like the end of the—

A huge puddle appeared dead ahead. More like a lake with waves and everything. Too late to swerve.

Whoosh!

The road disappeared. A wave of water flew into the windshield. He held his breath. The motor was running smoothly but he knew it would take a second before—

Stutter, stutter. He felt the engine dying. Then it revved up again. He slowed down. High beams in his rearview mirror. Now the guy was flashing his lights. Couldn't he see that he was having trouble?

Dan turned on his flashers and steered the Mercedes onto the breakdown lane. The motor was throbbing like a bad heart. Let it dry out, then get going again. Just in case, he better call the Auto Club. He popped his briefcase open and pawed through papers, looking for his planner.

What was this? He lifted out the inspection report he had

ordered on Malcolm Ravling. He'd been avoiding reading it. Veena had said there was something on it from Texas. Those people in Malcolm's office were from Texas. That hard-assed broad and—

A truck passed so close it felt like a bomb going off. The car shook violently and a wall of water covered the windshield. Got to get off this freeway. See if maybe—

Click.

It was a connection made in Dan's mind. A quiet but danger- ous little *click* as the little suspicions slid into place. Everything he felt about Malcolm matched with the dream he'd had about the gold embossed stationery, at the track in Texas. In Texas where Malcolm had been in trouble. In Texas where that hard-assed broad was from. Everything fit.

All Dan could think was, *Oh God, no. Please, no.*

Dan's suspicions had started when the guy called to complain about his life insurance policy. He called when he was rushing to the track to meet Malcolm. What was his name? Gastin? But when he returned the call, Mr. Gastin had said, "I'm not concerned about this anymore, Mr. Van Berg. I just got a statement here Mr. Ravling prepared for me and it all looks beautiful."

It all looks beautiful. What did he mean? The gold embossed stationery? Or the figures?

Dan saw he was near the Van Ness Exit. Well, if what he sus- pected was true, there was one way to find out. He dropped the Mercedes in gear.

And the engine died.

143

Walking through the stables, feeling the quiet of the horses around him, Cliff saw Emerson up ahead, carrying a bucket, moving stiffly but with purpose.

"Hey."

Emerson turned. He was wearing a clean pair of jeans, white shirt and sweater. His hair was combed back wet and his mustache was neatly trimmed.

"Mornin' Cliff." His whisper fit with the reverent quiet of the pre-race stables.

"Got him iced down yet?"

"I iced him for thirty minutes." Then Emerson lost his confidence and asked. "Thirty minutes is what you wanted. Right?"

"Thirty's good."

They heard a bumping noise and turned. Epic Honor's big head appeared over the stall door. His round, dark eyes looked at them, questioning, as if he might miss out on something important.

Emerson chuckled. "He's only run—what?— four races now? He knows the routine better than I do. He heard the trumpet for the first race, he wanted to bust out and run right then."

Cliff stroked the colt's nose. "Hot to trot. You'll get your turn, guy."

Emerson lifted the latch and they moved into the tight stall with the horse. He stripped the ice bags off the legs and dumped them into the bucket. He stood back.

"What's our post position?" Emerson asked, watching Cliff inspect the horse.

"Got us in the four hole. I'm gonna tell Roberto to hang back, let the other runners burn out, then charge late. This guy's a closer. He wants to come from behind rather than hold the lead."

Cliff crouched next to the horse, running his hands down the long, muscular legs, checking the joints.

"So, Roberto Torres is our jock today?" Emerson asked.

"Huh?"

Cliff's thumb probed a tiny bulge on the horse's leg, above the fetlock.

"You said Zacco was trying to get Roberto."

"Roberto turned him down flat. Said he'd always ride for me if I wanted him."

Cliff pressed the bulge and watched his horse's face for a reaction. Epic Honor didn't flinch. He didn't blink or nicker or toss his head. No reaction at all. Emerson stood by, watching carefully.

"Vet check him yet?"

"Yes."

Cliff thought of Voss's offer to buy a share of this horse. He thought of Zacco's counteroffer. He thought of Malcolm over in the clubhouse, waiting to watch Epic Honor run, probably acting like a big shot, telling the people around him, *I have a horse in the fourth race, Epic Honor, trained by a Cliff Dante. He's the best trainer in Northern Cal.* He couldn't let him down, even though his gut was telling him something different.

He decided to ignore it.

"Want me to call the vet?" Emerson asked.

Cliff slowly stood up. "Naw. He looks good to me."

They stood there silently, looking at the horse.

Emerson finally said, "This is a big race."

"Been a while since we won in Southern Cal. Be a nice way to show 'em we're back. And I really want Jamie to see us win."

"She's here?"

"Came down last night. She'll be in the box with me."

Emerson smiled and looked away.

They were quiet again, the horse breathing easy, his ears turning to catch distant sounds. Alert, ready. It suddenly occurred to Emerson that there was one too many people in the stall.

"I'm gonna go get the wraps." Emerson said, picking up the bucket. He shuffled out of the stall.

Cliff stood alone with the horse, their heads close. Then a strange thought came to him. There's how you feel on the surface of your life on any given day. But then there's something underneath all that, like a current in an ocean that you couldn't control. You tried like hell to control it, to make it speed up or change course—but forget all that. The ocean didn't give a damn about you or what you wanted. And the current was going someplace you could only guess at.

Epic Honor sensed Cliff's mind was elsewhere and leaned in close, mouthing him with his big lips, trying to get his attention. Cliff looked into his bottomless eyes.

"Everyone else lets me down, but not you—you're always ready to dance." He added, his voice firmer, "I want everything you've got today." The big eyes absorbed the words and the feeling behind them. "Understand? I want it all."

Dan left the warmth of his car and stepped out into the rain. He popped the umbrella open and walked along the shoulder of I-80, slogging through an inch of standing water. His shoes were instantly soaked. Each car that passed him brought a hissing comet tail of water. And the suction of passing trucks tried to pull him into traffic. But he was almost to the exit ramp. And from there he could probably see . . . .

Yes, there it was ahead of him through the rain, like a lighthouse beacon, just as Veena had described it when he called her. The neon sign throbbed in the wet air: Golden Gate Motel. As Dan stumbled on, he saw a man under the awning holding an umbrella. Veena's uncle was waiting to help him.

"Sid?" Dan called out to the Indian gentleman under the umbrella.

"Yes, hello. You must be Mr. Van Berg." He shouted back through the rain, walking out to meet him. "Would you like to step inside? Have a nice cup of hot tea?"

"No. Did Veena tell you? I have kind of an emergency."

"Yes, yes. She explained it all to me. My car is waiting to take you. A '98 Camry LX. Very good car."

They moved across the parking lot to a cranberry-red Toyota.

Dan said, "I'm soaked. I hope I don't get water all over—"

"Leather interior," Sid assured him. "Very rugged."

Inside, Sid referred to a slip of paper with an address handwritten on it. They rocketed out of the parking lot and into the rain.

"Out of the way you silly woman!" Sid shouted at an old woman threading her way through a puddled intersection. The Toyota's horn screamed.

Dan remembered that Veena once said her uncle, Sid, had been a cab driver in New Delhi. Over there the tolerances were much tighter —miss a pedestrian by inches, no one blinked.

Dan braced himself, watching the city outside under the pall of rain, feeling a shadow sliding over his life. There was still a chance it wasn't true. But everything fit too well. And, if it did, how much had Malcolm stolen? Dan dug out his phone and was going to call Cliff. But then he thought of the big race and decided against it.

"Here we go!" Sid announced proudly, screeching to a halt in front of a modest bungalow on a side street.

"Sid, would you mind waiting?"

"No, no. Veenabin said it was important. I'll listen to some tunes." Then, as if to put Dan at ease he added, "Four-speaker stereo with CD changer," and winked.

Dan took the umbrella and moved up the walkway, wondering what the hell he looked like, soaked to the skin, coming in out of the rain. Before he could knock, the door opened on a gray haired man in a cardigan, his face lined with anxiety.

"Mr. Gastin, I'm Dan Van Berg."

"Your assistant called—she said you'd be coming. Is there a problem?" He held the door open. Dan stepped in and felt the stuffy heat of an elderly person's house.

In another room, Dan heard a woman's voice: "Who's there, Stan?"

"Friend of Mr. Ravling." *Friend.* Dan winced. "He's here to talk about—about insurance."

"Insurance? Oh."

To Dan, he said, "I don't want to upset her. She worries, you know." He led Dan into the kitchen where a folder was lying on the plastic tablecloth.

"Mr. Gastin, when I talked to you last week, you mentioned that Malcolm—Mr. Ravling—had given you a statement."

"That's right."

"I'd like to look at that statement."

"It's right here." Mr. Gastin opened the folder and pulled out a single sheet of paper. Dan took it, thinking, *It could still be all right, everything could still be as good as it seems.* But when he saw the statement he knew it wasn't. And he felt sick.

"See how much our money's gone up?" the old man said, smiling hopefully.

Yes, it appeared that their investments were going up. Going through the roof, in fact. But this was according to Malcolm Ravling, because the statement was on his letterhead. A beautiful gold-embossed bond stationery, just like Dan had seen in his dream. The only problem was, the statement didn't come from a bank or an investment company. It came from Malcolm Ravling, himself. And he could put down anything he wanted.

Dan looked up and saw a woman moving by touch through the dining room, coming to the doorway and holding onto the frame. Then it hit him—she was blind. Malcolm had stolen the life savings from a blind woman. *Jesus.*

"Is everything all right?" she asked.

"Of course it's all right," Mr. Gastin said. "It's all right. Isn't it, Mr. Van Berg?"

But Mr. Van Berg didn't answer. He had his cell phone out and he was dialing, hoping like hell he could reach Cliff before he signed his life savings away to a fraud.

Cliff was walking toward the paddock at Santa Anita Race Track outside Los Angeles, moving along pathways through hedges, some of them cut to look like horses. This whole place was really classy. Kind of an old Hollywood feel to it, with black-and-white pictures of movie stars posing with jockeys and horses.

The paddock was a long, low building open on one side to risers. People stood on the risers watching the horses being saddled. A number was posted above each stall, empty now since the horses for the seventh hadn't been led in yet. But the railbirds were already gathering, checking racing forms, glancing at the changing odds posted on the side of the grandstands or on the video screens that were everywhere.

Cliff stood there shifting his weight; he had no interest in conversation. Jamie said, "I'm going to find a phone, see how Grandma's doing with the kids."

"Use this," Cliff said, pulling out his cell phone and handing it to her. Jamie took the phone and moved away.

Malcolm removed a Fed Ex pouch from his inside jacket pocket and unfolded it.

"Think I can get that check now, Cliff? I'm expressing some papers back to the office. Thought I'd send your check along, too."

Cliff was thinking, *Man, can't you see my mind's on other things?* But the paddock was empty and there was time to kill.

"The checks're in Jamie's purse."

"Brilliant. Must get this to the office. Gordon will make the deposit tomorrow."

"He's back?"

"Sorry?"

"Gordon. You said his mom was sick or something."

"Yes, yes. Everything's fine now," Malcolm said impatiently. "You said your lovely wife had the checks . . . ?"

Malcolm saw Cliff hesitate so he pulled out his own checkbook. "Tell you what—long as we're at it, I'll write you a check for the training fees. Say, ten thousand? I'll give you a check from another account for the horses when we get back up north."

Cliff saw that Jamie had Grandma on the cell phone and was chatting away. He interrupted, saying, "Got those IRA checks?" She opened her purse, pulled out a block of checks.

Cliff rejoined Malcolm and they sat next to each other on the bench.

"Jamie thought these were junk mail and threw them out. That's why they're boogered up like this." Cliff laughed, then added, "Lucky thing she found them."

"Indeed." Malcolm grunted, writing in his checkbook with a thick fountain pen that probably cost him a grand. And he'd find a way to let you know about it too, Cliff thought.

Nearby, Jamie was saying, "Hello? Hello?" into the phone, and pushing buttons. "Grandma? I better get going, I think the battery is dying."

Cliff didn't really want to explain what he was doing to Jamie, so he said, "How should I do this?"

"Just make it out to R.F.A."

"What was the amount again?"

"Forty."

Forty thousand pretty much wiped out their savings, Cliff realized, noting with some relief that Jamie was still on the line to Grandma.

"There you go," Cliff said, extending the check. Malcolm plucked it from his hand.

"And here *you* go," he said, handing a check to Cliff. "All cleared up now, aye?"

Cliff looked at the check, signed, Malcolm M. Ravling.

"What's the 'M' stand for?"

"Marquis." He smiled. "Family name—on my mother's side."

They stood up. Cliff saw the horses being led into the far end of the paddock. Emerson walked beside Epic Honor, carrying the saddle.

"Here comes our horse."

Malcolm glanced in that direction.

"You know, I think there's a Fed Ex box across the street. I'll just pop this in and be back for the race."

151

"Whatever you say." Cliff was starting toward Epic Honor when Malcolm did a strange thing. He held out his hand to Cliff.

"Best of luck," Malcolm said.

They shook hands. And Malcolm dissolved into the crowd.

PART FOUR

OFF & RUNNING

THE HORSE WAS SADDLED, the race strategy discussed and they began that long walk under the grandstands, through the tunnel and out onto the track. The groom was leading Epic Honor while Roberto sat high on his back, wearing blue silks, adjusting his goggles, getting the feel of the horse underneath him. And then they came out of the tunnel and there was the track. It looked twice the size of Bay Meadows, a huge sprawling field that gave way to trees in the distance and then sloped up to the purple mountains that loomed over the scene.

When they got to the track, Cliff reached up and shook Roberto's hand.

"Catch us a break out there, man," he told him.

"Go get 'em, Epic Honor," Jamie said. She knew better than to say "good luck" because luck was what they needed more than anything else. And to ask for what you needed never seemed to get it. Life was like that, Cliff thought. The only way to get something was to stop wanting it, or to try to sneak up on it.

A young woman on a chase pony trotted up beside Epic Honor and together they moved out onto the track. Cliff watched Epic Honor rise up and float above the earth, effortless and free. An easy mover. *Gonna be a shame to have to sell him—or even a share of him.*

A hand threaded itself into Cliff's and he turned to see Jamie's face looking up at him, excited, alive. "Been awhile since I came to the races with you. It's fun."

"I know," he said, wanting to add, *It sure is great to have you here.* But it didn't come out. The hell with it. She knew how he felt.

Looking up into the stands, Cliff saw Emerson waving them into a box up above the finish line. They moved up the aisle as the bugler played "Boots and Saddles." The signal sparked a wave of activity and people swarmed toward the betting windows.

"Ladies and gentlemen," the announcer's voice boomed over the loudspeaker, "the horses are on the field for the Santa Anita Handicap." A cheer rose up from the grandstands as the announcer read off the names of each horse.

"Want me to put a little something down?" Emerson asked as Cliff and Jamie moved into the box.

"The usual." Cliff slipped him two one-hundred dollar bills. "On the nose," he added, instinctively looking at the tote board. Word musta traveled south with them; Epic Honor, in the four hole, was going off at 7 to 1.

Emerson nodded and disappeared.

"Word's out on your horse, man." Cliff turned and saw Nik Zacco smiling at him, extending his hand. "Hi Jamie. Haven't seen you for a while."

"Hey Nik."

"Stopped by to see Epic Honor run," Zacco said. He lowered his voice and said, "People I was telling you about, they're very insistent. They authorized me to offer you a bonus to sweeten the deal. So we double Voss's offer, and we put a hundred grand in your pocket. What do you say?"

A hundred grand? Now, this was getting tough.

Zacco saw the wheels turning in Cliff's mind. A sly smile spread across his face as he added, "From what I hear, you can really use the bucks."

The words slapped Cliff in the face—and he sobered up real fast.

"A deal's a deal. I'm not goin' back on Eddie Voss."

Zacco gave him a look like, *Man, are you stupid.* He muttered, "Okay. Change your mind, I'll be in the bar."

Cliff watched him go, then turned to watch the grounds crew opening the rear doors of the starting gate. They would be running on the inner track, on turf—once around the track, a mile and a quarter. He picked out Roberto's blue silks and watched Epic Honor running easily, loosening up.

Then he realized something was missing. He looked around.

"Where the hell's Malcolm?"

Jamie said, "Probably at the window."

"So what do you think of the guy?" They had all had lunch together in the clubhouse and Malcolm had done his suave continental routine on her.

"His accent's really fun."

Figures, Cliff thought. *Women get off on that phony pip pip, cheerio bullshit.*

"Yeah, but what do you think of him?"

P H I L I P   R E E D

"Oh, I don't know . . . ," she said, biting her lip. Cliff gave her a look and she laughed. "Don't worry. I'm just giving you a hard time. You're so serious."

"Serious? I don't got to tell you what's riding on this race?"

"Cliff, it's this way with every race. When're you going to see that?"

The grooms were leading the horses into the gate now. Epic Honor tossed his head and ducked away as a groom reached for his bridle. Roberto turned the horse's head but Epic Honor fought him. All the other horses were in the gate now.

Emerson appeared at Cliff's side. He flashed the betting slip and said, "All set." He looked down at the track and said, "What's going on?"

"He's never been afraid of the gate before." Cliff wanted it all to go easy. He wanted Epic Honor to get in the gate and give Roberto a chance to set the reins the way he liked for a clean break. But the horse was still out there, fighting the grooms.

Jamie's hand tightened on his. One of the grooms caught the bridle and the other slapped his rump. He jumped forward and they ran him into the gate. They were slamming the rear door behind him when —

BBBRINNNGGG!

The doors flew open and the announcer called, "And they're off!"

The horses shot forward, digging for the rail. Epic Honor stumbled out a half stride behind the others and was three wide in dead last going into the first turn.

"Jesus!" Cliff said. "What the hell kind of start was that?"

"Never seen that before," Emerson wheezed.

"Glasses."

Emerson put the binoculars in Cliff's hands. Cliff had to see what the horses were doing on the back side. There was still a chance . . . .

As he lifted the binoculars to his eyes he saw the grounds crew drag the starting gate out of the way, saw the deep hoof prints in the soft grass. He screwed his eyes into the glasses and saw the pack moving along the rail across the way, thought *Where the hell's our horse?* Then he saw a flash of blue moving up between the other horses and saw Epic Honor's dark head straining forward and even from here he thought he could see the fire in his eyes, the fire of a true thoroughbred, a real competitor.

When the doors of the starting gate flew open, Roberto thought they didn't have a chance.

There was no time for him to get set in the gate. No time to lay the reins across the horse's neck. He felt Epic Honor resisting, saw the other horses go in first and then, *Holy shit,* the doors were open and they were tear-assing after them. Only a stride off the field, but a horse with this speed could make it up easy in the stretch.

Roberto thought maybe he should pull Epic Honor back, let him gallop out the race easy so he wouldn't hurt himself. But the horse was ready to run and Roberto knew Cliff had a lot on this race. There was no drawing off the lead for this horse. So go for it. Okay?

They caught the pack on the back side, where Epic Honor pulled forward with each stride. *Easy, easy. Keep the pace.* Roberto settled into fourth place and waited for a chance to make his move. They were in good shape now. Good shape after a real shitty start.

Into the turn, three wide and Epic Honor was starting to work now, his head straining forward, digging deeper and finding something at every level. Roberto nudged him and felt the horse change leads and saw the stretch ahead now. Time to hit the gas. This would be a hell of a win if he could pull it off. And Roberto felt he had what it took—a good position and a fast young horse.

Time to get it all. Now or never. He put the crop to him, ready to close and he got the feeling he was on top of a volcano. Energy, fire, strength. Man, this horse had it all.

They passed a gray in three strides, to take third. Passed the next horse in two, still picking up speed. The eight pole flashed by on Roberto's left. The lead horse felt them gaining and reached down for more—and came up empty.

Epic Honor had a ton of momentum now, barreling forward into the lead with fifty feet to the finish line. *Hang on baby!* Roberto thought. *Keep firing you son of a bitch. Keep firing!*

The rhythmic pounding underneath him was the feel of victory to Roberto. Hooves on turf. Until —

Crack!

One of his hooves went down and it just kept going, like it punched a hole in the earth's surface.

And they were falling.

The last thing Roberto remembered was trying to keep the horse's head up. If you could keep his head up you might have a chance.

Cliff knew better than to think it was a sure thing with fifty feet to go to the finish line. One second he was shouting his lungs out. The next he heard the crack and saw Epic Honor's head pitch forward, saw him throw Roberto, then somersault on top of him while the other horses thundered past on all sides. Riderless, Epic Honor jumped to his feet and tried to finish the race. But his right foreleg stuck out at a crazy angle, waving like a flag, broken at the fetlock.

Jamie screamed and covered her mouth.

Cliff heard himself say, *He's finished.*

But Epic Honor was still running, a grotesque loping gate on three legs, circling the track in front of the grandstands. The crowd watched the injured horse, silent and horrified.

Cliff found himself running down the stairs and out onto the soft dirt of the track, heading for Roberto. They had him on a stretcher and were moving him toward the ambulance when Roberto opened his eyes and saw Cliff coming and said, "I'm sorry, man," as he disappeared through the back doors of the ambulance.

Cliff turned and saw a woman on a palomino trying to catch Epic Honor. Cliff waved her away and advanced on the crippled horse, standing now by the inside rail, head down, breathing hard. The horse saw him coming, his big eyes filled with terror and a look of confusion that tore Cliff's heart out.

"It's okay boy," he said, as if talking to a child afraid in the night. "It's okay." But it wasn't okay, of course. He'd been at the track long enough to know how this would play out. It was all over for his horse. No more early morning workouts at the track, no more post parades with the other horses. No more trips to the winner's circle with flowers around his neck. It was all destroyed by one misstep on a soft track.

Epic Honor let Cliff hold him in place as the track vet ran up from behind, the hypodermic in his hand. In the distance, Cliff saw the big dark van lumbering toward them down the track. They would set up a tent around the horse while they winched him into the van and took him away. He'd seen Epic Honor come into this world and now he'd have to see him leave.

The vet held the needle up and looked to Cliff for permission. Cliff nodded, holding Epic Honor's bridle, stroking his nose and talking to him, and he felt like he was dying too.

The needle was in for one, two, three seconds when Epic Honor dropped. He hit the track and rolled on his side. But his eyes were still open and Cliff saw the fire was still in them, as if to say, *I gave you everything.*

Cliff felt a hand on his shoulder. He turned and saw Jamie with tears streaming down her face. She tried to take his hand but he pulled away. He couldn't deal with this shit right now.

Cliff crouched beside his fallen horse, thinking, *Why do I always lose the things I love?* He looked in Epic Honor's eyes and watched as the fire went out.

"Hello!" Malcolm called as he opened the front door of his house and walked in, setting his bag down.

Malcolm hoped like hell Becca wasn't here because he had to get in and out in a hurry. The limousine was waiting in the street. The first class reservation had been made. All he needed now was his traveling money and his files. As a good financial planner, he had been preparing for this moment for quite a while.

"Hello!" he called out again, moving down the long hallway toward his study.

"Malcolm?" She came in from the living room where she had been lying on the couch, watching a movie. Her hair was mussed, face puffy, and she wore the blue and white exercise suit. Seconds later the little dog rounded the corner, skidding on its nails and yapping.

"Where've you been?" she asked, raising her voice above the barking.

"In L.A., buying horses."

"You didn't tell me."

"Course I did. You didn't listen."

"No you didn't," she whined. "I've been here for two days wondering whether, like, you'd been like murdered or something."

"Murdered?" He looked at her for the first time.

"Well, I didn't know, you know?" She backed off a little, softened her tone and said, "Malcolm. What's going on?"

He knew she would try to hug him now. He let her do it, thinking that, in the long run, it would make it all go easier. Her doughy softness pressed into him, nauseating him.

The dog was biting his trouser leg. He kicked it away.

"*Malcolm!* He missed you, too. Didn't you, Nookie?"

She bent down to comfort the dog. Malcolm pushed past them, carrying his leather bag into his bedroom. He dumped the dirty clothes in a corner and began laying out white shirts and ties.

"What are you doing?"

"Now what does it *look* like I'm doing?"

"Where are you going?"

"To the airport."

"Why? Malcolm, is something wrong?"

"What could be wrong?"

"I don't know. But you're just like acting so *weird.*"

"I've got business," he growled. "I'll be gone for a while."

"How long?"

He whirled on her, roaring, "I don't know! Now *PISS OFF!*"

She stood there, stunned. Then it happened. He knew it would. She threw herself on the bed and began sobbing. Good, now she was out of the way. He pushed his shirts and ties and underwear into his bag, picked it up and headed into his study. He banged the door shut and locked it.

First, he pulled out all the statements from his various accounts. Most of the money had been moved overseas already. But he still had money in some of these accounts. He totaled them in his head, rounding them to the nearest thousand. Nearly a quarter of a million . . . . He had planned to wire this to himself overseas. But there wasn't time now.

He sat there thinking, listening to Becca crying in the other room.

He unlocked the door, went over and sat beside Becca on the big bed thinking, *Maybe there's a way* . . . . He stroked her back, saying, "Hush, lassie. Hush now." It was what he called her when they first met and he knew she adored it.

"I'm in a bit of a jam, you see. And I've got to make myself scarce for a time."

She sat up, face shiny with tears. "What happened?"

"Some clients that I'm working with, they got me into something . . . . I should have known better but—there you have it. I'm the one in the hot seat now."

"Is someone trying to, like, *get* you?"

"Get my money. And they probably will unless . . . ." He paused, knowing what she would say.

"Malcolm, if they're trying to cheat you, I'll—I'll do anything to help you."

He was silent, pretending to think it over carefully. He disappeared into his study and returned with the bank statements. "I could sign these checks over to you. Then, what I need you to do is wire them overseas to yourself at American Express." He wrote the name of the office on one of the statements. "Then, quick as you can, catch a flight. Check into this hotel and I'll call you. Can you do that for me, lassie?"

She nodded, biting her lip, her face filled with excitement and a sense of intrigue. He smoothed her hair back from her face and kissed her.

"Now I've got to get ready." He returned to the study and quietly locked the door. Taking a screw driver, he crouched near the electrical outlet behind his filing cabinet. He began loosening the screws on the face plate.

Movement behind him. Turning, he felt Nookie's tongue lashing his face. Somehow the fucking dog got locked in with him. He picked it up by the neck and was about to hurtle it out the door and relock it. But he didn't want to have to deal with Becca anymore. He tossed the dog to the side and bent to his task again.

This time he got the face plate removed. He took out the small box, the one containing the tightly rolled wad of $100 bills, his traveling money, when Nookie charged again. The dog knocked the box from his hand and bills scattered around the room.

"*Foock!*" Malcolm bellowed as rage swept through his system.

"Malcolm?" Becca's voice was faint through the door. "Everything okay?"

"Yes." Malcolm said, stalking the dog, saying softly, "Come here my little Nookie . . . . Come here Nookie. Nookie, Nookie." He had it trapped in a corner now. His hand was extended toward the trembling dog when—the needle-like teeth sank into the fleshy web between Malcolm's thumb and forefinger. He bellowed in pain, jerking his hand back, the dog dangling in the air.

"Malcolm?"

"Everything's fine," he said through clenched teeth. "Just shut the drawer on my hand."

Malcolm had hold of the dog now, one hand on its head, one on its body and—*yes*—one quick twist was all it took. The dog went limp in his hands. He hid poor little Nookie under a pile of clothes in the corner of the closet, stopping to find a T-shirt to wrap around his bleeding hand. Now, in peace and quiet, he returned to the task of gathering up all the bills that were strewn around the room.

"Gotta make a call before we hit the road," Cliff told Jamie. He didn't think she heard him at first, but then she nodded, kinda dead like, and said, "Yeah, okay."

Yeah. Okay. Whatever. She was sitting on a couch in the hotel lobby, staring out at the rain, which had started falling right after the race ended. They were waiting to drive to the airport.

Was she sad because their horse broke down in the stretch? Or was she pissed about the way he pulled away from her when she tried to comfort him? He didn't know. He didn't really care. He had to make a call.

Cliff was heading toward the pay phone, when he thought of something else.

"Hey Jamie. Would you check at the desk, see if Malcolm's around? I can't figure what happened to the guy. One minute he's all over me—next he disappears."

She said nothing, just got to her feet and moved toward the front desk.

He found a pay phone near a bar where a guy at the piano was playing some sad song. He dialed Dan's office number thinking how, as a trainer, he was always breaking bad news to someone.

"Insurance Services," a voice answered. It was that Indian lady, Veena, Dan's assistant.

"This is Cliff Dante calling for Dan, if he's in." Actually, he kinda hoped he wasn't.

"Mr. Dante! Dan's been trying to reach you. Hold please." Her voice was urgent. Guy must be anxious about the race. Hope he didn't put a bundle on our horse, Cliff thought.

"Cliff, I've been calling your cell phone all afternoon." His voice was coming through the receiver at him. "Where the hell've you been?"

"At the track, man, where else would I be? Look, we didn't do so good—"

"Something's come up. Is Malcolm there with you?"

That's weird, Cliff thought. *I'm here with bad news and he don't even want to hear it.*

"Malcolm? He was here but—why? What's up?"

"You didn't give him any money, did you?"

"Hell yes I did. You said the guy was cool."

"Look, I don't know for sure but—I checked one of Malcolm's other clients. Turns out Malcolm didn't set up the investments like he said."

All thoughts of Epic Honor, of the race, vanished. "You're saying the guy ripped me off? But he gave me a statement. My money's in mutual funds or something like that."

"The statement he gave you—is it from the investment company, or from Malcolm's company?"

"I don't know. Why?"

"That's what he did with these other people. Listen, it might be too late but—in the morning, you've got to stop payment on your check. Okay?"

"Yeah, sure."

"Are you flying back up here tonight?"

Cliff couldn't speak. He leaned his head against the wall next to the phone feeling the cold tile on his forehead. In the silence he heard someone in the bar laughing, could hear that sad song on the piano. He had thought he was tapped out, after seeing Epic Honor hit the dirt like that. But here he was, feeling like someone had just cut him off at the knees.

"Cliff, you there?"

"I'm leaving for the airport in a few minutes. Be back at eight."

"Come straight to my office. Bring any statements Malcolm gave you."

Jamie was beside him now, saying, "Malcolm checked out this morning." She saw his expression and said, "What's going on?"

"Tell you in a second." Then to Dan he said, "You sure about this?"

"No. But if you see him again, don't give him any more money."

"You don't worry about that. I never liked the guy's action in the first place. But you said —"

Dan waited.

Cliff said, "See you tonight." He hung up thinking, *He didn't even ask about the race.*

Jamie was standing there, waiting.

"What's going on?"

"Dan thinks Malcolm's ripping people off."

"*People?* Did you give him any of our money?"

"I'm not sure. Some maybe. Plus he owes me a bundle for boarding fees."

She processed the information.

"Well, at least we still have the IRA." She saw his reaction and her expression fell. "Oh God. You didn't give him *that* too, did you?"

There was this one time when Cliff was a kid, when he went swimming in the river that cut along the edge of his granddaddy's property and some field workers showed up. Teen-agers. This one fat kid named Umberto kept shoving him under the water and holding him down. Cliff tried to land one on his nose so he'd cut the shit but Umberto moved easy for a fat kid and Cliff's arm was slow through the swirling muddy water, so down he went, time after time, until part of him said, *You're gonna die—you're gonna go*

under and you won't come up. He was thinking of that time now, feeling trapped and suffocating, realizing most of his money was gone, only it wasn't Umberto shoving him down—it was Malcolm Ravling. Malcolm's face was in front of him, laughing at him with that sickening Scottish accent, the screwed-up eye looking at him sideways.

They were in Dan's office late at night, running the account numbers through the brokerage firm's Internet site. So far they had found that Cliff had a grand total of zip. But they had to try all the accounts because you never knew for sure.

"Man, look at this one mutual fund—it went up 26 percent last year," Dan said, holding the statement that Malcolm had given Cliff. He saw the look on Cliff's face and added, "Oh, sorry."

"What's the account number, please?" Veena was plugging in the numbers as the three of them sat clustered around the screen. Dan had told Veena to go home a couple of times but she ignored him. Somehow, having her here helped. Every time another account turned up dry she turned to Cliff and said, "I'm very, very sorry," and looked like she might cry.

Cliff's eyes were falling out of his head. He looked away from the screen to the black windows and the night outside. The rain had stopped and high winds had moved in behind the storm. Gusts hit the windows, making the glass flex like a monster was trying to get in. Yeah, there was a monster out there—it was the muddy river and they were shoving him down, down. One of these times he wouldn't bother to come back up again.

"We must hope for the best," Veena said, hitting the return key. It was what she said each time. So far, hoping for the best hadn't produced any miracles.

The little gizmo on the screen flashed, showing that information was being sent and received. The computer beeped and the words flashed on the screen:

Invalid Account Number!

"Son of a bitch took it all," Cliff said standing up, pacing, his fists clenching. "Every last penny. Got in there and sucked it dry."

"What's the next account number?" Dan asked Veena.

"We've checked them all," she answered.

Cliff looked at Dan. He was hunched over, shirt collar open, tie hanging loose.

"He get any of your money?" Cliff asked Dan.

"No."

"Well he got all of mine! All of it! Everything Jamie and I were saving. It's all gone."

And it's your fault! Cliff heard the angry words in his head. *You introduced me to him!* Dan waited, maybe hearing the unspoken words. But Cliff didn't say them. It was one thing to lose all your money—it was another thing to be a damn crybaby.

Veena sat there, the edges of her eyes pooling with tears. That cooled Cliff off.

Finally, Dan said, "I don't know what to tell you, man. I know he ripped off a lot of people, so the feds will go after him. But I don't know if you'll ever get your—"

"*Jesus!*" Cliff said, as the thought exploded in his head.

"What?"

"He was after my grandmother." Cliff looked at his watch. It was after midnight, too late to call her.

"If he got her money . . . . If that—"

The door at the bottom of the stairs banged. They looked at each other. Two sets of footsteps were heavy on the stairs, coming up.

"Who's this?" Dan walked through the outer office and opened the door. He spoke into the hallway. "Can I help you?"

"We're looking for Mr. Berg. Daniel Berg."

"*Van* Berg. That's me."

Cliff could see them now, two guys in suits, white shirts, clean-cut, expressionless faces. *Feds.* It flashed into his head as he heard one guy say, "Agent Rosski. FBI. And this is Agent Klemsky."

"FBI?" Dan said. "Man, am I glad to see you guys. Come on in."

The two men moved into the small office. Veena brought chairs in, saying, "Have a seat." They remained standing, big guys with arrogant expressions. Cliff had a hunch they weren't there to help him. But Dan, man, he was acting like the cavalry just rode in.

"We want to ask you about your relationship with Mr. Ravling," Rosski said, looking at Dan. He had thinning sandy hair, neatly cut, and freckles across his long sharp nose.

"Sure," Dan said. "But this is the guy you want to talk to. This is Cliff Dante, he's a horse trainer. We just found out Ravling took all his money."

Rosski stared coldly at Dan. After a moment he said, "Is it true that you entered into a business relationship with Mr. Ravling?"

"He wrote a few life insurance polices through my company, yeah."

"Can we see the contracts on those policies?" This was Klemsky talking now. He was a tall lanky guy, athletically put together; Cliff knew he probably felt good about how he looked in his fed suit. He had seen his share of feds at the track. They came around asking questions you couldn't answer without sticking a knife in your friend's back.

"Veena, would you dig out those files for me, please?" She

moved into the other room as Dan added, "You know, I talked to Ravling tonight. He was going to the airport. You guys should get a list of international flights. You could probably pick him up when he lands."

This suggestion was greeted with intense silence. Finally, Rosski said, "Tell you what, Mr. Berg. We won't tell you how to run your business. Don't tell us how to run our investigation."

Veena reappeared holding a stack of papers. Dan nodded to her and she handed them to Klemsky.

Rosski finally looked at Cliff and asked, "A horse trainer, huh? That means you buy and sell horses for people."

Cliff let the statement lie there for a moment, until it began to seem ridiculous. Then he said, "You figure that out all on your own?"

"Listen," Rosski said, pulling up one corner of his mouth, "I don't know where the attitude's coming from. We've got our investigation and we need to ask you some questions. What's so hard about that?"

"Oh, so this is an investigation? I thought you were here for a tip on a horse race." Felt good to mouth off a little, Cliff thought.

Dan motioned Cliff toward the hallway. "Talk to you for a sec?"

Out in the hall Dan said, "What the hell're you doing? These guys'll find Ravling."

"You think that's what they're doing?"

"What do you think?"

"They're looking for a sucker to nail. They're not about to run off to Europe or wherever Ravling is. They'll choose from who's left. And that could be you."

Dan looked at him for a long time and finally smiled. "You're protecting me. That means you don't think I had anything to do with taking your money."

"I didn't say that. But you and me, we can settle it on our own. These Feds, man, they act like they care—then they'll just shine you off. It was me, I'd tell Dumbski and Flunkski to pound sand up their asses."

Dan nodded. He walked back into the room and faced the two men. Everyone was standing now. He chose the husky one, Klemsky and invaded his space.

"Can I ask you something, Agent? Am I a suspect in your 'investigation?'" He put the word in finger quotes.

The two agents looked at each other. Then they looked at Cliff, realizing where this came from.

"Why? What've you done?"

"I'd like my contracts back," Dan said, holding out his hand.

They hesitated, then handed them over.

"Now I'd like you to leave my office."

They stood there chewing on what he said.

"Mr. Berg, it doesn't have to be like this. We hoped you would help us out."

Dan was breathing hard, his head jutted forward threateningly. The agents saw it was pointless. They gave Dan and Cliff a wide berth as they walked out. On the way through the door, Cliff heard one say, "A horse trainer and an insurance salesman—what do you expect?"

Back home, Cliff lay on his bed, fully clothed, and his thoughts eventually spun him into an hour or two of confused oblivion. He woke up, dizzy and exhausted, his head packed tight with trouble, aware that his grandmother was stirring in the kitchen below.

"Morning Grandma," Cliff said to her as he walked in. She was frying bacon, a tiny woman, her back bent by the years, but her eyes were still bright.

"Cliffie," she said, half turning, smiling. "I thought I heard you come in late last night."

"Grandma, I got some bad news for you."

"I heard about your horse. Emerson showed up, told me all about it. Damn shame." She was standing next to the stove, the spatula in one hand. She was worth a couple million bucks, but that didn't change the fact that she was basically a rancher's wife. To her, life was work, and to get your work done you woke up at dawn.

"It's worse than that, Grandma. You know that Malcolm Ravling, been out here a few times?" She nodded, waiting. "Looks like he's a crook. He ran off with some of my money."

"Malcolm?" The pain showed in her face, aging her suddenly.

"He claims he's investing people's money. Makes up fake statements to keep people happy. Meanwhile, he's spending their money, being a big shot."

"You mean, that nice boy with the English accent?"

"Well, I guess he was Scottish or something, but, yeah, that's him." Cliff paused, needing to know, but not wanting to ask. "Grandma, did you give him any money?"

"Me?"

"Yeah, did you invest with him?"

"Oh, you thought—" she laughed suddenly, then came over

and hugged him, thumping his back. "God bless you, Cliffie. No, I didn't give him a penny. I probably would have, but that guy that was with him—"

"Gordon."

"Gordon. I couldn't stand that skinny little queer. But Malcolm—such a nice boy. Such beautiful manners."

She went back to the sputtering bacon. Suddenly, Cliff felt hungry.

"I'm gonna go check on the horses. I'll be back for breakfast."

"You check on your horses, Cliff. I'll be here." She sadly added, "I can't believe that nice boy would do that to people. He had such beautiful manners."

Cliff stepped outside. The air was still cold and wet, but the sun was up, warming him. The barnyard was a sea of mud, pulling at his boots. But he was walking easy. It was one thing to shoulder his own loss. At least he hadn't spread the infection any further.

Inside the barn, Cliff looked the length of the building and could see into the tack room. Emerson was sitting on the edge of his cot. He looked up, saw Cliff and got to his feet, hurrying forward with his brittle sideways shuffle.

"Mornin' Cliff." Clouds of steam puffed out along with Emerson's husky voice. "Got somethin' to ask you."

"Fire away."

"I heard you talkin' to Jamie yesterday, at the hotel. About that Ravling fella."

"Yeah . . . ."

"I just want to know, everything's gonna be okay, isn't it?"

"What? With the money I invested?"

"No," Emerson said, "with *my* money."

"*Your* money?"

Emerson looked down, ashamed. "Yeah, I gave him my money to invest."

"You—*WHAT?*"

Emerson saw the anger on his boss's face. He shrank away, frightened.

"I'm sorry, Cliff. But, I figured, if you were going with him, he must be okay so . . . ."

"How much did you give him?"

"Not much really. See, I was putting some aside 'cause, few years from now, I figured I'd buy my own ranch. Breed some horses. I always wanted my own place."

"How much you give him?"

"Twenty-three."

Emerson saw the look on Cliff's face and stepped back.

"But it's okay, isn't it?" Emerson asked weakly.

"No, it's not okay! Guy's a fuckin' crook!"

"I know, but—I'll get it back eventually? Right? I mean, Cliff—it's all I have."

"You ain't listening to me, Emerson! The money's gone. He took it all! All of it."

Cliff looked around wildly, grabbed up a shovel and swung it like a baseball bat into a beam. It snapped off clean and the end flew across the barn into a row of tools.

"Son of a bitch!" Cliff smashed the broken end again and again. *"Son of a bitch!"*

"Cliff!" Emerson's voice strained to reach him. "Cliff! I'm not blaming you. I just thought—I don't know what I thought. But it's just money. I can still work for you. I mean, I still got my job, don't I?"

Cliff threw the broken handle aside and headed out of the barn.

"Cliff. Please. I still got my job, don't I?"

He knew he had to say something. But it was hard to make his voice work. Finally, he forced himself to look at the old man's face, child-like with fear and dependency.

"Oh yeah. You got your job, Emerson. Long as I've got a job to give you."

Later that morning Cliff was leaning on the rail next to the clocker's shack, waiting for Firecracker to start a quarter mile breeze. Ramon was on board because he always had a thing for that horse, said he was something special even though the times weren't the greatest. Said Firecracker was a great competitor and needed the other horses there to show his full potential. Some horses are like that, no doubt about it.

Truth of the matter was, Cliff just needed to be here at the track, to convince himself he had a future. So he was looking at his horses, trying to see a glimmer of hope there somewhere.

Laughter behind him.

Cliff turned and saw Zacco down the way, talkin' to a couple of guys. One of them held a newspaper folded back. He looked familiar but Cliff couldn't place him.

The hell with 'em.

After last night, Cliff's patience was gone, his energy was gone, his hope was just about gone. But he was at the track. That was something. Maybe he'd find a thread here he could pick up and follow through the darkness into his future.

More laughter. What the hell was so funny?

Cliff turned and saw the men doubled over. They saw him watching and turned away.

The hell with 'em.

Across the track he saw Ramon on Firecracker. The big gray was fighting him, trying to turn left into traffic, other horses exercising, getting ready to breeze. The horse needed a lot of work.

"Tough luck." Cliff looked around and saw Zacco walking up. He didn't really need to be reminded of the race yesterday.

"So what're you going to do?" Zacco pressed.

"I'm workin' the rest of my stable. I still got a few winners." That was bullshit, but Cliff had to say it. Last thing he wanted from Zacco was sympathy.

They looked over and saw Firecracker coming. Ramon had him movin' nice, runnin' easy. Maybe Ramon was right about the horse. A spark of hope stirred.

"Always liked that horse," Zacco said, nodding at the Gray. "Want to liquidate your inventory?"

"No way, man. That there's my future." He looked at Zacco and thought how this conversation wasn't tracking. He thought of Zacco and the other guy laughing. Then he remembered where he'd seen the other guy. He was a reporter for the *Daily Racing Form*.

"Why would I want to sell him?" Cliff asked.

"I just figured, since you wouldn't be racing for a while, you might need the cash."

Cliff forgot about his horse breezing. Forgot about everything else except the fact that Zacco knew something he didn't.

Zacco said, "You haven't heard, have you?"

He handed him the *Racing Form*, folded to the article. The head-line read TRAINER RULED OFF and there was Cliff's photo.

Zacco said, "With the FBI after your owner, the stewards won't let you run."

Ruled off. The words were ringing in Cliff's ears. It meant his trainer's license was suspended. He could barely hear Zacco talking. Finally he tuned back in.

". . . I was even gonna say something to you, Cliff, about Ravling. I mean, he approached me, he approached half the trainers out here. We all knew he was dirty."

"Bullshit you did." If Zacco didn't shut his mouth Cliff was gonna shut it for him.

"Hell, I threw his ass out of my office six months ago. I won't take that kind of money."

"No Nik, not when you can go down to Hollywood, suck dick and get anything you want."

Zacco stepped back, shook his head sadly. "Jesus, Cliff. That's way out of line. I know this's been rough. But, come on, man, that's way out of line."

Zacco turned away, then came back. "You want to sell that gray, lemme know."

Cliff watched Zacco walking away, fighting the urge to put his boot up the guy's ass, send him face down in the mud. Maybe he would have if his phone hadn't started ringing. He dug the phone out of the inside pocket of his windbreaker thinking, *What now?*

"Hello."

"Cliff? Tommy Boyd, at the Hawley-Cooke Ranch."

"Yeah, Tommy." Cliff tried to focus. He was still reeling. He pulled himself together and asked, "How's the weather down there in Florida? Nice and hot for the Relaunch colt?"

"Weather's fine, Cliff. But we got a problem"

"I don't need no more problems, Tommy. What's up?"

"Your horse, that Relaunch colt you were shipping us? The pin hook?"

"He's okay, ain't he?"

"I wouldn't know. He never got here."

Dan's wife stood in the doorway of their mobile home looking Cliff over. Finally she said, "So you're Cliff Dante."

"Yeah, that's me." He didn't need this, didn't need to be kept on the front stoop in the dark, like some magazine salesman. Besides, he never imagined Dan lived in a trailer. The guy made out like he was a high roller.

"Look, is Dan in? I tried to get him at the office. But everything's shut down."

She was a tall woman with pretty eyes, eyes that were real hot right now, roasting him. Cliff felt he'd probably like her under normal circumstances. But there was nothing normal about what was happening to him now.

"I don't know why you can't just leave Dan alone."

"I'm not here to cause trouble," Cliff was feeling his way along. "Some new stuff happened he's got to know about."

"*New* stuff? Haven't you done enough already?"

She tried to pull her anger back, placed a hand on her round belly—and the baby inside—and took a deep breath. Now her pretty eyes turned sad. "Don't you know Dan can't say *No*? He tries so hard to be a big shot. Someone like you comes along with a bright idea and takes money he doesn't have. Does that make you proud?"

Jesus. What's going on here? Cliff wondered. *I'm the one who took a big hit.*

"Look, I'll get out of your life, soon as I talk to him one more time."

"He's up at the property."

"Property?"

"We own a lot, at the top of the road. Or at least we *used* to. After what happened, he's going to sell it off. That means we'll be stuck here the rest of our lives—in a god-damned trailer."

The door closed in his face.

A few minutes later, Cliff's headlights found Dan standing next to the lone tree in the middle of the vacant lot. He was facing down the hill, toward the lights of Silicon Valley. And he didn't turn when Cliff approached across the freshly graded dirt.

"I'm gonna be gone awhile," Cliff said. "Didn't want you to think I ran out on you."

"Where ya going?" Dan spoke without turning. He really didn't sound interested.

"I'm gonna find him." Cliff didn't need to say who he was talking about. "He took our horse, man, the Relaunch colt, our pin hook."

Dan turned and Cliff could see his face now. His expression lifeless and hard. His skin looked like cardboard.

"I gave him the papers so he could try to sell our horse overseas, remember? Instead of shipping it to Florida, he shipped it to England somewhere. I checked with the shipper. It left the country under one name, never got to England. He musta doctored the papers, changed the name."

Dan smiled and shook his head as if to say, *What do you expect?*
He kicked the dirt with his toe, digging a little trough.

"The guy shafted me four ways," Cliff said. "A regular cluster-fuck."

"He left a little surprise for me, too." Dan's voice was broken.
"I'm about to close a deal with Fidelity West, okay? As soon as the
ink's dry, I get twenty grand, and from here on out, I get a percent
of all the premiums sold. That's huge, ya know? I tell the contractor I'm ready to break ground. Well, this afternoon, a process serv-
er walks into my office with a cease-and-desist order."

"What's that mean?" Cliff asked.

"Means I'm out of business—means Fidelity drops me like a
stinking piece of shit. I don't need to tell you, the suit was filed by
our *friend*."

They were quiet for a minute or two, staring down the hill at
the lights below, and thinking their separate thoughts, thoughts
that eventually led to the same conclusion. Cliff said, "This is getting personal."

"He didn't have to do that to me, he gets nothing out of it,
except a little personal *fuck you* as he leaves town."

Cliff said, "I thought I'd get personal too."

"What do you mean?"

"I'm gonna find him—" Cliff was breathing hard, so he had to
wait before he could continue, before he could say the words he
had never said before: "I could do it. I know people over there. I'm
gonna find him—and then I'm gonna kill the motherfucker."

Dan nodded. He understood.

Cliff saw the look on Dan's face and said, "You want a piece of
him too, don't you?"

"Yeah. But I'm not gonna spend the rest of my life rotting in prison."

"Guy took everything I got. Made me the laughingstock of the backside. I'm gonna take him out." He paused, breathing hard, clenching his fists. "Because, I'll tell you something—there's always a winner and a loser. And I'm not losing this one."

"Maybe, but where's the finish line?" Dan asked. Then he thought of something and his face began changing, losing the cardboard look. There was life in it—or at least anger. "I've got a better idea about how to win. Here's what we do . . . ." He licked his lips. "We track him down. We get our horse back. Then we destroy him."

"How is that different than killing him?"

"Killing him is too final. We'll destroy him *financially*. He's ripped off a ton of people, right? We find the money and we give it back."

"After we pay me back first. Me and Emerson."

It hit Dan what Cliff had just told him. "No way, man. You gotta be kidding me."

"Wish I was. He stung Emerson for twenty-three. That's every penny the old guy ever made. Malcolm took it all with the stroke of pen."

They fell silent, running scenarios in their heads. It was a clear night and they could almost see the length of the Peninsula. They were looking at the view but their thoughts were thousands of miles away.

"I know a couple of jockeys over there in England," Cliff said. "We could call the shipper, find out what stables the horse went to. Racing's a tight world. I think we could do it. Besides, Malcolm probably just figures we're not gonna come after him."

"Okay. But how're we gonna finance the trip? Plastic?"

"Yeah, well," Cliff took off his hat and scratched his head. "That's a problem for me. I've lived the last three months on plastic—I'm maxed out."

"So what are you going to do?"

It suddenly hit Cliff what he had to do. *This is really hitting the bottom,* he thought, *I can't go any lower than this.*

"What are you going to do?" Dan asked for the second time.

"I have to go see *the man,*" Cliff said, realizing that, at least when you hit bottom, there's only one way you can go from there.

"Looky here. Kinda figured she'd come back before long." Ellis's easy drawl brought Linda back from her daydreams to the present. She looked out the windshield of the rented Chevy Lumina parked down the street from Malcolm Ravling's house. They had been waiting about six hours hoping Becca would appear. Before that they watched a pair of feds ring the doorbell about 15 times. Seemed everyone wanted to know where Mr. Malcolm Ravling had gone to.

"Time to do your thing," Ellis said. "And remember, be sympathetic."

"I am sympathetic," Linda answered. "I'm a victim. Remember?"

Linda caught up with Becca as she was putting her key in the front door. Linda hoped she presented the right image, a business-woman in a skirt, blouse and jacket. Purse over her shoulder, briefcase in her hand. Probably looked like a real estate agent or something.

"Mrs. Ravling?"

Becca turned apprehensively. "Yes?"

"I'm Linda Powell, I'm a friend of your husband's."

"He's not here right now. He's—he's on a business trip."

"I'm here to see you," Linda said keeping her voice even. "Your husband's in a lot of trouble. I think I can help."

"I don't know what you're talking about," Becca said, pushing the door open and stepping inside.

She was about to close the door, when Linda said sharply, "Becca! You need my help." Then, softer, she added, "Let's just sit a while and talk."

They moved inside into the stuffy air of a house that had been empty for some time. Sun was streaming through the large windows, and it was warm—very warm. Linda felt her nostrils pull back at the edges sensing a smell just bursting into ripeness.

Linda followed Becca into the living room, their heels clicking on the hardwood floor.

"I've been away for a few days, at my parents'," Becca said. "I just came back to get some clothes. And to try to find my dog. He wandered away a few nights ago . . . . I told all the neighbors, put up signs, but no one's seen him."

Becca sat on the big leather couch and Linda sat nearby on a matching easy chair.

"You look very unhappy," Linda said, setting her briefcase on the floor.

Becca's expression clouded. "Why do you say that?"

"I think I might know something of what you're going through." The air was stifling, the faint but repugnant smell making her feel claustrophobic, so she asked, "Mind if I smoke?"

Becca looked ready to say no, then thought better of it, and nodded.

"I invested money with your husband," Linda said, waving out the match and dropping it in a saucer holding a potted plant. "I lost a lot of money. I live in Houston, you see, this happened some years back."

"Malcolm never lived in Houston."

"Yes he did," she said. She watched Becca carefully, not wanting to lose her. "It's okay honey, even a good man lies now and then. Anyway, I hired an accountant, a man who specializes in tracing money, to see what went wrong. He came back with an interesting report. Your husband took our money because he was being blackmailed."

"Blackmailed?" It wasn't what she expected.

Linda nodded solemnly. "The guy he was working with, Gordon Pinsker—does that ring a bell?"

"Gordon. Yes, he still works with him!"

"This Gordon must have had something on your husband. The money would go through your husband's accounts, and into Gordon's control."

Linda watched relief and understanding flickering across the young woman's face. She was buying the story—it was playing right in with her pathetic belief that her husband just couldn't be a crook.

"This is like *so* weird. Gordon, the guy you're asking about, he just disappeared, last week. He told Malcolm he was like going up to Portland to take care of his mother. Right? Uh huh, *sure.*"

Linda nodded understandingly. "Fits now, doesn't it?" She wanted Becca to feel they were two detectives working on the same problem. She slowly reached into the leather briefcase she was carrying with her.

"I've got quite a file on this Mr. Pinsker." Linda casually opened the report that she had prepared along with Ellis, based on information he had gotten off the hard drive he lifted. The report was bogus, of course, but Becca didn't know that. Linda looked up to find Becca's eyes fastened on the "report."

"I really think your husband would be interested in reading this," Linda said.

"I could give it to him," Becca eagerly volunteered.

"Oh. So you know where he is?"

Becca realized she had been trapped. Before she could react, though, Linda said, "Of course you do. I sensed that you two are very close."

Becca bit her lip and nodded, her eyes tearing. Linda stubbed out her cigarette and moved to sit on the couch next to Becca. She put her arm around the younger woman.

"Becca, I'm going to tell you the worst of it, so it will all be out in the open. Malcolm was caught up in a Ponzi scheme. He—"

Becca shook her head, confused. "A *what* scheme?"

"Ponzi. It's when you keep the money people give you to invest. Then, if they get suspicious, you pay them off with money from new investors. So you always have to keep getting new investors to pay off the old ones. Now, who else invested with him? Your friends? Your parents, maybe?"

Linda felt Becca's shoulders begin to heave, and soon the tears were flowing. This would be good; a few tears, a little girl talk, and complete trust.

Becca shook her head miserably. "My dad gave him everything he had."

"This Gordon Pinsker is getting all the money, and your husband will get all the blame." Linda let it sink in. "That's why it's important you let me talk to Malcolm."

Becca dropped her head into her hands and rubbed her face. She nodded, not looking at Linda. "I need a little time to think. I'm going to be seeing Malcolm next week, in London, I don't think he'd mind me telling you that. After I talk to him, maybe he'll agree to meet with you. I could let you know, you could fly over."

Linda let a disapproving silence settle on the still room. The cigarette smoke was no longer masking that awful smell.

"Becca, I don't think you realize how urgent this all is. I'm offering you a way out. If you don't believe me, have your parents check on the money Malcolm invested for them."

"Oh God, *please* don't say that."

"There really isn't time to think this over." She stood up and crossed back to her briefcase and tucked away the "report." She put her purse back over her shoulder and picked up the briefcase.

Becca looked up at her from the couch. A fresh outbreak of tears was brewing.

"I lied to you," she said miserably. "I don't know where Malcolm is, per se, but he'll be calling me, when I get to London. If you were, like, *there*—I could convince him to talk to you."

Linda smiled down at her, trying to stay in character, "Sounds like a plan. What's the name of the hotel you'll be staying at?"

She tried to keep the excitement out of her voice. But all she could think of was the image of Malcolm's smiling face bisected by the barrel of her gun. She wouldn't hesitate this time.

"Hotel Continental. Across from Hyde Park." Becca stood up, sniffing. "I have to go pack."

"Sure. I'll let myself out."

Turning, Becca walked down the hallway toward her bedroom. Linda waited a moment, then turned and left. Moments later, when she was out in the street, she thought she heard a scream. She stood there, listening for more, and decided it was just her imagination.

The big gray horse named Firecracker was looking at Cliff like he couldn't figure out what he was doing in his stall, why he was just standing there stroking his neck, not saying anything, just looking at him in a sad way.

It was late afternoon, and it was quiet here in the stables at Bay Meadows. Firecracker toed the straw, shook his head and looked again at Cliff, nudging him as if to try to get an answer. Then, his ears pricked up as he heard footsteps. He turned as another man entered the stall.

"Hey Cliff."

"Nik."

Zacco handed him the envelope. "Cash, like you wanted."

Cliff handed him the ownership papers for Firecracker.

"Everything looks good," Zacco said, skimming the papers. "Surprised you're letting him go so cheap."

"I guess we both know why," Cliff said, wanting to say more, but knowing it was pointless now. He always knew Zacco moved in like a vulture on broken trainers, sensing their need for money, exploiting their weakness. Guy was a clearinghouse for losers on their way out of town.

"He's a good guy," Cliff said, stroking Firecracker's neck. "He'll win some races for you."

"When he does, I'll give you all the credit."

"Bullshit you will." Cliff picked up the duffel bag, lying nearby in the straw.

"Going somewhere?"

"Got some business to take care of." Cliff stroked the horse's neck once more. "Okay. So the horse is yours. So I'm outta here."

Cliff walked slowly through the stables and out into the fading sunlight. Down the way, in the parking lot, Cliff could see Dan's Mercedes with two figures inside. He glanced at his watch—it was still three hours before their plane took off. He walked slowly, wondering if this would be his last look at the world where he was raised, the world he loved.

"Hello, Mr. Dante," Veena said as he slid into the back seat of the Mercedes.

"Veena. Dan."

Dan handed a set of papers back to him along with a pen. "Need your John Hancock on this."

Cliff saw it was a life insurance policy. "Thought you needed a physical—the whole nine yards for this kind of deal."

"A friend of mine's gonna put it through for us." He glanced at Veena and smiled. "You can get covered for about 90 days on just your signature. I put your wife down as a beneficiary."

Cliff had skimmed the papers and found the bottom line. "If I get killed over there, a half-million bucks will do a lot to cheer my wife up."

"Funny how that works," Dan said. He fired up the Mercedes, dropped it into gear and pulled out. "Veena will put it through for us on her way back from the airport." Turning to her, smiling, he added, "She just got her license. This is her first sale."

PART FIVE

PURSUIT

STANDING IN FRONT of the grandstands at Lingfield Park, south of London, Cliff felt the bite of the March wind on his face as he looked out over the race course. The track climbed a hill, nearly disappeared in the distance, then came back downhill and over a series of jumps and finished in front of the clubhouse. The center of the track, a grassy meadow, was used for parking and a stream of cars lumbered into the area and disgorged race fans carrying picnic baskets, umbrellas and binoculars.

"Ready for some proper racing, then?"

Cliff turned and saw Adrian Sellwood walking toward him, smiling.

"You call this racing?" Cliff said, shaking his hand. "I call it a obstacle course."

"Eight jumps, two and a half miles—now that's a proper horse race. None of that flat racing, like you have in the States. When did you get in?"

"Landed yesterday at noon. I called you, then crashed."

"Staying in London?"

"For now anyway." Cliff took in Adrian's suit and tie, his overcoat. He was about Cliff's age and height. His brown hair was neatly cut, coming to a widow's peak on his forehead.

"So where're your silks, Adrian?"

"I'm not riding anymore."

"Why not?"

"Too fat and ugly," Adrian laughed. "Besides, I was no bloody good at it. I work for a bookmaker now—public relations."

"You?"

"Yes *me!*" Adrian said straightening his cuffs.

"A bookie, huh?" Cliff said, slapping his racing program into his hand. "We're gonna have a lot to talk about."

Adrian looked around. "Where's your mate?"

"My wife stayed at—" Cliff caught himself. He couldn't get used to the way these Brits talked. "Over there," he pointed at Dan, who stood in a line of people—no, a *queue*—buying pork sandwiches. A pig was impaled on a spit and a woman was cutting slabs right off the carcass, putting them on fresh-baked buns.

Adrian watched Dan joking with the woman running the sandwich stand. "Big lad, isn't he? How do you know him?"

"He owns part of this horse we're looking for. You get a copy of the Tattersall's catalog?"

Adrian handed him a thick book listing all the horses for sale at the spring auction. "And here's the late entries." He handed him a faxed sheet.

Cliff skimmed the list of horse names, owners and trainers. Maybe the Relaunch colt was here somewhere. But what was he looking for? He already knew the name was changed.

"What about the shipper? Did he know where our horse went?"

Adrian smiled like he was holding out on him, bouncing lightly on the balls of his feet.

"*What?*" Cliff asked.

"I'm expecting a call back any time."

"Oh. I thought you were gonna charge me for it. I told you I spent the last of my money on a one-way ticket here."

"Just what we need, more bloody immigrants."

"I'm not staying."

"Well, it's a long swim back." Adrian must have seen the glint in Cliff's eye. Either that or he saw the way Cliff opened his racing program and reviewed the horses he had circled with bold slashes of his pencil.

"Oh no," Adrian said. "Don't tell me—you feel lucky today?"

"Where is the Regis Fountain?" Becca asked the doorman at the Hotel Continental. He was dressed up like a soldier of some kind with a sword hanging down and everything. Very cool.

"Right," he said, searching his memory. "That's in the middle of Hyde Park now, isn't it?"

She shrugged. "Someone told me to meet him there."

"Right. What you want to do is . . ." he gave her about a million *lefts* and *rights* and she wasn't like really listening until he said, Tell you what, luv—" *Luv*, she liked that—"I'll put you in a cab, drop you near the fountain. It'll be a short stroll from there."

A half-hour later she was walking across a broad, grassy field, filled with daisies. Ahead was a grove of trees and a small fountain. She stood by the fountain, staring down into the water, the sound of the gurgling blended with birds singing and making her like zone out or something. Maybe it was the jet lag, or the pills she was taking to help her sleep, but she didn't hear him coming. She saw his feet in front of her, looked up and there he was, smiling at her, his expression asking her how much she knew. He was very handsome in a gray suit with a silver tie and an overcoat.

"Rebecca." Malcolm's eyes swept over her, taking in the flowery spring dress. "You look ravishing."

He held his arms open and she rushed into them. She hugged him tightly, desperately, trying to forget what he had done, trying just to, like, concentrate on her love for him, on this moment in this beautiful park in London. Yes, that felt right, it felt good.

"Why so sad?" He took her chin and gently raised her face to look into his eyes.

She shook her head.

"They're saying nasty things about me, are they, back in the States?"

Actually, she was thinking about her little dog, poor Nookie. He must have killed her dog. But she would have to pick the right time to confront him.

"Are there stories about me in the newspapers?"

She looked him in the eye. "It's all over the Chronicle. Your clients are calling. People keep coming to the house."

When she said this, she saw a frightening change. It was as if a clear plastic shield had slid down over his face, changing him into someone else.

"Who came to the house?" he demanded.

"How should I know? I'm not exactly about to answer the door, you know."

He relaxed. "Good girl." He slowly smiled, his naughty boy smile, and said, "Christ, I want you. I'm as randy as a flippin' schoolboy." He grabbed her roughly.

"*Malcolm!*" She pushed him away playfully.

"What have you got on under the dress, aye?"

"Well . . ." She bit her lip and looked away.

"Nothing," he guessed. "Am I right?"

Becca giggled. Malcolm made a low growling noise. "You're torturing me."

This was working, she thought. All she had to do was focus on how she felt at this moment. Then the other questions went away.

"Let's go back to the hotel," she said.

"No." His voice was firm. "The car should be here any moment."

He turned away, looking toward the road that ran through the park that carried a steady parade of London cabs.

Becca saw the big silver-gray car with a hood ornament pulling to the curb. "That's for us?"

"Of course."

He took her hand and they began walking.

"You're never going to forget this day. Remember how you used to ask me all those questions about where I was from, what it was like here? You'll see it all today."

She watched the chauffeur get out of the car in his cute little uniform and open the back door for them. He was an older man, gray hair, a faint smile on his lips. Inside she could see the cut glass vase, the silverware, the champagne on ice.

Casually, Malcolm asked, "Get that bit of business taken care of like I asked you?"

"Hmmm?"

"The money. Did you wire it over here?"

"Oh yes, the money."

"Thought we'd stop by American Express, get that taken care of before we move on to other things."

The chauffeur nodded and smiled to Becca as she ducked into the Rolls, smelling the flowers and underlying scent of the leather upholstery.

"You know, Malcolm," Becca said. She was surprised by what she was thinking, what she was about to say. She was doing it all by instinct, her instinct telling her that to do this would extend the happiness she was feeling right now. "There was a little problem with the money."

Malcolm faced her, the shield sliding down over his eyes again. His voice was tight as he asked, "What *sort* of a problem?"

"Not a problem, really," she said feeling her way along. "More like, sort of a delay."

"I could eat about five of these," Dan said, pushing the last of another pork sandwich into his mouth and licking his fingers. They were at the paddock now, watching the horses in the Post Parade for the fourth race. They had watched the first three races, and hadn't seen anything worth betting on.

"Want one, Cliff? Adrian?"

Dan looked ready to disappear again. Cliff held him back. "You're the banker. Stick around."

Cliff watched the horses circling the paddock, checked his racing program. Most of the entries for this race had slashes through them.

Dan put his arm around Cliff and said to Adrian. "If anyone can pick a winner, it's my man right here."

"I know," Adrian said. "I used to ride for him in the States."

Cliff ignored them. "What's the turf track here like? Soft?"

"A bit hard, actually. Hasn't rained for a fortnight."

"Favors speed then," he muttered.

"I fancy Number Four," Adrian said, pointing at a gray parading in front of them, its mane in tight braids. Cliff thought of Firecracker, how Nik Zacco stole him for the price of one-way ticket out of town. He watched the gray walk, saw the way his lead feet circled. Wasted motion.

"That horse's got a hitch in its get-along," Cliff said, and drew an angry slash through the entry. He had only three entries left.

"Now there's a runner," Cliff said, nodding at a small bay with a white diamond in the center of his forehead.

"Too small," Adrian said. He handed a racing sheet to Cliff, "Look, he lost his last three races."

Cliff studied the sheet, "Yeah, but his last three races were in the rain. Means he's not a mudder."

"Actually," Adrian said, "I know these jockeys that rode him. Right piss artists, each one."

"Who's on board today? Femright? You know him?"

Adrian looked up from the racing sheet and smiled. "Femright's brilliant—one of the top jump jockeys. He's got great instinct—knows just when to make his move."

Cliff looked at the other two men. "So what we've got here is a fast track, a fast horse who's only run in the mud. And he's never had a good jockey."

"Big casino, baby," Dan said, his eyes narrowing. He looked around for the odds. "Where's the tote board?"

Adrian laughed. "'The tote board.' You're in England now, lad. The bookies are 'round front. But look, Cliff, don't be daft. This horse probably doesn't have a chance."

"Then why'd they put a good jockey on him?" Cliff said. "Just show me where the bookies are."

They walked past the concession stands selling fish and chips and meat pasties, past pubs packed with men in herringbone coats and women in tweed skirts, with peaches and cream complexions and bad teeth. Here, going to the races was like a day in the country, Cliff thought. Not like back in America, where the track was all dirt and concrete, with video screens plastered everywhere.

They rounded the side of the old white clapboard clubhouse. Adrian frowned, looking up at the sky. A leaden bank of clouds marched toward them. "I hope that rain holds off till post."

The grandstands were a series of stone steps looking down on the grassy race track. Between the stands and the white railing of the race course, laid out on cobblestones, Cliff saw a bizarre crowd of men, all engaged in frantic activity. It looked like a flea market without any stuff to sell.

"You want odds on Number 6," Adrian said, "take your pick. Each bookie out there will give you different odds. And the odds will keep changing, right up to race time."

Dan pulled Cliff aside and lowered his voice.

"How much cash you got?" Dan asked.

"Two hundred and twenty four pounds," Cliff said. "And I

might have about five hundred still left on one of my credit cards."

"Fuck the credit cards," Dan said. "How much you want to bet?"

"Two hundred and twenty four pounds."

"Come on, let's not be stupid about this."

"Why not? I done a lot of stupid things to get here. Maybe one more stupid thing will break my losing streak."

Dan looked away, then back, his voice changing. "I've got about 700 pounds. But we're gonna need a lot more than that if we're going to pull this off, get our horse and ship him home. You know, I like to talk about big casino and everything, but that's just bullshit, okay?"

"What are you saying?"

"The golden rule is, don't bet money you can't afford to lose."

Cliff thought it over. "Way I figure it, there ain't a golden rule that applies to me anymore."

Dan's eyes seemed to bore into him. "Okay, how much're you putting down?"

"Big casino, baby—gonna bet the farm," Cliff said in his monotone voice. "Stop me if you want, 'cause if I lose, you're gonna have to carry me."

Cliff took all the cash out of his wallet and slapped it into Dan's palm. He put his wallet back in his hip pocket—it was so thin he could hardly feel it.

Dan nodded solemnly and walked off. Cliff watched him threading his way through the packed area. Dan spoke to several bookies, making notes on his racing program. He finally handed his money to a bookie standing on a wooden crate next to a sign that read "Larry Perry, Bookmaker." Cliff saw the bookie take the cash and put it into a worn briefcase under his sign. That's the bank?

Cliff heard a cellular phone ringing. Instinctively, he reached into his windbreaker pocket. It was empty. He looked over and saw Adrian on the phone saying, "No, that can't be. I mean—why?" Adrian nodded and said, "Thanks. Cheers."

Cliff waited, glancing through the auction catalog Adrian had given him.

Adrian put his phone away, saying, "That was the shipper handled your horse."

"What?" Cliff put his thumb in the catalog to mark his place.

"It doesn't make sense," Adrian said slowly. "The shipper delivered the horse to another transport service. So he didn't know where it went."

"Trying to cover their tracks," Cliff said. "The more hands the horse goes through, the harder it is to trace. Hey, who's this?" He held out the faxed pages of the late entries at the Tattersall's Auction. He had found a two-year-old roan named Marquis' Millions. Why did that sound familiar?

"It's being sold by Peter Turnbull," Adrian said, and started laughing.

"What's so funny about that?"

"He's only the best trainer in the U.K."

"Maybe this Turnbull thinks the horse is legit."

"Well, ask him yourself," Adrian said. "He's standing right over there." He pointed to a short, powerful-looking man in a tan trench coat with a big, shining bald head. "But I'd watch your step. They don't call him 'The Bull' for nothing."

They watched as Turnbull greeted another man, pumping

his hand, looking up into the taller man's face with a big predatory grin.

"I'll introduce you to him later," Adrian said. "He's not going anywhere—he's got a horse in this race too."

Cliff glanced down onto the track and saw their horse, the horse they put everything on, the six horse being led into the gate. The horse walked nice, looked alert, athletic—an easy traveler. The jockey on board wore red silks with yellow sleeves. Cliff felt his hopes rising—if they hit big casino, it would take a lotta pressure off this trip.

Dan reappeared holding a brightly colored cardboard betting ticket. He stood in front of Cliff, his eyes like slits, and said, "Fucker wasn't going to take my bet. I asked for his odds on the six horse and he just laughs. Finally he goes, 'If you wager 300 pounds, I'll give you 75 to 1.' So I kicked in a hundred." He shook his head. "This is nuts. I sure hope you know what you're doing."

Adrian looked up at the sky again. Cliff followed his gaze and saw the clouds were coming in dark and low. From behind the grandstands he heard a deep *thump, thump, thump.* If he were back home, Cliff would have thought it was the bass in some gangbanger's lowrider. Seconds later a helicopter swooped into sight, moving low over the tree tops and setting down in the center of the race course near the parked cars.

"Someone's arriving in style," Adrian said. "Probably some sheik. Come with me, I'll show you the best spot to watch the race from."

They walked around the grandstands toward the paddock. A cameraman was videotaping a sports announcer who stood next to a large monitor. As they approached, Cliff heard the announcer saying, ". . . And of course this presents a wonderful opportunity for Peter Turnbull to get back in the game. He's had such a run of bad luck, and he's such a wonderful chap, that we all wish him the very best of luck."

There's another difference for you, Cliff thought. The media guys would never say that on American TV. They sink their teeth into your jugular and suck you dry.

"Meet a couple of my friends from America," Adrian said to the announcer. "Cliff Dante, Dan Van Berg this is Richard Maxwell, the voice of Channel Six."

"Pleasure," Maxwell said, then holding up a finger to silence them, he spoke into the microphone: "Oh, I think his chances are excellent in this race. And there they go," he said, looking at his monitor, "all the horses breaking cleanly at the start of this two mile, three furlong, Gold Cup Hurtle."

Maxwell's commentary droned on, as Cliff watched the action on the screen. He saw that they must have had a camera moving next to the track because, in one continuous shot, Cliff could see the horses taking the first jump, flowing over the hedge in a wave of muscles, colors, riders, and whips. Cliff looked for the red and yellow silks of the jockey, and saw their horse holding his position along the rail with three horses in the front of the pack. The second jump was cleared easily and several of the horses fell off the pace and began to lose ground.

"Well done, boy! Go on! That's it!" Shouted a woman nearby, watching the race on the TV monitor.

Adrian nodded at the woman and said to Cliff: "Cory Marsh. She trained the six horse—the one you're betting on. And she's never had a win."

"Now you tell me," Cliff said. He felt a few drops of cold rain on his face and looked up, "Shit, here it comes." A moment later it was raining hard. Yeah, but how long before it turned the track to mud? We still got a chance here, Cliff thought, turning back to the TV.

"He's hanging in there," Dan murmured, clenching his fists, watching the horses clear another jump.

The field had narrowed to three front-runners: six, four and one. They closed in on another jump. Three horses went up. One hit hard, pitched forward, throwing its jockey. Cliff searched the screen and saw the six horse was still up and running. The thrown jockey scrambled to his feet and ran off the course while his horse got to his feet and, riderless, continued to run next to the two remaining leaders.

"Oh dear," Cliff heard Maxwell saying, "This loose horse could be trouble. And now the riders have to contend with a bit of mud from this rain too."

From the other side of the grandstands they heard a roar. "They've gone around once now," Adrian explained. "One more lap."

The riderless horse veered off, and disappeared from the screen, leaving just the two front runners.

"You can do it! *Please!*" Cory Marsh pleaded.

"Just three more jumps and this race is done," Maxwell said into his microphone. "And what a race it is! A marvelous perform-ance by these four-year-olds, Peter Turnbull's horse facing an unexpected challenge from this long shot."

The two lead horses were running one foot apart as if fastened at the shoulder. At the next jump, the one horse narrowly cleared the hedge, his legs crashing through the wickets. He landed hard, but kept going, without losing any ground. He took the next jump the same way, everyone holding their breath to see whether he could keep going.

"That other horse is done," Cliff said to Cory. "He's workin' too hard, head moving up and down. Your horse'll blow his doors off in the stretch."

She glanced at Cliff, her expression flashing thanks, then she turned back at the screen, and said, "You've got him now! Come on!"

Dan was shaking his big fist at the screen. "Go you son-of-a-bitch, go!"

Cliff saw the last jump coming up, and felt himself bracing inside, holding himself tight as the horse vaulted into the air, over the hedge, hit hard, but found his stride again and surged forward. The one horse had gotten a second wind and cleared the jump nicely, and they were, once again, dead even. Cliff saw the jockeys trying to make a move now, arms back, whips slashing, and he knew the horses were reaching deep for everything they had, looking for one last burst of energy. They heard the roar of the fans in the grandstands swell, Maxwell's voice calling the race, Cory pleading with her horse, and without meaning to, Cliff heard his own voice join the others, as he said, "You got it! Finish him off you son-of-a-gun!"

Same old story, Cliff thought, two horses in a dead heat. Which one of them had something extra, more energy, more desire, more pride—more heart—and could claim victory?

Then it happened. With each stride one of the horses gained a few inches, enough to pull ahead by a nose, a head, and finally, half a length. Cliff saw the white number six on the saddle and the yellow and red of the jockey's silks emerging ahead of the other horse, as it came down the stretch and thundered across the finish line in first.

Cory screamed with joy, her eyes alive as she turned to Cliff, hugged him and kissed him on the lips. She pulled back, said, "I'm so happy!" and dashed off around the building, heading for her horse.

Adrian pumped Cliff's hand furiously. "Well done! Well done!"

"You made the pick, man," Cliff said.

"Let's go get our dough before that guy with the suitcase leaves town," Dan said.

The horses were coming around the side of the grandstands now, breathing hard, the jockeys sliding off and jumping to the ground. Cliff watched as the jockeys took their saddles with them and stood on the scales outside the weighing room. The winning horse appeared with Cory Marsh leading it. She was in tears, holding the horse's bridle, hugging him and kissing him passionately. She steadied the horse as the jockey, Femright, removed the saddle. The horse's back steamed in the cold air.

"Nice race," Cliff said as Femright passed him.

The jockey met his eyes, maybe hearing the American accent, and gave him a nod. Cocky. What the hell, Cliff thought, he's the winner, he deserves it.

"Here comes *The Bull*," Adrian said. "Maybe I can introduce you."

But then they saw the look on Turnbull's face as he charged toward the jockey who had ridden his horse. The Bull chewed him out pretty good. The jockey answered angrily, then strode away.

The tall man they'd seen with Turnbull earlier reappeared. He whispered something to Turnbull and they moved off into the crowd. As the tall man turned, Cliff saw his face—pudgy and boyish and vaguely familiar. A mop of brown hair fell in his face.

"Where're they off to in such a hurry?" Cliff asked.

"Follow them if you like, I'm getting out of this rain," Adrian said. "Meet you in the Oaks Bar, round front."

Cliff stuck with Turnbull and the tall man as they hurried around the grandstands and past the concession stands. Cliff saw the pig on the skewer had been reduced to a skeleton with tatters of meat clinging to its ribs, the whole ghastly sight being soaked in the rain.

Turnbull and his friend had reached a gate that led to a path across the race track. He showed some sort of identification to the attendant and the two men were allowed to cross the track and enter the area where the cars were parked. The helicopter was still there, the doors open.

"Sorry sir," a track official said blocking Cliff's way as he tried to follow.

"Need to get to my car over there," Cliff lied.

"Horses are in the field now. Sorry."

The horses had been led onto the track for the next race and were running up and down in front of the grandstands, their hooves churning the turf into mud as the rain beat down. Cliff returned to the grandstands and stood under the roof, wiping the cold water off his face. He saw Turnbull was standing alongside the helicopter among a cluster of umbrellas.

"Can I borrow your binoculars?" Cliff asked a ruddy-faced man standing nearby.

"I'll need 'em back for the race, mind you," the man said, handing them over.

Cliff raised the glasses, and found the men under the umbrellas next to the helicopter. Their faces were blurred, shaky through the binoculars. He quickly focused. That was a little better. There was Peter Turnbull's bald head . . . the tall man with the brown hair . . . . They were talking to someone inside the helicopter. Cliff could see a pale face inside . . . a woman beside him . . . .

"And they're off!" came a voice over the loudspeaker.

Cliff felt a tug on his sleeve. "My binoculars . . . . if you don't mind . . . ?"

One last glimpse, Cliff thought, feeling the rage building inside him.

He felt sure Malcolm was inside the helicopter.

I'm gonna kill the motherfucker. Cliff heard the words in his head, as if he had shouted them out. *Wait a second*—he stopped the flow of thoughts—*The game has changed.* He looked around for Dan, hoping he was there to pull him back to sanity.

Another tug on his sleeve. "If you don't mind . . . ? My binoculars?"

Cliff handed them over. He found himself running through the rain toward the track, saw the official still blocking the way, ran along the rail, looking for an opening, thinking, *There's got to be a way to get across.* But security was tight. And looking across, he saw the helicopter blades were beginning to turn. He stood and watched as Turnbull climbed on board and the doors closed. The helicopter rose into the air and passed overhead, the deep *thump* of the blades was like a fist in his gut.

"Cliff! Over here!"

The warm smoky air hit Cliff full in the face as he came into the pub out of the rain. He worked his way through the crowd to the bar where Adrian and Dan were drinking with Cory Marsh. She was maybe thirty years old, lean and tough, with square shoulders and straight brown hair pulled back. She drew on a cigarette, then flicked the match on the floor. Cliff could tell by looking at her she'd come up the hard way, probably as an exercise rider or jockey.

"Nice race," Cliff told her.

"Bloody fantastic, that!" She was still pumped from the race.

"I told Cory a bit about your horse," Adrian said to Cliff.

Dan cocked his head at her, and said, "Listen to what she says about Turnbull."

"He's a dodgy motherfucker," Cory said. "Wouldn't surprise me to hear he's got a stable full of stolen horses."

Cliff felt nervous about having their mission exposed—he knew how fast word spread around the track. He wanted to back off, but he had to learn more.

Dan saw Cliff was without a drink, turned and slammed his hand on the bar. "Mr. Bartender-man!" The bartender appeared and Dan indicated Cliff.

"I'll have a Guinness."

"Very good." The bartender said.

Dan reached into his pocket to pay for the beer. He slowly drew his hand out, nudged Cliff and pointed down at the wad of bills, shielding it from view. The roll was as thick as a paperback book.

"Is this unbelievable or what?" Dan laughed. "I'm telling you, man, this is a sign—our luck's turning."

Cliff's beer arrived and he scooped it off the bar, toasted Dan, saying, "Tell you something else unbelievable."

Dan's eyes narrowed. He waited.

"Malcolm was here."

"No way."

"He was the big shot flew in on that helicopter. He came to pick up Turnbull."

Dan processed the news, fitting it in with other things, and said, "Turnbull's got to be our man. So how do we get to him?"

"Hey Cory," Cliff said, interrupting Adrian, who was hitting on her. "How well do you know Peter Turnbull?"

"Quite well, I should think. I was his assistant trainer until he gave me the boot six months ago."

"Wait a second," Dan said. "So you just kicked your ex-boss's ass?"

Cory took a big pull on her beer. "Doesn't get any better than that."

"Can we buy you another drink?" Cliff said, then, before she could answer, "The hell with a drink—we'll buy you dinner. We owe it to you, seeing as how we made a bundle on your horse."

"So that's what this is all about," Cory said. "I get it now."

"I get it too," Adrian said, seeing he was out of the loop. "Must dash. If not I'll get stuck in London traffic. Best of luck." He shook their hands. "Cheers!"

Adrian disappeared into the crowd.

"I'm starved." Dan looked around. "Let's get a booth, order some food."

"Not in this shit hole," Cory said. "You're taking me to a proper restaurant. And you're buying for my assistant trainer too. Oy! Pam!" She waved to a woman coming through the door. As she walked toward them, Cliff checked her out. He figured her for a hard forty—wearing a big red coat and a baseball cap. She had ruddy cheeks and a lined face. But her eyes were carefully made up. Still a lady under those stable rags.

"Pam—I snagged a couple of rich Americans."

"Howja do?" Pam asked shaking their hands.

"They made a killing on our horse so they're taking us to dinner," Cory announced.

"Bring on the filet mignon," Pam said.

"How about it, lads?" Cory asked. "Celebrate with us? Or are the wives back at the hotel watching the clock?"

"The wives are six thousand miles away," Dan said.

"And they're pissed at us now," Cliff added.

"I can see why," Pam said, poking Dan in the ribs. "Couple of regular punters, you are, runnin' off like that."

Dan laughed until he stepped out the door and the cold rain slapped him in the face. Then they all pulled up their collars and ran for it.

"What do you call this?" Dan said, chewing a big mouthful of food.

They were packed into a high-backed booth in a place called the Bag o' Nails Pub across the street from the railroad station where the train from London had dropped them off that morning. Cliff sat across from Cory. Dan faced Pam.

"That? Steak and kidney pie," Pam answered.

"Tasty. But it's not big enough."

"Typical Yank," Cory said, stabbing her food and eating furiously. "Where are you from then? Texas?"

"California," Cliff said. Then, pointing at his dish, a thin slice of meat bordered by mushy peas, he added, "Back home, this'd be on the kiddie menu."

"Get out," Cory said. Then to Pam she added, "They aren't half obnoxious, are they?"

"How'd you become a trainer?" Dan asked.

Cliff was glad Dan was here. He was an easy talker—let him ask the questions, draw people out. Then he could sit back and figure it all out.

"I was a jockey—first woman to ride in the Cheltenham Cup. Pam and me, they think we're a bit daft, two women in a man's game. I'll tell you something, for woman to make it, you have to haul ass, same as the lads."

Dan asked, "So how did you hook up with Peter Turnbull?"

Cliff heard the slur in Dan's voice. He could feel the strong beer spreading warmth through his own blood stream. Or was that hope that he felt? They were on the trail and they had money in their pockets.

Cory looked at Pam. "Hear that? They're pumping us."

"Just an innocent question," Cliff said.

"Nothing with you is innocent." She took a drink of her beer. "When my old dad died, we had to sell the stables to pay off the debts. I was through riding—sick of gettin' injured, I was. Broke my collarbone three times, three bumps on it. I never could get the hang of landing on the shoulder and rolling. I was always putting my hand down to break the fall and, *Snap*. Got knocked out five times, fractured my skull, broke every bone in my hands, and got a pin in my knee."

Dan whistled. "That beats my football injuries."

"The Bull—Peter Turnbull—he came to our auction and bought some of my dad's horses. He says to me, 'Why'n't you come be my assistant trainer?' I goes, 'You're too hard on your people.' 'Give it a try,' he says, 'you never know.'"

"How long did you last? Cliff asked.

"Long enough to buy my first horse. Best day of my life was when I walked in and I told him, I says, 'I've learned everything you know. Now I don't have to take your shit anymore.'"

"And he said?" Dan asked.

"He said, 'You may know everything I taught you, but you don't know everything I know.' I reckon I showed him different today, aye?" She raised her glass. "Drink up lads. It's a great day."

Dan leaned across the table and asked Pam, "What about you? How'd you meet Cory?"

"You don't want hear it. That's a right boring story."

"Sure I do."

"I never had my leg over a horse until I was fifteen. I was raised in the West End. I was a naughty girl and they sent me out to the country to sort things out . . . ."

Listening to Pam talk, Cliff saw the age disappear from her face. She was lookin' pretty good. He saw that Dan probably felt the same way—he was leaning in, smiling, laughing, his voice warm and friendly.

Stay focused, he thought and turned back to Cory. He found her staring at him, her eyes dark and filled with energy.

"Can you get us into Turnbull's barn?" Cliff asked Cory.

"I could ring him up, tell him I've met two rich Americans I'm sending to him." Her eyes hardened. "But if you muck things up, you're on your own. Understood?"

"Comin' through loud and clear," Cliff said. "But say we find our horse is there, what're our chances of getting it away from Turnbull?"

"You mean convincing him it's stolen and getting him to give it to you?" Cory laughed harshly. "Your chances are slim to none. Turnbull is as tight as bark to a tree. You'd have to kill him to get your horse back."

"Maybe we will," Cliff said. "If he don't kill us first."

Cory looked at him for a long time. There wasn't any room in her expression. She took another long pull on her beer, looked over at Pam chatting with Dan, then back at Cliff.

"They're gettin' friendly."

Cliff saw she was right. He glanced at his watch and stood up. "About time for our train."

Cliff and Cory walked along the dark railroad platform. He could feel her arm brushing his and he wanted to put his hand around her waist, he wanted to feel her fingers in his hair. Up ahead, Pam was leaning back against the wall as Dan stood in close to her. He said something and Pam laughed softly.

It could happen, Cliff realized as he ran a scenario in his head. He could tell Cory, "What do you say we get a hotel room here and . . . ."

Stay focused, he thought. *You got what you need, now get the hell out of here.*

But another part of Cliff was saying that he didn't get *everything* he needed from Cory. There was still a big *need* inside him and the booze had made it rise to the surface and burn like a tongue of flame.

Cliff was surprised to hear himself say, "I can still feel that kiss you gave me this afternoon. I ain't been kissed like that for a while."

He probably shouldn't have said that, he thought. 'Course, when you're half gassed, the separation between thinking and speaking is much smaller. Cory wasn't thinking about that or anything else. She stopped walking and faced him, breathing hard. She seemed to be moving inside herself, getting ready for something. She grabbed his coat and dragged him back into the shadows, pulled him hard to her. Light filtered in from someplace, a distant street light maybe, but it wasn't the light that helped him find her lips. It was her breathing—hot and ragged. Her lips were wet and eager and he thought this might be the most erotic kiss he'd ever gotten.

He felt like they were falling together, falling through the night, rolling downhill through the darkness, thrown from a horse and landing in each other's arms, tearing at each other, the pain turning to pleasure.

A whistle in the distance, down the tracks somewhere.

"You're not getting' on that train," she said, tonguing his ear.

He pulled back, looked down the rails, lit by the piercing light.

"Tomorrow morning we'll both be glad I did," Cliff said.

"The hell we will. I'll be alone and needing you."

"Or someone like me."

He thought she was going to slug him. And, what the hell, maybe he felt he deserved it.

Instead she laughed, grabbed him and pulled him back tight. Her lips were against his ear as she said, "Watch out for The Bull. He's got Glasgow money behind him. They're a bad lot up there."

Cliff backed away, standing on his own again. "Hey Dan! Let's go."

The train pounded into the station and bumped to a stop. The silence was intense. Cliff pulled the door open and they stepped inside, into the glare of the compartment lights, which blinded him to what he was leaving behind.

When they got back to their hotel in London, there was a message from Adrian. It was almost midnight but Cliff called him anyway.

A sleepy voice came on the line: "Thought you should know—my friend called just about every van service in England. Your horse went through three transport services and two stables."

"Where did it wind up?"

"I still can't believe it. There's got to be a mistake."

"Where'd it go?"

"Graycroft Stables. Peter Turnbull."

"Right then, let's just see what you've got on under that pretty little dress," Malcolm said as the door to his hotel room swung shut behind him.

Becca squealed and ran to the other side of the room, putting the double bed with the faded brown bedspread between them. Facing him, she saw lust in his eyes. She'd seen the look many times, but now it reminded her of a very bad time—the night he came out of his study after Nookie disappeared.

Malcolm dove across the bed and grabbed her leg. She

screamed and pulled back. He got a fist full of her dress and would-
n't let go.

"Don't tear it!" She cried. "I don't have anything else with me.
Pleasssse!"

"Bugger that!" he growled.

Ripppppp!

The thin dress came away easily, leaving her naked in the cold
room. She cupped her breasts with her hands as she danced away
from him.

The clear plastic shield was lowered across Malcolm's face now,
the glassy look in place as he stalked her, playing "Bitch and Sire."
They played it when they came to a new hotel room, in the Grand
Caymans, in Aspen, in Switzerland. But there, they were staying in
five-star hotels where she could pick up the phone afterwards and
order herself a whole new outfit. She'd lounge naked or wrapped in
a big fluffy bathrobe until the man came to the door with the
bright packages.

But it was different here. This place was drab and cold—not
his style at all. And it sure didn't fit with the Rolls-Royce or their
flight in the helicopter over the English countryside to that cute
little race track.

"*Ooomphf!*"

With a flying tackle, he pinned her to the bed. He was still dressed—
she didn't have a stitch on. At least with him on top it was warmer.

"*There are things you can buy on time and other things you have
to pay up front. The higher you go, the more things are taken on faith.*"
That was the motto he had lived by since she met him two years
ago. And it served him well most of the time, the joy of their life
only occasionally punctuated by angry calls demanding money, by

shouting from behind his closed study door, by threatening notices from credit card companies.

His shirt was open down the front and she felt the hair of his chest tickling her nipples. *Now my thoughts will slide away, as they always do when I have sex,* she thought. Slide away like a pleasant wave lifting her higher, up to the place she liked to be. The highs of life. That's what she and Malcolm had experienced.

Grunting and wrestling, he tore his pants open and—she knew the next move—he rammed it in with a satisfied grunt. She was nailed to the bed now. He had what he wanted; he possessed her.

As he moved on top of her she noticed that her thoughts weren't sliding away. They were staying with her, nagging her like a bitchy mother. Why couldn't she just go with the flow like before? Ride that big wave—the way they rode the stock market as it went up and up, the money rolling in.

She looked up into his face, his eyes on her, but not on her, and she suddenly pictured what his face had looked like as he had killed her dog. It was hard to forget the sight of Nookie under that pile of dirty clothes in the corner of the closet, his decaying lips pulled back tight on his little teeth. Snarling at her. It was harder still to forget the smell. She saw the right moment, she would get even with Malcolm for what he did.

He was slamming it into her now, his tempo increasing, each grunt getting a little louder until, *Yeah! Oh yeah . . . ! Yeah! Yeah! Yeeahhh!*

He rolled to the side, throwing one arm over his eyes and she knew he might conk out now. But for once she didn't want to let him sleep.

"Malcolm."

"Uh?"

"We need to talk."

"Later."

She spun and slapped her hand down hard on his chest— *SMACK!*

"*Now*, you bastard!"

"Ow!"

He sat up, dazed, then furious. But she was pissed too.

"Listen to me! What'd you do with my dad's money?"

Malcolm looked at her a long time, realizing things had changed.

"What did I do with his money? I took it and made him a bloody fortune, that's what I did."

"I called him before I left. I told him to check everything. *Everything.* If it's not there, and you're lying, I'll find out about it."

She watched him carefully, focusing on his good eye, trying to see the truth in there somewhere.

"That's why you're stalling on the money?" he asked at last. "Holding me hostage?"

Actually, she had gone with a bank instead of an American Express by accident. But it was working out in her favor because the banks were closed during the weekend. He couldn't get the money till Monday. And now she saw that the longer she held out on him, the more she needed to.

"I know more than you think I know. I know you're in some, like, really big trouble. And—and you need me. I know things that could help you. So you better start by telling me everything."

Malcolm stood up and put himself back together. Then he sat

217

down again with his back to her, shoulders slumped. And when he spoke his voice was broken. She hadn't been prepared for this. She shivered, pulling the blankets around her.

"I can't tell you everything, just now. I don't know how all this will wind up and, if you knew too much, it could hurt you." He turned and looked at her with an expression she'd never seen before.

"You're saying, if I knew too much, they might, like, try to get me too?"

"It's . . . possible. So all I can say is this." He paused, thinking, then continued. "I've made a lot of mistakes. I've let other people lead me to do things I shouldn't have."

"Gordon?"

That surprised him. But he agreed. "Gordon. Yes Gordon. How did you know?"

She thought about telling him about Linda, the woman from Texas who was probably back in her hotel lobby right now. Becca had called her and set up a meeting. But at the last minute she ducked out the side door. Why not leave all her options open? No, this wasn't the time to tell Malcolm about her. There would be time for that later. It was time to hear his side.

"Tell you later. Go on."

"I have a plan . . . " Malcolm said. "I have the chance to make a lot of money. A *lot* of money. It's enough to pay back most of what is—is missing. But I don't have that money just yet. And I need cash to pull off my plan. That's why I need that money you had wired over."

It was beginning to make sense now. And she felt he really was telling the truth. But she needed to be careful. And she needed to retain some control. As long as the money was in her name, he had to do what she said.

"Malcolm, I'll help you. But I want you to promise me one thing."

"What's that?"

"When you get this money, I want you to pay back my dad first. I want you to make whatever investments you told him you were going to make. I don't want him to know anything's wrong. He, like, trusts you sooo much. Will you promise to do that?"

"Aye. I will," he said softly. Then he took her hand. "Rebecca?"

"Yes."

"Thanks for standing by me. I won't let you down."

He left the bed and disappeared into bathroom. And, while he was in the shower, she knew this might be her only chance. She dug his wallet out of his pants and saw he had a list of banks and account numbers written on the back of an old business card. By the time the water in the shower stopped she had copied the account numbers and put his wallet back in his pants. Then she hopped back under the covers. When he appeared at the bathroom door, rubbing his wet hair with a towel, she stretched, yawned and smiled at him. It was easy to smile now because it was so cool. For once she knew more than he did.

"Got an idea," Ellis said, leaning forward in his chair in the hotel lobby.

"What's that?" Linda asked. They had been there quite a while and she knew he was getting restless. He was like that. A lot of men were.

"When she sets up this meeting with Ravling, once we get

them both together, how about I stick my knife in his face and tell him to come up with the money?"

"And if he doesn't?"

"I'll cut off his fingers, one by one, till he does."

Linda thought it over. "You know what he's gonna say. He'll tell you he can't get the money right then."

"Then we'll tell him we'll keep the girl as collateral till he gets back with the cash."

"Too crude."

"Okay, what's your idea?"

"I'm waiting to see what she tells us."

"Looks to me like she's a no-show."

"Maybe. But she'll be back. She wants to clear her man." Linda smiled.

Ellis bounced his foot, one leg over the other. He wasn't wearing his Stetson, but he still wore the cowboy boots. She was noticing how he stood out among these Londoners. She hoped that didn't go against them. They would probably be leaving the country in a hurry and she didn't want to get stopped at customs.

"Tell you what, Linda. I'm a little tired of all this waiting around. I think we need to take action—even if it's crude."

"Ellis. The longer we wait—"

But he didn't stay to hear the end of the sentence. He stood and walked past her and out onto the street. She really hated it when he did that. But he was the restless type. She had always known that about him. In this case, it was a damn shame he hadn't stayed to hear what she had to say, because he would have liked it.

She was going to tell him, "The longer the wait, the bigger the payoff."

It was early Sunday morning and Charing Cross Station was nearly empty. Cliff was off buying their tickets to Cambridge, where they would catch a second train to New Market and visit Peter Turnbull's stables. Dan leaned against a pillar sipping a cup of coffee and looking around, watching a pigeon fly up to the glassed-in ceiling arching above the waiting trains.

Dan saw a newsstand nearby and thought about buying a paper. He drifted over to see what they had. English rags. They all looked the same, pictures of bodacious women on the cover. Or photos of soccer games. Here was one with racing news . . . .

Hey, they had a copy of the *San Francisco Chronicle.* Friday's paper but still—that was only two days ago.

"See that after you?" Cliff asked, handing Dan his ticket. "Want to check the races at Bay Meadows. See if Zacco is running Firecracker yet. Bet he is, money hungry son-of-a-buck."

Flipping through the paper, Dan stopped, staring at a head-line: *MARIN EXEC INDICTED FOR FRAUD.*

"Whoa," Dan said. "Look at this—a story about Malcolm."

Cliff looked over his shoulder. "Hope my name's not in there."

They read in silence, Dan digesting the facts . . . . Malcolm M. Ravling indicted on 15 counts of fraud . . . . An estimated 40 investors cheated . . . . $15 million missing . . . . Lavish lifestyle . . . . Race horses . . . . Expensive cars . . . . Two paragraphs jumped out at him from the end of the story:

> The fraud is thought to have led to the suicide
> of one investor. Irene Gastin was found dead of an
> overdose of insulin in her modest Fremont bunga-

low. Her husband recently invested their life savings with Ravling, money he said was needed for her expensive medical treatments for diabetes.

Stanley Gastin, her husband said, "Last time I talked to her, she said, 'It's my fault our money's gone.' She liked him so much. Trusted him. And then he did this to us. What kind of a monster is he?"

Dan handed the paper to Cliff and walked away, recalling the feel of the Gastin's stuffy house on the rainy day he had been there just last week. Had it been like that when her husband found her? Hot and stuffy and quiet in the house where they spent their life together.

"You okay?" Cliff asked.

Dan didn't answer. He stood in the middle of the vast station, watching the pigeon trapped by the glass, unable to fly to freedom in the sky.

"A rich American horse owner arriving by taxi?" Cliff asked. "You think The Bull's gonna buy that?"

"Depends on how we sell it," Dan said, watching mansions glide past outside the taxi's window. "I used to go door to door when I was a kid selling Fuller Brush. But I didn't approach people like I was some little jerk-off—I focused on all the great stuff I had for them. It's all in how you present yourself."

"I guess everyone's got their own style," Cliff muttered.

"All we have to do is find out if our horse is there," Dan said. "This opens the door. So believe it."

The cabbie slowed down and looked back through the glass, "Which house you reckon it is?"

"They said it would be the last on the left before the turnoff. This is it, my good man," Dan told the driver. Cliff waited for the cabbie to give him a look, something like, *Are you having me on?* But the cabbie didn't seem to notice. Maybe Dan was right. You had to sell it.

Problem was, Cliff always hated lying—it just wasn't in his nature. His approach would be to go straight at the guy: *Hey, you got my horse or what?* But they were strangers in this country, with no legal power. One false move, they could get their asses thrown in the slammer.

They slowed, passing a brick wall with hedges rising behind it. Appearing in the middle of this was a pair of solid wooden gates with a sign that read Graycroft Stables.

"I'll open it for you," Cliff said. He jumped out and pushed a button beside the gates. The doors swung open slowly, powerfully, like they were entering a bank vault. Maybe they were, Cliff thought, as he saw the house ahead of them. It was a stone manor house surrounded by sculpted hedges and gardens. An English wolfhound, the size of a pony, was relaxing in the sun. The beast jumped to his feet with a deep-throated *woof* and bounded toward him.

"I'd say this guy's won a few races," Cliff said, back in the cab as it rolled forward, tires crunching on the gravel drive.

"But remember what Adrian said, he's in a slump now. He's hungry. I mean, look at the overhead he's carrying."

Cliff remembered something else, what Cory had told him, her voice hot in his ear as she hissed, *He's got Glasgow money behind him.* What did that mean?

The cab's brakes screamed as it ground to a stop at the front door, a sound so inappropriate on this sunny Sunday spring morning.

"Here you are, my good man," Dan said, paying the driver from the wad they won at the races yesterday. The driver took the payment and tip, and quickly took off, circling the drive and disappearing through the gates.

A discrete sign said "Office" and pointed through a door in a brick wall to their left. From over the wall Cliff heard the cheerful sound of horses' hooves on pavement. He instinctively headed for the sound.

"Where are you going?" Dan asked. "We're big shots. We start at the top." He pointed toward the front door.

The wolfhound saw them coming and blocked their way barking loudly. Cliff walked past the dog, saying, "We get the message, loudmouth."

They climbed a set of stone steps to a massive front door with frosted panes of glass. Dan rang the bell. The wolfhound had followed them and was barking, his huge mouth even with Cliff's hip. He could feel his hot, slobbery breath through the material of his pants.

"That's enough!" Cliff yelled at the dog. "Now get back over there!"

The dog circled away, still barking.

The door opened. The woman standing in the doorway smiled with her mouth but her eyes were cold, as if they had committed a faux pas—like farting at high tea.

"You're the Americans who called?" she asked. "I'm Bonnie Turnbull."

"I'm Dan Van Berg and this is Cliff Dante."

"Yes, well, usually visitors go to the office straight-away." They followed her through a second doorway and then they were inside, at the base of a long staircase. "Peter's back at the stables now, I'll ring back there and have him come up."

The words were friendly enough, but Cliff felt everything was a big imposition with her.

"Wait in here," she said, indicating a room to the side. "Would you like some tea?"

Cliff was about to say no—he hated the stuff—but Dan jumped in.

"That would be lovely. Thank you."

After she left, Dan laughed, looked around the room and whispered, "Is this unbelievable or what? We're in the epicenter of British racing."

The walls were covered with racing photographs, shots of The Bull reaching up and shaking jockeys' hands, swarms of reporters pressing in. The mantelpiece held several trophies. But Cliff saw something more interesting than any of this—a board covered one wall listing all the horses Turnbull had in training. The board, with plastic letters stuck onto the felt, listed about sixty horses, the races they were scheduled for and the money they had won. Cliff wondered if it was legit, or just there for suckers like them to drool over.

A door banged shut somewhere and Cliff heard footsteps coming. The doorframe was filled by Peter Turnbull. The wolfhound trailed behind.

"Gentlemen!" Turnbull boomed extending a hand that Cliff

found impossible to grip. It was like a baseball with sausages sticking out. Up close, Cliff saw why they called him 'The Bull.' His bald head was set on massive shoulders which gave way to a thick trunk. He was like a testicle with legs.

"It's a pleasure to meet you," Dan was saying. "This is Cliff Dante, a trainer I've been working with for years."

"Oh oh! You're not plannin' on racing over here are you?" Turnbull asked, laughing.

"Got my hands full at home," Cliff said.

"Last thing I need is more bloody competition," Turnbull said and roared.

Bonnie entered the room carrying a tray. Cliff noticed she was probably twenty years younger. She was slim, attractive, with thick red hair and hard eyes.

"Lovely," Turnbull said, smacking his lips at the sight of tea and chocolates. "Bonnie, did you meet the Americans?"

"I did indeed, Peter," she answered without looking at him. "They came right to the front door. I thought Beowulf would eat them."

"He tried," Dan said. "Cliff talked him out of it."

"Whatcha train in the states then?" Turnbull said to Cliff. "Quarter horses?"

Quarter horses? Cliff thought. *He thinks I'm a fuckin' cowboy.*

"Thoroughbreds," Cliff answered. "I got about fifteen racing, maybe four or five babies we're gettin' ready to run."

"I been over there a few times," Turnbull said, slurping his tea. "Took a horse to your Kentucky Darby one year. Thing about going to the Colonies, you got to take your own water."

"Really? Why?" Dan asked, drawing him out.

226

But it was obvious to Cliff. Every trainer knew that stuff about traveling a horse with local water—and a lot of it was just horseshit to impress the owners.

"Keep 'em fit till race time—that's half the battle, aye Cliff?" Turnbull said. Then, looking up, he said sharply, "Where're you off to, Bonnie? Sit a while with us. Bonnie's as much a part of the team here as anyone. Got a good eye for horses and people, she does."

"Must get those things in the village," she said, lingering near the door.

Turnbull looked back at Dan, sensing he was the money man. "So you're friends of Cory Marsh then, aye? Oh, she's a live one."

"I represent a group of investors in the U.S.," Dan said. "We told Cory we wanted to buy some horses and create a presence here in the UK." Dan spoke slowly and confidently. They were getting close to it now and Cliff felt Turnbull sniffing out the money. At least he hoped that's what he was sniffing.

"Tell you what, seeing as how Bonnie's desertin' us, I'll take you 'round the yard. We'll finish our tea later. Maybe have something with a bit more kick to it."

They all rose and moved to the door. Cliff pointed to the board and said, "These all your horses?"

"All that's fit to race," Turnbull said. "Plus, I got a few going off to auction."

Cliff remained in the room, staring at the board, hearing Turnbull's voice fade down the hallway as he escorted Dan outside. Cliff was skimming the names of the horses. There were a few with no race winnings listed after their names. One was called "Marquis' Millions." *Marquis.* Why did that jump out at him?

The door boomed shut and the house fell silent. He'd been left behind. He turned and saw Bonnie leaning in the door frame watching him with a stare that seemed to peel his skin away.

"You're the one with the eye, aren't you?" she asked.

"What do you mean?"

"The quiet one is the one who's always watching." She paused. "Am I right?"

Her accent was beautiful, but the sound of it made him tense, his pulse accelerating. Why?

"I'm just a dumb horse trainer," Cliff said. "If I had any brains I'd be in another line of work."

"Oh, you're dumb all right," she said evaluating him. Then, without smiling, she began laughing, a deliberate, superior laugh that echoed through the big cold house.

He laughed with her for a second, but when her laugh didn't die, he turned toward the door she had indicated. His hand was on the knob when he turned back.

"Where're you from?" Cliff said.

"Why do you ask?"

"Your accent . . . ."

"Little village called Ayr. Know where that is?"

"No."

"Thirty miles south of Glasgow. There's a race course there."

Cliff suddenly understood why her accent pissed him off. Now he had to keep from showing it to a woman who seemed to see everything.

"You're from Scotland."

"Why do you say it like that?"

Cliff thought how long it would take to answer that question. Finally, he said, "I've always wanted to go there."

"Maybe this trip. Who knows?" She began laughing again.

"Yeah, who the hell knows?" he said, and stepped out the door.

"We thought we lost you," Turnbull shouted as Cliff came around the corner of a long row of stables.

From where Cliff stood, he could see stall doors open and horses eagerly reaching their heads out. There must be fifty horses here, Cliff estimated, and not just any horses—the top thoroughbreds in the world.

Turnbull was standing next to a bay colt with a coppery red coat, stroking its neck and talking to Dan. Around them, exercise riders, stable hands and grooms walked past, leading horses, pushing wheelbarrows or carrying long wooden rakes. Cliff felt he had died and gone to trainer heaven. Man, what he could do if he had this guy's money, this layout.

"I was telling Daniel here," Turnbull said as Cliff joined them, "I check each horse twice a day—morning and night. I go round to every door with a sweet. That way, they hear me coming, they come to the door, straightaway. Soon as I start my round, every head is out. If not, something could be wrong. I put my hand up under the blanket. Are they warm? Bit of colic coming? If so, I send 'em to the isolation stalls straight away."

"You have that here?" Cliff asked.

"I've got *everything* here. Like my transport vans—" he pointed at a large van parked nearby "—specially designed. Holds seven horses. Every weekend I'm loadin' it up to head to the races in England, or maybe Germany or France."

Turnbull saw someone coming. "Julie, meet a couple of your fellow countrymen."

A young woman with straight blond hair was pushing a wheelbarrow past them. She stopped and smiled.

"This is Mr. Van Berg and Mr. Dante. They're from the states. Where're you from, Julie?"

"Tennessee."

"Tenn-*ah*-see." Dan laughed, imitating her accent. "I could never tell."

Cliff pointed at the peat moss in the wheel barrow, "Got a horse with sore feet?"

Turnbull plunged his hand into the soft, dark material, lifting it out and crumbling it with his thick fingers. "A horse just came in with a bad case of thrush. Phosphorus kills the infection. Can't be too careful—no feet, no horse, you know." He laughed.

"Where're you from?" Julie asked them.

"San Francisco area," Dan said.

"*Really?*" Turnbull asked. "San Francisco? I didn't know that."

"Well, Pleasanton," Cliff quickly added. "That's where my ranch is."

Dan had caught Turnbull's reaction. "That's about 30 miles away—across the Bay. A whole different world there."

"I wouldn't know," Turnbull said softly. Turning to Julie he said. "Right then. Has Donny got the string ready to go?"

"They're in the yard now."

"Tell Stephen to meet me at the end of the gallop—in the old stables."

He turned back, saying, "Like to come along, see the horses work?"

"Sure," Dan said.

Cliff watched Julie pushing the wheelbarrow toward a brick building away from the others. The old wall had newer sections, as if the stable doors had been bricked in recently.

"Is that your isolation stables?" Cliff asked Turnbull.

"Huh? No. We don't keep horses in there—it's strictly for storage."

They followed Turnbull to a green Land Rover. Cliff hung back, noticing a trail of peat moss leading around the corner where Julie had disappeared with the wheel barrow.

"Here! Cliff! Jump in!" Turnbull shouted, holding the door open for him.

They all piled in and Turnbull fired up the Rover.

They drove into a courtyard and Cliff saw a dozen horses with riders walking in a circle. The lead rider saw Turnbull arrive and nodded to him. He turned his horse down a lane toward a barn at the rear of the property.

"We've got the use of the farmer's land across the way," Turnbull said. "Nice bit of land, that. We take the horses we're racing, canter them a mile down, walk them around a bit, then canter back."

He stabbed the horn. An old man appeared, a hammer and chisel in one hand. Turnbull opened the window and shouted, "Hey Jerry! Finger on the button! There's a good lad." Closing the window he said, "We have a flashing light installed down the road. Otherwise these bloody maniacs come around the corner at 100 kilometers an hour."

Turnbull drove behind the horses, crossing the road. Cliff saw the flashing signal. Several cars were stopped in each direction. Bumping forward, they climbed a rise into a broad meadow with a path meandering through it toward a huge tree in the distance. Behind the tree, partially hidden, was a stone shed.

The last horse in the string kept fighting the rider, rearing, turning, tossing its head.

"That's what we call an outlaw," Cliff said noticing the horse's coat was very short, not like the shaggy winter coats of the other horses.

"A right mean animal, that one," Turnbull agreed. "But we'll get him sorted out."

The riders gave their horses a slap and they jumped forward, rising off the ground and floating as they ran effortlessly. Cliff had seen this a million times, but it always excited him—it was like speed was always in the horses, all the rider had to do was release it.

Turnbull gave the Rover some gas and pulled alongside the horses, watching them work. Cliff saw Turnbull's sharp little eyes taking it all in, noting the way each animal moved, looking for injuries, for hitches, smiling satisfied as they finally reached the turnaround by the huge tree in the middle of the meadow. Turnbull waved to one of the riders and turned the Rover off down a second track. Ahead was the stone shed they had seen from a distance.

"Come along then," Turnbull said, stepping out. He disappeared into the shed.

"I guess that means we're supposed to follow him," Dan said opening his door.

Cliff watched the horses heading back toward the stables now, the last horse still fighting the rider. He turned back toward the stone shed in front of them, saw Dan at the doorway and wondered what the hell was going on. This didn't have the feel of a tour stop for potential owners.

Dan stooped to move through the low doorway. Cliff followed

and saw it was dark inside, a single shaft of light slanting through a hole in the roof. Straw was trampled flat underfoot and a dank, earthy smell hung in the air. His eyes adjusting, he saw Turnbull flanked by a tall man, the man they'd seen at the track yesterday. He wore a long black leather coat and gloves. A horse was tethered behind him, nervously tossing its head.

"Right then," Turnbull said, exposing his teeth menacingly. His cannonball head jutted forward on the stumpy neck. "Time for you lot to come straight. You must think I'm *stupid* or something."

"I'm not following you," Dan said evenly.

Cliff felt a tightening in his gut. But he also felt relief. He didn't have to lie anymore, didn't have to take shit off this windbag. Plus, he was pissed at how life was treating him. It might feel good to land a few punches—it'd even feel good to take a few. He was in that kind of a mood.

"Problem one," Turnbull said, sticking a rail-spike finger in the air. "Cory'd never send clients to me. The bitch wouldn't give me fuck-all. Problem two, horse racin' is a small world, lads. I heard about this bloke from San Francisco comin' round with his horses, trying to get someone to take him on. But word is, there's somethin' dodgy about him. Now I get you two comin' here from San Francisco. I'd have to be *stu-pid* not to see what's goin' on here."

"Our horse was stolen. The shipper told us our horse was brought here," Cliff said.

"*Your* horse?" Turnbull cocked his head, smiling. "You're after *one* horse?"

"A colt," Cliff said. "Dan, show him the papers."

Dan was reaching into his pocket for copies of the Relaunch ownership papers.

Turnbull said. "Get stuffed. I don't have your flippin' colt."

"How do you know?" Cliff asked. "Look at the papers."

Dan held out the papers but Turnbull ignored them. His massive chest began heaving. His face turned blotchy red. In the silence, the horse behind him nickered.

"I didn't take any stolen horses," Turnbull rasped. "Your pal from San Francisco come around, I told him to take his horses and bugger off."

"You're not gonna look at the papers?" Cliff asked. "That's how it is with you?"

"Damn right." Turnbull laughed. "Only question is, how well can you walk with my boot up your backside? Cause we're gonna kick your arses all the way back to the Colonies."

"Who? You and limp dick over there." Cliff pointed at the tall man.

The tall man came to life finally. "Ah, you're talkin' shit now." But when he said it came out *shite.* "I'll be puttin' the hammer ta the both of ya."

"Just look at our papers," Dan said, still holding out a copy of the Relaunch papers. "If you don't have the colt, we go away."

Turnbull spat on the papers.

"You Yanks make me sick," Turnbull said. "Comin' in to my stables, with an accusation like this, to a trainer like me."

"*A trainer like you.*" Cliff laughed. "You couldn't train a goat to eat shit."

"Fuck your papers, mate," Turnbull said to Cliff. He turned back to Dan. "And fuck you too."

Turnbull shoved the papers aside and smashed Dan in the jaw. Dan staggered back on his heels but didn't go down. The Bull charged. Dan let him come and hit him with a forearm smash, throwing him up and back. He staggered, trying to stay on his feet. Dan hit him again, *crack, crack,* turning with the punches. The Bull was rocked but didn't fall. He growled and charged again.

Cliff nailed the tall man in the gut, then brought his fist up as the guy's head came down. Right on the chin, nice and clean. Only trouble was, the guy was onto him, working in close. Cliff drove his fist into the man's nose. He staggered back, toward his waiting horse. A length of chain flashed out from under the coat. He smiled, his nose dripping blood, whirling the chain as he moved in on Cliff.

Beside Cliff, Dan took a big punch from Turnbull, backed up, then drove in hard with his fist. The Bull saw it coming and leaned into it, catching it on his thick-boned forehead. Dan grunted in pain, but came back with a left to Turnbull's jaw.

Cliff ducked as the chain *wooshed* toward him. He circled to one side, skirting the man, picked up an old rake handle lying in the straw. He jabbed the handle into the chain's arch, wrapping it around the handle, then yanking the man toward him. The man pulled the chain free and came at him again. He lashed Cliff with the chain, heavy steel biting into his ribs. The man saw Cliff weaken and started to move in. Cliff moved to the side, watching the horse in the background, seeing his ears were back, his rear legs dancing.

Cliff lunged at the man who instinctively jumped back. Near—too near—the waiting horse. A hoof shot out, caught the man in the side of the knee. He screamed in pain and crumpled in the straw.

Cliff turned to find Dan and The Bull wrestling in the straw, tumbling over each other, grunting. He waited for a clear shot, seeing the back of the Bull's head come around. He swung the rake handle, *smack*, into the bald pate, seeing the flesh on his crown open up and the blood flow. Dan shook him off and stood up.

Cliff looked down at the two men in the dirt, gasping in pain.

"You shoulda looked at our papers, like we asked you to," Cliff said. "Our horse is here. And we're gonna get him."

"Hey," Dan said, jabbing Turnbull with his foot. "Read this." He threw a copy of the clipping from the *Chronicle* down next to him, the one that showed the FBI was chasing Ravling. "This is who you're dealing with. Malcolm Ravling has fifteen felony counts for fraud against him. Give us our horse, or the FBI's gonna be after you next."

"Becca, I'm beginning to get the feeling that you're giving me the runaround," Linda said, setting her teacup back onto its saucer and firmly holding the young woman's eyes. Lately, those naive blue eyes held a knowing quality Linda found unsettling.

They had spent the afternoon strolling through Hyde Park, lounging in striped lawn chairs, listening to the speakers on their soapboxes, seeing the sights. But Linda was tired of playing girl-friend because, back in the room, or somewhere nearby, Ellis was restlessly awaiting her return.

Now they were having afternoon tea, another fun thing for girls to do in London, sitting over a platter of cookies and white bread sandwiches, washed down with milky tea. Linda decided to apply some pressure.

"Surely you can convince Malcolm to meet with us," Linda said. "Is he in your hotel room now?"

Becca shook her head. "He's not staying with me. I have to, like, wait for him to call me. It's so *boring*. As usual, he's totally crazed."

"Crazed?"

"Busy. Malcolm's always incredibly busy. That's why he's so successful."

"But what could he be doing? He has no clients here."

Becca frowned, a sign Linda took to mean that she was about to receive a half truth. "Something to do with his race horses."

This was news to Linda. "He brought his horses over here?"

"I'm not like positive *which* horses these are. But I think he's trying to sell them. When he does he'll make a ton of money."

Linda pictured Ellis hearing this news. He surely would be interested.

Becca continued: "I'm worried that if I like interrupt him or something? If I try to get him to meet with you guys? I'll upset his plan and then there'll be no money to pay you back with."

Time to raise the stakes, Linda thought. "Well, there's always that risk. But this accountant I'm working with, he used to work for the FBI. He knows the agents on the case." Linda was impressed with the way the lies sprang so quickly to her lips. "The FBI is real interested to know whether Malcolm will agree to a restitution schedule."

"The rest of what?" Becca wrinkled her forehead.

"Restitution schedule—it's a promise to pay back the money that he's taken. It could keep him out of prison. I'm due to call the FBI back tonight. I wish I had something more promising to relate."

Becca stared glumly into her tea. She scooped out a large helping of clotted cream and smeared it on top of a scone. She stuffed the combination into her mouth, some of the cream dotting her lips. "This stuff will go, like, straight to my thighs. *Zoom.*"

"Oh, right. I'd kill to have your figure, even for a day."

"You've got a good body for a—" Becca stopped herself.

"—for an old lady," Linda finished the sentence for her. She saw Becca scramble to undo the damage. Before Becca could speak she pressed her advantage, leaning on her guilt. "Are we going to work together or not? What am I going to tell the FBI?"

"I suppose that when Malcolm comes to pick me up tomorrow morning —"

Linda tried not to seem too excited. "He's going to come get you tomorrow? He told you that?"

"No, but I know he will."

"Why?"

"The banks will be open then."

"What's that have to do with it?"

"I wired money to myself over here. Some of Malcolm's money. He hasn't been able to get at it this weekend while the banks were closed. I know Malcolm is like stressed out about it. So I know he'll be here first thing in the morning."

As casually as she could Linda said, "Money? How much?"

"Oh, not much at all. About two hundred thousand. But he said he needs it for this plan of his. Anyway, I'm supposed to meet him downstairs, but I'm—" she giggled "—never ready to go on time, you know? He would come up to the room to get me—"

"—and we would be waiting there for him."

"Right. But—you're not going to, like, hurt him are you?"

"Hurt him? What do you mean?"

"Well, I know a lot of people are really pissed at Malcolm."

"Honey, we're just going to show him how he can stay out of jail. And of course I'll ask him to pay me the money he took from me."

"Okay," she said, brightening, "because, when you said you were working with another guy I pictured like, a detective or whatever."

"The guy I'm with is an accountant. You know what those guys are like, right?"

"Yeah," she giggled. "Pencil-necked geeks."

"Are you worried he'll hit Malcolm with his pocket calculator?"

Later, when Linda got back to her room, Ellis was lying on the bed, a drink and cigarette in one hand. His eyes were closed but Linda knew he wasn't asleep. She sat beside him and took his hand in hers, feeling the dusting of talcum powder on his fingers and realizing he must have been out shooting pool.

"I don't like the person you turned me into," Linda said.

He opened his eyes, waiting for her to elaborate.

Instead she said, "I have news."

He sat up, his back against the head of the bed, long legs stretched out. Linda wondered, *What was it with him?* Sometimes it seemed his sole ambition in life was to talk as little as possible. She decided to wait him out. Finally he said, "News? From the blonde?"

"Right." She stroked his long cool fingers. She pictured the cue sliding through his fingers, heard the crack of the balls, the satisfying *thunk* as they dropped in the pockets. She knew he was a beautiful pool player. But her man had lost his confidence.

"How'd you do?" she asked.

"They play a different game here. Billiards. Table's bigger, and there's only three balls."

She touched his lips with her finger. "I don't give a damn about the game, Ellis. I asked you how you did."

"Won a few bucks." He reached in his pocket and spilled a collection of bills out onto the bedspread. "Or whatever you call this stuff."

He won. Good, Linda thought. She leaned over and kissed him. "I'm not sure I like the person you turned me into."

"We're back to that now, are we?"

Why didn't he ask what she meant by that? She was losing control, she realized, saying things she regretted, wanting more from him than he would give. *Oh hell,* she thought, *I can't stop myself.* "Honey, I want to kiss you all the time. I want to hold you. I'm getting as soft as that bitch we're chasing."

He chuckled, a deep rumbling sound. "*You? Soft?*"

That hurt. But she wouldn't show it, she'd just lean in and kiss him, kiss him while he was here because he'd probably be going soon. She held his lips with hers and, after a time, he was there with her, his kisses returning her passion, and in between their exchanges she told him that tomorrow morning they would see some action. And, she added, there was much more money at stake than he realized.

Afterward, they lay breathing hard in a room which had become dark as the day outside faded. She asked him, "When all this is over, when you have the money you want, when I know the son of a bitch is dead, what's going to happen to us?"

He may have been thinking about billiards, picturing the

angles in his head, feeling the cue glide through his fingers, wondering if maybe he'd gotten his touch back, because, after a long silence, his only response was, "Us?"

Lying on their stomachs beside a stream, Cliff and Dan washed the blood off their faces like cowboys in a Western. Dan's hand hurt like a son-of-a-bitch and he had a purple welt on his jaw. Cliff's ribs were bruised and he had a few cuts on his face that stopped oozing after he splashed cold water on them. They inspected each other, decided it would have to do, and stood up.

It was nearly dark when they started walking again, crossing farmers' fields, moving along hedges between meadows. Approaching the village, they waited awhile, watching from a distance in case Turnbull had called the local police. The coast looked clear. They walked into town, sticking to the shadows, and retrieved their bags from the railroad station where they had left them that morning.

Cliff realized it was a battle between the pain in his ribs, where the guy clobbered him with the chain, and the gnawing hunger in his belly. His belly won out and a few minutes later, carrying their suitcases, they walked through the doors of a pub called The Bell. Silence greeted their entrance. Well, we're strangers in a local joint in a small town, Cliff thought, what do you expect?

They found empty stools at the bar. A young woman with a white apron approached them and set her hands palm-down on the counter. She took in their bruised faces but knew it was none of her business and waited silently, ready to take their orders.

"Plowman's sandwich," Dan said after scanning the list of specialties on a chalk board. He added, "and a pint a' Guinness." He was starting to sound like a local.

The barmaid nodded, filing his order in her memory. She looked at Cliff.

"I want one of those steak and kidney pie deals. A shot of your best Irish whiskey, and a Guinness. And bring a whiskey for my friend here too."

The barmaid nodded and disappeared through a pair of double doors. They saw her reappear almost immediately, and begin drawing their drinks. Groups of men stood around the bar talking softly, occasionally bursting into laughter. A darts game was being played in a nearby room and soccer highlights were on the television.

"What do you think?" Dan asked. "Time to get the fuck out of Dodge?"

The barmaid set their drinks in front of them. "Here you go, gentlemen."

When she moved out of earshot, Cliff sipped the whiskey and said, "We don't have our horse."

Dan nodded and said, "Fuckin' A right."

"We put some heat on The Bull. Now, how's he gonna react?"

"You're a trainer. What would you do if you had a hot horse, and two guys like us showed up?"

Cliff shrugged. "Ship the horse."

"But we don't even know for sure it's there."

"I do."

"How?"

Cliff was about to answer when the barmaid appeared and set

their dinners in front of them. She took up her position again, palms-down on the bar waiting to see if they wanted anything else. Cliff saw she had pretty, reddish-brown shoulder-length hair.

"Do you know a horse trainer near here named Peter Turnbull?" Cliff asked her.

She shot a look at the group of men down at the end of the bar. Cliff noticed one of the guys had a silver loop dangling from the top of his ear.

The barmaid lowered her voice and said, "I reckon everyone in towns knows Turnbull."

"You know anyone that works for him?" Cliff asked. The whiskey took some of the hurt from his ribs. Made him feel warm and good, shrinking his world down to just this room. Maybe the best thing to do would be stay here and get half-gassed.

"Aye. I used to work for him."

"Really," Dan said, surprised. "Reason we're asking all these questions is, we're visiting from America—I guess you knew that— and we're thinking about having Turnbull train our horses."

Cliff took over: "We were out at his stables today. Since you worked for Turnbull, you might know something I was wondering about."

She waited.

"The isolation area at the stables, brick building off to the side."

"I know it."

"Does he keep horses in there?"

"No," she said firmly.

"He doesn't?" *Well, shit,* Cliff thought. *Kinda shoots my theory.*

The barmaid stared at him, pulling back inside herself, listening without a smile or a reaction.

Dan set his sandwich down and said softly, "What's your name?"

"Eveleen."

"Eveleen. Like Eve?"

She nodded.

"That's a beautiful name. Is it Irish?"

"Aye."

"Eveleen, we've got this horse we really think is great. You probably know how that is. It's almost like our kid or something. And we don't want to send it to a trainer that might put on a big show, but not treat it right when the owner's not around. So, what's the deal? Is Turnbull good to his horses or not?"

She glanced at the group of men nearby. Then she said, "His horses win."

"What're you telling us?"

"If you're like most owners you don't give a *foock* about your horse. You just want it to win."

"We're not like that, Eveleen," Dan said. "We care about our horse. This guy here is a trainer in the States. He buys young horses and trains them to race. He knows horses so well it's like he knows what they're thinking."

"You're a pin hooker," she said to Cliff.

"Yeah, well, it's a sideline to my racing."

"So you're rich."

"If I was, I wouldn't pin hook. I'd just buy any horse with a fast time and a good pedigree. Guess you could say I'm at the low end of the spectrum."

The group of men behind them had finished their drinks and headed out the door. Eveleen watched them go, then breathed out.

"Why did you ask that about the isolation area?" she asked Cliff.

"It didn't look like a place I'd want any horse of mine."

"It isn't. But they don't keep 'em there for long."

For long? Cliff thought. *The hell's that mean?*

"Sometimes though, he gets a horse for just a day or two. I don't know why. He sticks 'em in there. Sadistic sod."

"So okay," Cliff said, understanding. "So he doesn't stable horses in there —permanently is what you're saying."

"Excuse me," she said.

One of the men who just left had reappeared, the one with the silver loop in his ear. He called her down to the end of the bar. She leaned across the bar to talk to him. They heard his low voice. She looked back at them. Dan leaned over to Cliff.

"What's all this about the isolation area?"

"Remember that groom, takin' in a load of peat moss?"

"Yeah."

"Relaunch had thrush—it's a hoof infection. It wasn't bad, but it coulda gotten a lot worse if it's not treated right. You don't get one horse in a hundred with that. When you do, peat moss is the only thing for it."

"Okay. So how're we going to find out if our horse is in there?"

Cliff tossed down the last of his whiskey. "Go out and take a look."

This time they wouldn't go through the front door like a couple of big shot horse owners. Dan and Cliff would silently approach Graycroft Stables the way they had left that afternoon, through the meadows and along the exercise trails.

They had spent the evening in the pub, drinking whiskey and building their courage. At 10 p.m. they began walking, the cold night air sobering them up and quieting them down. When they reached the edges of Turnbull's property, they waited in the woods near a stream and watched the big house as the lights went out one by one and the noises of the day died away.

Sometime later they heard a church bell in town ring midnight. It was a lonely sound, the sound of one day dying and another beginning. An hour later, when complete silence had fallen on the stables and even the sound of horses shuffling in their stalls had stopped, Cliff motioned to Dan and they moved forward.

It all seemed simple to Cliff now, and he felt almost relaxed. No more bullshit, no more lying or pretending. It was a simple matter of getting what belonged to him. A matter of winning.

A half moon had risen above the trees and patches of light fell through the leaves as they moved down the banks of the stream and across the stepping stones to the other side. A paddock appeared ahead, bordered by a white fence, the grass inside clumped and heavy. A wet-dirt smell rose from the ground, rich and fertile, and it reminded Cliff of spring, of being young, and wanting to do something new and dangerous. An owl hooted. In the distant town a dog barked. Somewhere a truck accelerated through the gears.

Ahead, the big house was a block of darkness. A lone bulb, high on a stable wall, sent shafts of light slanting along the cobblestone lane between the stable buildings that housed the best horses in all of Europe. Including one colt with crooked legs and a lot of promise.

They skirted the paddock to a corrugated tin shed containing a walker, for exercising horses. They moved around the edges of this contraption and saw the old brick stable building across the way, where Cliff thought the Relaunch colt was hidden.

The lane between the shed-rows was exposed and brightly lit. Cliff paused, his senses alive, listening, feeling, smelling. Last thing he needed was for that wolfhound to sound the alarm on him.

He leaned in close to Dan and whispered, "Wait here. If our horse's in there, I'll bring him out."

Dan gave Cliff thumbs up and patted him on the back.

Nothing to do except go for it, Cliff thought, moving steadily, confidently across the open space. His feet scraped the cobblestones, his breath caught in his throat. He felt exposed and vulnerable but—a moment later—his hands felt the cold bricks of the old stables and he felt along the wall for an entrance into the old building.

At the far end he found a large wooden door with wrought iron strap hinges. Pulling on the door, he expected the hinges to scream. But it opened quietly, easily—a good sign, he thought. The door must have been opened recently. He stepped inside and found himself wrapped in darkness. He stood still, listening for the heavy breathing of a horse. Silence. The only encouraging sign was the sweet smell of fresh straw.

He moved forward through the darkness, his arms groping ahead of him. Soon, he felt a wooden wall, his fingertips touching peeling paint. He moved to his left, where he imagined there would be another door leading deeper into the long building. He touched a half door, the kind that were common in stables. Working like a blind man, he lifted the latch and pushed his way into a new space.

He felt dank, cold air on his face. He stood still, listening, hoping.

Was that it? He held his breath and, in the darkness, he heard what he had come for—the long, heavy sigh of a horse breathing.

"Hey boy . . . . Hey guy . . . . Hey, Relaunch . . . " he kept his voice low, gentle, soothing.

Pause. Then, the snuffling murmur of a horse answering him. He heard hooves shuffling toward him then—big wet lips were pressing into the side of his neck. A huge tongue lashed his face. A big nose bumped him, begging for affection.

"I'm here now," he said, hugging him back, thinking *I'd be lonely too, locked up here in the cold and dark by myself.*

Cliff couldn't see the horse. But in his heart he knew it was his colt. He put his arm around the horse's neck, buried his face in the warm, coarse hair of his mane.

"I'm gonna take you home now, pal," he told him, feeling a wave of emotion rise up inside him, feeling reconnected with something that he loved that had been lost. Cliff breathed in the smell of his horse, ran his fingers over his coat, snarled and unwashed.

"They ain't takin' good care of you, are they? We're gonna change all that."

Grabbing a handful of the horse's mane, Cliff led him toward the door through which he had come. They stopped at the outer door and Cliff looked out to make sure the coast was clear.

Looking down the lane, he stopped.

The scene was bathed in a red light. There was the low murmur of a powerful engine. He left Relaunch inside the stable doorway and crept toward the end of the building. He looked around the corner. A transport van was idling, its parking lights throwing a red light on the scene. Its headlights silhouetted two figures standing beside the van talking. As he watched, a groom led a horse out of a stall and into the van.

One of the men was obviously Turnbull. Cliff could recognize that fire-plug body anywhere. The other man had his back to him, his head cocked toward Turnbull, talking— no, arguing. His hands chopped the air with angry gestures.

"What you fail to see," Turnbull was telling him, "is that there's just as much money for your horses up north, as there would be sellin' 'em at Tattersall's."

The other man refuted this, but his voice was blotted out by the idling van.

". . . A proper genius he is, best bloodstock agent in Scotland," Turnbull said. "Your sister knows 'im. Ask her."

Another horse was led onto the transport van. The other man watched, turning his face so Cliff could finally see him. In the red light, Cliff found himself looking at Malcolm Ravling.

Turnbull was getting hot now. "Look, you can sell 'em at Tattersall's if you want, but not under my name. I had two Yanks here today snoopin' around. Who else knew?"

"Let me handle them," Malcolm growled.

Another horse was led into view and stood quietly beside the van. There was something familiar about the animal. He was a youngster, probably a two-year-old, with a narrow face and an easy walk, kind of like the horse he'd just bought at the Barretts auction last week.

Wait a second! Cliff thought. That *is* the horse I bought at Barretts. Did that mean Malcolm controlled all the horses on the van? Cliff flashed back on his conversation with Zacco: "He approached me six months ago—he's approached half the guys out here." Maybe he owned a lot more horses than Cliff realized. He thought of all those business trips Malcolm had taken overseas. He must have been here in England buying horses with the money he took off his American clients.

Turnbull said, "All I'm saying is, a nice quiet little country auction will do you just as well."

The tall man who Cliff had fought in the deserted stable that afternoon appeared from behind the van. With satisfaction Cliff saw he was hobbling on crutches after getting kicked by that horse. He said something to Turnbull, who looked back in the direction where Cliff was hidden.

"Right then," Turnbull said. "Let's go get that colt. Not that the ugly brute will fetch much with those crooked legs."

Good time to cut and run, Cliff thought, and he was about to turn away when—*Holy Jesus!*—he saw two stable hands approaching the transport van shoving Dan in front of them.

"Look what we found hiding back by the shed," one of the stable hands said. A glint of light caught the silver loop in his ear— they'd seen him in the pub in the village.

"Where's your mate?" Turnbull growled at Dan.

"Back in town, telling the cops all about you."

"Bullshit!" He turned to the stable hands. "Look around! He's here somewhere." Then, to Malcolm he said, "Let's shove off then."

Dan stood there staring at Malcolm and breathing hard.

"I just thought of something," Dan said, looking from Malcolm to Turnbull. He laughed, "This is what I call the '*The Bull*' and '*The Shit.*' That makes this all bullshit!" He laughed and— *crack!*—decked Malcolm with a short hard punch to his jaw.

Two stable hands jumped in and held Dan as he tried to kick the fallen man. Malcolm rose slowly, massaging his jaw.

"Stephen, mind if I borrow one of these?" Malcolm took one of the aluminum crutches and swung it like an axe, chopping down on Dan's head. Dan turned aside and the crutch landed on his shoulder. Malcolm swung it again and again, chopping firewood, beating Dan to his knees, then to the ground. The sound of metal crashing down on Dan's skull made Cliff sick to his stomach.

"Enough!" Turnbull roared, stepping in. Malcolm backed off, breathing hard.

Cliff saw they were leading the Relaunch colt out of a stable and onto the transport van. The three men grabbed Dan's feet and dragged him toward the transport van. They swung Dan up into one of the stalls in the van. The body landed, *thump*, rocking the van. Inside, the horses shifted restlessly in their stalls.

Okay, what's my move here? Cliff's mind was racing. *Charge in and complete the suicide mission?* But what if Dan was only unconscious? Maybe he could get him out later—if only he knew where the van was headed.

A groom approached Malcolm carrying a pump shotgun.

"Thought you might want to do some hunting while you're up there."

"Never know," Malcolm laughed, taking the gun.

The men piled into the van. The engine revved, then dropped into gear. As the van began rolling forward, Cliff felt himself being separated from Dan. Instinctively, he began moving, running behind the stables, back toward the road, where he knew the van would stop at the caution light, to check for oncoming traffic. Then, the van would pull out, heading for—where? A destination

Cliff might never find. Cliff knew what he had to do. He got there before the van and waited for the right moment. The only question now was, would Dan still be alive to rescue?

Becca sat alone in her hotel room and counted backwards on her fingers. Was San Diego ten hours or nine hours behind London?

Of course, she knew that she was just putting off making what would be like the hardest call of her life. But she had to do it, and do it fast. Maybe there was some money left her parents could save. Maybe, if they heard the bad news from her, it wouldn't hit them so hard. Maybe she would keep sitting here and trying to figure out what time it was back home.

So okay. So here goes.

She picked up the receiver and dialed. As she waited, she imagined her dad outside on the patio sipping a beer, flipping burgers, telling mom how he birdied the last hole to win all the quarters from his golf buddies. When she visited them last week her dad looked so happy. Now she would be ruining all that.

Ring . . . ring . . . ring . . . .

"Hello?"

"Hi Dad, it's me!"

"Becky? How are you?" They still called her Becky. It made her feel like she was back in high school or something. And that had been like *sooo* long ago, almost six years ago.

"Well, isn't this a surprise? First Malcolm calls—now you."

Her stomach flip-flopped. "Malcolm called you? When?"

"Couple hours ago."

"What—what did he say?"

"Said he was in trouble of some sort. Said his partner pulled some shady deals, then ran out on him. That why you're calling?"

"Yeah. I wanted you to hear it from me, in case you read something in the paper. 'Cause I didn't want you to think that Malcolm had, like, cheated you."

"Cheated me?" he laughed. Then there was a pause, which meant he was taking a sip of beer. From the slur in his voice she knew this was probably his third.

"Becky, I'll tell you what I told Malcolm. I said, 'I trust you one hundred percent.' Everything he's done for us, all the funds and whatnot he's set up for us—it's just beyond belief." In the background Becca heard her mom's voice. Her dad said: "Your mom says he's a miracle-maker. We don't know how he's done it, but we're rolling in dough."

"Did Malcolm say anything else?"

"He said, because of this deal with his partner, some of our accounts might show empty. But he said he'd send us a check to cover it." She heard her mom again.

"Exactly," her father said. "It's terrible what some people will do for money. But, Becky, your mom and me want you to know, we're so proud of the way Malcolm has handled this. So relax and enjoy the rest of your trip to merry old England."

"I will, Dad."

"Mom says she loves you."

"Love you both. Bye Dad."

Becca hung up and felt like she was floating off her chair. Malcolm really was trying to fix things, like he said. So he probably would agree to meet with those Texas people in the morning. They would give him what he needed to show that Gordon was the one to blame for all this.

She looked out her fourth floor window down into the street. Not much traffic this time of night. Just a cab passing now and then. Looked like it was raining. Drops of water on her window caught the light. She yawned, sleepy now that she knew everything was going to be all right.

Brrrriiinnnnnng! The shrill ring of an English telephone.

"Hello?"

"Hello Rebecca." It was Malcolm. And it sounded like he was on a cellular phone, driving somewhere. At this hour? "Change of plans. A car will come 'round to get you. Be there within the hour, so you need to get cracking."

"Where am I going?"

"Driver will take you to Heathrow. A ticket's waiting for you at the British Midlands counter. First-class, of course."

"But where am I going?"

"You'll find out when you get your ticket. And I'll be waiting at the other end to pick you up."

"Malcolm, what's going on?"

"Do you trust me?"

Becca thought of how Malcolm had called her parents, how happy they sounded.

"I don't know."

"Do you want your parents to get their money back?"

"Of course, but—" *But I have control of enough money to take care of that,* she suddenly thought. "But this is all so, like, weird and everything."

"Give me three more days to sort things out," he said softly.

"Then your parents will get their money. And we'll be set for life. Can you trust me that long, lassie? What's three days for a lifetime?"

"Okay Malcolm."

"That's a girl. See you in the morning. Cheers."

She hung up and stared at the phone, as if it might reveal where Malcolm was and what he was really doing. He was up to something, that was obvious. But what? And would it get her parents' money back?

She started to pack, then realized she would have to tell Linda, the woman from Texas, that she had to bail. Well, actually, she didn't have to *tell* her anything. Just leave her a note at the desk. That would be the easiest thing to do. She wrote: "Things have changed. Sorry. I'll call you soon. Becca." She reread the note and felt it was too abrupt. So she added a little smiley face.

She sat there at the desk, looking out into the rainy night and realized she was going somewhere she had never been before. Someplace cold and frightening. Would Malcolm follow through on his promise? Or would he—what? What was she afraid of?

Well, it wouldn't hurt to protect her parents, she thought. And herself.

She picked up the pen and began writing a second note:

Dear Cliff:

I'm not sure what's going on with me and Malcolm. But it's really important that I try to get my parents' money back. So I'm writing to you, in case something happens to me. Here are a list of account numbers Malcolm has that might be hard for you to

255

find. If something happens to me, please get this
money and give some of it back to my mom and dad.
I also wanted to say, I'm sorry I never got that rid-
ing lesson from you. I think you're a really good guy.
Becca

When she finished writing out all the account numbers, she packed her suitcase and left the room. At the front desk a serious young man stood behind the counter ready to help. She gave him the note for Linda. Then she took out the letter to Cliff and told him to mail it if she didn't return—or call—in one week. He nodded solemnly. Then he transferred all this information to a sticky note and stuck it on the envelope.

He looked up at her and cleared his throat.

"Right then. I'm to post this in one week unless you come back and get it."

"Or I call you."

"Or you call me," he said, writing again on the sticky note. "Right then. All done."

"I can count on you?" she asked, smiling rather sadly.

"You can count on me," he said, matching her mood. "Right down the line."

A horn sounded in the street. She looked through the front windows and saw a waiting car and the driver standing beside the open back door.

"I will be back, of course," she said to the clerk. "This is just, you know, in case."

"Right-o."

"I will be back."

"Very good. See you then."

"See you then."

She pushed through the revolving door and the awful cold air hit her in the face.

Where the hell're we going? Cliff wondered, lying on the rear tailgate of Turnbull's transport van as it hauled ass down dark country roads.

Cliff had jumped onto the rear platform as the van stopped at the caution light outside Turnbull's stables. Now he was hanging on for dear life, diesel exhaust mixing with the cold wind swirling around him. How long could he hang on before his fingers froze and he fell off? He looked down at the road as it sped by—a dark blur with circles of red from the tail lights. If he hit the road at this speed he'd be hamburger.

They might stop any time and find me here, Cliff thought. Or they could keep going for hours. Better assume they were going to stop soon and get Dan the hell out of there.

If he's still alive.

Cliff stood on the tailgate and inspected the backside of the van. It was like a huge delivery truck, but with three doors across the back. Inside were the separate stalls for the horses. And there were three or four other stalls that were loaded from the sides. He thought he had seen them throw Dan into one of these back compartments. Experimenting, Cliff found he could stand on the wrought iron tailgate, which was about two feet wide, and cling to the door handles of the stalls as he moved around.

He tried turning the knob of one of the stall doors. It was locked. Of course it was locked. He looked at the latch. There was about a half-inch between the door jam and the paneling. Maybe he could force something in there—if he only had something to pry it with. A screwdriver? Crowbar? *What about a tire iron?*

The van slowed and stopped at a crossroads. Cliff was glad for a chance to warm up, to look around without being blown off the back of this thing. The light changed and they started off again, rolling through a sleeping village, then circling a roundabout. Cliff saw a sign: M-1 NORTH. The van took the ramp and pulled onto a divided highway.

Great—a new problem. Cars would be coming up from behind, their lights on the back of the van. They would see Cliff. *Look at that, luv—why there's a man on the back of that lorry up there!*

But at least for now they had the road to themselves. Time to explore some of the other doors in the back.

The first door held the ramps they used to unload the horses. They figured no one would want to steal the ramps so the door was unlocked. Cliff was encouraged. Opening other doors he found there were lots of things stored back here: sacks of feed, water, blankets—everything but a jack and tire iron.

Headlights gaining on them. *Shit!*

He pulled a blanket out of one of the compartments and wrapped himself in it. Then, lying face down on the platform he tried to position himself so he looked like— what?—a sack of grain maybe. Through a gap in the blanket he watched the lights grow brighter . . . brighter . . . then—darkness again as the car passed.

Cliff started to unwrap himself. More headlights. He lay back down. He could see the road two feet below him. One good bump and he'd fly off, land under the wheels of the car behind them. *Thump-thump!* Check-out time.

Here I am worrying if Dan's alive, he thought, *and I'm the one that's probably going to wind up as a greasy spot in the road.*

Cliff pictured his wife hearing about his death and maybe crying a little. Then she'd get a call from Veena about the insurance policy, hear how a check for a half million bucks was on the way. He saw Jamie drying her eyes, picking up the phone and calling Dan's wife: "Too bad about Cliff and Dan . . . . Ready to go shopping?"

Lying there on the back of the van, Cliff laughed. Then, forgetting where he was for a second, he had the impulse to describe this scene to Dan—he'd laugh his ass off.

If he was alive.

The car came right up on their bumper and stayed there. Did they see something? Cliff held his breath, watching the road rushing past below him.

Hey wait a second! Cliff found he was looking at a black metal box located below the rear bumper. *I bet that's where they keep the jack and the tire iron.*

The car following them pulled out and passed. Cliff reached down and opened the door of the box. He felt inside and his hand gripped a canvas pouch, metal clanking inside. Tools? *Haul it up and take a look.* But his hands were like frozen slabs of meat. What if he dropped the tools? He wrapped his hands in the blanket. Get some feeling back in them before he tried that again.

But it might be too late now, he realized, seeing that the van's turn signal was flashing. They were turning off the road, heading into a rest area. A yellow sign blazed above a parking lot of trucks and cars and a small restaurant, "Cafe, Open 24 Hours."

The van stopped. The engine died and Cliff heard doors opening, voices. He rolled off the tailgate and fell to the ground, ready to scramble away and hide. But his legs wouldn't cooperate—they were frozen stiff.

Voices. Coming closer.

He rolled under the back of the van.

Looking out from under the van he saw four pairs of feet. Boots . . . boots . . . that guy on crutches . . . and someone in dress shoes. Seconds later he heard a key in a lock and a compartment door opened above him.

"He's still out cold," a voice said. It wasn't Turnbull. Maybe that other guy from this afternoon. Stephen? Or the guy with the silver ring in his ear.

"Out? Or—is he done for?" Turnbull asked. "You thumped him good."

Cliff waited for the answer, holding his breath.

"Dunno. Doesn't really matter now, does it?"

"Don't reckon it does. Have to get rid of him one way or another."

"Dump him when we get there. That'd be easy enough."

"We're not going to Ayr straight away," said a new voice. Cliff was sure it was Malcolm. "You're forgettin'. You're lettin' me off in Glasgow. I'll meet you in Ayr once I've got the money."

Cliff watched as the feet turned away, toward the restaurant. He heard Turnbull saying, "Let's get a bite. But no beans for you, Stephen. You'll asphyxiate us, you will."

Their laughter died as they walked out of earshot.

Cliff rolled out from under the back of the van. He glanced toward the cafe and saw the four men standing inside, at the counter, ordering.

He knelt at the back of the van, opened the metal box and found that, yes, it held the jack and some tools. The tire iron had a lug wrench on one end and a narrow, tapered screwdriver blade on the other. He jammed the blade end into the door latch and pried. The metal door frame began bending, crushing the fiberglass paneling. If he could only bend the frame a little more, the latch might pop. He threw his weight against the bar. The siding began crumbling, snapping, buckling. The door frame was pulling away, the latch nearly free.

Come on, you son of a bitch, just another quarter inch . . . .

He tried levering the door frame farther down, biting into a new section of metal. Dammit, this thing was tough. Cliff searched in the tool bag and found a hammer. He slammed the tire iron into the frame, then pounded on it with the hammer.

It was starting to move. Another few good shots and—

The sound of a door slamming shut.

Cliff whirled and saw the guy on crutches was coming back into the parking lot. He gimped his way around the building and disappeared into a door marked WC. Cliff saw Malcolm and the others were still at the counter. They were being handed bags of food. *Shit.* They ordered something to go.

He slammed the hammer into the opening and pushed. The lock still held. Looking back in the tool bag he found a length of pipe. He slid this over the end of the tire iron, giving him a longer lever. He threw his body against the pry bar. The door frame seemed to give. He did it again . . . one . . . two . . . three times . . . then—

261

Crunch! The door popped open and the tire iron shot out of his hands, landing on the pavement with a ringing clatter. He looked back toward the cafe. Crutches came out of the john, drying his hands on his coat. The others were still inside, paying the cashier.

No time to waste. Cliff opened the compartment door. In the weak light he saw the still form of a man, face down in the straw. When he picked him up would his skin be cold? Cliff grabbed Dan's feet and dragged him out, easing him onto the ground. He tried to hoist him over his shoulder like a sack of grain but he was too heavy. He dragged Dan by the legs, around a truck parked next to the van.

Then it hit him. *He had left the door open!*

If they saw that, they'd know Dan was gone. And they'd search the parking lot for him.

Cliff left Dan on the ground, beside the truck's tires. He ran back to the rear of the van and shut the door, praying the mangled latch would hold. It did.

No time to skirt the truck. Cliff hit the ground and rolled under the truck's trailer, coming out on the other side where he had left Dan. He held his breath, listening. The men were talking in low tones. Doors opened and banged shut. The van started up. Headlights flashed on, sweeping the parking lot as the van started moving. It rolled down the ramp, then accelerated onto the highway and drove out of sight.

Cliff let out a long breath. Then he turned to Dan, almost afraid of what he would see. Dried blood covered his face and matted his hair. His faced was bruised and swollen. His breath rasped in his throat.

But he *was* breathing. He was alive.

Cliff shook him. "Dan." He waited, watching the bloodied face. "Hey Dan."

Dan coughed. Groaned.

"Dan. Wake up. We gotta get moving."

Dan frowned, his expression showed pain. He was returning to contact with his body. He began shivering.

"Freezing," Dan muttered. His lids opened. He looked around, focusing on Cliff.

"How ya feelin'?" Cliff asked, waves of relief sweeping over him.

"Shitty," Dan said, wincing. "How long was I out?"

"Couple hours."

Cliff could see Dan working it out, picking up the pieces and remembering what happened. "That son of a bitch hit me with his crutch," Dan said. Then: "Malcolm was there."

"I know. I saw him."

Dan squinted, trying to remember something. "I came to for a while and—I was in the van, huh? That's how we got here?" Cliff nodded. "Where's the van going?"

"Glasgow, I think. Then it's going on to a place called Ayr. Look, we gotta get you fixed up. Wanna try walking?"

"Walking . . . . What's that?"

Cliff helped Dan to his feet. Dan groaned and wobbled but he kept standing.

"There's a bathroom over there, get you washed up. Then we'll get some warm food, some coffee. You'll feel better."

Dan ran a hand through his hair, felt the clotted blood. "I must look like shit."

"Yeah, you do," Cliff said, laughing. "Sorry, man. I know it's not funny but—but—" It was great to have his friend back. But how the hell was he supposed to put that into words?

They were sitting by a fountain in a square in Glasgow, the pigeons swirling around them looking like ash flying off a trash fire. The morning seemed so dark, so gray. This whole city was *so weird,* Becca thought. Not like Rio, or Paris or the fun places Malcolm had taken her. But this was where Malcolm was raised. Maybe she would finally learn something about the man she married.

Across the street were the gigantic doors of Barclay Bank of England. It was almost 9 a.m., at which time the bank would open for business. She would walk through those doors, then return with the money she had wired to herself. In cash. "Why did it have to be in cash?" she asked Malcolm. "Cash travels easier," he told her, smiling the way he did when he wanted something from her.

Malcolm was holding her hand, staring down at her fingers, and she couldn't help noticing the circles under his eyes.

"Malcolm?"

"I'm right here, Rebecca." He looked up slowly, darkness in his tired eyes.

"Before I get the money I want to know what you are going do with it."

"We've gone over all that already. I'll write your mummy and daddy a check for forty thousand dollars—express it to them straight away."

"But the rest of the money. What's that for?"

He looked like he was about to blow up, but then he said, "I told you I have a plan. Once it goes through, we'll head back to California and begin damage control."

"I know all that," she said. "What I'm asking you is: What is this incredible plan of yours?"

"You wouldn't understand if I told you," he snarled.

"Oh yeah? Then maybe I'll just like go and get the money myself, make damn sure my parents get paid back. I could do that and you couldn't stop me."

He looked at her, startled. "I've kept you in the dark too much then, is that it?"

"Only like about *everything*."

He was arranging it in his head, replacing things, inventing new things. Then he began: "The money I made in America I used to buy racehorses over here. See, you can take a race horse anywhere and sell it. It's an international currency. That's the beauty of it."

"You used *all* that money to buy horses?"

"No. A lot of it I just spent. On you and me—travel, fun and games. But I still have seven thoroughbreds. They're in a stable in Ayrshire—30 miles south of here. They're going to go on the auction block tomorrow noon. After the sale, I'll probably have about two million pounds. You know how much that is?"

"Three, three and a half million dollars, depending on the exchange rate."

"Right you are," he nodded approvingly. "I've had a lot of expenses, transport, boarding, the bloodstock agent. This money you're going to get will be used to set up the auction."

"Without this money you can't sell the horses?"

"Exactly."

Church bells began ringing somewhere, sounding the hour. He stood up.

"Let's get that cash now, shall we?"

Her heart began beating faster as she said, "What if I told you I have something that would show you're innocent in this whole thing?"

That stopped him.

"What's that?"

"A woman from Texas came to the house last week. She says your company cheated her out of thirty-five thousand dollars. She said she hired an accountant to investigate the whole thing. But she says it was all Gordon's fault—he was blackmailing you. That's why you did it, took the money. Is that true?"

He thought it over carefully, then he nodded, regretfully. "Aye. True enough. But what can I do?"

Becca stood up and moved to him. She put her arms around his waist, feeling his warmth through the dark overcoat. Her knee worked between his legs.

"Malcolm, I want you to meet with this lady, give her her money back, and hear what this accountant knows."

His eyes narrowed as he said, "Tell me something. This woman—is she tall? Thin? Straight blond hair?"

"Yes. So you remember her?"

"Vividly."

"Would you meet with her and her accountant? For me, please?"

"Of course. But tell me, does she know where I am now?"

"*Yeah right. As if I knew where you were.*"

"Good point." He nodded thoughtfully. "You know, Becca, after you get the money, I thought you might like to see where I grew up. We could drive through the old neighborhood, then head down along the coast to Ayrshire for the auction. Lovely drive."

She threw her arms around him, kissed him, standing there in the square, the gray pigeons circling around them. She lay her head on his chest and said, "I'd love that." Then as they began walking toward the bank doors she said, "I think things are going to be very different between us from now on."

He said, "Becca, you're absolutely right."

The hard part was keeping Dan awake.

Cliff knew from talking to jockeys that when you took a good shot to your head, you shouldn't sleep much in the next 24 hours. He'd heard of jockeys who got thrown or kicked by a horse who went to sleep and just floated away into coma-land.

So now, here they were on a train, heading up to Scotland, and it looked like all Dan wanted to do was let his eyes slam shut and take the big dive. So Cliff had to keep waking him up every hour and walking him around the train, or sending him to the club car for coffee. As he moved down the aisle he saw people stare at the purple bruises decorating Dan's face, wondering what kind of a fight he had been in. If they only knew.

As the train thundered along, Cliff stared out the window at the changing landscape. At one point they were running alongside the ocean, the North Sea, he heard someone say. They had been in and out of the rain all morning, and now the sky pressed down like a low

PHILIP REED

ceiling, a ceiling that might fall in on them at any moment. The waves looked like scrap metal—cold and hard. And he couldn't help noticing that there always seemed to be the hulking stacks of nuclear power plants in the distance. Somehow it all matched his mood.

The morning passed in a blur. Dan was in and out of consciousness; the train was in and out of rainstorms. Cliff couldn't wait to get into a hotel somewhere, hose himself down good, and eat a decent meal.

At one point Cliff found himself standing in between the railroad cars, where the bags were stowed, leaning against the wall next to a window looking out. The window was partly open and the wind came in strong and felt good on his face. The train slowed and stopped on a high bridge over a river in the middle of a city somewhere. It was then that he realized he was thinking of how things might have turned out last night.

Dan came back from the club car carrying two coffees, handed one to Cliff.

"I want to tell you something," Cliff said.

The train bumped forward and Cliff spilled hot coffee on his hand. "Ah! Sonovabitch, that's hot!" He wiped his hand on his jeans and said, "That's not what I was going to say."

Dan smiled. But he still looked awful—one eye swollen, purple bruises. It hurt Cliff to see him like this. The train started rolling again, still on the long high bridge above rowhouses with wash hanging in the tiny back yards.

"One thing about you," Cliff said, "you're a good talker."

"A real bullshit artist," Dan grunted.

"No. When you got something to say, you get the job done.

Me, I'm here thinkin' this thing I need to get said, and it won't get arranged into words."

Dan sipped his coffee and looked out the window. They were in the country again and now they were running beside the river.

Cliff took a deep breath and said: "Last week, when all this shit went down, I was pretty hot about how you were the guy introduced me to Malcolm. I can tell you now, I had some bad thoughts about you, is what I'm saying."

"I deserved it."

"The point of what I'm saying here is this, you didn't have to come chasin' this horse with me. Lotta guys woulda just said, 'Hey, shine this—it ain't my problem.' But you put it on the line. I mean, when I saw them throw you in the back of the van, I thought you weren't gonna make it, I thought you were gonna die 'cause of me."

"Yeah, but if it wasn't for you, I'd probably be under Turnbull's compost pile right now, or dead in the woods somewhere. Maybe in that river down there." Dan's eyes were suddenly intense. His voice was thick when he said, "That's a powerful thing to say to another guy—I wouldn't be here now if it weren't for you. So I guess we can call it even, okay?"

"Okay," Cliff said, looking away and thinking how he hadn't come close to saying all the things he felt.

A moment later, Dan said, "Man, I sure wish we were back home, and this was all over. Thing is, we still don't have our horse."

"No," Cliff said. "But I'm pretty sure I know where it is. And I got a rough idea how to get it. Thing is, I can't do what it takes to pull it off."

"What's it take?" Dan asked, trying to follow what he was saying.

"It's gonna take someone who's a good talker. Someone who knows how to work the phones. Someone who can spin a good yarn." Cliff let that sink in.

"I get it now. All that stuff you just said about me being a good talker, that was just to butter me up for this."

Cliff was serious when he said, "It just came out that way. I meant what I said."

"I know you did, man. Now what's this about spinning a yarn?"

"We gotta stop Malcolm from selling those horses, right? It sounds like he's taking them to an auction up in Scotland. Well, how about this for an idea?"

Cliff sipped his coffee, took a deep breath and began talking. He wasn't even half done before Dan started smiling and nodding, saying, "Yeah, that'd work. That'd be beautiful."

In Edinburgh they changed trains for Glasgow. Cliff was standing in the train station, groggy and exhausted, when the train announcer's voice suddenly boomed over the speakers: "Trains to Stirling, Perth and Inverness, track three. Trains to Dundee and Aberdeen, track five. Trains to the West . . . ."

It was like someone had slapped Cliff across the face. He had entered a new country, a place where the people rolled their R's and talked like they were clearing their throats, where the men were tall, red-haired and ruddy-faced, tough-looking guys in black leather jackets with cigarettes hanging from their lips, their eyes hard and cold.

Feel like I fell through a hole in time, Cliff thought. This place isn't connected to anywhere I've ever been. I have no idea what to expect.

They boarded the train to Glasgow. Their car had cramped, stuffy compartments with narrow seats, the upholstery dirty and frayed. Cliff immediately fell into deep sleep, then woke suddenly, an unknown amount of time later. Dan sat across from him, so tired he didn't attempt conversation. Cliff looked out the window and saw they were pulling into a station in a small town. It was raining again, and as he watched, it beat down even harder and then turned to hail. Cliff watched the hailstones bounce on the platform. As the train pulled out, he could see the houses of the town, all identical, with drab gray siding, splotched by the driving rain and hail. Outside the town, a mountain had been torn in half, and the debris of mining left abandoned and rusting.

Where the hell's the quaint Scotland you always hear about? Cliff wondered.

And then he was asleep again, his exhausted brain throwing out jagged memories and violent images. He was arguing with someone . . . fighting . . . . Then someone shook him awake. He opened his eyes. Dan said, "You were dreaming, buddy. Better stay awake now, we're almost there."

Cliff looked out and saw the train was crawling along a submerged bed with graffiti-spattered, soot-blasted walls that sucked the light out of the air. Trash lay knee-deep in the weeds along the tracks.

They stood by the exit door and jumped off as soon as the train stopped. They took the first exit they found and emerged into a square with a fountain in the middle. As they stood there, getting their bearings, a sick lookin' young guy tried to sell them a magazine from a stack he was lugging around. His accent was so thick Cliff could hardly understand what he was saying, something about donations to help the needy of Glasgow. Cliff mumbled his refusal, turning away and thinking, *Guy looks like a junkie.*

They walked along the edge of the square, past the fountain, around which dirty pigeons wheeled and dove. Across the street was a huge, dark bank building. Bone tired, they stumbled downhill, hoping to find a place to sleep before they collapsed.

One block from the river they found a hotel that looked passable in the lobby, but which got worse with each step they climbed to their room. Inside, they found two lumpy double beds, mismatched furniture and a cracked linoleum floor. Cliff ran the water in the shower for ten minutes before he realized it was never going to warm up. He got in anyway, so frozen by the icy blast he could hardly breathe, just to bring an end to this nightmare episode. Shivering convulsively, he returned to the bedroom, his wet feet sticking to the linoleum. He peeled back the covers and found he wouldn't be the first person to sleep on these sheets. Or even the second.

As Cliff let go of consciousness, he heard Dan on the phone, saying, "What's your name?" Then, with great sincerity, Dan said, "That's a beautiful name. Well Mary McGwire, I've got one hell of a news story for you. It's about fraud, it's about an international chase, and it's about horse racing." Cliff was just about asleep when he heard Dan add, "Hell yes, there's a local angle—the guy who did all this is from Glasgow."

"Anything else then?" the managing editor asked, squaring a stack of papers in front of him. Several editors were already pushing back from the big meeting table in the offices of *Scotland Today* in Edinburgh.

"I just got a wee tip," Mary said in her innocent way. She was well known in the room and everyone was immediately attentive. "If I can only confirm it, it'll be a fantastic story."

"Let's have it then," the managing editor said, hands on the table, looking out from under eyebrows that were gathering like storm clouds.

"A lad from Glasgow has gotten himself in trouble over in the States."

"Ah, that won't do. What's he done?"

"He took money as investments, then stole it."

"How much money did he get from the Americans?" the managing editor asked, a smile lurking in his expression.

Mary referred to the fax in front of her, a news clipping from the *Chronicle*. "Only fourteen million dollars. I reckon that's about six million pounds."

A murmur of approval greeted this. Someone muttered, *Well done,* and others chuckled.

"A naughty boy, he was." The managing editor stood up, saying, "Three graphs on the back of Metro."

"That's what I thought," Mary said in her wicked little voice. "But it seems this lad has bought a great lot of racehorses—he aims to sell them at auction Thursday."

"Horses he bought with stolen American money?"

"Aye."

"Can you verify it?"

"That's the problem. I can verify the charges against—" She

273

referred to the fax again, "— Malcolm Ravling. But not the auction. Not yet anyway. The horse crowd is a dodgy bunch. I'm supposed to meet with a couple of Americans who are chasing him."

A woman named Anne spoke up. "What'd you say his name was?"

"Malcolm Ravling. Doesn't sound like a Scots name. But he was raised in Glasgow. Still got family there." Mary looked at the surprise on Anne's face. "What? Do you know him then?"

"I went to university with his sister, Bonnie."

"Can you put me in touch with her?"

"Aye, sure. But you know who she's married to, don't you?" She looked around the room, pleased to see she had everyone's attention. It was moments like this that reporters lived for. "Peter Turnbull, the trainer."

"Ah, I see," the managing editor said, sitting down as he realized what they were onto here. "I saw him take the roses at the Cheltenham Cup two years ago." He frowned, kneading his forehead like a slab of dough. "Go ahead then, meet with these Americans. But please, Mary, you must be discreet—reputations are at stake."

The meeting broke up, everyone heading for the door.

"Do you have that number for Turnbull?" Mary asked Anne as they were leaving.

"At my desk." Then, as they walked together, Anne added, "Best let me call first. You're attacking her brother and her husband—no telling how the bitch will react."

"No telling." Mary agreed. "So you weren't great friends with this Bonnie then?"

"Bonnie? I should say not. She's a real cunt, she is."

"Then you don't mind me puttin' the hammer to her husband."

"Be a pleasure to watch him squirm."

Becca realized she'd made a mistake. As soon she handed the cash to Malcolm, she felt him change. He seemed preoccupied, not listening to what she said. In London during the past few days, it was great, like it had been in the beginning. He was romantic, passionate, attentive. She thought he had changed. *Right.* He was just waiting to get the money. *Duh.*

Now they were driving through Glasgow in his rented Vauxhall, the cash in the trunk. He had already stopped like three or four times to call someone. When she asked him what he was doing, he totally ignored her. It was like he had slammed the door in her face.

It was time for her to take action on her own. Maybe the only thing he understood was pressure.

"Malcolm, you were going to show me where you were raised."

"That's where we're headed," he muttered, glancing at his watch.

They were tearing down a narrow street, past grim, four-story stone row houses. They rounded a corner and, dead ahead, was a cluster of modern high-rise buildings, eight of them, all identical and oddly dilapidated, as if they began to deteriorate as soon as they were built. Many windows were broken and those that weren't were boarded up. The siding was paneled with sections that might have once been colorful but were now a chalky gray, stained with black splotches from the rain that had begun falling again. Laundry hung on the balcony railings and men slouched in doorways, arms folded, cigarettes dangling from slack lips. A pack of children played soccer with a tin can.

The sight struck Malcolm silent. He eased the car to the curb in front of a pub. He killed the ignition and stared dully through the windshield at his boyhood home.

"The Gorbals," he said, nodding toward the buildings. "When I was a wean, they tore down our building. Put up those dirty great piles of *shite*. Elevators always broken. Power kept going out. No heat in the dead of winter. All of us huddled around the gas stove for warmth. On wash day, my mum had to drag the laundry to the steamers. Came back hackin' and coughin'. All I knew was I had to get the hell out—and go as far away as I could from this."

Becca forgot her resentment for a moment. She looked at Malcolm, seeing the anger in his eyes, hearing the bitterness in his voice, and saw what he had once been. But as quickly as he had revealed himself, he closed himself off again.

"Thought we'd pick up something to eat," he said, opening the car door. She followed him into the pub and he muttered, "Order what you like, I'm not hungry," and picked up a pay phone in the back.

She wasn't hungry either, so she sat on a stool waiting for him to finish his call. The pub was empty in the late afternoon. She moved close so she could catch phrases of his conversation. His voice was animated, as he said to someone, "It's taken you long enough. Now I've got to figure out how to deal with them before the auction. Yes, yes, I have it. Yes, in *cash*. Now give me the name of this place where they're meeting. St. Enoch Hotel. And the bitch's name? Mary McGwire. Phone number?"

He banged the receiver down and headed for the door. She followed and they climbed back in the car and began heading south along the ocean, Becca making several more attempts at conversation. *Boom*, he slammed the door shut on her each time. It was clear that, now that he controlled the money, she was worthless to him. She no longer had anything left to negotiate with.

Well, maybe that wasn't completely true, she thought, looking in her purse for the phone number written on a scrap of paper. Thinking about what she was going to do, she felt better. Taking action always made her feel stronger.

"Malcolm, I need to use the phone."

"What? Now?"

"Yes, now. I forgot it's Mom's birthday."

"Bloody hell. Can't it wait?"

"It'll just take a second. Please."

He had stopped the car at a red light and she glanced around frantically for a pay phone.

"There!" She said, opening the door and jumping out before he could stop her.

She found a pay phone in a quiet corner of the store. She quickly dialed a long string of numbers for her credit card, and then the telephone number she read off a small slip of paper.

The phone rang several times, and then a woman's voice answered.

"Linda? It's Becca. I have a time you could meet with Malcolm. No, he doesn't know you'll be there but— I found out where he's going to be and when." She listened, then said, "Yes, he'll have the money with him. It's in the trunk of his car."

"You saw where I was raised, you saw the Gorbals, so now

maybe this will make sense to you," Malcolm said to Becca as he pulled the car to the side of the country road. They had driven about thirty miles southwest of Glasgow on a road that followed the coast. The sun had come out and it was really quite a beautiful afternoon.

"Come on, then," Malcolm said, smiling and slipping on his prescription sunglasses. They followed a footpath that led to a cliff overlooking the ocean. "When I was a boy, every Saturday morning, I'd catch the bus and spend the entire day here. It was my escape."

"It's soooo pretty," Becca said, looking out at the ocean. The wind snatched at her colorful dress, whipping it around her bare legs.

"Is that Ireland over there?" she pointed at an island offshore, blue and hazy and magical in the afternoon light.

"No, no," he laughed. "Still Scotland. That's the Isle of Arran. Mainly fishermen there."

"So you'd come here for the view?"

"No. For the eggs."

"Eggs?" she wrinkled her nose. "To eat?"

"To collect. It was my hobby. See all the birds," he pointed at the gulls and terns soaring in the wind just off the cliffs. "I used to scramble around, take the eggs right out of their nests. It's a wonder I didn't get killed. Here, I'll show you."

He took her hand and led her along the path. It descended between two rock outcroppings so they were no longer visible from the road. Now, they could look right down on the waves crashing and foaming two hundred feet below.

"One day I came here," Malcolm said. "And I found an old

woman looking out at the view. She says to me, 'I've traveled all over the world. This is the most beautiful place I've ever seen. When I come here, and look out at that, I feel I've died and gone to heaven.'"

Becca shielded her eyes from the sunlight and gazed out at the view.

"I think she's right," she said softly, the wind moving in her hair.

Malcolm thought how Becca's voice sounded suddenly different—not like a silly girl, but like a mature woman, intelligent and strong. He felt close to her at this moment, even as conflicting emotions rose and fell inside him.

"Rebecca, I'm sorry."

"Sorry for what?"

"For the way things have turned out."

She was startled by the finality of this statement. She said, "It's not too late to do something about it."

"I'm afraid it is," he said, and gave her a good shove.

"*Malcolm!*" she screamed as she spun, clutching wildly, trying to get her balance, and in that instant, turned full face to him, her eyes were filled with betrayal. Her hands clawed at him, reaching for a hold, so he stepped out of range, and watched as she went over backward, still facing him, her face shrinking in his vision until she hit the rocks far below.

The colorful dress was easy to spot. But he knew the tide was coming in and she would be lifted up and set adrift. The waves were already touching her, bathing her in foam that swept in white and drained off pale red.

Malcolm watched until she began floating away from

shore. As the colorful dress became smaller and harder to see, he found that most of his sadness had also disappeared. She had no place in his new life. And this was the cleanest resolution to a relationship that was over. Regrettable. But true.

He walked slowly back to the car, thinking what a fine day it was, so bright and sunny. He walked along, patting his pockets, searching for his sunglasses.

Ellis was on a nice run—he'd made five billiards in a row—when Linda came steaming through the door with that look on her face.

Well, she'd just have to wait. He needed one more billiard to close out this guy and take the money. With Linda standing there, he knew his mind might drift into the future. Big mistake. *Bear down now*, he told himself, taking a moment to chalk the cue, line up the shot . . . .

The trick was to *feel* the shot before you made it. He saw the cue ball banking off the cushion, striking the first white ball, changing direction and continuing on to hit the other white ball and complete the billiard. If he made this shot the game was over. He saw the shot, felt it happening.

He bent over the table, his long fingers snaked out on the green felt. The cue moved like a deadbolt sliding home and —

Thump . . . click . . . click. The game was over.

"Well done," the guy muttered, pulling out his wallet. He was probably burning inside, but he handled it. Ellis had been there before. Today, his luck turned.

An hour later, they were settled in their seats on the British Midlands flight to Glasgow's Prestwick Airport. Ellis was still feeling the glow of victory. His touch was back. Or maybe it had been there all along, living somewhere in his mind or his body. It had been out of reach, that was all. A change of scenery, a change of games and it all came back to him again.

Ellis took Linda's hand, thinking, *Bodes well for the business at hand.* She looked down at their hands, fingers laced together. Then her eyes came up to meet his, and smiled. Now that they were moving toward a conclusion of all this, he felt easy with her again. Tonight they'd close out Ravling. Get the money, finally give Linda the satisfaction that justice had been done. Then, they'd pay cash at the airport and catch the first flight home.

And when they got back to Houston? There was an old boy there he needed to see. Same guy ran him out of town a few years ago when he started slipping. He imagined the guy standing by the table, big old gut hangin' out, watching as Ellis dominated, dropping shot after shot.

Payback's a bitch, Ellis thought. Speaking of which . . . .

"She gonna be there tonight?" Ellis asked.

"Who?"

"The blonde."

"Didn't say."

"Because, remember, she saw me that one time at the track. She sees me again, cat's out of the bag."

"You don't think she'll just think you're this accountant I've been telling her about?"

Ellis gave her a look. "Me? A damn bean counter?"

"You're right," she said. "I don't think that would fly. She was pretty upset when she called—I think Ravling is really going to be there this time. I think this is for real."

He leaned back in his seat and looked out the window. They were in and out of the clouds, moving along above green pastures and hills. In the distance the sun reflected gold off the ocean.

"What's our plan?" Linda asked, an edge to her voice.

"We get a car, we go to the hotel, we see what the lay of the land is. Then we'll figure out how to take him." His thoughts were shifting now, away from billiards to this new game. One thing was coming to the surface now. It would be dicey trying to take him without a gun. He'd have to work in close and that was always risky.

"In a situation like this," he added, "you don't want to try to get too cute. Once we know the money's there, then —"

She waited for him to say it.

"—I take him out. I'm to do it. Right?"

She nodded. "I want you to do it. I don't want any more mistakes."

He closed his eyes, thinking how good it would be to be heading home again. He hoped that, when they got back to Houston, it would be stinking hot. On the edge of sleep he felt the heat of the night, could hear the locusts calling in the trees in the darkness.

Then he realized something. They were still holding hands. He opened his eyes and found Linda gazing at him.

"What?"

"Nothing," she said. "Just looking at you."

Something was rising in his mind, something other than thoughts of billiards and money and danger.

"I've enjoyed this," he told her.

She seemed surprised. "Enjoyed what?"

"This," he paused, feeling exposed. "Being together."

He must have said something that fit with what she was thinking because she smiled and said, "So have I."

Her voice was easy on his ears. Low and sweet. Not like so many of the women he had known who were desirable at first, then grated on your nerves the next morning.

"When we get back to Houston, I hope we can keep in touch," Ellis said, settling back and closing his eyes.

"Me too, sugar. Me too."

"Fine-looking animals," bloodstock agent Donald Cameron said, closing the stall door at the Ayr Race Course after reviewing the last of Malcolm's horses. "Fine-looking animals. You must have done quite well for yourself in the States. Good to see a Glasgow lad making a success of himself—in the land of opportunity, no less."

"The market's been very good to me," Malcolm said softly, adopting the humble tone he felt suited him best.

Turnbull stood by, hands clasped behind him, attentive to both men. He cleared his throat, and spoke, "So, Donnie, you'll fit these in tomorrow, then?"

"Can do," Cameron said, his head of curly gray locks bent over the ownership papers, reviewing the information and muttering, "Uh huh . . . yes . . . very good . . . ." He stopped, "This colt . . . came over from the States, did he?"

"California, yes."

"There's something about him . . . . " he left the statement hanging there.

"He was an experiment," Malcolm said quickly. "Bought him on a lark, messing about with pin hooking."

"That's not what I meant," Cameron said, cocking one eyebrow. "Oh sure, he has no pedigree, and he's got bowed legs. But still, there's always the freak of nature you know, maybe a recessive gene reappearing after generations." He tucked the papers away. "Now, the payment for the auction fees. I'm afraid I must ask for cash so close to the auction. But I don't suppose that will be a problem for you."

Malcolm's hand slid into his inside coat pocket, and he withdrew an envelope. Cameron accepted it, slapping it thoughtfully into the palm of his hand.

"Your horses should fetch a handsome figure. This time tomorrow, it'll be me paying you," Cameron said, his raised eyebrow giving the statement a playful twist. "Aye?" He added, and began chuckling.

Turnbull and Malcolm joined in the laughter, which Cameron kept bubbling by saying, "Aye? Aye? Aye?"

Walking back to their cars, Turnbull spoke under his breath. "Crazy old sod. But he knows what he is doing, best bloodstock agent in Scotland. Buyers come here from all over Europe."

"All I can think of is how much more we would have gotten if we sold them at Tattersall's," Malcolm said.

Turnbull stopped in his tracks. Malcolm turned to find his face swollen with rage.

"You ungrateful shit!" Turnbull hissed. "My dick's on the chopping block, all you can talk about is how much *more* you could've made. If you weren't Bonnie's brother, I'd—"

Turnbull looked like he was ready to plant his fist in Malcolm's smiling face. But he just muttered, "You could lose your limbs talking like that." He opened his car door and was getting in when he thought of something else.

"You better hope this deal goes through," Turnbull said. "You better hope those Yanks don't cause any more trouble for you."

"After the beating I gave him, he probably turned tail and headed for home."

"Don't be so sure. The pry marks on the door were on the *outside*. Someone followed the van and got him out. Who was that?"

"Ah, you're worrying about nothing," Malcolm waved his concerns away. "Those two are done."

"You better hope so. You better hope there isn't a word about this in the newspaper. Because if there is, you're going to have to take your horses and bloody well go back to the Colonies."

Malcolm sat over a pint of lager in his local pub, down the street from the Gorbals, sorting through the events of the day. It was important to step back occasionally and look at things analytically. The way he saw it, he was very close to something wonderful, but also close to something terrible. Success and failure were out there, right next to each other, in the very near future.

You better hope those Yanks don't cause any more trouble. You better hope there isn't a word about this in the newspaper.

Turnbull was right. But maybe, Malcolm thought, maybe he should do something more active than just *hoping*. His sister told him the name of the hotel where Dante and Van Berg were staying. She said the reporter had called her and was planning to meet them there tonight to verify the charges against her husband. Malcolm thought that he really must prevent that meeting. Van Berg was a persuasive speaker. Dante played that salt-of-the-earth cowboy role convincingly.

But what to do?

Toward the bottom of his pint Malcolm found the answer. And the answer filled him with regret. How had it come to this? He wasn't sure. And he didn't like it. But he had come this far and he would close the deal. He'd take care of business. Then, with five million pounds at his disposal, he could bloody well choose what to do with the rest of his life. Switzerland? The Grand Caymans? Manhattan? Tough choice. Maybe he'd keep an address in each place. He pictured a business card with those three addresses on it. Now there was an image to motivate you, he thought, standing and moving toward the pay phone.

In his pocket he found the mobile phone number for the reporter from *Scotland Today* that Bonnie, his sister, had given him. Mary McGwire answered on the first ring. In the background, Malcolm heard a voice calling out what he knew to be train stops between Edinburgh and Glasgow. He had caught her just in time.

Malcolm politely told the reporter he was phoning for Mr. Van Berg, who was unavailable at this time. He regretted to inform her that Mr. Van Berg couldn't meet tonight as scheduled. He was having difficulty confirming the information he had given her earlier and would need to check some things before he could continue. Mr. Van Berg deeply regretted causing her any inconvenience.

Hanging up, Malcolm had the urge for another pint, or a wee

goldie. The whiskey would fortify me, he thought. But then he rejected the urge. There would be time for drinking later.

Outside, Malcolm popped the rental car's boot. The briefcase of money was lying there untouched. It was lighter now, after paying Cameron. Only about twenty thousand quid left. But that was enough to get the job done.

Beside the briefcase was the pump shotgun he had taken out of Turnbull's horse transport van. It was a thick, ugly gun. But effective. It reminded him of the American movies he used to watch with Becca in the big living room in their house in Marin County. The bad guys always came through the door with their shotguns blasting. He'd always wanted to do that. Maybe he had picked up a few bad habits in the states.

Then, turning the phrase over in his mind, he thought, *Tonight, I know two bad habits I'm going to drop.*

Sitting in the hotel bar, waiting for Dan to return, Cliff was listening to the people around him singing along with that Patsy Cline song, "Crazy."

Yeah, crazy, Cliff thought. *I'm crazy. Outta my mind, and out of money.* Even worse, he hadn't gotten his horse back. He flashed on the last time he'd been with the Relaunch colt—dirty and cold in the dark stall at Turnbull's stables. He hoped they were taking better care of him now in Ayr.

They had been waiting for the reporter to show up, the one Dan had called, when the hotel's desk clerk came into the bar and said the reporter had just phoned with a message. She had said she was down at the railroad station, several blocks away, because she had trouble finding the hotel. Dan, always the gentleman, had left to find the lady and escort her back here.

Cliff looked around the small bar, which was off the lobby of their shitty hotel. Two guys stood against the wall with pints in their fists, something tattooed in faded purple, a letter on each of their fingers. A drunk in a three-piece suit was perched on a stool at the bar, eyelids at half mast. Billy, the bartender had a face that seemed to be collapsing, eyes disappearing under a dark brow, his mouth a line of disappointment. His arms were like two-by-fours with tattoos on them.

"We Glaswegians are very big country-western fans," Billy told Cliff.

"There's only two kinds of music worth listening to," Cliff said. "Country and western."

Billy nodded. He took Cliff's empty pint glass off the bar, held it under the spout and began working the long tap handles, filling Cliff's glass with tepid lager. So that's how he gets arms like that, Cliff thought, watching him work.

"They'll play this song at my funeral," Billy said. "This, or 'Blue Skies,' by Willie Nelson. Ya know it?"

"Do I know it? Had a horse once called Blue Skies, named after that tune."

"There's a right proper name for a horse. How'd it run?"

"Like a dream," Cliff said. Then, remembering, he added, "Till it bucked its shins." He fell silent, picturing a race, years ago, as though it was happening now, right in front of him. He saw Blue Skies in the stretch, closing out the favorite with a late charge. Why was it that he could remember every race so vividly? But he couldn't pay his bills, or keep his family together. Racing's all I'm good at, he thought. I'm not much of a provider, or husband, or even a father. I'm just a track rat, chasing winners. And this chase is just about over. Here I am, 7,000 miles from home, alone in a bar with a glow on.

Like an ugly drunk picking a fight he couldn't win, Cliff turned on himself, wading in with a flurry of punishing images—losing his retirement money, losing his horse, getting ruled off by the racing commission. Yeah, he thought, I'm worth more to Jamie dead than alive. She could take all the insurance money and start over, find a new husband, some suit who worked in a bank, type of guy who worried about what kind of fertilizer to use on the lawn, what kind of minivan to buy.

The vision of his wife rose before Cliff. She stood there, Emily in her arms, holding Davie by the hand, shaking her head and saying, "I thought you'd be winning by now."

He wanted to tell her: "I would, but I never get the good horses."

"Right," she said, disgusted. "So you chase some freak all the way to Scotland? Does that make sense?"

"You don't understand," he told this vision of his wife (he always seemed to start sentences this way). "It's not about making sense—it's about winning."

And what would winning be in this case? Getting the Relaunch colt back? Getting his money back?

Killing the motherfucker?

Where did that come from? It was the impulse that started this journey, the impulse Dan replaced with more acceptable goals. But the urge was still there, in the deep wild part of his mind. And if he had the chance, one clear shot, he'd—

"Cliff Dante?" A thin, disheveled young man stood in the doorway of the bar holding a stack of magazines under his arm. The same kind of kid who panhandled them at the station that afternoon, selling some rag to benefit a drug rehab joint.

"Cliff Dante?"

"Yeah. Over here."

"Got a message from your mate. Dan? He wants you ta meet him 'round back."

"Where?"

"I'm ta bring you there."

Cliff pulled out his wallet to pay. The bartender frowned, pushing the money away, "Ah, no. Drink's on me. For luck," Billy said, as if a man with a face like that could bring luck to anyone.

"Thanks, man." Cliff turned to the messenger. But the kid was gone. He stepped into the lobby and saw the street door closing, saw a figure moving through the glass of the front window. He followed the vision out into the night.

Cold rain hit Cliff in the face. He zipped his windbreaker, shoved his hands deep into his pockets. He hurried, and caught up with the skinny kid.

"Is he far?"

"No. No. Right 'round the corner."

They were one block off the hotel, moving toward the river. It was dark down here, not many stores, just big black, stone warehouses pressing in on the narrow street. They passed a fish and chips shop and, for an instant, a hot, soggy cloud of fried-food smell swirled around him.

The messenger stopped, and pointed. "Your mate's just over there."

"Where?"

"Across the street, over the bridge."

The kid began to move away.

"Hey. Who sent you?"

The kid broke into a run and disappeared around the corner.

The rain was ice water on Cliff's face, trickling down through his hair, dripping off his nose and chin. He crossed the street and found the opening to a pedestrian bridge. He glanced around—no one was on the streets, no cars were passing.

Cliff turned toward the narrow bridge. It stretched across the black river and led to the other shore where a wall of five-story stone buildings rose, recently sandblasted but still smudged with patches of soot. He wiped the rain out of his eyes and squinted. A figure stood at the far end of the bridge.

Dan?

Cliff began walking, his footsteps ringing on the wrought iron bridge. Looking down, he saw the metal beneath his feet had rusted through in spots and he could see the rain-choked river below, moving fast. Eddies here and there snarled hungrily.

Why was Dan over there? It didn't feel right.

Cliff was close enough now to see the man ahead of him, wearing a dark overcoat, leaning on the bridge railing, staring into water below.

When Cliff approached, the man turned and faced him, smiling.

"You spent a lot of money chasing an ugly horse," Malcolm said, laughing. "The nag's only worth 17K."

Cliff nodded, trying to stay inside himself. Finally he started his own laughter.

"That's funny?" Malcolm said. "I call it bloody pathetic."

"I was just thinking how typical that is—you always know how much things cost, but you have no fuckin' idea what they're really worth."

Rain was drumming on the car roof, streaming down the windshield, making it hard for Linda to see out into the street as she watched the entrance of the St. Enoch Hotel, waiting for Malcolm Ravling to arrive. They had seen him circling the block, watching the front entrance, but he wouldn't go in. Why not? Becca said the meeting was set for 9 p.m. It was past that now. What was going on?

Ellis sat silently in the passenger seat. When cars passed she watched the lights move on his face. He looked like a hunter lying in wait.

"I want him out of the car," Ellis said at one point when Ravling's car pulled to the curb. "I ain't moving until he's out of the car."

But then Ravling's headlights flared and his car pulled out and drove off.

And so they settled in and kept waiting.

Some time later Linda said, "Ellis?"

"Yes ma'am."

"Don't worry about getting his money. The main thing is him. Make sure he doesn't get away this time."

"I can do both."

"But if you have to choose—"

"Linda, that's your brother's money—money he stole from honest folks."

"Does that change anything?"

"I think it does."

"I can give you money—I have enough for us both."

He smiled, as if to say, *You just don't get it.* "A chance for a score like this doesn't come along every day. You want him dead, you wanna recover Sonny's dough, and I get the rest of the money. It's beautiful."

Oh yes, so beautiful, she thought, realizing it was the play that interested him, making the right move, finessing the other guy. Like making a combination shot in pool, like holding a winning hand at cards, or sinking a long putt on the 18th green. This was a beautiful chance to take someone else's money and not call it stealing.

Headlights splintered water droplets on the windshield. Ravling's car again, the Vauxhall. It stopped and Ravling stepped out onto the street. Ellis's hand was on the door handle. Then the car's passenger door opened and a second man stepped out, a young street punk with a load of magazines under his arm. Ravling pulled out his wallet, handed the kid a bill, and pointed toward the hotel. He stepped back into the car and drove off.

They waited, feeling something was about to break. In the stillness Linda could hear Ellis breathing, faster now.

The hotel door opened and a man stepped out, following the kid with magazines.

"I know that guy," Ellis said at once. "He's that horse trainer pal of Ravling's." Then, putting it together, he added, "The meeting must've been moved. *Follow him.*"

Linda groped for the keys in the dark, unfamiliar rental car. She fired it up, found the stick shift and pulled out. Coming around the corner they saw the horse trainer start walking across a pedestrian bridge over the river.

"Stop here!" Ellis said.

Linda hit the brakes. Ellis stepped out and peered through the rain. He ducked back into the car.

"I think Ravling's on the bridge. We gotta get across the river."

"How?"

"There." He pointed at a bridge down river. "Go."

She revved the car and took off. The bridge was coming up now and—*shit!*—it was one-way.

"I can't."

"Screw it. Go!"

No traffic coming. She pulled onto the bridge. Halfway across, headlights came around the corner toward them. A huge truck flew past them on the right, horn blaring, lights flashing. They were across the river now, among dark stone buildings.

Ellis pointed down a side street, "Turn here. *Here!*"

She turned left down a narrow dark street, splashing through puddles.

"Left! Left!"

They swung around another corner and headed back toward the river again.

"Slow down now. Slow . . . ."

She saw they were approaching the street fronting the river. She could see the pedestrian bridge, two figures walking toward them. Ravling and the horse trainer.

"Park here. Cut the lights."

She pulled to the curb, turned off the ignition. The engine died. It was quiet. Just their breathing. And the rain on the roof. Ellis's hand was on the door handle, eyes watching. *He's ready,* she thought, seeing him slide the knife out of his boot. Damn blade was about a foot long.

She looked at his face in profile as he took in the scene. He nodded and said, "Okay. This is good . . . ."

He smiled, never taking his eyes off Ravling, and said, "*Beautiful.* Here goes."

She watched as Ellis opened the door and stepped out into the rain.

Dan had looked everywhere at the train station and couldn't find the reporter. Just those junkies trying to sell magazines. He found a pay phone and dialed the reporter's cellular phone number.

Mary McGwire came on the line. And she was pissed. "First you want to meet, then you don't. Now you want to meet again. I'm losing my patience with you."

"You called us at the hotel. You said you were at the train station."

"I certainly did not. Look, what kind of game are you playing? My deadline is midnight. If I miss that, I can't get anything in tomorrow's paper."

Dan was quiet, realizing he'd been set up.

"I'm going to have to call you back—a half-hour max. Then I'll give you everything. *Everything.* Okay?"

Dan hung up before she could answer. He began running back to the hotel.

"You didn't really think I'd run out on you, did you?" Malcolm asked, facing Cliff on the bridge. Malcolm's voice was soft and sad, his accent sounded thicker.

"Running out's one thing, takin' my horse—all my money—that's another," Cliff said.

"So you come all this way, *foock up* the auction at Tattersall's. I was going to use that money, come back to San Francisco and square everything with my clients."

A wave of anger swept over Cliff. "That's all bullshit, man. Bullshit and lies. That's all you ever gave me." He was breathing hard, hands flexing at his sides. He hated seeing Malcolm's face again, hated the smug, soft voice with the syrupy accent. He saw himself grabbing the lapels of that $500 overcoat, hurling the sack of shit into the polluted ditch down below.

Maybe Malcolm saw the rage in Cliff's face, because he backed away a step and said, "I'm here to give you your horse back. It means nothing to me."

He turned and began walking in the direction he had come. Cliff followed as Malcolm added, "Only thing I ask is that you let the auction go through."

"And forget the fact you bought those horses with stolen money?"

"Best thing for everyone is if I turn these horses back into cash. Then I'll pay back as much as I can."

A car was parked up ahead. Looked like no one was inside, Cliff thought, trying to guess what Malcolm was up to.

"Why'd you send Dan off on a wild goose chase?"

"I reckon this is between you and me. I've got the papers on your horse in the car. Tomorrow, after the auction, you can pick up your horse at the Ayr Race Course. And I've got some good-faith money for you, too."

I'll believe it when I see it, Cliff thought.

They began walking toward the car now, and Cliff realized the rain had tapered off. Their heels clicked on the pavement and echoed off nearby buildings. They were almost to the car when they heard movement, turned and saw a tall, thin white-haired man move out of the shadows and glide toward them. In a moment, he had reached them, opened his coat and, as he extended his arm, the long blade of a hunting knife flashed in the street light.

"You again," Cliff said to the man.

"Easy pal," the guy said in a lazy Texas drawl. He pointed at Cliff with his free hand. "Beat it. This doesn't concern you."

"If you're after his money, it damn well does," Cliff said. He stayed put, waiting for a chance to make his move.

The Texan stepped in close to Malcolm, stuck the knife up under his chin, lifting him up onto his tippy-toes. "Open the trunk, Mr. Butler, Mr. Ravling, Mr. Whoever-the-fuck-you-really-are."

"The trunk? Oh, you mean the boot. That's what we call it over here, *partner.* You want the trunk open, I need my keys," Malcolm said.

"Nice and slow," the guy said, aiming the point of the knife at Malcolm's throat. "Do everything nice and slow."

Malcolm reached into his pants pocket and drew out the keys, dangling them. "Okay, *pal?*" he asked, sneering, imitating the Texan's accent.

"Just open the trunk."

Malcolm fed the key into the lock. The trunk lid sprung open, bobbed on its hinges. Malcolm lifted the trunk lid and stood there, waiting.

"Reach in and take out the briefcase now. If it's not a briefcase I see coming out, this knife'll be in your gut. Got it?"

"But the briefcase has his papers in it, too," Malcolm said.

"What papers?"

"On my horse," Cliff said. "They're no good to you."

"Your horse? He stole your horse?" the Texan asked Cliff. "That's why you're here?"

"He got my money, too," Cliff said. "But I'll take my horse for starters."

The tall man turned a twisted smile on Malcolm. "In Texas, we hang horse thieves. String 'em up in public, so everyone gets the message—you don't steal another man's horse."

The Texan thought it over. "Okay. Here's the deal. You—" he said to Malcolm, "you lift the briefcase out of the trunk. You hold the briefcase out in front of you. You open the briefcase and show me there's money in it. Then you," he nodded at Cliff, "You reach in and get the papers for your horse. Then take off." To Malcolm again, "Then you, you're going to close the briefcase and hand it to me. You got all that?"

"I got it, *pal*," Malcolm said, smiling.

"Then do it."

Malcolm leaned over the trunk and reached in. As he straightened, Cliff saw the briefcase appear. Malcolm turned and held it toward the guy.

"Open it."

One latch popped open. Then the other. Malcolm raised the lid. It had packets of bills. Just bills. No papers.

"How much is in there?" the guy asked.

"About twenty thousand quid."

"What's that in dollars?"

"Thirty thousand bucks," Malcolm said. "Understand what I'm sayin', *pal?*"

"Got ya. Close it."

Malcolm snapped the lid shut.

"Give it to me."

The briefcase changed hands. The tall man smiled, satisfied. Then his voice turned cold again.

"Where're the papers for his horse?"

"In the boot, you know what I mean?" Malcolm said, mimicking the Texan. "I thought they were in the briefcase. But they're in my folder and my folder is in the boot, or should I say, the trunk."

Cliff listened to Malcolm smart-mouthing and wanted to say, *Watch him! Watch him!* But now that the Texan had the money, he just wanted to wrap up this deal and split.

"So, *pal,* whaddya say?" Malcolm said. "Get the folder out of the boot? Yes? No? Whaddya say?"

"Shut up and get it."

Malcolm bent over the trunk. He straightened and turned, the shotgun in his hands. The Texan lunged, driving the knife at Malcolm's chest but Malcolm twisted away and—

BOOM!

The blast caught the Texan square in his chest, blew out his heart and lungs. He dropped in the street.

Cliff dove for the shotgun, grabbed the barrel and knocked

Malcolm sprawling to the street. He rammed the muzzle into the bridge of Malcolm's nose. Terror flooded Malcolm's eyes. His feet back pedaled, sliding him along the pavement, his throat making whimpering noises like a dog.

Kill the motherfucker! a voice in Cliff's head screamed. *Go on! Kill him!* The need was rising in him, out of control. He racked the shotgun and aimed.

"Cliff!"

He looked toward the voice—Dan was running across the bridge.

Malcolm swatted the gun barrel away.

BOOM! The shotgun fired into the pavement.

Malcolm scrambled to his feet, crouching low behind the car. Cliff pumped and fired, blowing out the rear window. Malcolm jumped in and the car engine whined, the tires screamed as he pulled away.

Cliff turned to the fallen man. He knew it should have been him lying there dead. That was why Malcolm had split them up, lured him here with lies about returning the Relaunch colt. He lured him here to kill him. And this stranger died in his place.

A woman was running toward them from a side street. Faltering, gasping, she fell to her knees next to the still body, which lay there like a pile of laundry someone dropped in the rain. A stream of blood flowed out from under the crumpled form, steaming in the cold air, mixing with puddles, flowing down the sewer and into the black river.

"*No . . .*" she moaned, touching the dead man's face. "*Oh God no . . . no . . . .*"

Across the river, the wail of a police siren rose and fell, echoing off the stone buildings.Cliff picked up the briefcase. He offered it to the woman.

"Take this. It's yours."

She didn't answer.

"The money," Cliff said. "It's yours. Take it."

Her face slowly turned to him and Cliff saw she was broken.

"My man is dead, and you offer me money?" She turned back to the dead man as if she would never leave him.

The siren was louder now. They saw flashing lights on the traffic bridge, coming toward them.

"Come on!" Dan said. "Let's go!"

The briefcase in one hand, the shotgun in the other, Cliff ran for the pedestrian bridge. Looking back, he saw police cars converge from opposite directions, their headlights catching the woman and the fallen man like actors on a stage.

At the other end of the bridge, Cliff threw the shotgun over the railing and down into the cold black water.

A ringing broke the early morning stillness. A piercing light came from the north, shining down along the rails that curved into the station. The train appeared, rolled along beside the platform, then bumped to a stop.

A burly teen-ager stepped off the train and slung a bundle of newspapers toward a closed window under a sign reading, "Ayr Station News Agent, Confectionery, Tobacconist." The teen-ager stepped back aboard the train. It pulled out, gathered speed and disappeared to the south.

Cliff stepped into sight and crouched next to the bundled newspapers. He worked loose a single copy of the newspaper and left behind several coins for payment. He stood on the quiet platform overlooking the village, turning the pages with unsteady hands, the paper rustling in the quiet morning, looking for Mary McGwire's story. They had called her last night after the shooting by the river. She said her editors had been holding space, but by then it was after midnight so she didn't know if it would see print.

When Cliff reached the end of the newspaper without finding the story, he swore. He began leafing through the paper again, turning the pages faster and faster. At the end he swore again. He was about to throw the newspaper aside when something caught his eye. He began reading a short story on the back page:

WOMAN'S BODY FOUND

The unidentified body of a young woman was discovered floating in the ocean by fishermen off the Isle of Arran Wednesday afternoon.

The Ayrshire Coroner's office said it appeared the woman, clad in a coloured dress, had only been in the water for a short time.

The woman was described as being in her early 20s, about 5'6", with blond hair. She was carrying no identification but investigators said she held a pair of men's sunglasses in her hand. A tattoo of a butterfly was on her left hip.

Anyone with information about the identification of this woman is asked to call 171-748-3131.

Cliff read the article several times. Each time he kept seeing that tattoo, remembering the rainy night and his close encounter with Becca at her house, how she asked him to teach her to ride horses, how warm she was when he touched her, how sexy she was, how full of laughter she was. Sure, she was kinda dingy, but she was a good kid. And now the butterfly tattoo was on cold flesh in a morgue somewhere, like a broken promise. It made him sad and angry and full of feelings he couldn't control.

He slapped his pockets, searching for change. When he found none, he retrieved the coins he had left for the newspaper and fed them into a pay phone.

"Hello," he said when someone answered. "I'm calling about a story I read in the paper, about a woman's body found in the ocean. It says here to call this number if I had any information. Well, I do."

Cliff listened, then said, "No. I ain't gonna give you my name. But I can tell you —" He listened again and said, "Look, I'm just gonna talk, and you're either gonna listen or not. But I'm not giving you my name. Okay? Now, I know who this woman is that got killed. And I know who did it."

Cliff paused as an idea struck him. "I can even tell you where to pick this guy up. How's that? You interested?" He smiled. "I thought you would be."

Standing in a paddock on the back side of the Ayr Race Course, Cliff watched as the auctioneer mounted the steps to a wooden platform where Donald Cameron, the bloodstock agent, was waiting for him.

It was almost noon, and the auction for two-year-old thoroughbreds was about to begin. The first horse had been led in and was standing on the platform blinking at the crowd, switching his tail. The enclosure was crowded with perhaps three hundred people, mostly men, wearing dark overcoats or leather jackets to keep off the cold which swept in off the nearby ocean. Scanning the sales sheet, Cliff saw that Marquis' Millions and six other horses were listed under the name of P. Turnbull.

The bidding began, and Cliff listened as the auctioneer's voice droned over the crackling sound system: "I've got a bid of 12,000 guineas from the gentleman on my left. 12,000 guineas. Any bid?"

"What the hell's a guinea?" Dan asked, leaning close to Cliff.

"Over here horses're always sold in guineas. It's one pound and five percent. Five percent is commission for the auctioneers."

"Can I make it five—12,500 guineas. Any bid? Thank you, sir. 13,000 guineas is the bid. Thank you, sir. The bid is 13,500 guineas. Any bid? Can I make it fourteen on my left? Thank you sir. The bid is 14,000 guineas. Any bid?"

The auctioneer paused momentarily, glancing toward the nearby parking lot. A dark car pulled up and four men stepped out. Heads turned as Malcolm and his entourage arrived—the tall man on crutches, Peter Turnbull, and an assistant trainer. They shouldered their way through the crowd and stood near the front.

The auctioneer nodded to Turnbull and resumed his banter. "Yes, very well. The bid stands at 14,000 guineas from the gentleman the rear, 14,000 guineas. Can I make it five? 14,500 guineas in the rear. Any bid?"

Cliff tuned out the auctioneer and watched Malcolm. He saw Malcolm's eyes rove through the audience, maybe looking for him.

Then their eyes met. They stared at each other for a moment. Malcolm began to move toward him but Turnbull held him back with a hand on his arm. A satisfied smile spread across Malcolm's lips as if to say, "Nice try, but you couldn't stop me."

But then, the auctioneer broke off his banter again, looking out over the heads of the crowd to the parking lot. Two cars pulled up, one of them with a police shield on the side. Several uniformed officers and a detective emerged from the cars. They walked through the center of the crowd and up onto the auctioneer's platform. They spoke with Donald Cameron, who shook his head several times. Finally, the police officer in charge moved to the microphone.

"Ladies and gentlemen, we apologize for this intrusion. However, we are attempting to contact an individual by the name of Malcolm Ravling. Would Mr. Ravling please make himself known to us?"

The officer looked out into the sea of faces.

No one moved. Cliff waited, holding his breath.

"This is of the utmost importance," the detective said. "Now, would Mr. Malcolm Ravling make himself known to us immediately?"

Still no response. People turned to each other and exchanged words, glancing around.

The detective spoke with Cameron again, who shook his head firmly.

The detective raised the microphone again. "We must speak with a Mr. Malcolm Ravling. If he's here, would he please make himself known? That's Malcolm Marquis Ravling."

The cops are gonna leave, Cliff thought. *They're gonna walk out of here without getting him. 'Cause no one wants to finger him.*

"He's right there!" Cliff heard himself shout. He extended his arm, pointing at Malcolm. The crowd slowly parted until Cliff and Malcolm faced each other through a corridor of people.

The cops moved down off the platform and surrounded Malcolm. Cliff could see Malcolm reddening, acting indignant, then belligerent. One of the officers took his arm, guiding him away.

"Please be patient. The bidding will continue momentarily," the auctioneer told the crowd.

Cameron whispered something to the auctioneer, who told the crowd, "Before we proceed, Mr. Cameron wishes to inform you of the withdrawal of a number of horses for sale here today."

Cliff looked over to where Malcolm was being led to a police car. Malcolm stopped, listening to the auctioneer.

"Six horses in all will be withdrawn," the auctioneer said. "The six horses beginning with Marquis' Millions."

The detective at Malcolm's arm pushed him forward. And, as he began to walk again, Cliff saw Malcolm's head was bowed.

Who's winning now? Cliff thought, feeling good for the first time in a long while.

It was after dark when Cliff finally reached Mary McGwire on her mobile phone. She was in Glasgow writing a story on Malcolm's arrest for her newspaper. And she had bad news.

The police had tried to question Malcolm about Becca's death, but he kept his mouth shut, saying he would only talk with his lawyer present. His lawyer, it turned out, was notorious for defending criminals in Glasgow's organized crime world.

Mary said the word was that this lawyer had all the judges in his pocket.

"So what you're saying is, it doesn't look good for puttin' him away?" Cliff slumped against the wall of the phone booth outside their hotel near the Ayr racetrack.

"Putting him away?" Mary laughed. "Oh no. They'll not do that. In fact, he's out already."

"Shit," Cliff caught himself. "Sorry."

"That's okay," she answered brightly, "We often use that word when referring to the judicial system. But take heart, after my story runs, no one will have anything to do with Ravling and no one will buy his horses."

"But that's a long way from getting my horse back. I can't hold out much longer. I've got to get back home."

"What about that dodgy motherfucker, Turnbull?" she asked.

"The horses are with Cameron right now, at the track here. Me and Dan have been hammering him and Turnbull pretty good—neither of them will release the horse."

Mary laughed. "This is a right fine mess. They've got five million pounds worth of thoroughbred horses. But they can't sell them and they can't race them. They're *foocked*." She laughed sweetly. Then, when she heard nothing but heavy sighs from Cliff's end of the phone she added, "Ah, poor Mr. Dante. My advice to you is to sit tight. Wait for my article to run. See if it doesn't shake a few loose apples from the tree."

The next morning Cliff read Mary's article as he plowed

through a plate of eggs, ham, fried tomatoes and beans. The story said Malcolm Ravling was indicted for 14 counts of fraud in San Francisco, fled to the U.K. with a string of horses and attempted to sell them with the help of Peter Turnbull.

It also said Malcolm had been questioned in connection with his wife's death. But it didn't say the one thing Cliff wanted to see in print.

"It doesn't say he stole my horse," Cliff told Dan, who was bent over the paper reading, still shoveling food into his mouth.

"Not directly, but it's here."

"Where?"

"It's implied."

"*Implied*. Great. That'll help a lot," Cliff said, disgusted.

Dan was still reading. "I don't know . . . This article might do more than you think. Look at it this way: What's he going to do with those horses?"

"If he can get away with murder, he can sell stolen horses."

Dan slowly laid down the newspaper. He spread his hands out on the table, a salesman making a point: "He's got to make a move, right? So we've gotta be there when he does."

"What do we do?"

Dan pushed his plate away. "Let's go see if Turnbull's ready to make a deal."

"I'm telling you one thing right now, man. I'm not buying my own horse back."

Dan rolled his eyes. "Don't be an asshole, Cliff. Come on, let's go find Turnbull."

They walked to the race course and by the time they got there they were ready to kick ass. Problem was, it didn't look like Turnbull was around. They walked between the long shed rows, asking grooms, exercise riders, where they could find the trainer. Then, out of nowhere, a jockey approached them.

"You the Americans? Been askin' about Peter Turnbull?"

"That's us," Dan said, his head jutting forward. "Where is he?"

"I've got someone wants to talk to you."

The jockey led them to an open stall door at the end of a row of brick stables. They were both about to enter when the jockey blocked Dan's way.

"Sorry, sir. Only Mr. Dante's to be allowed in."

Cliff stepped into the darkness of the stall. Donald Cameron stood there in the straw, in the empty stall, slapping a rolled up newspaper into the palm of his hand. He moved behind Cliff and closed the door. When he turned, his face was red.

"Mr. Dante," his voice filled the stall. "I've lived my life by two simple rules. I've never knowingly stolen anything from anyone. And, if anyone steals from me, I will go to the end of the earth to recover what is rightfully mine."

Cameron paused, watching Cliff carefully, tapping the newspaper into his hand. He drew a deep breath. "I realize now I've been an unwitting participant in a terrible fraud. And I must repay you."

"Just give me my horse," Cliff said quickly. "That's all I want."

"I cannot do that."

"Why?"

"I cannot give you something that's not mine. As far as the law of this land goes, the horse belongs to Peter Turnbull."

Cliff opened his mouth to speak, but Cameron held up his hand.

"I'm going to give you something more valuable than just your horse—a way for you to solve your problem. And also to bring about some measure of justice."

Cliff waited, thinking, *Well, the guy's saying all the right words.*

"A local groom has told me that he's been hired to fly to the U.S. with six horses. He's to fly in storage with the horses, take care of them on the flight. This groom tells me that a certain individual—he won't say who—has offered him a large sum of money to use his passport and make the flight in his stead."

"They're gonna switch places? So this guy can get in the country without anyone knowing?"

"Actually," Cameron said, enjoying this, "it's more a matter of getting *out* of this country. You see, he's been a naughty boy."

"I'd say he's more like a fuckin' asshole."

"You could say that," Cameron allowed.

Cliff played it out in his mind, putting what Cameron told him with things he already knew. And other things he would do, once he got home and dropped a dime on a pair of guys who had no sense of humor.

As Cliff turned to leave, Cameron added, "You're the trainer that picked him, aren't you? For a pin hook?"

"Who?"

"That colt with the bowed legs."

"I did."

"He's no beauty. But I like the way he moves. I think you've got a runner there."

Cliff nodded, and walked out.

Now this was flying in style, Malcolm thought, stretching his legs out in front of him. No beautiful flight attendants, no gourmet food and champagne, but he had plenty of room and no one to bother him. It was just him, the two pilots, the horses and a whole lot of cargo. The long hours of silence had left him free to plan out his next couple of moves.

He had called a trainer before he left Prestwick Airport near Glasgow. The trainer would take the horses and trailer them down to the Lone Star Park in Grand Prairie, Texas. They had a two-year-old-in-training sale there next month. He didn't really think his earlier trouble would follow him to Texas. He knew for a fact there would be one less angry investor chasing him.

At first, when things fell apart in Glasgow, Malcolm thought the game was up. But then he saw his chances of making a killing in Texas were actually pretty good. And he really didn't want to go through another interrogation session with the Glasgow police concerning poor Rebecca. So it was time to head back to the States again.

The jet engines eased back. Malcolm breathed in the stuffy air, heavy with the odor of horses, and caught a faint whiff of smog. Malcolm glanced at his watch. They had been in the air for ten hours, so they must be getting ready to land at San Francisco International Airport. Oddly, the smell of smog was a pleasant one. It meant sunshine. The weeks of cold and rain had left Malcolm yearning for the California sun.

He strapped himself in for landing and a half-hour later the plane came to a stop at the docking area. The ramp at the rear of the plane cracked open, then slowly lowered revealing, *yes*, golden sunlight. It was so bright he slapped his pockets instinctively for his sunglasses. They weren't there, of course. They were in the evidence locker at Glasgow Police Investigations linking him to

Becca. Investigators had released him after he relinquished his passport and gave him strict orders not to leave the area. But now, after his departure, they would need a warrant for his arrest and extradition papers to get him back. For that they would need more than a pair of sunglasses to build a murder case.

The ramp opened and slanted down to the pavement. He squinted until his eyes got used to the light. Taking shape in front of him, at the bottom of the ramp, were two men. The trainer and his assistant?

The men walked toward him. Must be customs officers. He was ready for this. He reached inside his coat and pulled out the passport he had gotten from the groom at the Ayr Race Course. He extended it to the men as they advanced. They didn't even look at it.

"Malcolm Ravling, I'm Special Agent Demski, FBI. I have a warrant for your arrest for fourteen counts of fraud, seven counts of money laundering and twenty-five counts of making false statements."

When Demski was done reading him his rights, a second agent stepped forward, holding a pair of handcuffs. "Forty million bucks—you had a nice run. But the game's over. Place your hands on your head. And spread your legs."

"Who told you I was here?" Malcolm asked.

The agent smiled. "*As if . . . .*"

The other agent said, "Let me put it this way: you fucked with the wrong guy."

PART SIX

THE WINNER'S CIRCLE

"LOOK AT HIM, he's glad to be home," Emerson told Cliff as they watched the Relaunch colt run the boundary of the field at the ranch, tossing his head, smelling the familiar air, the eucalyptus trees nearby, the ocean in the distance and the dry summer coming on.

Cliff leaned on the railing and watched the colt closely. He'd grown a lot, like a teen-ager who left an awkward phase behind and matured into a man. Gone was the feeling of the red-headed kid with freckles. In fact, the Relaunch colt had changed so much he almost looked like a different horse.

The colt was running toward them when Cliff saw Emerson looking closely at the way he was moving.

"His legs—" Emerson said turning to Cliff. "They're straight."

"He grew up," Cliff shrugged. "He matured. It can happen."

"Yeah, but not that much. You sure you got the right horse? Maybe they got switched somehow."

They both laughed a little, thinking how funny that would be.

"Well," Cliff said, "I was thinking about ordering a blood test."

"Then you'd be sure."

"Yeah, but I ain't gonna do it."

Emerson nodded toward the romping colt and asked, "Gonna race him?"

"You mean, if I ever start racing again," Cliff said bitterly. "Frickin' stewards still got me ruled off."

"Why?"

"Shithead's name is still on some of our horses. They have to hold an auction to sell off Malcolm's share, make a public announcement—the whole nine yards. You know how them stewards are."

Cliff had to stop talking for a second to catch his breath. Whenever he thought about Malcolm his pulse shot up, he breathed hard. He often flashed on that night in Glasgow, looking at Malcolm's face over the sights of the shotgun. Sometimes, he played out the scene in his mind with a different ending. He pictured Malcolm's head a pulp of blood and tissue on the streets of Glasgow, his body next to the Texan's. And he thought, *Yeah, that's the way it should have been.*

"Naw, I'm not gonna race Relaunch," Cliff said, returning to the earlier question. "Got him as a pin hook—gonna sell him as a pin hook. Besides, all the publicity on him might bring a good price. You know how people like something to talk about."

Emerson nodded.

"Thought I'd give him a name that lets people know what he went through."

"Such as?"

Cliff smiled. "I was thinking 'Marquis de Fraud' might suit him."

Emerson was a master of the slow take. He turned it over his head, then said, "I like it." A slow laugh built in his chest, turning into a wheezing cough. "I like it a lot."

They watched the horse in silence. Sometime later Emerson noticed Cliff was extending an envelope to him.

"What's this?"

"The money Malcolm took off you." Cliff added, "I'm givin' it to you under one condition. When you get that ranch, you gotta promise to send me your best horses."

Emerson took the envelope, leafed through the bills and saw it was all there. He looked at Cliff. "You get your money back?"

"Interpol is tracking Malcolm's accounts in Europe."

Emerson thumped the envelope, feeling the weight of the bills. "How'd they find his money?"

Cliff hesitated. So Emerson took a guess. "Someone sold him out. Right? I bet it was that Gordon, his assistant."

"Naw. It wasn't him. They pulled that guy out of a lake up north. Looks like he ran off the road—in Malcolm's BMW. Cops're tryin' to connect it to Malcolm too. But so far, nothin'."

"So I'm curious. Who sold out the Slimy Limey?"

Cliff smiled sadly, thinking of the letter he received from Becca when he got home. It was tough, knowing she was already dead by that time. The words in her simple note were like a voice from beyond the grave. And it meant that his anger just wasn't going to go away. Malcolm had hurt too many people not to pay for it.

Cliff turned away, saying, "Look, I gotta take off. I'm goin' into the city—they're sentencing him today."

"Who? Malcolm?"

"Yeah, I been looking forward to that for a long time."

Walking up to the house, Cliff decided he should change into something decent, a shirt and tie maybe. The prosecutor was trying to get him to make a statement, tell how Malcolm cleaned him out. It struck Cliff as kind of a crybaby thing to do. He preferred a more direct response, he thought, opening his safe and taking out the big nickel-plated Colt .45 his grandfather had given him along with the deed to his ranch. His grandfather, like all ranchers, knew you had to be ready to defend what was yours. Including your reputation.

It was a strange feeling, not being able to stop himself from doing this. It seemed someone else was moving his hands, sliding fat bullets into the waiting chambers.

Dan was flipping through his calendar when he saw a note he had made several weeks ago. He grabbed his phone and pressed his speed dialer. As he waited for an answer, he listened to Veena in the other room, setting up a meeting with Trans-Pacific, a new company to take the place of Fidelity West. Once Malcolm pleaded guilty to fraud, the cease-and-desist order was automatically dropped against Dan's company. Things were slow at first, but they were picking up again now.

"Hello?"

"Cliff? It's Dan. How ya been, man? You racing again?"

"Not yet. Frickin' lawyers are jackin' me around."

Dan heard bitterness and anger in Cliff's voice.

"Hey, it's almost lunch. Let's get some Mexican food, have a couple of beers."

"Can't do it. I'm on my way downtown. Going to the courthouse."

"What's up?"

Dan could hear Cliff's breathing over the phone.

"Gonna see the motherfucker get sentenced."

"That'll be good. After the sentencing, you can put all this behind you."

Cliff said nothing, but Dan could hear him breathing.

"You taking the Relaunch colt to the Barrett's auction?" Dan asked.

"That's the plan."

"Thought I'd go with you. I want to be there when he sells for big bucks."

Cliff was silent.

"Big casino, baby!" Dan said, hoping to get Cliff laughing. Nothing. "Hey Cliff, call me after the sentencing, will ya?"

"Sure thing."

Dan hung up and sat there looking at the phone. See the *motherfucker* get sentenced. He hadn't heard Cliff use that word for a while. A terrible thought occurred to him—but then he pushed it aside. No, he thought, Cliff wouldn't do that.

Things are gettin' out of hand, Cliff thought, sitting on a hard bench in the federal courtroom in San Francisco, surrounded by a couple dozen other "clients" whom Malcolm had ripped off. *If this judge doesn't watch out, they're gonna lynch him right here,* Cliff thought. The rage was raw and ugly in this sterile room, filled with all the trappings of justice—the U.S. flag, the lady holding the scales—but none of the real stuff.

"If these outbursts continue, I'll clear the courtroom," the judge said. She was a middle-aged gal with a bad dye job on her short black hair. She kept banging her gavel down and yelling at the crowd. But the people didn't give a damn—Malcolm was right there in front of them (trying to look pathetic and sorry in that orange prison jumpsuit) and they wanted a piece of him before he was sent to Club Fed.

The judge turned back to listen to Malcolm's attorney.

"As I was saying, my client had no idea an FBI investigation was in motion. He went to England on business and—"

"He's lying!" a woman yelled, standing up.

"Silence!" the judge said. "I've warned you that these outbursts—"

"I can't stand his lies anymore!" the woman screamed.

The judge motioned to a bailiff and he wrestled her back into her seat.

"So, your honor," the defense attorney continued, "I submit that if the victims in this case are interested in any form of restitution, my client should be a candidate for E.C. You could put an electronic bracelet on him and release him so he would have the opportunity to put his affairs in order, to see what is left and make that money available to those who deserve it most."

"Yeah! Where's our money?" a man shouted.

Cliff saw Malcolm glance at the crowd. Something caught Malcolm's eye and his face reddened. Cliff followed his gaze and saw someone slip through the courtroom door and take a seat in the rear.

The judge waited for the crowd to quiet down, then turned to Malcolm and said, "Does the defendant wish to make a statement?"

Malcolm rose slowly, his head bowed, voice broken. "I wish there was something I could say that was meaningful to my victims." He paused as people leaned forward, trying to catch his words. "I can only say that I am deeply sorry for the suffering I've caused. And I do hope that the people who trusted me will find it in their hearts to forgive me."

"We don't!" a woman blurted out.

"You're scum!" someone else shouted.

"Where's our money?"

"Quiet! Quiet please," the judge said, banging her gavel several more times.

Then, as if she wanted to get this over with, she said, "The court has heard the testimony. The court acknowledges the suffering of the victims. The evidence before it is compelling and the case is complicated. Therefore, the maximum penalty for fraud will be served in a federal prison. But first, the defendant is instructed to use every recourse possible to prepare a list of assets which can be provided for restitution. Because the risk of flight is real, the defendant will be released under the conditions of Electronic Confinement. He will wear an electronic bracelet and will not be allowed to leave the state without permission. He will report to the corrections facility at Oakland in one week to begin serving his sentence."

The judge stood up and, without looking back, disappeared through a door and was gone. The crowd began pushing forward. Three bailiffs blocked their way as Malcolm was led out through a different door.

Cliff stood up and turned, thinking, *Better get movin'.* He saw the courtroom door open and a woman slip out. Around him, the crowd muttered angrily.

"You're that horse trainer, aren't you?"

A tubby man with a round, smiling face stood in Cliff's way, holding a slim notepad. Cliff tried to move past him, toward the door. The man walked next to him.

"Todd Pollack, *Chronicle.* What do you think of the sentence—Mr. Dante, is it?"

"I think it stinks."

"But he got the maximum sentence."

"Big deal. He ripped me off on the horses, destroyed my livelihood and stole my life savings. Now he'll be a good little prisoner for three to five, then go back to England and have a nice little nest egg waiting for him. You think that's justice?"

The guy was writing as fast as he could, so Cliff took the opportunity to duck out the door. Walking down the long marble hallway, he thought about what he had said to the reporter. Actually, the worst part of all this was that Malcolm probably thought he had *won*—he probably thought he had beaten Cliff, not to mention Becca and the tall man he had dropped in the back streets of Glasgow. When Cliff thought of this, he got a choking feeling as the rage boiled up inside him too fast to contain.

Passing back out through the metal detectors, Cliff ran to his car. Inside, he unlocked the glove compartment and took out the Colt .45, getting that feeling again, that feeling that someone else was doing this, someone who had a sense of justice that wouldn't be denied.

It was over now, Malcolm thought, calmly watching the corrections officer secure the electronic device on his ankle. He was back in his own clothes, and he was about to be released. The shouting was over, the angry red faces of his clients were only an unpleasant memory. It was over and he knew now the price he would pay—eight years in federal prison (actually, his lawyer predicted he'd serve only five). That meant he'd be out when he was about 37 years old. Not bad. By then the investments he had made in Europe, under a variety of names, would have grown and he'd be back in the game.

So, there you have it. Five years in prison for the ten years he'd spent traveling the world—top cabin all the way. Not bad, considering the fun he'd had. Not many people could say they'd done the things he'd done, owned the finest horses, slept with the most beautiful women, tasted the best wines. The luxury, the *excess*. What a sense of power that had given him.

"There you go," the officer said to Malcolm, completing his work on the electronic monitoring device, the small box on a leather strap. "Now, wherever you go, Big Brother is watching you."

Then, to Malcolm's lawyer, the officer said, "You know the drill. He can't leave the county without permission. If he leaves the state he's subject to automatic arrest with additional charges. In one week he is to report to the federal prison in Oakland for . . . ."

Malcolm tuned out the rest of this little speech. His mind was already on the money, trying to remember what was left, where to put it. Must give up some, of course, for appearance's sake. But some could be moved around, perhaps, could be discreetly hidden so that . . . .

"Be good now," the officer said as Malcolm rose and, with his attorney, walked out the door and into the hallway.

"Better take the back way," his attorney muttered. "You never know . . . ."

They wound their way through the labyrinthine corridors as Malcolm's thoughts took a new turn. He found himself actually looking forward to the predictability of prison. A chance to read, to think, to savor the experiences of the past ten years.

"Here we go," his attorney said, opening the door. Fresh air greeted him, the smell of the ocean.

Malcolm stepped out into an alley. Across the street was a parking garage where his attorney's car waited. They moved toward it as Malcolm realized that, after five years in prison, this would all be fresh to him again. Where would he go, that first day out of prison? In a jail cell one day, eating in the finest restaurant the next? He'd lived like a king for the past ten years. He would be a king once more.

Almost to the parking garage now . . . . Movement to his left. Malcolm turned. A figure moved toward him down the alley.

"Hey! Hey, Malcolm!"

It was Cliff. *Shit!* He thought all this was over.

"Who's this?" his attorney asked.

"An old friend," Malcolm said, turning.

Cliff was about five feet away now, holding out something that looked like a letter.

"You're done, Malcolm," Cliff said. "Don't think you're gonna do easy time, then go get your nest egg, 'Cause it ain't gonna be there. We know about all your accounts. And we're gonna get 'em."

Malcolm felt like the ground under his feet was crumbling.

Like he had been dropped and was falling through space. Falling back into the oblivion he had come from as a boy in the Gorbals.

Cliff saw Malcolm going pale, looking like he might keel over. An expression of relief spread across Cliff's face, as if he was letting go of something he had carried for a long time.

"Know how they found your accounts?" Cliff asked. "It was Becca. She put it all down in a letter to me. You pushed her off that cliff, but you couldn't shut her up."

The lawyer looked at Malcolm sharply. "What's all this about?"

"Rubbish," Malcolm said. "He's just talking shit."

"Think about that in prison, Malcolm," Cliff continued. "When you get out. You've got nothing. We're gonna get it all. And give it back to the people you stole it from."

"Let's go," Malcolm said, starting to turn away.

"Not so fast," Cliff said. "I want to thank you for something. You taught me a lesson."

"And what might that be?" Malcolm sneered.

"Sometimes, winning is really losing."

"Meaning?"

"I got you right where I want you. That's enough for me."

The smile was complete on Cliff's face. He slowly unbuttoned his coat and reached inside.

Halfway through eating a big sloppy burrito, Dan still couldn't shake what Cliff had said to him on the phone.

I'm gonna watch the motherfucker get sentenced. Why did that give him a bad feeling? He played it back in his head a few times.

Finally, he matched the tone with that night on the hill, Cliff standing there in the dark saying, *I'm gonna kill the motherfucker.*

He left the burrito unfinished and walked out to his car. He drove toward downtown San Francisco. He drove fast, then faster. By the time he reached the courthouse, his feeling of dread had grown so strong that he left his car double-parked in the street with the flashers on.

Dan spoke to the security guard at the metal detector, who made a call to the courtroom. He was told the sentencing hearing was over. The guard said prisoners were sometimes released through a rear door.

Back in the street, Dan ran down the block, then turned into an alley. He saw Malcolm emerge from the door, escorted by his attorney.

Made it in time, Dan thought. Then he saw Cliff in front of him, talking to Malcolm, his hand in his coat. He started running. He was almost there when he looked to his right, saw a woman come out of the parking garage.

Jesus, it's her! Dan remembered that rainy night in Glasgow as she crouched next to the white-haired man, his chest blown apart by the shotgun blast.

"No!" Dan shouted. But she raised her arm, and a pistol appeared.

Cliff watched Malcolm's eyes as he pulled back his jacket to reveal the pistol tucked in his belt. Malcolm saw the glint of light on the weapon and then looked back up at Cliff, as if to see if he had the ability to kill. But before their eyes met they both sensed motion—frantic motion—to their right and turned to see a blond woman running toward them, her face a hideous mask of rage. And as Cliff thought *Jesus, it's the woman from Texas!* she raised her arm, there was a flash of light and—

Bang!

Malcolm's lawyer screamed in pain and staggered back, clutching his hand where the bullet had torn away three fingers.

Malcolm turned to run for the parking garage across the street when—

Bang!

Malcolm pitched forward, rolled, then scrambled to his feet and, limping desperately disappeared into a stairwell.

Cliff yelled, "Hey!" at the blond woman and she spun, leveling the gun at him. She recognized him and turned away, running for the stairwell. Cliff sprinted after her, realizing that he didn't want to miss seeing real justice done. Not the state's justice of eight years in prison. But the ancient blood-letting of a public execution. Cliff bounded up the stairs, glancing back to see Dan helping the wounded attorney, then he was on a landing to the second level and was moving out among rows of parked cars. He stopped, breathing hard, and looked to his left. The woman was working her way down the long row of cars, checking between cars, the gun pointing the way, ready to fire. In the distance Cliff heard sirens and running feet and shouting and he wondered if Malcolm would slip away yet again—wounded but alive.

But then Cliff saw a glistening footstep of blood. And another and another leading off to his right. He followed the footsteps five cars down. Then he stopped, staring. Malcolm was slouched against the concrete wall between two cars, holding his right leg, his hands slippery with blood, his chest heaving in pain and terror.

Cliff felt his hand reaching for his gun. Yeah, okay, I'll finish what she began. And no one'll know it was me. Cliff could imagine the weight of the gun in his hand, his finger on the trigger squeezing, squeezing and—

"Please," Malcolm hissed through clenched teeth, looking up at Cliff. "Please help me. She finds me, she'll kill me."

Cliff looked across the parking garage and saw the woman walking back in this direction.

"Is he there?" she yelled to Cliff.

Cliff said nothing. He looked back down at Malcolm whose eyes were wide with fear. Tears streamed down his cheeks and his face quivered uncontrollably.

"For the love of G–God!" Malcolm whispered. "Help me!"

The sirens were louder now. And there were shouts from the alley. A voice yelled, "He went up those stairs!"

There might not be time for her to finish this, Cliff thought, checking again to see where the blond woman was. He felt his hand straying toward his gun once more, felt the smooth wooden handle as his hand closed around it. This had to end now. But he knew that if he killed Malcolm, he'd be destroyed too.

"Do you see him?" she yelled.

Cliff nodded. And she began running toward him with that killing look in her eyes, a look of primitive lust at the prospect of taking another person's life.

Cliff stepped aside as she ran up and looked down at Malcolm, cowering and whimpering against the wall. She raised the gun.

A high-pitched whine came from deep inside Malcolm as his eyes fixed on the gun. She aimed low and put the first one in his left leg, the bullet exploding in his thigh. Blood gurgled up and filled Malcolm's lap as he writhed in pain. She relished the sight for a moment, then aimed higher and fired into Malcolm's shoulder. His head whipped back, then drooped as he looked down at his ruined, blood soaked body. Then, once more, his eyes came up, pleading for mercy.

"Drop the gun!"

Cliff turned. A cop stood near the stairwell with his gun raised. "I said drop it!"

Cops and courthouse guards were running toward them and Cliff saw Dan a few paces behind. Cliff turned back to see the woman aim for the last time and fire. The bullet blew away part of Malcolm's jaw and fountain of blood rose from the hole in his throat. Malcolm's body pitched sideways, then he rolled onto his back as Cliff stood over him and saw that, miraculously, his eyes still held light and fear and understanding.

Shouting voices surrounded them. A cop struggled with the woman from Texas, who was still clutching the gun. Cliff watched her try to fight her way free, try to fire again, then lose the gun to a cop. Screams and more sounds of running.

Cliff turned back to Malcolm, who was looking up, an expression of agony and terror in his eyes. Dan had Cliff's arm now, was trying to haul him away, but Cliff fought him off because he had to make sure, had to see it happen for himself. Cliff held his ground so he could look into Malcolm's eyes, where life was still flickering, growing dimmer, dimmer, but still flickering until finally—

Cliff looked into Malcolm's eyes and watched as the fire went out.

And then it all passed away from Cliff. All the bitterness and frustration. All the rage and hatred. It passed away in a moment, like mist burned off by the sun, and he felt himself being pulled away by Dan, guiding him through the parking garage as more people came running in the opposite direction. Cliff's last image was of the woman from Texas, held by two burly guards, smiling down at Malcolm's corpse at her feet.

Cliff and Dan made it back to Dan's car and took off. When they were safely out of the area, Cliff said, "I want you to know something, so everything's real clear between us."

"Yeah?" Dan looked shaken. He kept his eyes on the road.

"I went there to kill him. But at the last second I realized I'd be the loser. I'd lose everything—my family, my freedom, my chance to train a Derby winner someday. So I just looked him in the eye, I said, 'I got you right where I want you,' and I showed him my gun, to let him know he was mine if I wanted him. Then that lady from Texas did the job for me."

Sometime later, as if talking to himself, Cliff added, "What scares me, though, is how much I loved watching him die. I never thought I could feel that way about someone."

"And now we come to Hip No. 83—the Relaunch colt," the auctioneer said, looking down from his table at the young horse being led onto the Barrett's auction stage.

Cliff sat up in his seat in the back of the room and looked at the young horse. It had been almost two months since they got him back into the country, and he was lookin' real good. Looking good, Cliff thought, but not running so good. That's why he hadn't posted any new workout times. The times listed in the auction catalog were posted before he was taken to Scotland. Because of all the rain, they'll have to stand as his official times.

It was late in the afternoon, and from where Cliff sat he could look out the window at the golden sky over Los Angeles. Hard to believe that two months ago El Nino-style rains were drowning the state. Hard to believe a lot of the things that happened two months ago. It was like his life went into a tailspin for a while, then straightened out.

Life was like that. So was horse racing. It was enough to make you superstitious.

Across the auction room, Cliff could see Dan, sitting alone. At the other end of the room, Cliff checked to make sure Emerson was positioned to look like yet another bidder. Dan and Emerson were there to drive the bidding up or—God forbid—buy the horse back if they couldn't get their price.

So what is my price? Cliff wondered, running the numbers again in his head. A hundred and a half'd be nice. That would cover a lot of expenses. It would even pay for Malcolm's share, which they had bought at a sheriff's auction last week along with the other horses that were seized at LAX. He picked up some good horses for cheap. So, if he could get hundred and a half, he'd come out of the whole thing all right. Of course, there was always the chance the horse could sell for more. A whole lot more. Cliff saw that Zacco was here, with his guys. The sheiks were here, too, and the Japanese. There was money all over the room.

"You may have heard about this horse," the auctioneer said. "He was bred in Texas by Relaunch—in fact it was the stallion's last crop. This is the last Relaunch. He was being trained in Northern Cal before he was stolen and shipped to Scotland. Eventually the colt was recovered and returned to trainer Cliff Dante who said, 'This horse has more frequent-flier miles than I do.'" Laughter. "I saw Cliff before the auction, and he told me they were thinking about renaming the colt 'The Marquis de Fraud.'" More laughter. Applause. People turned and nodded at Cliff, smiling.

They're laughing *with* me now, Cliff thought, remembering how it felt—all too recently—when they were laughing *at* him. Yeah, everyone loves a winner.

"This colt has posted some impressive times—breezed at 10.2 in March."

In March, Cliff thought, when its legs were crooked. Before it took the trip to the U.K. and came back looking better—but running slower. Funny how that was, a freak of nature outrunning a good-looking horse like this.

Cliff saw Zacco moving up the aisle, taking his customary spot at the rear of the room. Good sign. That meant he'd probably be bidding.

"Okay. Who'll start us off?" the auctioneer asked. The spotters, in green blazers, were in place, their keen eyes surveying the room for bids. "Let's start at fifty thousand." The auctioneer's voice slid into that machine-gun style, rattling off numbers rapid-fire.

"Fifty thousand. Anyone give us fifty thousand for the Relaunch colt? Okay then, forty-five thousand? Who'll give us forty-five thousand then. No? Let's try forty thousand. Forty thousand to start us off. Come on folks—he's a beauty! Just look at him! Thirty-five thousand then. Who'll give me thirty-five. Thirty-five?"

"Ho!" the spotter yelled, pointing at Dan, who had raised a finger to make his bid.

Shit, Cliff thought. Startin' too low.

"Thirty-five. Do I have forty? Thirty-five—"

"Ho!" The spotter pointed at Emerson.

"Forty! We have forty. Do we have forty-five?"

Don't even have a real bid yet, Cliff realized.

"Ho!"

"Forty-five!"

Cliff looked and saw a guy in the third row on a cell phone who had just made the bid. Looked like Ricky Diaz. He looked back and saw Zacco was on his cellular phone, too. Was Diaz shilling for him? Zacco rotated his guys so no one knew who was bidding. It was a safe bet they were talking to each other.

"Fifty thousand! We have fifty. Do we have sixty?" the auctioneer said, moving the bidding by tens now.

"Ho!"

"Sixty! Do I have seventy?"

"Ho!" the spotter yelled, pointing to a gray-haired gal in a denim jacket. Don't recognize her, Cliff thought. This is gettin' good.

"Seventy, do I have eighty?"

"Ho!" One of Zacco's guys bid again.

"Eighty! Do I have ninety? Ninety thousand. Eighty, do I have ninety?"

The spotter looked at Diaz for a bid. He spoke into the phone—no bid.

"Eighty thousand, do I have ninety?"

"Ho!" The spotter pointed at Dan! *Shit, man! I told you not to bid over fifty!*

But now the bidding was moving again.

"Ninety. Do I have one hundred? One hundred. One-ten.

One-ten, one-twenty. One-thirty? Do I have one-thirty? One-thirty! Do I have one-forty? One-thirty, can I get one-forty?"

"One-thirty-five," Diaz said.

Gettin' cute now, Cliff thought. Okay, that's a good price. Let's close now.

"One-thirty-five—one-forty?"

Cliff watched in horror as Dan casually raised a finger.

"Ho!"

Oh man, you really screwed us! Cliff thought, slumping in the seat. We were almost there. Now we gotta buy our own horse back at —

"One-forty-five! One-fifty? One-forty-five. Can I get one-fifty?"

The spotter, a bald guy with eyes like lasers, extended his hand to Diaz, wiggling his fingers, trying to tease a bid out of him. Diaz looked away. Across the room, another spotter looked at the old gal in the denim jacket. She folded her arms.

Cliff frantically looked at Diaz. He was talking into his cell phone.

"Going once at one-forty-five. Going twice . . . ."

Diaz looked up at the spotter and nodded.

"Ho!" the spotter yelled, snapping his fingers.

"One-forty-five!" the auctioneer shouted.

Now for Christ's sake, keep your hands down! Cliff thought, giving Dan the hairy eyeball. Dan smiled back, and folded his hands across his chest.

"One-fifty? Do we have one-fifty? Okay then, one-forty-five once. One-forty-five twice. Sold for one hundred and forty-five *thousand* dollars."

Cliff worked his way across the room, shaking hands, accepting congratulations. When he got there, Dan had a big grin on his face. "I knew the guy was good for one more bump."

"How the hell could you know that?"

"He was giving me a buying signal—the way he was sitting. I could tell."

"Well, your bump almost blew the deal," Cliff said as they moved into the bar.

"But it didn't and the horse is sold. So it's okay. Okay? Let's get a beer." He turned and shouted, "Hey Mr. Bartender-man!"

Cliff felt a hand on his arm, turned and found Zacco shaking his hand.

"That was me bought your horse," Zacco said grinning. The guy was always smiling. "I had one of my guys buy it for me. If they'd known it was me bidding, I woulda had to pay you double for it."

"You bought Relaunch?" Cliff said, trying to act surprised, and maybe hamming it up just a little too much. "Jeez Nik, you outfoxed me again."

Zacco dissolved back into the crowd. Dan let out one of his big laughs and said, "What an asshole."

"But I love the color of his money." Cliff downed half his beer in one swig.

They toasted and drank some more, feeling good.

"So now you can cover your expenses, start racing with a clean slate," Dan said, stifling a burp.

"Huh?" Cliff said. He had his nose in the auction catalog.

"Your expenses. For the trip to England, for boarding Relaunch, your profit will cover that."

Cliff looked up at the TV monitor on the wall. "What number are they up to?"

"93. Why?"

"We looked at 95 this morning. Good lookin' animal."

"*We?*" Dan asked, catching something in his tone.

"Me 'n' Jamie. She came down for the auction, helped me look over the horses. She's got a good eye for the young ones. You know, it helps to have a vet in the family."

"You guys patch things up? She come back home?"

"Not yet. But things are lookin' up." Then, with a catch in his throat Cliff added, "I think we're gonna make it."

"I'm glad to hear that, man," Dan said, nodding. "I'm really glad to hear that."

"Yeah, well . . . ," Cliff turned back to the video monitor, all business. "So, like I was saying, this 95's got Northern Dancer blood in him. He might go cheap. If I could get him for under eighty he'd be a steal."

Dan dropped his head into his hands. "No . . . no . . . no . . . ."

"With the right jock on board, we could win some races with him," Cliff said, deadpan. "So how much you in for?"

Dan smiled, shaking his head, but then, thinking about it, said, "I could go ten. I'd go higher but, ya know, now that the baby's here we got expenses out the wazoo. My wife would kill me if she knew."

"Ten's good," Cliff said, shutting the auction catalog. "I'll see what I can do."

Cliff finished his beer and headed back into the auction. On his way he slid the envelope out of his back pocket. It contained the results of the blood test he had ordered on the Relaunch colt.

And it would answer whether or not they got the right horse back from Scotland. Like he told Dan when this whole deal started, there's a story behind every horse you pin hook. Sometimes you're lucky just to get your money back. Other times you hit big casino. But, like a lot of stories, there's always a part you have to leave out, he thought as he ripped the envelope into pieces and dropped it in the trash. Besides, no one would ever believe me if I told them.